NEW STORIES FROM THE MIDWEST
2013

NEW STORIES FROM THE MIDWEST

2013

ROSELLEN BROWN
Guest Editor

JASON LEE BROWN AND SHANIE LATHAM
Series Editors

newamericanpress
Milwaukee, Wis. • Urbana, Ill.

n e w a m e r i c a n p r e s s

www.NewAmericanPress.com

Printed in the United States of America
ISBN 978-0-9849439-7-5

For ordering information, please contact:
Ingram Book Group
One Ingram Blvd.
La Vergne, TN 37086
(800) 937-8000
orders@ingrambook.com

All stories reprinted by permission of the individual authors. Grateful acknowledgment is made to the journals and magazines where the stories first appeared:

"Tracks" © 2011 by Kate Blakinger. First published in *Harpur Palate 10*.2 (Winter 2011).

"Mulligan" © 2011 by Steve De Jarnatt. First published in *Cincinnati Review 8*.2 (Winter 2011).

"Here Is What You Do" © 2011 by Chris Dennis. First published in *Granta* 114 (Spring 2011).

"The Garden of Earthly Delights" © 2011 by Gina Frangello. First published in the *Fifth Wednesday Journal* (Spring 2011).

"North Country" © 2011 by Roxane Gay. First published in *Hobart* 12 (June 2011).

"The Speed of Sound" © 2011 by Elizabeth Gonzalez. First published in *Hunger Mountain* 16 (November 2011).

For Jay

CONTENTS

EDITORS' NOTE

NEW STORIES FROM THE MIDWEST 2013 showcases twenty stories set in the Midwest by midwestern and non-midwestern authors. The goals of *New Stories from the Midwest* are to celebrate an American region that is often ignored in discussions about distinctive regional literature and to demonstrate how the quality of fiction from and about the Midwest (Illinois, Indiana, Iowa, Kansas, Michigan, Minnesota, Missouri, Nebraska, North Dakota, Ohio, South Dakota, and Wisconsin) rivals that of any other region.

To collect the stories, we solicited via flyers, letters, and e-mails for contributions from more than three hundred magazines, literary journals, and small presses. We received more than three hundred nominations from more than one hundred publications and editors. We narrowed the selection to fifty finalists, which were passed on to the guest editor, Rosellen Brown, who chose twenty stories for inclusion. The thirty finalists not chosen for inclusion in the anthology are listed at the end of the book.

— Jason Lee Brown and Shanie Latham
Series Editors

INTRODUCTION

PICTURE THIS: At the 2012 conference of the Association of Writers and Writing Programs (AWP) in Chicago, the editor of *New Stories from the Midwest*, Jason Brown, organized a panel optimistically titled "The Renaissance of Midwest Writing." I always pity the people whose job it is to assign such panels the proper size room: they range from the intimate—a few modest rows—to grand ballrooms with chandeliers. Deciding which presentations warrant which space seems to me more challenging than a restaurant's reservation scheduler guessing at the unpredictable habits of diners.

This time they got it spectacularly wrong: The mid-sized room (in a corridor named for the Great Lakes) was so packed a fire inspector would have ejected us for the number of floor sitters and exit-blocking wall-warmers. Unprepared for this demonstration of Midwestern solidarity, I arrived just in time to get the last seat in the house.

What drew more than a hundred people to this event? Who, in fact, were they? Natives of the Midwest eager to renew their sense of heritage? Current inhabitants, studying or teaching in a nearby MFA program? Escapees (if that's not too harsh an epithet?)—though why, if they'd fled, would they subject themselves to what would most likely be a celebration? I never did find out the reason(s) for this prodigious audience's attendance, but after fanning my way through an hour and a half of crowd-induced body heat, I could certainly see why Jason had saluted a renaissance.

*

Now picture this: The new students in my writing program at the
School of the Art Institute of Chicago are gathered to introduce
themselves on opening day of their first semester. When it comes
time to tell us where they're from, one young woman says "Texas"
and a young man says "Massachusetts" and this curmudgeon
remonstrates with them from the back of the room. "I have lived
in both Texas and Massachusetts and I have no idea what we
are supposed to imagine. Dallas? Austin? Crawford?" (For those
of blessedly short memory, that was the bedraggled little town
famous a few years ago for housing our brush-clearer-in-chief).
"As for Massachusetts! Cambridge? Portuguese Fall River? A
Berkshire town of 200? You are writers," I remind them. "Honor
the details. Differentiate!"

Faced with the task of choosing, and here describing, these
stories from the Midwest, I find myself recalcitrant once again.
Distinctions must be made, because "Midwest" is larger even than
Texas, and more varied.

More pictures: The El crawls along the track—this is
Chicago—beside an ancient, vibrating wooden platform. The trees
in North Dakota are fairly few and fairly far between. Youngstown,
Ohio, is one abandoned steel mill after another but Yellow Springs
is still home to the '60s, Birkenstocks, acoustic guitars, sprouts.
Which Iowa should we envision: good citizens caucusing for the
presidential primaries or a sea of cornfields, or shall we suffer the
sight of meth addicts with rotted teeth? Minneapolis's buildings
are linked by skyways to fend off icy winds and St. Louis sweats in
summer as if it were Florida. And so on, pictures proliferating, not
canceling each other out but co-existing in an imaginary exhibit
twelve states wide and (at the last census) 66, 927,001 people high.

And so these stories represent a shaky proposition, not
untenable but a challenge to defend: Emanating from a geographic
mash-up, do they have anything in common? Is there a recognizable
"vibe" that might be traced to their provenance or that of their
creators? Where should we look for an answer, assuming there

is one, or something that comes close to explaining why all those writers assembled to share a connection? Are we looking at setting or sensibility? And finally—a good possibility—might we be defining them more by what they are not than by what they are?

Whenever I read a list of representatives of something under scrutiny—women CEO's, Asian-American Ivy League graduates in the NBA—I can't help but see it as defensive: these are exceptions, remarkable for having broken a barrier, overcome expectations. No one, for example, compiles lists of "New York writers past and present"—it would be laughable to imagine even trying to define any congruence among such a herd of mavericks, beginning with, say, Washington Irving and ending up in the recently rehabbed precincts of Brooklyn.

Does the same apply to a ledger-full of Great Writers of the Midwest? Are they all too easily countable? (Do we hear denizens of both coasts asking behind their hands, "Are they worth counting?") And if they need a renaissance—why? I can only think it's because midwesterners don't actually know their own histories or value them as they should because they've bought into the reputation of "mid-ness," of mildness and characterlessness. The opening lines of Michael Cunningham's superb story "White Angel" speak derisively of Cleveland: "We lived then in Cleveland, in the middle of everything. It was the sixties—our radios sang out love all day long. This of course is history. It was before the city of Cleveland went broke, before its river caught fire." Like the jokes about the Greyhound buses making their way out of the Dakotas or the mockeries of the Coen brothers' *Fargo*—with such rancid memories in the popular imagination, no wonder the middle of the country sometimes seems to provoke one apology after another.

Yet, even leaving aside a history that goes back beyond Dreiser, Henry Blake Fuller, William Dean Howells, Hamlin Garland, Sherwood Anderson—a big bunch of guys, isn't it?*—if

I turn to some of the writers I love most, I cannot think of them as exceptions; their quality is absolute. Two of the greatest books of the last, say, 50 years—William Maxwell's *So Long, See You Tomorrow* and Evan Connell's *Mrs. Bridge*—are so clearly born of smalltown Illinois and Kansas City they are unimaginable set anywhere else. A small town in Maine—see Olive Kittredge—is not the same as Lincoln, Illinois. Is Toni Morrison's *Bluest Eye* transferable to the east coast or—impossible!—California? Could Saul Bellow have celebrated Augie March by having him cry "I am an American, Miami born?" Or even "Manhattan" born? Consider the implications that would have been lost, and, just as important, would have been imposed, had Augie not come from the rawer, less sophisticated and less familiar middle of the country? Or right this minute: Could the particular combination of the sweetness and saltiness of Charles Baxter survive a change of venue—Boston, or maybe Mississippi instead of Minnesota (with some Ann Arbor on the side)? I don't think so. None of these extraordinary writers hesitated at the alleged blandness of their hometowns or could have imagined their characters in more "fashion forward" venues.

Ditto the stories you are about to read. The Upper Peninsula, the lake at the thumb of Michigan, the neighborhood bar where an out-of-work father flees from the pain of his depressed household, the Chicago of old tradition and half-eclipsed memory, Chicago as a city of refuge and of new beginnings, Milwaukee through the weary eyes of an immigrant from an unlikely place, the heat and languor of a Kansas summer afternoon when "we can feel ourselves sliding right off this map."

In one story, a very young man, caught with a pocketful of pills, is exiled to a Texas prison. There is a heartbreaking moment when he phones his grandmother back in Indiana—he'd told her he was going to hear a seminar on the Miami Indians of the Midwest but instead took her car and lighted out for Mexico. Not understanding where he's calling from, she asks if she can come to get him. From Woodville, Texas, home has become a vague shadow, almost invisible. The story's author, Chris Dennis, says in an interview: "I live in St. Louis, Missouri, but I grew up in southern Illinois. Everything I write about is influenced by that place. Most of my work is set there. I'll pretend it's somewhere else—that I'm writing about a place that isn't home—but it always is."

The concerns of these writers—love, sex, children, animals—growing up, growing old, going crazy—are universal. We don't read them for ethnographic information but for proof that, after all the concrete details and local habits fall away, we are similar in our needs, our refusals and our allegiances. Still the ethnography is there to be read; it's a cliché too easily simplified to say that the particular is universal. It isn't, or at least that's only half the story—"Honor the details. Differentiate!" It's what's under and behind the particular that's universal, and the understanding that where you live and what you see day in, day out makes you, to a great extent, who you become and, maybe, who you don't. The specificity is where an author's personality resides, her voice, his quirks.

Renaissance? Do we need one or have the good writers of the Midwest been here all along, unacknowledged because they tend to speak quietly and not assume much of the world is listening? No wonder those hundred people gathered for some company—they've got a secret and they wanted to be with others who know it too.

— **Rosellen Brown**
Guest Editor

* *Willa Cather's Nebraska gets counted as technically Midwestern, though that always feels unlikely to me. Left to my own devices, I'd call it a plains state.*

HEARTLAND

Alexander Weinstein

MY SON IS DOING FANTASTIC until the elimination round. Then he
gets to the quiz questions and I watch him fall apart. His little face
goes tight, the way it does when he gets near a barking dog, and
he starts haphazardly punching the buzzer—not even listening to
the questions. For a moment I want to bury my face in my hands,
almost do, but then I realize it'd be me and not some other poor
schmuck on the TV crying. So I sit up straight and keep my eyes
on Sam, trying to look supportive as I watch him lose ten thousand
bucks.

There are papers to sign and hands to shake when the show
is over, and then we're driving home. Sam's strapped into his
booster seat with the *Scaredy Cat Home Version* DVD in his lap.
By now it's dark. Only six p.m., but Indiana's late October light is
long gone. I hold both hands on the steering wheel and stare out
at the headlights of the opposite lanes and the blackness of the clay
fields around us.

Sam's been quiet the whole ride. He can feel when I'm upset.
Finally he speaks, his voice small from the backseat. "Daddy, are
you angry?"

"No," I say.

"I thought I knew the answers."

"Yeah, I know," and before I can stop myself I add, "but you've
got to listen to the questions."

"I know. I'm sorry."

"I mean, you weren't even listening to the questions. You were just hitting the buttons."

"I was trying to listen...I mean, I was...well, I mean..."

Then there's just silence. I look in the rearview mirror to see Sam staring out his window, tears falling down his cheeks. "It's OK," I say. It's too late though.

Sam was a beautiful baby, which is what landed him the diaper ads, but ever since he turned seven he's become a normal kid. *Scaredy Cat* was his one big shot. The winner of the show always lands a TV ad, sometimes even an appearance on KidMTV. That's how Mindy Sands got so big. But that's never going to happen to Sam. He doesn't even know how to play an instrument. I let out a deep sigh. "It's OK, Sam," I say again. "You did the best you could."

The darkness of the backseat is broken only by the passing bands of light from the overhead streetlights. In those momentary flashes I can see he's still staring out the window, crying. I put on my signal and head for the exit where I'll find a place to pull over and give him a hug.

At home Cindy hasn't started dinner yet. She's got Laurie in the crib where she's gumming on the corner of my old iPhone. Cindy's at the computer, uploading photos of our furniture and Sam's older toys on e-auction. "Hey," she says, clicking the screen onto solitaire when Sam runs into the room. "I saw you on TV, little man."

"Sorry," Sam says.

"Don't be sorry; you were great. Was it gross to eat worms?"

Sam smiles. "Kinda. Sorta like spaghetti that kept wiggling."

"Ew!" she says, scrunching her nose together, and gives him a hug. Over his shoulder she mouths to me, *other room*.

"Come on, Sam, let's go make some funny home videos," I say, so Cindy can finish uploading the photos.

"All right," Sam says.

We do a couple classic knock-down gags in his bedroom: Sam standing on his tippy toes, trying to hit the light switch and falling back onto his ass, Sam jumping on the bed and falling off the edge. Decent stuff that probably won't make the cut. As a reward I let him play GameCube.

Cindy's playing solitaire when I walk into the living room.

"Dinner?" I ask.

"Laurie just stopped crying and I've been nursing for the past hour. Let's order in pizza."

I feel the familiar flush of irritation beneath my skin. "I thought you were going to make dinner tonight. It's not like we have money to order in."

"Yeah, well it sucks about *Scaredy Cat*. Quiz questions: your department."

"Thanks, you've got a real gift for compassion." I walk into the kitchen to get a beer. Cindy's up from her chair, following me. I open the fridge and take a Corona.

"I thought you were quitting."

That was our deal. She would quit coffee, I'd quit drinking. I pop the bottle with a lighter and toss the cap into the garbage under the sink where we keep our bucket of compost. A swarm of fruit flies is buzzing in the murky darkness of sponges and Brillo pads. "Can't you at least take out the compost?" I say.

Laurie starts crying from the other room. Cindy looks at me. "It's your turn to take her."

"Fine, I'll take her and the compost out."

I put my beer on the counter and sweep Laurie from the crib. I turn her so she's facing me, then go into the kitchen and crouch to get the bucket. Laurie begins to cry again.

"Give me her," Cindy says.

"I've got her."

"She's not happy how you're holding her. Give her to me." Cindy puts her hands around Laurie and pulls her from me. I'm left with the bucket of compost and the fruit flies. I take the compost, step outside, and slam the door behind me.

What's left of our yard is a mess from yesterday's rain. Ever since we sold off the topsoil, the clay makes walking treacherous. It's the same for every yard in our neighborhood. I put on muck boots and climb down the makeshift steps that Heartland Gardens put in when they carted our soil away, then I sludge through the slippery clay to the corner of our yard where we're trying to make dirt. Blackened banana peels, old coffee grounds, and moldy vegetables sit in the wired-off compost pile. At this rate we'll have usable soil a decade from now.

I hear Laurie still wailing inside. She's been wailing ever since she came into this world. Laurie was born with a stray eye. Minor corrective surgery would've fixed it, except minor corrective surgery when you're not covered means no minor corrective surgery. Which meant no baby commercials for Laurie.

I crouch down next to the compost and look up at the sky, which is covered by gray clouds. Seems like it rains every day now. When I was a kid we used to have these long, beautiful Indiana summers. Now we just have a drawn out rainy fall—all year long. With the soil gone, it turns our backyards into clay pits. The clay runs off onto the streets, where it hardens between rains until the city comes and sprays the sludge into the sewers. I look at the telephone and electric wires cutting across our patch of sky, feeling like the whole world is coming down around me.

Cindy is nursing Laurie when I come back in. I lean over the chair and give her a kiss. "Sorry," I say. "I just don't know what we're going to do."

"I know," she says. Her skin smells like apricot, a familiar smell that I'd somehow forgotten, and for a moment I feel our closeness. "Did you remember to take out the recycling?" she says.

The moment is gone. I force myself not to say anything. I'll just be an asshole, she'll get angry, Sam will see us fighting, and we'll all be miserable. I can't go there. Not tonight. I take out my wallet and put a twenty by the computer.

"What's this for?"

"Pizza for you and Sam."

"Huh?" she says and looks at me.

I go into the kitchen and finish what's left of my beer. Then I put the bottle in our recycling bin which is overflowing with containers of biodegradable dish soap and empty cans of beans. "I'm going out," I say.

"What do you mean you're going out? I've been taking care of Laurie all day."

"Sorry," I say. "I need some time alone." I tote the recycling past her through the living room to the front door.

"What about me? You ever consider I need a break too?"

I'm already out the door, closing it behind me. By the time I get to the curb, I imagine she's going to be in the doorway yelling at me for the entire neighborhood to hear. Not that it matters. Most of the houses have been empty for years. The only houses with signs of life are at the end of the cul-de-sac where blue recycling bins have been set out in the mud. But Cindy doesn't come out. Not by the time I've separated the cardboard from plastics, not by the time I've gotten to the car and unlocked it, not even when I pull out of our driveway and leave.

The Shovel is located down 37, just north of Martinsville. It's fashioned to look like the interior of a potting shed, a real note of irony for all us who no longer have our yards. The walls sport fake bags of potting soil, shovels, hoes, chicken wire, and dirt-stained terracotta pots. Jim's sitting at the bar, waiting for me with a pitcher of stout in front of him. He's my only friend left from the old job.

"Tough night, huh?" he says, filling a second pint and pushing it in front of me.

"Every time I think I'm gonna quit drinking, the fighting starts up again. That's all we do now: fight, fuck, make up, then do it again."

"Look at the bright side, at least you're fucking," Jim says and lifts his glass. "Here's to quitting."

We clink and I take a sip of beer. There's the familiar tang of alcohol against the tongue, the molasses sweetness of the stout. *Dream Girls* is on the flat screen hanging over the bar. One of the frumpy wives has undergone reconstructive surgery to appear identical to her husband's favorite movie star.

"I just don't know what's wrong with us," I say. "We used to have it good together. Now it's like we're not even a couple. I come home, I want to be with her, and she just hands me the baby. She thinks I'm an asshole. I don't know, maybe I am. Tell me the truth: I sound like an asshole, right?"

"Nah," Jim says and takes a sip of his beer. "You just need a job, that's all. And you got to learn to swallow your pride."

Which is true. One of the things I like about Jim is that he's not sentimental. Me, I can over-think things. Jim watches shows like *Dream Girls* and doesn't give a shit. "How are things at work?" I ask. "Same crew?"

"More or less. The kid who got hired after you—he got canned yesterday. Larry caught him stealing topsoil. Had his trunk filled with it."

"What a stupid way to go," I say and realize we're both thinking the same thing. "You know, I was just standing up for my family."

"Forget it," Jim says, looking down at his glass. "It's history."

"What would you have done? Just smile at him and take it?"

"Don't know what I'd have done, but I sure as hell wouldn't

have hit the boss," Jim says. Then he turns his eyes back to the TV. On the screen, the husband is making out with his reconstructed wife.

Jim's answer is more or less the same one Cindy gave me when I told her what had happened. There had been a car issue that day; Cindy needed it, so she dropped me off at work. Sam and Laurie were in the backseat. Larry had been out front, straightening lawn displays, and had seen Laurie. On my way inside to clock-in he'd joked, "I think your baby girl was giving me the eye."

"What did you say?" I asked, turning to face him across the small square of lawn.

"Hey now, don't you start looking at me cockeyed too," he said. That's when I hit him. There was no conscious decision about it—just this surge of heat and a streak of green beneath me. Then he was flat on his back and I was on top of him, driving my fist into his face. Jim said I was lucky I only lost my job. Cindy said I was a fucking idiot. Which I guess was true, because we were already behind on our second mortgage. Still, it was one of the few things I can remember doing in the past couple years that I actually felt good about.

"You think there's any way I can get back delivering?" I ask.

"Not a fucking chance. You're blacklisted from Fort Wayne to Bedford."

"It's been two years."

"People remember. Only way you're gonna get a job installing gardens is to move."

"How am I going to do that? I can't sell our house in this market. We're lucky we still have it. You've seen downtown Indy—tent city."

"That's what I'm saying, move. Leave it all behind. Start fresh."

"Move where? Michigan? Illinois? They're straight sheets of clay." Jim doesn't answer. "You know, I thought we were going to have a break today. Sam was on—"

"Yeah, Fran told me what happened," Jim says. "Real sorry to hear it. Here, let me fill you up." Jim pours the rest of the pitcher into my glass. "You know, there are still some jobs in Kentucky—they've got patches down there. South America's got some green, places in Brazil."

"Brazil's finished."

"So try something new, switch professions."

"And do what? Nobody's hiring. Do you know how long the list is to even get a job at this place?" I say tapping the bar.

Above us *Dream Girls* is finished and the news has come on. It's day nine-hundred of the oil spill. There's a picture of the Pacific Ocean, black as soil, followed by photos of obsidian waves crashing against the California coastline. Hawaii is on fire. A company spokesman is standing on a freighter, saying he believes they'll be able to cap the underwater well by July of next year.

"God," I say. "This is really the end, isn't it?"

"Nah," Jim says. "People have been saying the world's gonna end for years. It never does."

"Yeah, but this time it's for real. I mean look at that." I point to the screen with my glass. "The land's gone, the water's going. The Northeast doesn't even have decent drinking water anymore. We're done for."

"That's just how it feels 'cause you're in the dumps. Fran and I still got it good. Plenty of people still got it good."

"Yeah, well we don't have it good," I say, looking into what's left of my pint. The alcohol is hitting me now, dragging me downward. My brain feels like it's full of dirt. "I think we're gonna lose the house by Christmas." Above us are rolling photos of the earthquakes in Chile, followed by the recent floods in Japan. I take a long sip of beer.

"Listen," Jim says, "Fran and I were in a rough spot last spring. Nothing too serious, but cell phone, internet, cable, 24/7 GPS, online debt, those kinda things..." He takes a sip of his beer and lowers his voice. "You know, you've got a couple of good looking kids. Really good looking kids. You ever consider putting photos online?"

I grimace as though my drink's rancid. "What the hell are you talking about?"

"Don't give me that look," Jim says. "I'm not talking porn—just photos of them in the bathtub, Cindy changing her diaper. Mild stuff, practically family photos. No big deal."

I empty my pint glass, put it down on the counter, and face Jim, looking him square in the eyes. "No," I say.

"Look, it wasn't my first choice either, but I know a guy—completely confidential—you email him the attachments, he sends you a check. You don't have to have any contact with his clients. Two hundred full frontal for boys, three hundred for girls. You get a shot of them together he'd probably pay six."

"I'm not putting naked photos of my kids out there."

"Who's it hurting? So a couple perverts are willing to pay good money to see them—so what? We're talking a lot of money for a few snapshots. Sure, it's not what anybody wants to do—I didn't want to do it—but it got us through a tough spot. Look, nobody's going to see the photos except whoever he sells them to. And I'll tell you something, the market's gonna be flooded before you know it. A year from now those pictures will be gone. You need money—this is where the money is."

"I'm not interested," I say.

"OK, so you're not interested now, but at least let me give you his e-mail in case you change your mind." Jim writes the address down on a napkin and shoves it in my shirt pocket.

"I'm throwing it out," I tell him.

"Do what you need to do," Jim says. "As for me, I'm gonna treat us to another pitcher." Which is kind of him, and though I ought to pay, I just nod my head and say thanks.

*

Really, I shouldn't be driving, and for this reason I take the long back road home, up old 67. Out here on the forgotten highway I'm alone in the darkness watching my high beams cut across the land and the great pits. Twenty years ago it was all cornfields out here. Indiana soil so rich you could put anything in the dirt and it would grow. Then they came for the soil, followed by the clay, and finally the bedrock. All that's left are these pits, abandoned and sinking. They talked for a while of filling the canyons with water, turning the place into a second series of great lakes—private ponds for the rich to float their sailboats on and their children to jet-ski across. Then the rich moved on—away from this endless stretch of exposed rock and dead earth. Perhaps years from now, when we're all gone, some new creature will step forth on these canyons and gaze out at the abyss, never knowing there were once cornfields here.

The rains have started again. The drops splatter against the windshield and make the roads muddy. At one point the mud gets so bad the wipers can't cut it and I have to pull over to the side of the road. I park beside the tall chain-link fence that separates the state road from the pits. I pop the trunk and take the squeegee from the back. The rain feels good against my skin, sobering, and I take my time, running the rubber blade against the glass and flicking the mud onto the road. Across from the pits, all the foreclosed houses are abandoned. The empty sockets of front yards, yanked from the ground like teeth, are filled with rain. It's kind of beautiful in the darkness, as though the neighborhood is floating. Soon it will be dawn and everything will be ugly, but for now there's an eerie radiance to the world. Perhaps it will be OK, I think. The Earth will recover; the world won't ever truly end. Perhaps it will be green again someday. I put the squeegee back in the trunk and start on the road toward home.

There's a story I would like to tell to my children. In this story a boy meets a girl and they fall in love. They both have good jobs and enough money to buy a nice house with acres of land. There are old trees on their land—apples and pears, cherries and plums, blueberry bushes and grape vines. In the late fall the grass gets sticky with the pulp of fallen fruit, and bees buzz amid the fermenting cores. The family makes pies and the children's fingers get stained from the blueberries, a light purple hue that remains even after their baths that night. In this home the parents love one another. Sometimes the children see their parents kiss and they feel embarrassed. They are good children, healthy and happy. They ride bicycles with other kids; they grow up, fall in love, and have children of their own who they bring back to the land. And at night, when the moon rises full above their home, the family goes to sleep to the sound of crickets chirping in the high grass.

In this story there is no car pulling into the driveway at four a.m., there is no father stumbling to the door as he struggles to find his keys. In this story, when the father goes into his son's room to make sure he's sleeping, he kisses the small boy on his forehead and tucks the blankets up beneath his son's chin, never considering, not even for a moment, rolling the blankets down past the boy's small chest which rises and falls with every breath, where deep inside there's a heart that loves his father and trusts he will protect him against the monsters of this world.

HERE IS WHAT YOU DO

Chris Dennis

You wet your hair in the sink, then comb it back, slick as a new trash bag. You look nice. OK, so your name is Ricky. You are twenty-three years old. People say you're sweet. You say to them, "No, I'm not." But you are. You know you are. You can't help it. It's like there's a piece of candy hidden deep inside you and everyone is trying to find the easiest way to get it out.

Your cellmate, Donald Budke, he's like Rasputin, or Genghis Khan, maybe even Napoleon Bonaparte. No one tells Donald he's sweet. His motives are serious, and he's got acne scars which make him look like a criminal. He is a criminal. He's ten years older than you, is on his fourth year of a fifteen-year sentence for manslaughter. You're just a high school history teacher from southern Indiana, or at least you used to be.

On the day you were arrested, the US Customs agent said, "What the hell are you doing, Ricky?" like he knew you or something, like he was really disappointed. "Who's the vehicle registered to, Ricky?" You told him it was your grandmother's. You gave him your driver's license, your car keys. He asked you to sit in the back of his patrol car while he searched your trunk. You watched through the windshield, waiting for him to find the five cottage cheese containers full of oxycodone you'd hidden beneath the spare tire. The sky was pink, like a drop of blood in a glass of water. You thought, *Mexico is like an art film.* You thought about the ten or so pills in the pocket of your pants, wished there was some way of keeping them so you could eat them later, in the event you were placed under arrest. You didn't want to eat any of them right then. You were already as high as a butterfly. You fished the handful out of your jeans pocket and put two in your mouth anyway, waited for the spit to come, swallowed. The rest you chewed into a paste and spat on to the floorboard of the patrol car while the customs agent rifled through your roadside emergency kit.

The man came back and said, "You need to step out of the car, Ricky." You stood beside the highway while families in minivans drove by, the early evening heat like needles pricking your face.

Before the customs agent put you back in the car, he said, "Anything else hidden on your person becomes a felony inside the jail. Is there anything else, Ricky?" You stared at his ears, which were so big and red. They suited him, you thought.

"No, sir," you said. "Where else would I put it?"

"Never mind," he said, looking away.

You could hardly hold your eyes open.

Hours later inside the customs office, another man—not much older than you, his eyes pale as pool water—told you to relax your hand while he rolled your fingers across an ink pad, pressing the fingertips on to a little index card with your name on it. The fingerprinting station was fascinating, and you told him so. You talked to him about Henry Faulds, a squat man, you said, who wore funny hats, credited with being the first person to use fingerprints for identification. "He used a greasy print left on a bottle of alcohol," you said.

"Well, all right then," the man said.

He put you in a small room by yourself, a concrete cell with pale green walls and no windows. You lay down on a metal bench that was bolted to the floor. You drifted in and out of the thing the pills made you feel. You thought about Horatio Nelson and the final moments in the battle of Cape Saint Vincent—the fleets falling out of formation on the water, gunsmoke rising toward the sails, Nelson reaching out to take the surrendering sword of San Jose. You slept, turning constantly on the hard bench, shaking the whole time from nervousness and the thought of never going home and the thought of not having any more pills to take. The lights went off, and then later came back on again. A man opened the door to say you could use the phone. You followed him into the racket of the booking office and called your nanny.

"Good afternoon," Nanny said when she answered the phone. You tried to explain about the pills but she kept saying, "Ricky, how did this happen? Should I come get you?" When you said you were in Texas she started to cry. That wasn't the worst part.

"Who's done this to you? Should I call the police?" she asked. There was a loud crash on the other end of the phone, something breaking.

"What was that, Nanny?"

"I dropped a plate of food. Where's the car, Ricky?"

"I'm being arrested, Nanny. I have the car. I'll bring it back." And you meant it, without even realizing you wouldn't be able to. She said she'd call the secretary at Woodrow Wilson High School to tell them you wouldn't be at work on Monday. She told you not to worry about the dogs, she'd find someone else to walk them. This made you feel deserted, and damned. Nanny didn't get it. "Can the neighbors do it?" you asked. Nanny said she had to go, to clean up the food. "Nanny! Nanny!" you said, after she hung up. The officer next to you reached for his Taser. You dropped to the floor and hid your face. "Jesus," he said, before helping you up.

After two weeks in the Webb County Jail, Judge Henry Travers of the eleventh circuit court sentenced you to one year at Lewis

Prison in Woodville, Texas. "You'll only serve four months," your public defender said afterward.

You spent eight days in a holding cell with a car thief named Teddy from Houston, then down a long, loud hall full of men yelling and watching as the guard took you to your room. Donald was sitting on the edge of the bunk reading. The guard handed you your toiletries. The door made a shocking click-clicking noise when it closed. Donald moved his hair out of his eyes, held out his hand for you to shake.

"You like Tom Clancy?" Donald said, showing you the cover of his book.

Most of the cells here are two-man rooms with bunk beds, like the one you're in. There are three dormitories with around seventy men in each and people get moved all of the time but you've been in the two-man cell with Donald since your intake. Everywhere you turn there are black men. They huddle in the dorms, or else move through the block like schools of shimmering fish spotted by the rare scrawl of a white face. When the white men smile, their slim mouths are filled with rotten teeth. At first there is a lot of crying and vomiting and shaking, coming off the beautiful pain pills you'd grown, over the past year and a half, to love enormously. This is prison. Donald says he can't find you pills in here and that anyone who can is looking for a hook-up. Sometimes the old dudes will offer something boring at the canteen, Effexor or Ambien. These do not help.

You look at yourself a lot in the mirror. You're lanky—bony and gaunt. Your hair is too blond, the cut pathetically neat. Everyone in here seems taller than you. Even the shortest felon seems like a giant.

Donald tells you that some of the other inmates have offered him money for the chance to get at you. "What do you mean?" you ask.

"What do you call a blond with half a brain?" he asks.

Two months in and already you are ashamed of so many things, things you had no idea a person could be ashamed of. One, for being educated, because most of the men here never made it through high school. You feel embarrassed around them, like Louis XVI must have felt after his arrest, surrounded by the working class in the Temple Prison—not condescending but humiliated.

Your cell has a toilet with a sink attached. The sink is attached to the top of the toilet where you think the tank should be. At first this made you uncomfortable about washing your hands. You're used to it now. You have to straddle the toilet facing the tank or stand to the side of it when you brush your teeth, or wash, or get a drink. You push a button above the faucet and the water comes.

The recreation room reminds you of the teachers' lounge at Woodrow Wilson High. One of the dudes in there, he can hardly read the newspaper. When you first saw him, sitting with the paper open, sounding out the words to himself, you thought you'd help him. He was skipping the words he couldn't figure out. You went over and pulled up a chair. "Can I have a look?" you said. This was before you knew how things worked.

He said, "Get your own fucking paper."

"It's nay-bourhood," you told him, "not neeg-bourhood."

"I got it," he said, sliding his chair away. "Now get the fuck off me you faggoty fuck."

"Sorry," you said.

Your lip was trembling. You couldn't think of anything good to say. You got up and went to the other side of the room. You sat in one of the yellow vinyl lounge chairs next to the window pretending to read *People* magazine. You sit there a lot now. You try not to make eye contact with anyone you suspect might be illiterate.

You told Donald the story and he laughed. You pretended to

laugh too, but also you were crying a little. You didn't let Donald know.

Donald has long black hair. Many tattoos. His teeth aren't perfect, but you've seen worse. There is something dim and monumental in his eyes—the irises gray as tombstones. He grew up in Iowa. You can hear it when he talks. He calls cola "pop," and other things like that. This is not the only reason you like Donald but it has a lot to do with it. He says he's in for manslaughter, but he won't say anything else. You ask him what happened but instead he talks about his hair. "There were a few guys in here that used to fuck with me," he says, "because I wouldn't cut my hair and because sometimes I put it up in a ponytail. They used to say to me, 'What's under the ponytail, Donald, a horse's ass?' All I have to do now is give them the look."

He stands up really fast, like something bad has just happened. You're not sure what's going on. He gets right up in front of you like he's considering the quickest way to crack open your face. "That's what I do," he says. "That's the look I give them." He starts laughing. "Works, don't it?"

You nod. Your pulse knocks inside your ears. "It does. For real."

He says now he tells them to shut the fuck up and they shut the fuck up. You're sure you're not capable of this.

"Try it," he says.

"I don't think so. I'll just be cool. I'll stay out of their way or else give them my dessert at dinner."

Donald points his finger at you. "Shut the fuck up!" he yells. He makes a fist, brings it up to your mouth and presses the knuckles against your lips. "Stop fucking talking right now!"

"Why? What did I do wrong?" you say into his knuckles.

"No, Ricky. Damn it. That's what you're supposed to say to them. I'm not telling you to shut the fuck up. Shit, dude, you've got to stop being such a giant pussy." Donald shakes his head, like he can't believe people like you exist. "I'm trying to help you." he says. "You're going to be in here a really long time. You've got to at least try."

You've been here two months now. "Yeah," you say, "two more months."

"You'll be lucky if they ever let you out," Donald says. He picks up his book. *Without Remorse* it's called, and it must be serious because Donald will sometimes talk aloud while he's reading, usually to cuss out the bad guys who he says are always corrupt cops. He lies down on the bed holding the book open in front of his face. "It's gonna suck without you here, man."

You've been with him almost every hour of every day since you got here and you're still not sure what to do when he says these things.

He lays the book down on his chest. He says, "Some dudes make friends in here and then get all depressed if they leave. You're lucky I'm not like that. I'd never try to kill myself or anything." He picks up the book again. "I'm reading now—don't talk to me." He stares at it, turns a page. "Bitch," he says, and then: "Just kidding."

Another thing you feel ashamed for is Donald. You can't remember ever thinking of a man in this way. You had a girlfriend for a while in college, Janice Pickett. You looked at her and you liked what you saw. She was short, breasts like half-filled water balloons, strawberry-blonde hair. On the old couch in your dorm room, spring of sophomore year, she took your virginity. She took off your clothes and sat on your lap. There was a sudden wetness on you, like maybe she'd just spilled warm soup on your penis. You made an awkward groan and came inside her. She got up and ran to the bathroom. After that you went on dates together to the movies and to sports bars. You bought flavored condoms and laid a blanket down on the dorm-room floor, thought about important moments of the American Civil War and tried not to come as soon as she climbed on top of you. You liked her, thought about asking if she wanted to move in together. Right before graduation she showed up saying, "Let's keep in touch, Ricky. Sound good?" But it sounded awful, like she was making fun of you or something. That was two years ago. You haven't had a woman since. The female teachers at Woodrow Wilson made you nervous when they started acting sexy, cornering you in front of the faculty microwave. You just never thought about guys. One time in college a drunk guy at a house party showed his penis to everyone in the room. It made your face hot, caused a tingling feeling in your stomach, but you didn't want to touch it or anything. Why would you? You only thought it looked weird. It was big.

When you find out that Nanny reported the car stolen, her car, which you drove from Indiana to Mexico to the buy the pills, you aren't angry exactly, just frustrated. Frustrated is a better word for it. Nanny forgets things. She can't help it.

She can't come to visit but you call her on Thursdays. At first she only asked about the car, kept telling you that someone had stolen it. "Can you believe someone would do that to me?" she said. Two months in and she's finally stopped with that. Instead she tells you she hopes you're doing well, that she's proud of you, and proud of your new job in Pittsburgh, where she says you're teaching history again. She says you should go and straighten up the desks before class every day, pick up all the little bits of paper trash off the floor so that the Lord can come into a nice clean classroom before each session, inspiring the children to learn and truly love their lessons. "Will you do that for me, Ricky? Will you try it and see if it makes a difference?"

"Yes," you say, "I'll do that, for sure, what a good idea." Then you walk back down the hall, through all the loud and mechanical doors toward your cell, where Donald is playing rummy against himself or watching *The Maury Povich Show*. "How was it?" he says.

"Oh, it was whack," you tell him.

At 9 p.m. the lights and the television are shut off. Sometimes it takes a while for the cell block to quiet down. The other inmates are always laughing or yelling. Eventually one of the guards calls for everyone to knock it off. Donald has the bottom bunk, and he usually waits fifteen or so minutes before he asks if you're asleep. You say, "No, I'm still awake," and then Donald asks if you want to come down there.

"Whatever," you say.

You'd been in here maybe a month when Donald first said it, and now after a few weeks of it, you just climb down from your bunk and try not to look nervous. You wait for him to make a spot for you next to the wall. You lie stiff as a book against the cold concrete and wait. You both lie there for a minute without touching until he asks if you want to suck. That's when the tingling in your stomach starts. If you want to suck you put your hand on his penis, which is already so hard that it sticks up out of his underwear, flat against his stomach under the tight elastic of his briefs. You play with it for a minute before putting your face under the covers. Sometimes he asks if you'd rather fuck, in which case you roll over and face the wall. It's nothing, really. Just a heavy weight. A heat in your joints. A current travelling. This is what cellmates do.

About the pills. You had an abscessed tooth, right—a cavity and then a pain like a wide throb across your face that woke you up one morning before work. Your dentist—the same one Nanny had been taking you to since you were little—scolded you for letting it get that bad, prescribed ten days' worth of antibiotics and twenty Vicodin, told you to come back in a week and a half. The first pain pill made you dizzy and tired. You slept straight through the night. The second one made you vomit. The third one lit a glorious fire in your head that eventually spread to your chest and arms and groin until it had invaded your whole body. Everything was right in the world. Nanny was a thin, white angel mixing vanilla pudding at the kitchen table. The children at school were blurs of pink and green with flesh tones in between. Instead of reading aloud from the textbook every day you wrote lectures for the first time. History books became the things they used to be on sunnier days alone in your old dorm room. The surge of those sagas opened up to you like ancient mausoleums.

You read:

The Life of Wilhelm Conrad Röntgen.

The Sephardim in the Ottoman Empire.

A History of the American Privateers During Our War with England in the years 1812, '13 and '14. You could put your hand over your eyes and see battlefields, crowded infirmaries, the torch-lit corridors of Nubian pyramids.

After that you were making appointments at the doctor's office all the time, complaining of back pain, neck pain, chronic headaches, a burning sensation in your kneecaps. You'd take Lortab, Vicodin, Percocet, Percodan, Tylox. It was like learning a secret language. Some of the pills were more exciting than others. You saw three different doctors, had prescriptions filled at every drugstore in town, until finally Shirley Lynn Dobbs at Dobbs' Drugstore started asking questions, making calls.

It was maybe a week later that you saw the article about pharmaceuticals and drug laws in *Newsweek*—they mentioned Mexico, speedy clinics in the backs of grocery stores and novelty shops, prescriptions for anything a patient was willing to pay for in cash. You thought of nineteenth-century China, of the thriving opium trade and those covert smoking divans. It sounded like the most perfect retreat.

It was the Thanksgiving holiday. You told Nanny you were going to Indianapolis to hear a seminar on the Miami Indians of the Midwest. You emptied your savings, cashed in a couple of bonds. You had enough pills to last three days. You got in Nanny's car and drove. And drove. And drove. The sun and the moon came and went.

The day before Thanksgiving, in Nuevo Laredo, you rented a room at the Red Roof Inn. You got lost two days in a row, ate too many cheap enchiladas, asked the wrong people the wrong questions in the wrong language until you finally decided that the back-door pharmacies were made up, were more like small invisible cities of El Dorado than the luxurious opium dens of China.

On the last night, at the Chaser Lounge, you let Kenny Voglar from Carson City, Nevada, buy you too many strawberry margaritas. Kenny wore a lime-green tank top and a diamond ring. He claimed he was once the president of the Rod Stewart fan club. He had a soft spot for GHB and Xanax. He said he knew a man who had exactly what you were looking for. You could see your reflection in the mirror behind the bar. The Christmas lights strung around the alcohol bottles made little flashes of color across your face like so many blue and red stars blinking off and on.

The man who had exactly what you were looking for was actually a seventeen-year-old Mexican kid in short-shorts with a Madonna tattoo. Kenny talked. The Mexican kid turned up "Like a Prayer" on the stereo and danced. Kenny watched. You stood by the door, pretending to read the ingredients on a package of gum. After the song was over the kid went into the bathroom, made some noise, brought out five cottage cheese containers full of pills. He handed you one of the pills. You took it, and sat on the floor watching the Hispanic boy and Kenny Voglar snort something off the bedside table. They danced around to the music while you waited for the pill to do its stuff. After twenty minutes or so you decided you maybe liked Madonna. "Vogue" seemed like an interesting song. The Hispanic kid did a special dance for it. He seemed very talented. You gave him all of your money. He gave you all of his cottage cheese containers.

If you don't answer Donald when he asks if you're asleep, he says, "I see how it is. What? You mad at me? You got a problem, Ricky?" But you're never mad at him. You're just worried. You lie in your bed and fake the loud, steady breaths of deep sleep. You feel the bed start to shake, Donald furiously taking care of himself on the bunk beneath. He's only touched your penis once, wrapped his hand around it and squeezed for a second. After he finishes in your mouth or on your back he quickly pulls up his pants and rolls over and you climb up to your bunk.

Once, after he was finished fucking, you started to get up and he said, "Don't move." He put his arms around you, pressed his face into your back, touched you neatly on the spine with his nose. You might have stayed like that all night except Donald woke you up later, smacking you in the head, saying, "Go back to your own bed, faggot." An inmate a couple cells down was yelling, "It's my stomach. I think it's the pancreas! I need a doctor!"

"Shut the hell up," someone else yelled.

"No shit," Donald called back, "because you don't even know what a pancreas is!"

You met with your drug counselor for the first time and he told you your official release date. May 14. It is now the fifth of April. He said he was proud of you, which was odd since you'd only met with him once. Still, it was nice to hear. You asked when you would have to appear before the parole board. He said, "This is a kind of parole hearing right now. You've done everything right. Good job, Ricky."

You come back into the cell and tell Donald that things went great with the counselor. Donald is sitting on the floor, shuffling the cards. "Where's *Rainbow Six*?"

"Where's what?"

"My new Clancy book, idiot. Where the fuck is it?"

"I haven't seen it."

Donald holds up the deck of cards with one hand, presses them between his thumb and index finger so that the cards go flying. There's something in his mouth. He looks up at you while the cards fly. He spits hard across the room, hitting you, perfectly, on the mouth. He says, "Don't think you're better than anyone else in here! You fucking drug addict. If you get out you'll be back on drugs in no time. Then you'll be dead."

You stand with his spit running down your chin. You want to say something but the spit clings. You don't wipe it away. Just stare at the wall with your mouth closed tight. You think about the Korean War. Think about President Harry S. Truman or picture old Douglas MacArthur standing on the grassy banks of the Nakdong River polishing his sunglasses with a handkerchief. Wait for Donald to look away and then use your shirtsleeve to wipe away the spit. You go and put your mouth under the spigot. You wonder how much tobacco it must have taken General MacArthur to fill his gigantic pipe. Think about your counselor. Think: Good job, Ricky. Good job.

Nanny is your mother, or she might as well be. There has never been anyone else, at least not that you can remember. You remember a day years ago, before the pills, right after you moved home from college. You were in the living room with Nanny. The dogs, Ashley and Lyle, were asleep under the coffee table, their noses at Nanny's feet. She sat her Dr Pepper down on the china saucer she used for a coaster. You loved the sound it made after each drink, when she returned the can to the saucer, the warbled ping of aluminum to china. "You know, honey, to me Dr Pepper tastes like vanilla extract. And you know what else? I think you have always been this way. You have always been like you are now, even as a little boy. A criminal mind, some people call it, but I think you could be a minister. Your great-grandfather was insane. He used to choke rabbits to death in the shed. He enjoyed it. You remind me of him." You were flattered, even though it was clearly one of her less coherent days and you weren't entirely sure what she meant. She kept calling you Larry, who was maybe an old friend of hers. She'd go through a short list of names—her grandfather, distant cousins—before she called you by the right one. It made you proud to know you reminded her of a dangerous person. You only wished you were the sort of person who could choke a bunny. You wonder if Nanny somehow knew this was coming.

The day after Donald spat in your face the two of you sit on the floor and play spades as if none of it happened. Donald has a tattoo of a black knife surrounded by a spiral of thorns directly over his Adam's apple. You stare at his throat, not at the tattoo, but at the thick apex of bone there. It reminds you of something. A pill. A tree. An erection.

"One time I choked a rabbit to death," you tell him.

"My lawyer fucked me over, really did a number on me," he says.

"What do you mean?"

"Just did, man. Just did."

This isn't good enough. You want the history. The timeline of events. You want the body count. But before you can ask him, Donald reaches into his pants and takes out an oatmeal cookie. "I saved it from lunch. It's all yours." It's against the rules to leave the mainline with food, and you don't like oatmeal cookies. But you eat it anyway. Donald says, "Ricky, I was trying to help you. That's why I spit on you. Every motherfucker in here is going to try and spit in your face, or worse. They don't give a shit whether you live or die. You're not free yet, man. You're still an inmate. I just want you to be prepared. I just really care about you. I take care of me and mine."

During the last few weeks you keep your hands clean. Shave every day. When you shower, you always use more soap on the parts of you Donald pays most attention to: hands, butt, hands.

Nanny sends many cards. The last one: Life is well in Pike County. Ashley is eight! Lyle has been injured! Those crazy people down the street with the camouflage golf cart! Ashley whines at your bedroom door. Lyle always thought so much of you. You didn't forget about him, did you? He would always follow you around when you killed the flies so he could eat up the dead ones! Went to lunch at Long John Silver's with my sister. She's been coming over to walk the dogs. I might get tired of her soon! Been thinking of you. Been thinking of you so much. Submitted your name to the prayer chain at church.

Climb into bed. Get back up. Read the last chapter in all of Donald's books. Write a letter to Nanny. Drink water from the sink. Wet your hair. Comb it straight back. Look at yourself in the metal of the sink and think: Not bad, Ricky.

You like the black guys but sometimes they throw pieces of food at each other during dinner. They make a mess. They ask you what you're looking at and you offer them your fruit cup. One of them comes and takes it. "Thank you," he says. Apparently he doesn't like the pear chunks, because he spends the rest of the time throwing them back at you every time the guard looks away. Finally Donald comes in and sits down, sees the pear chunks on the table, a piece stuck to the front of your jumpsuit. He looks over at the black dudes but they're looking at their food, pushing it around with their spoons. "What the fuck?" Donald says. Eventually someone lifts their head. Donald points at him, picks up some of the pear, throws it and hits him right on the forehead. They both stand up.

"Fuck no," Donald says. "Sit right back down." When the guy doesn't sit down, you say to Donald, "Don't. Just forget about it. I don't care about the pears," but Donald is walking over with his tray in his hands and breaking it over the guy's head. One swift crack against the man's face and the guards are dragging Donald out of the mainline. You're just standing there, not saying a word, with fruit still stuck on your jumpsuit.

Donald's skin is tan and tough from years of working in the sun. He was a laborer. He roofed hotels in Cleveland, worked as a garbage man in Louisville, did other things in Chicago. "You go where the work is," he always says.

He is gone for over a week. In solitary confinement. You can only wonder what is happening to him. Sometimes men will spend months in the hole. No television. No books. No one to talk to. Donald came on you the night before he hit the guy in the face with the food tray. You don't take a bath while he's gone. You keep the smell on you. Put your hands on your back, between your legs, up to your nose. It is the smell of something old, something unclean and sour and terribly personal. This is what it's like with him.

Several inmates approach you in the yard. They enclose you, dark and scary as a basement. They want to know if you're looking for anything. One of them gets right up in your face. He says, "You're fair game now that your dude is gone." He tells you, "This way, buddy. Walk over here." But one of the senior guards, Clint maybe, or Gary, comes and stands between the two of you. He says, "Come on, Ricky. That's enough. Let's go." He takes you through the gymnasium, and all the way back to your cell. "You need to get your shit together," he says. He wants to know how a kid like you ended up in Woodville.

"Drugs," you tell him.

He laughs at that. "What else," he says. It's not a question.

You lie in bed the rest of the time smelling yourself and thinking about Donald: how he only sleeps on his back; how the blood pools in the sink after he brushes his teeth; how he always cleans under his fingernails with an envelope, how his semen tastes, how it sprays over you in varying arcs—the distance it goes, the sheer and warm amount of it shooting across your body.

When he finally comes back you're in the recreation room sitting in your chair by the window, reading a magazine. You watch him walk in. He's freshly shaven. His hair is pulled back, combed and wet. You're not sure if you should smile. You know you pay too much attention to him in front of other people. He stands on the other side of the room talking to some of the other men from your block. He looks so clean, just back from the showers. You're still dirty. You walk over and stand next to him. You don't speak. It takes him a minute. "What's up?" he says, like he hardly knows you. You have to keep your hands tucked into your waistband to keep from reaching out and stroking his ponytail. Here you are, like Hephaestion standing in the court of Alexander the Great, pretending to listen to the strategies but instead thinking of how he's going to make you feel after the troops disperse.

When you're both back in the cell Donald says, "They'll put someone else in here as soon as you're gone. I wonder who it will be? I hope they're cool."

You imagine another man in the cell. You imagine the lights going out, the room quiet for a few minutes before Donald asks this other man if he's asleep. You wonder what Donald means by "cool."

At lights out you take all of your clothes off and wait for him to ask you. After maybe half an hour has passed and he hasn't said anything you climb down and get into his bed. For the first time, you kiss him. Maybe you shouldn't but you want to try.

"What the hell?" he says, jerking back, like he doesn't understand. "I'm not your fucking boyfriend." He grabs your head, pushes you down toward his crotch. "Do me a favor," he says.

For the rest of the week, after lights out, Donald says nothing or else he just comes up to your bunk. He says, "Turn over." He presses his fist against the small of your back and whispers in your ear. He says, "You like it now, don't you? You love it. You want me to own it." He says, "You like it when it hurts?"

You tell him you like it when it hurts. You tell him you want him to own you.

You talk to Nanny on the phone. You tell her you need a way to get back to Indiana. You tell her the car was impounded, you don't have the car, she'll have to pick it up.

Nanny is upset. "Ricky, you've got a good job there in Pittsburgh. It's a friendly city. I don't know why you're quitting. This is nonsense." So many times you've explained to Nanny. It was easier to go along at first, but now you realize the problem with that.

You tell her it's the end of the school year and you might go back in the fall but you're not sure yet. You say there's been some conflict among the faculty members over trash in the classrooms. "I don't know what to do," you say. You ask for money to buy a plane ticket. You tell her she can send it to the same address she sends the letters. She says she has to get the dog off of her lap. "I have an ink pen right here," she says. You've given her the address four other times, but you tell her again. She says, "Why on earth would I mail a check to someplace in Texas, Ricky? That doesn't make any sense to me." You get the dreadful feeling that maybe she chooses her moments of sanity. Nanny says that Ashley is going crazy over something in the kitchen, probably a mouse behind the refrigerator. She has to get off the phone to see what the ruckus is about. "I can't have her hurting herself. They're all I've got, Ricky. These sweet little dogs." She hangs up and for a while you keep the receiver to your ear, listening to the droning static of the open line until the guard taps on the door to say your time is up.

After dinner you and Donald play cards and drink milk, sharing the same styrofoam cup, taking little sips so that there is always another drink left. You always do it this way when you have milk before bed, and there is always one last sip. Even before the lights are turned off you put your hands down the front of Donald's underwear. You hold his penis. Donald punches you in the arm and then puts his hand in your underwear too. He tries jacking you off. You each hold the other's penis. Donald doesn't know what he's doing. He gets too rough. You think he's trying to make it hurt. You don't say it hurts though and, eventually, it starts to feel good.

The lights go out before you're done.

"Stay here," he says.

"Where?"

"Here, idiot. With me."

"I don't think I can."

"Then do something," he says, smiling.

"What do you mean?"

"I already said."

You get in Donald's bed. He puts his head under the cover. Puts you in his mouth. He bites you. You're wishing you knew how to help him. You're wishing he knew what he was doing, that he meant it. His teeth get in the way. He's going too fast.

"Are you close?" he says.

"I think so," you say.

He moves around for a few minutes. He presses his thumbs into your thighs. Eventually he gives up, slides back on to the pillow and props his head on an arm. He uses his other hand on you. He stares at you while he does it. He's never let you be this close to his face but after a minute he is finally putting his lips close to yours, easing his tongue in your mouth. He opens too wide and breathes across your teeth until you are running out over his knuckles and down on to your stomach. He's right there in front of you and you can feel his mouth widening into a smile. Something shifts, spreads through your body like a vivid fluid crowding out your limbs.

"You don't want to leave." he says. "I've got fifteen more years of this fucking place. Think about that."

"Eleven," you say. "You've got eleven more years."

"Yeah," he says. "Eleven. That's what I meant."

"Why?"

"I ran over a dog."

"Did the dog belong to someone famous?"

"No. Moron." He's quiet. He sits up, then lies down again. "Do you have kids?" he says.

"You know I don't." It's like he's forgotten who he's even talking to.

"That's right, you don't. They're not what you expect. It's not like how you imagine. You think you can look at someone else's kids and know what it's like." Donald lets down his ponytail. The hair falls forward, hiding his face. "When they're yours it's like they're wild animals or something and you have to clean up their shit and keep them from burning the house down or running into the street during traffic."

You want to get up. "I should sleep," you say.

Donald grabs you. "You're a fucking moron, Ricky."

"No, I'm not."

"You're like every other motherfucker in here."

You're thinking he's going to hit you. You get up but he just sits there with his hair in his eyes. "Why are you like the way you are?" you ask, but he doesn't talk now. You reach out to touch him, but you smack him instead, without even thinking, across the face. You hit him in the head, and arms, then on the chest. You're right up on him and both of your arms and hands are throbbing with the way it feels to touch him like this. You're on top and he's on the bed and you're trying to give him what he wants. He's yelling. He wants it to hurt. He wants it to hurt bad. He's covering his face and moving toward the wall and pretending. He's doing you a favor. He's saying you're crazy, someone help, you're fucking nuts. The door opens and the guard is saying, "Ricky, get off. Back up!" The guard is in the room and he's bending your arms behind you. He is pushing you out and holding your wrists against the middle of your back as he leads you into the long, loud hallway of men who are watching and whistling as you go by.

He takes you out of the cell block and into a room with pictures on the walls. There are chairs all around, like in a waiting area. Another guard drags one of the chairs toward the middle and handcuffs you to it. You're in there alone for a long time, sitting in the chair, with a fiery and disordered ache still in your arms and face. Every so often you can hear the sound of something mechanical, an engine of some kind on the other side of the wall. There are shelves filled with magazines and thick paperbacks, and a small window, high up, with a white curtain. It is different in here, not like the rest of the prison. It is for employees, you think. That you're handcuffed to the meager chair seems like a joke.

Eventually you hear the door, and the guard comes, with two little cups. "Here," he says. One of the cups is full of water, and the other has a pill in the bottom, something small and yellow, and unfamiliar. "I can't," you say. "I can't take it."

"Yeah, you can. It's fine." He sounds bored, like he's said this before. "I promise. Just swallow it. It's so you can sleep."

Stare at the pill, and then the guard. Recall the distant rapture of pharmaceuticals. "People get nervous, Ricky. You're a kid. Shit is scary. Take the pill."

Dump the pill out of the cup into your hand and put it in your mouth. Drink the water and swallow. The guard says to stand up and come with him. He walks you out of the room, down another hall into a different cell where there's just a cot and a toilet. This is the hole. You know it once you're inside. The door is closed and then it's too dark to see. You feel your way around. The guard says he'll see you later. You find the cot and lie down and think about Nanny for a long time until, finally, you're seized by the miraculous buoyancy of the little pill. After that, there's not much.

There is a long corridor of solid metal doors that eventually open to the prison yard, and then to an enormous parking lot, and beyond that the grass and the interstate where the cars pass all day long like birds migrating in both directions. In the morning no one talks about what happened. They give you a bus ticket and eighty-six dollars. "For food," the man says, after he explains how long the trip will take, and the various stops, on the way back to Indiana. They give you the same clothes you were wearing when you came in. You don't know how to feel about this. It's like you're supposed to walk out and pick up where you left off. You sit down on the floor and tie your shoes. You have forgotten about them. You see them on your feet and you're shocked by the way they look. A stocky lady wearing red lipstick and big sunglasses comes out from behind the desk she's sitting at and says, "Come on, Ricky. I guess I'm taking you." She talks into her radio. She says some numbers. You don't know what they mean. You follow her out of the door and to a car. You're not sure if you should open the car door yourself or wait for her to do it. She comes up behind you and puts her hand on your back and says, "You can sit up front—if you want."

You get in the front seat of the car. The interior is hot. It feels good against the backs of your legs. Go with her, down the service road, on to the interstate. It's a few miles to the bus stop where there's a sign in the window that reads, "Give Us Your Hungry," which seems very silly to you. This is not prison. This is a bus stop. Here the shoe meets the grass. After she drives off, you stand there for a long time. If you wanted you could stare down at the gravel parking lot all day. This is where people get up from their seats any time they want and maybe even walk to the North Pole if they think there's something there worth walking to. It smells like dirt, and the bitter exhaust of so many buses. You're like John Smith, you think, or William Clark, or Amerigo Vespucci, an eager frontiersman plodding off toward the darkest places.

STANDARDS

Mary Morris

WHEN I WAS A GIRL, GROWING UP in Illinois, my father belonged to a men's club. It was the only one in Chicago that catered to German Jews. My father prided himself on the fact that he was the first Russian Jew ever to be accepted into this prestigious establishment. The Standard Club was that kind of a place. I loved the Club, as we called it, with its sweeping marble staircase, its second floor with the library, the enormous public spaces that I raced up and down as a child.

Everything about the Club was huge. It suggested wealth and largess and a secret world of men and privilege. Women weren't allowed to be members. There were whole floors that excluded women, and my mother complained, often bitterly, about this. But to me, as I dashed through the second floor, my patent leather shoes clicking on the marble, with the strong scent of cigars and men's cologne wafting my way, that made the Club all the more mysterious.

At the Standard Club they always knew where my father was. When we walked in, the front desk clerk, who sat at a round table in the middle of the lobby, would say, before we even announced who we were, "Hello, Mrs. Bernstein. Mr. Bernstein is on 6 playing cards." Or that he was on 3 having his hair cut. Sometimes he was at the gym or in the library, but the front desk knew. "Mr.

Bernstein," the desk clerk would pick up the phone and say, "your family is here." This just added one more mystery for me—that a stranger sitting behind a desk knew exactly where to find my father while we often did not. But this was so.

A short while later my father would join us in the library or in the huge dining room. He looked rested and pampered, spotless and trim. He acted as if he owned the place and in a sense I suppose he did. My father attributed his success to his good grooming and polished demeanor, a cover-up for his peasant roots. But he had Cary Grant good looks and a lot of charm and people were drawn to him wherever he was.

On Friday nights we went to the Club for the buffet dinner. Often we dragged along one of my great aunts or uncles or a grandparent who ate heartily, then inevitably complained that the food at their club was better and they didn't serve trafe. Though the Standard Club was a Jewish club, it is true that there were long tables, overflowing with shrimp and oysters. There was a carving table where roast beef (they drew the line at pork) was carved thin as you liked it by a black man in white gloves.

The appetizer table was a medley of sliced vegetables with radishes sculpted into intricate flowers and dips and mushroom caps with crispy cheese that I devoured by the handfuls if my father wasn't around. Dessert was a child's fantasy of bowls of strawberries and whipped cream, flans and coconut pie, and a thick German chocolate cake. Here my father was very strict and we were only allowed the smallest of helpings. I often wondered why he brought us to this splendid buffet, then would not let us partake.

All the waiters were black or Hispanic and they had worked at the Club for years. Some had known my father for decades before I was even born. They worked at the Club from the time they were boys until they were old men. "We treat them well," my father used to say. "So they like it here."

On Fridays after school my mother, dressed in her white gloves, drove along the Edens Highway to the Club. I was their only child, though she had wanted more, but none came, and she clutched the steering wheel as if someone held a gun to her head. Those days my father left work early to play raquetball or ping-pong, at which he was a champion. Then he greeted us all spiffy, smelling of talc and cologne.

My father never missed a Friday night dinner if he could help it. He liked to smooze and make the scene and he went from table to table, shaking hands with his buddies. My mother did the same, greeting Melanie Carter who owned an art gallery and her husband Eddie, Sal Pearson whose wife had just left him, or the recently widowed, though hardly grieving, Ed Kolowitz. "Oh, look," my father would say to my mother as he scanned the room, "the Greens are here tonight." And she'd sigh: "You go say hello. I can't stand her." Or "There's Glenn Edelstone." I looked over and saw Mr. Edelstone and his wife, Lorraine, and their daughters, Lucy and Laurel. "Well, we should go over and say hello," my father said.

"You can go if you want," my mother replied.

Glenn Edelstone was a big Chicago developer. A man of great wealth, unlike my father who put on a good facade, but in truth we were merely comfortable. And after that it was more smoke and mirrors. But Mr. Edelstone was truly rich and powerful. He owned whole swaths of Chicago. He and my father were once involved in an important business deal, but something happened before I was born.

My father was an architect and he had his own firm. Once, he told me, when he was just starting out and working late, an older man, wearing a cape, walked into his drafting room. He told my father that this had been his first studio and he wanted to look around. "Be my guest," my father said. The man introduced himself as Frank Lloyd Wright. He gave my father some tips on his drawing which my father ignored.

"That's typical," my mother would say.

At any rate, one day, many years later, my father and Mr. Edelstone were driving down Michigan Avenue and, as they approached the old McCormick Mansion on the corner of Oak, Mr. Edelstone said, "I'm going to buy that corner, Arnie, and you're going to build the first residential skyscraper on Michigan Avenue."

And my father, in his impeccable way, replied, "Glenn, no one is going to want to come and live in downtown Chicago."

"You build it," Mr. Edelstone said, "and people will come." So they built the building and the rest is history. Many people came to live in downtown Chicago. And for a time we profited from this. When the building was about five years old, Mr. Edelstone convinced my father, who was in need of cash for one reason or another, to sell him his shares. "I'll take these off your hands," were Mr. Edelstone's exact words. Two months later Mr. Edelstone turned around and sold the entire building for millions.

"Of course he knew he was going to sell it," my mother complained. "And we'd be rich now." But my father bore no grudge. "It was just business," he said. He and Mr. Edelstone remained friends, though my mother was bitter about this and added it to a list that would grow as the years went on.

That evening at the Club, Mr. Edelstone came up to our table, along with his wife, Lorraine. He carried a plate, heaped with a slab of rare roast beef, swimming in its own blood, and Yorkshire pudding and green beans while Lorraine had opted for a simple platter of poached salmon and a boiled parsley potato. My father jumped up to shake his hand. "It's great to see you," he said.

"How're you doing, Arnie?" Mr. Edelstone was a man with

one of those great big handshakes, and he liked to slap people on the back. He was huge the way the Standard Club was huge and even as a child I thought he filled the space well. "Ready to build another building with me?" Glenn laughed and my father nodded.

"You know I am. Anytime."

Lorraine wore a plain navy blue suit. I only recall Lorraine in muted or dark colors. She leaned over, giving my mother air kisses while holding her plate erect. "Margie," she said, "you're looking well." My mother patted her hair. She was looking well. My mother, who tended to be heavy, had lost some weight, but Lorraine was too polite to say this. "Hello, Eve," she said to me, "My, Eve, you are getting to be a very pretty young lady." She gave us each a kiss and stood there chatting with my mother for a few minutes, even as her salmon got cold.

Lorraine Edelston was a petite woman, not pretty exactly, but she had a compact, concise way about her. She was an efficient woman who seemed to manage her husband, her life, and her two daughters quite well. Whereas her husband had eyes that were blue watery pools that seemed capable of the greatest sorrows and joys, Lorraine's were more dark and opaque. But she seemed like the kind of woman who could get any job done. Their daughters were dark like her, but both had the largeness of their father.

Suddenly Lucy appeared. "Mom," she tugged on her mother's arm, trying to pull her away. Lucy was a tall, looming young woman, big like her father, but with large, ample breasts. With her dark hair and red lips, she reminded me of Snow White. "Mom," she said, "Come on. Let's eat. They have crème brûlée for dessert and I don't want it to be gone."

"Oh, Lucy, they always have plenty of crème brûlée. You've just been away too long." Lucy was already in college somewhere in the East. Whenever someone from our town went East to school, it implied big plans, a serious future, and I envied it. "And you are being rude. You haven't said hello to the Bernsteins."

Lucy looked at me. "Is that you, Eve? My god, you're almost grown up."

I blushed. "I'm in eighth grade," I said.

"I haven't seen you since you were this high." And she held her hand close to the ground. "Mummy, let's eat," and she tugged once more on her mother's arm, blowing us kisses as she left.

"Well, it's lovely to see you, as always," Lorraine said. "We'll make a plan and have dinner soon." And she made that sign for making a phone call.

"Definitely," my mother replied, giving Lorraine a big wave. My mother waited until Lorraine was out of earshot, then she shook her head, whispering under her breath loud enough so that we could hear. "Oh," my mother sighed. "I think it's terrible..."

"What?" my father asked, sipping his vodka tonic, adding more ice with his spoon from his drinking glass.

"You know what. The way he..."

"Be quiet," my father snapped. He got that tense look he sometimes had around his mouth, and it was clear that the conversation was done. "I'm not discussing this." My mother pursed her lips, shaking her head, and I stared at my father, wanting to know what it was about Mr. Edelstone that he wouldn't let my mother say. My father glared back at me, then pointed to my plate. "And don't eat any more of that cake."

It was at about that time that my father began to travel more. He was on the road for business, searching for empty stretches of the Midwest where he could build retail stores and shopping centers. J. C. Penney, Montgomery Ward. He had a deal to close in Green Bay or a site to inspect in Evansville. My mother didn't seem to mind his absences. Quite the contrary, the little projects she worked on—scrapbooks she kept, curtains she sewed—seemed to take up more and more room, spreading themselves across the dining room table and into the living room until days before my father announced he was coming home. Then she'd fold everything up and put it away until he was gone again.

Once or twice a week he called from the road. One day I picked up the phone and the operator said, "Would you accept a collect call from Arnold Bernstein?"

I had never accepted a collect call before so I didn't know what was required of me, but I heard my father shouting in the background, "Say yes. Just accept the charges."

When the operator got off, my father said, "Eve, is this you?" He sounded as if he was playing that game when you talk through a tin cup.

Of course it was me. Who else could it be? But I just said, "Yes, Daddy. It's me."

"So you're already home from school."

I glanced at the clock. It was five o'clock. "Yes, I am. When are you coming home?" I wanted to know where my father was. I tried to imagine the motel room where he slept. The twin beds, the plaid spreads. I wondered if he called us from phone booths on the road or from inside his room on a black dial-up phone, and he was wearing a white hard hat the way he sometimes did on the job. I thought I could hear traffic zooming past as we spoke.

But he was all business. "How's school?" "Did you have your math test?" "How did you do?" "Did you go to baton practice this morning?" He barely waited for my answers and there was none of the nuanced speech, the dry humor I heard when he was at home. Or the anger too. Then after I answered the questions to his satisfaction, he said, "Put your mother on."

She was on the phone for only a few minutes, jotting notes of what he needed her to do. They exchanged very few pleasantries, though she ended each conversation with, "I love you too," which she said with the same inflection one might use to call the plumber about a leak.

When she got off, I asked her where he was. I wished I had a map so I could chart his movements as he traveled through the world, or at least the limited world of four farmland states. But my mother just shrugged. She flicked her wrist toward the evening and the darkness and the outside world. "Actually I have no idea."

The Edelstones were a fixture in our home. They came for card parties when my mother set up tables and served sandwiches without the crust, and they came for the big parties my parents sometimes threw for the Jewish Federation, and often they were at our smaller dinner parties, even if my mother didn't always want them on the guest list. Despite whatever difference had occurred between them, my father still considered Glenn and Lorraine among his closest friends.

One night when I had just entered high school I ran into Mr. Edelstone at the seafood table on a Friday night at the Club. My father and Mr. Edelstone had gotten involved in another small venture together ("Because he feels guilty," my mother said) and they were chatting about some engineering problem (support beams, I believe it was, and a ventilation shaft) that needed tending to. My father was nodding, shaking his head. "I know. I know," he said, as if he was a school boy, being chastised.

As I was spooning cocktail sauce on my shrimp, I felt Mr. Edelstone's eyes upon me. He wasn't just staring. His watery blue eyes roved across my body. He looked at me in a way that a man had never looked at me before and suddenly I was ashamed of my rounded hips, my burgeoning breasts. "Now if you'd built the building the way you built her, Arnie, we wouldn't be in this mess. And you'd be a rich man."

It was a joke, of course, and my father laughed, but somehow I missed the funny part. When we sat down with our plates filled with roast chicken and mashed potatoes and steamed carrots, my father repeated the joke to my mother and, though she wasn't a fan of Mr. Edelstone, my mother laughed and laughed. When she saw that I wasn't joining in, she turned to me. "It's a compliment, dear," she told me. "Don't take things so seriously."

I can't say that I was a model child. By the time I was fourteen I was living a secret life of my own. There was a group of boys—bad boys, my father would say—who smoked and drank and hung out at what our town called with some affection "the idiot's circle" in front of the railroad station. Most of these boys lived on the "wrong" side of the tracks, though some were just posing. That is, they were wealthier Jewish boys who wore leather jackets and held their cigarettes pinched at the filter. This was my preferred crowd when I began high school and, when I could, I would sneak away and joined them.

There was one boy in particular with whom I spent my time. Bobby G was tall and thin with jet black hair that he slicked back into a pompadour. He wore a black leather jacket before anyone else did and his face was utterly without expression. When he came into the classroom, usually late, he slid his body along the wall as if he was on a mission for a SWAT team, then slipped into his seat.

Our romance began over fractions. Bobby G was some kind of genius at math. Once in study hall I asked him a question and he solved it within seconds, not even bothering to write the problem down. That night I called him and read him my math problems, and he rattled off the answers like an auctioneer. "You must be using a calculator," I teased.

"Meet me and I'll show you."

Bobby G lived with his mother in Highwood above a bar and, given his jacket and cigarettes and slicked back hair, my father never would have allowed him to set foot in our house. So we made an arrangement. I had a piano lesson every Tuesday night. My father dropped me off at 7:20 just before my lesson, and Bobby G waited for me in the stairwell.

For five minutes as I tossed numbers at him, he did multiplication of fractions and long division in his head, just to prove that he could. "We can finish this on the phone," he said; then he grabbed me. He groped for my hips, kissing me, smelling my hair. His hardness pressed against me, though I must admit that I confused it with his wallet, and I pressed back against him until I had to dash, breathlessly, upstairs for my lesson. "Don't let my father see you," I warned him. "He'll kill me."

Soon I had my father dropping me off earlier and coming back later. I explained that my lessons were taking longer because Mr. LaTate thought I was gifted. My father didn't seem to notice that my hair was ruffled or that my piano playing never improved. This arrangement continued until Bobby G's mother moved them south, after Bobby got kicked out of school, to be near some grandparents. But, by then, I had my driver's licence and didn't need my father to drive me around any more.

That spring I had a paper to write about an Egyptian goddess. Isis, I believe. On weekends I went with my father into the city. He went to play racquetball at the Club while I spent the afternoon at the Chicago Public Library, doing research. I liked sitting in the big reading room of the library, enjoying the cool air and reading about ancient Egypt. One day a man in a dark suit sat down at the same table, adjacent to me. He wore glasses and had a briefcase which he snapped open. He removed some papers and began to read.

After a while he turned to ask about my book and if I was enjoying myself. As I looked his way, I realized that his fly was unzipped and his penis was sticking straight out, I had never seen an erect penis before and I knew I shouldn't look, but I did. I was transfixed by the large, pink cock protruding like an eel from its sea cave in the darkness of that man's suit. The way it seemed to be aching just for me. There was something oddly flattering in this. I had no idea what the man expected or what I was supposed to do so I turned, shaking and sweaty, back to my book as the man snapped his briefcase shut and scurried away.

The year we were turning sixteen, my friend, Annie Lerner, convinced her parents to have her Sweet Sixteen at the Club. The party was to be a sleepover in a large double suite ("Money's no object to the Lerners," my mother quipped), followed by a Saturday morning brunch. Annie's father was a longtime member and they had a lot of money. Perhaps they thought it would be better to allow the girls to stay at the Club than to have to deal with them in their home or drive us to the roller rink. And probably they were right.

Within moments of arriving, we took over that suite. We put on our pajamas and dragged mattresses to the floor. We ordered pizzas and broke into the mini-bar, drinking everything in sight. Somehow Annie had gotten her hands on a bottle of champagne which we guzzled until we were sick. I had never really had anything to drink before except a sip or two from my father's beer, and I spent much of the night with my head bent over the toilet. Sometime before midnight I descended into the darkness of my first hangover with little recollection of anything around me.

In the morning I had a tremendous headache, as did most of my friends. I thought I was going to die. I'd never had a pain like that before and didn't even know what to make of it. "I have two heads," I moaned to one of my friends and she agreed.

"I do too."

Somehow we all got dressed and made our way downstairs for brunch. I walked into the dining room wearing jeans and a pajama top, and we rowdy girls were ushered into the back of the dining room whose vaulted ceiling hung over us like a cathedral. I had never been in the dining room in daylight before, and I could see that the enormous Persian carpets that had seemed miles long when I was younger were faded and worn and the chandeliers needed a good dusting. Perhaps it was my hangover, but as the morning sun poured in, the Club had a slightly tawdry, shabby feel like an aging actress who has seen better days.

Still there were the usual long tables, though this time they consisted of sliced melon and strawberries and kiwi, a fruit I'd never tasted before, pastries and bagels, silver coffee urns, an omelette and egg station, a bowl of creamy porridge, chafing dishes filled with bacon (which, of course, is pork), sausage, fried potatoes. Because we were hungover none of us were hungry. Still we could not resist. We heaped food onto our plates. I took everything in sight. It was a classic case, as my father would say, of my eyes being bigger than my stomach.

As I was returning to our table, I spotted Mr. Edelstone in a far corner of the big room. He was tucked at a table way in the back and he had his family with him. He was eating his breakfast and talking in an animated way with his two girls. I thought I should go over and say hello, even though I was hardly dressed for the Club, but as I approached, I noticed that these girls seemed younger than his two daughters. They were wearing neatly pressed fall suits, and they both had red hair, as did the woman who was with them.

Mr. Edelstone was having a good time. He was enjoying himself immensely. He was laughing when suddenly he looked right at me. He stared for a moment, then his expression changed and looked away. I could tell that he saw me out of the corner of his eye as I saw him. But he acted as if he had no idea who I was.

Indeed he looked at me as if I wasn't even there. Something told me not to move any closer. I had never had this feeling before—that I should not acknowledge another person I know well; that I should pretend that person isn't even there. With my plate of food I turned, heading back to my table where I shoved scrambled eggs around on my plate and sipped black coffee as my head throbbed.

Later when my parents, who had been shopping in the city, came to pick me up, they asked how the party went. I told them about the sleepover and how we ordered room service and I told them about our rowdy breakfast. "We went into the dining room, wearing jeans and our pajama tops," I announced proudly.

"Oh, I won't be able to live that down," my father said.

"We weren't so bad," I told them, though I thought we were. I hesitated because I wasn't sure if I should say something more or not, but then I did. "Mr. Edelstone was there," I told my parents and they were silent for a moment with their eyes fixed on the road.

"Oh really," my father said.

"Yes, I saw him in a corner. He was with a woman and two girls. I'd never seen them before." No one spoke so I went on. "I'm not sure he recognized me."

My father cleared his throat even as my mother hissed under her breath. "That's his Rush Street whore."

"His Rush Street what...?"

"Margie, please," my father said.

"Why? She's old enough. She can know..."

I hated it when my parents spoke about me in the third person, even though I was with them in the car. But I was willing to overlook it now. "Know what?" I asked, because in truth I wanted to.

"Oh, never mind," my mother replied. "Another time." And we drove the rest of the way in silence.

A few weeks later my mother came into my room where I had

my homework spread all over my bed. My father was away on one of his business trips, which seemed to be getting more and more frequent, and he'd just called from some outpost in the Middle West, some empty stretch of land where he was going to tear up the landscape and build a block of stores. My mother stood in the doorway, just staring at me. I had no idea what she wanted or why she was there. She said nothing for a few moments.

Then she sat on my bed. "I want to explain something to you." She looked tired and her robe was open. I could see her sagging breasts and I watched them rise and fall as my mother puffed on a cigarette and explained to me that Mr. Edelstone had another family. "He has Lorraine and their two girls. And he has Mitzie. And their two girls."

I shook my head. "But how is this possible?"

"It just is—men can do this kind of thing," my mother said. Ruminating, she went on: "A woman could never pull this off, could she?" She tilted her head and gazed gaze out the window, as if she was talking to someone who was far away. "How could a woman have another family? And even if she somehow could, where would she find the time?" With a sigh my mother searched for an ashtray, then held her cigarette by the filter. Her other hand was cupped below to catch the ash when it fell, which it did. Then she looked at her watch. "Ask your father. He'll tell you more."

That weekend before my father returned, my mother sent me to the store. She wanted to have a picnic that evening so I rode my bicycle to pick up some things. Cole slaw, hot dogs, buns, pickle relish. After parking my bike in front, I went into the store. It was a warm summer day and I only had on a pair of shorts and a sleeveless shirt. I shivered as I walked past frozen foods. That was when I heard a man's voice call my name. "Eve? Eve, is that you?"

I turned and there he was, dressed for golf, buying frozen pizza. "Hello, Mr. Edelstone," I said.

"I wish you'd call me Glenn," he replied. "We've known one another a long time now, haven't we?" He gave me an odd look that I find difficult to describe, and I was afraid he was going to mention my seeing him at the Club. But he didn't. Instead he looked at my legs and my arms before his gaze settled on my face. It was as if he was floating on water and now he could relax. I covered my breasts, trembling from the cold. "I haven't seen you in a while."

I pretended to be looking for a frozen pizza. "Oh, I've been busy. At school with things." And in truth we hadn't been going to the Club as often as we had in earlier years.

"Well, you are very grown up now."

"I'm sorry, Mr. Edelstone, but I've got to run."

"Tell your folks we're going to have a card game soon," he shouted as I dashed away. I bought what I needed and left the store without looking back to see if he was still there.

We had our picnic that evening and on Sunday my father invited me out to Green Meadows to hit golf balls. We didn't go that often, but in the summer, if he was around, he'd sometimes ask me to come with him. One late summer afternoon when it was still hot, we were standing, both admiring a pretty good drive I'd clobbered down the fairway. As he reached to put another ball on the tee, I asked him. "Dad," I said, "is it true about Mr. Edelstone? That he has two families?"

My father pursed his lips in the way he did just before he got angry. And I was afraid he would now. "I suppose your mother told you?" He didn't wait for me to answer. "I guess you're old enough to understand. After all you've seen him with her, haven't you?" We hit a few more balls. Then my father bought me a Coke from the soda machine. We sat together on a bench as the night lights of the driving range were turned on.

Slowly he explained to me that Mr. Edelstone had two

families—the respectable one to whom he was married and legally bound, and the other family which he also took care of.

"Do the families know about one another?"

My father shook his head. "Lorraine and the daughters don't know about the other family. But Mitzie, that's her name, obviously she knows about Lorraine. Anyway he takes good care of them all."

I really didn't know what to say. But I knew I had entered unknown territory, something I had never imagined I would ever explore. I had many questions about this arrangement, but, not knowing what else to say, I asked my father, "But isn't that expensive?"

My father shook his head. "If you've got the money, you can do pretty much anything." He went on to say that every Friday night for years Mr. Edelstone had shown up at the Club with his legal family and every Saturday morning he brought his other family to lunch. I tried to picture Mr. Edelstone, so well coiffed and groomed, hanging out on Rush Street, a street of bars and jazz and apparently women of ill-repute. And I tried to imagine him coming to the Club every weekend with his two separate families.

"But no one ever said anything?" I asked, stunned. I thought of all those black men in their white gloves who worked there.

"Oh, no," my father said. "No one would dare."

The rest of the story unfolded as I was older and had gone off to college. It seemed that Mr. Edelstone's oldest daughter, Lucy, became ill with breast cancer. I didn't think much about it at the time. I was a junior in college and it was the '60s. That same year Abby Hoffman (who was standing trial in Chicago as one of the Chicago Seven) was invited to the Club by one of his lawyers. Apparently Judge Julius Hoffman (no relation), who was presiding at Abby Hoffman's trial, was a member of the Standard Club as well, and defendant and judge dined within yards of one another—a fact that tickled the subversive Hoffman to no end and that the Club gossiped about for months. I am sorry that I missed this historic event.

At any rate I probably would have been too stoned to notice. I had become a rather drunken, wild girl. I was high much of the time during college, listening to Jefferson Airplane, and probably had some minor substance abuse issues. I also became pregnant that year. I had been in love since college began with my lab partner named Doug.

Doug had large blue eyes and very black hair. He came from the working class neighborhoods of Boston, while I was a child of the Chicago North Shore. Doug had one of those accents people liked to imitate. I used to make him say "Park your car in Harvard Yard" over and over again. Our affair began the night of the Boston Blackout. It was 1965 and we were working on in the biology department on an experiment. Doug had devised a way to watch chicken embryos grow. He and I made little windows in their shells and under warm lights we charted their growth.

That night we had gone to check on our eggs when the lights went out. Not knowing what else to do, we walked over to the roof of the school library and stayed there all night. By the time the lights came back, we were wrapped in each other's arms.

Though Doug and I saw one another all the time, and slept together when we felt like it, he was engaged to Cindy. Cindy was his girlfriend back home and she had a mysterious ailment that prevented her from attending college, but it did not keep her from mailing him brownies during exams and hand-knitted sweaters when the weather turned cold. When Cindy came to visit Doug on campus, I made myself scarce. It was understood that Doug would marry Cindy (which he did, though they divorced several years later) and that I would go on to graduate school in French or something like that.

Then in our junior year I got pregnant. I struggled with Doug over what to do, but it was clear to me that he was not only not interested, but he was terrified of this baby. He wanted nothing to do with it. Or with me for that matter.

As I was heading out the door to the Boston hospital where I would terminate this unwanted pregnancy, my mother phoned. I only picked it up because I was hoping it was Doug, saying that he'd had a change of heart. That he wanted to marry me and "do the right thing." Instead it was my mother, calling to tell me that Lucy Edelstone had breast cancer. "That's terrible," I said, too focused on my own misery to record the news.

"Yes, it is," my mother replied. "You should drop her a card." My mother was always asking me to drop people cards. She gave me Lucy's address which I pretended to write it down. "I think she'll be all right," my mother said. "But it would be nice if you wrote to her." My mother waited for me to say something such as "I will" and when I didn't she went on. "And how are you doing?"

What could I tell my mother? That I was on my way to have an abortion. "I'm doing great, Mom. Just fine." My mother accepted this description of my state of my mind and told me she loved me as I hurried to get off the phone. The next afternoon, as I lay in my hospital room, with my roommate beside me studying for an econ exam, I did think of Lucy. I had only seen her a few times over the years, usually at the Club, but she was always kind to me. She embodied the largess of her father with none of the delicate bones or coolness of her mother. There was something about Lucy with her full breasts and wide red lips that seemed bigger than life.

Lucy had come to our house a few times with her husband, who was as dark and handsome as she was pretty. He too had a big, warm laugh. She brought her first baby for us to see and my mother had given the baby a soft yellow blanket. "Eve, my god," Lucy said the last time I saw her, "what a beautiful young woman you've become." Lucy and her husband set a kind of standard for me of what a perfect couple should look and act like as I lay in my white gown that tied up the back, the antiseptic odor of hospitals around me, my lover nowhere in sight.

Not long after my abortion my mother phoned again to tell me that Lucy was very ill and the cancer more serious than previously thought. She asked if I had written her a card and I lied, saying I had, and telling myself that I would. Then my mother asked once more how I was doing, but I was evasive, buried in my misery and drugs. While I was still caught up in my private dramas and stoned much of the time, Lucy died, leaving two children and her bereft husband, not to mention her grieving parents.

Mr. Edelstone, my father told me, was heartbroken. "Inconsolable" was his exact word. He could not seem to get on track. Nothing seemed to matter to him anymore. It was as if some link in a chain had been broken and he was left holding the pieces. Then, as my mother told it, Glenn Edelstone came up with an idea. He decided he wanted to bring his two families together. All the girls were grown. Everyone was a consenting adult. Both he and Lorraine were in their eighties and he told her about it first. He had assumed that Lorraine knew anyway and that she had been a monument of discretion. But, as it turned out, Lorraine knew nothing. She had no idea her husband had another family. In fact it had never occurred to her at all.

I came home for the summer holidays, the last time I would ever really spend much time at home. Outside of a secretarial job I had at a swimming club, most of the summer before my senior year I was holed up in my room, feeling sorry for myself. I could not get past Doug's abandonment, the fact that I had gone through that abortion on my own. Both our friendship and our lab partnership had come to a screeching halt. For the time being I'd sworn off men. I was sitting in my room, not doing very much, when the phone rang.

I picked up at the same moment that my mother did downstairs, a phenomena no longer possible in this world of cell phones, and heard an icy voice, which I recognized as Lorraine Edelstone, saying, "Margie, I need to ask you something..." And then she asked my mother in a methodical way if she knew that Glenn had another family. That he had daughters he had helped raise and send to school. He had even had these daughters bat mitzvahed. My mother must have handed the phone over to my father who took charge of this call and told Lorraine that he knew all of this.

"And how long have you know, Arnie?" I cupped my hand over the receiver, concealing my breath.

My father gulped on the other end. "Lorraine, I've known for years."

"And why didn't you tell me?" she asked. "Why didn't you ever mention this to me? We have been friends for almost fifty years."

"I assumed," my father said, "that you already knew."

Apparently this was what everyone assumed.

"I knew nothing," Lorraine told him. She slammed the phone down, crossing yet one more set of friends off her list. I never saw Lorraine or Glenn or any of their family after that, though every once in a while, when I was visiting my parents in Chicago or later in Florida where they'd move, the phone would ring and it would be Glenn on the other end. He was always very nice to me. "Hello, Eve," he'd say. "Are you still a beautiful girl? It's a shame you never married."

Glenn always called with the same thing. He was offering my father, whose own fortunes had declined, a deal. "You say when, Arnie, and we'll make something happen." They talked of building new buildings, of real estate. But they never made another deal. My mother hated Glenn for what he had done, but my father always forgave him. "He was good to those girls. He educated them. He bat mitzvahed them. He made them good Jews."

"You'd forgive Hitler," I heard her say.

Many years later I was married at the Club. This was after I'd had an "out of wedlock" child, as my father used to refer to my son, but I went on to meet a wonderful man and when my parents asked where I wanted to be married, I did not hesitate. "At the Club." For various reasons our wedding was a rather chaotic affair. We had trouble finding a rabbi who would marry me to a non-Jew. Then my mother grew weary of the cocktail hour and made the kitchen serve dinner before it was ready, resulting in a rush of salads and undercooked meat.

I had wanted a picture of my husband and me, with my little boy, walking down the marble staircase, but in the busyness of the occasion we forgot to get that shot. Shortly after my marriage my parents moved to a retirement community away from Chicago and, while my father often spoke of driving down to Chicago and visiting the Club, he never did, though at one point he had the honor of being its oldest surviving member. He received a kind of diploma which I found in his briefcase after he died. In the late '80s when he received this reward, my father was the only living member who had been on the Board of Trade when the market crashed in 1929.

Still, after he died, we lost our privileges and neither my mother nor I ever returned. I moved East years ago. Friends back home tell me that now women, and even blacks, are free to join the Club. And that this has been true for a very long time.

MITZ'S THEORY OF
EVERYTHING SERIES

by Rachel Swearingen

IT WAS MITZ WHO WAS IN Ona's drawings, over and over again.
See? That's Mitz lying on a bed, her arms detached at the elbows
and reaching up to Ona from the floor. That's Mitz with her
narrow hips, and her hair falling out in monstrous, feral clumps.
And look, there's Ona. The old Ona. Wholesome Ona. Mitz's
Midwestern Apple Pie Girl. Mitz's Peaches and Cream. So tall, her
arms reach out of the frame, her breasts balloon to the ceiling.
When one grows thin, the other must grow full. It's a law of nature.
Symbiotic. Mitz would call it neurotic, codependent.

But where was Mitz now? And why wouldn't she call Ona?
Nearly two years as inseparable roommates at the "Harvard of the
Midwest," or as Mitz called it, "College for East Coast Fuckups,"
and not a single phone call or e-mail. Nearly two years together
before Ona transferred to a state school, before Mitz dropped
out, went AWOL. Even her parents didn't know where she was.
Child of science and math camps. Daughter of Manhattan bank
executive and psychiatrist. Everyone saw it coming, especially
Mitz. "It's the stereotype you fear most that you can't escape," she
would say.

Ona tried to escape. Those first weeks at college, she told
herself she wouldn't be like the other Midwesterners—the ones

Mitz impersonated, the ones who worked in the cafeteria, who apologized their way through lecture halls. Clothing was for reinvention and Ona made herself SoHo Boho chic. She razored holes in dresses from Goodwill and wore them over jeans with baubles and beads. She practiced disaffected like Mitz practiced sane.

Now, when Ona walked through her new campus, past its squat modern buildings, she thought she saw her father, his hands thrust in his pockets, a newspaper tucked under his arm. She grew thin from working double shifts at the bookstore café and skipping meals, from staying up all night to draw. When she caught her reflection in a shop window and saw her dress hanging from her bony shoulders, she told herself Mitz was eating somewhere, her hair growing thick.

Ona called Mitz's parents. "Just let me talk to her." She didn't say please. She didn't apologize for not telling them about the food stuffed into Kleenex boxes and thrown into the trash, about Mitz's endless project to discover a theory for all human activity, a theory that as the months passed connected African famines with the changing shape of the earth's core, Navy sonar, aquatic crustaceans, the Monsanto seed bank, and the hypothalamus gland.

Mitz's mother's voice was so calm it bordered on hysterical. "We don't know where she is," she said. "She left the hospital. She isn't using her cell phone or her credit cards. You must know something. Someone she trusted? A friend?"

Ona was the friend. There were even rumors they had been lovers. Mitz had encouraged them. She took Ona's hand when they walked across the quad. She showered Ona with pet names. Dumpling. My little chick. My big hunk of Wisconsin cheddar. At night, when Mitz couldn't sleep, she crawled into Ona's bed and asked Ona to tell her stories. She wanted to hear about skating on rivers and Friday night fish fries. Mitz was the only one Ona told about her father, how his exposure to asbestos was both killing him and paying for her education. She dreaded his calls. She couldn't bear his making a joke of everything just to spare her. He never uttered the words mesothelioma or settlement. "How's life at Harvard?" he'd ask. "You doing us proud?"

"He sounds gallant," Mitz said. "You won't get it, you know. It's not catchy."

But Mitz was catchy. Look, there's Mitz on the vintage Nakishima dining table, an apple between her teeth. There's Ona reaching over with the serving fork. She prefers a leg. The man to her right, with the tall top hat and the banker tie, his arm raised high? That's Mitz's father. "Send it back!" he cries. "Give me something with a little meat."

"Creepy," said the guy behind the easel next to Ona. He whispered to her all through class. "You're supposed to paint what's on the table. It's a still life. You're not supposed to improvise."

But look at the broken chair, Ona pointed. Look at the silver platter, the empty pant leg hanging over the edge.

She should have said, it's there, all there, between the objects, rising up. If she had one more hour, she could even resurrect Mitz's parents' ramshackle cottage on Martha's Vineyard. Its chairs with unraveling rush seats, its leather loungers and end tables loaded with modern pottery, Victorian silver, and coffee-stained books and magazines. "We're terrible," Mitz's mother, Simone, admitted when she caught Ona staring at a glued-together Gambone vase. "There are pieces missing. I can't bring myself to throw it away."

Mitz said, "You wanted to know the difference between old and new money? This is it."

The walls were covered with framed portraits of ancestors and unframed canvases. Mitz's parents had collected art when they were younger. Agnes Martin. Richard Tuttle. Frank Stella. Even an

O'Keeffe, the paint cracking from sun and mist. And photographs. Mitz's mother standing knee-deep in the ocean in a long dress, her hair flying. Mitz as a baby, pouring sand into the air. There were no pictures of Mitz as a teenager. "The grim years," Mitz said. "I wasn't pretty then."

Two weeks of blind life-drawings. Ona's instructor stood next to the wooden platform inside their circle of easels. "Eyes on the model, folks." He whacked a yardstick on the metal chair next to Ona. "Up, off the paper. You're not feeling. Feel her mass."

When Ona looked down at her sketch, she saw two misshapen eyes, arms floating, hair unmoored, and only the faintest notion of a torso dripping. So unlike the fleshy model before her. Ona was getting closer. But still she couldn't quite capture Mitz. She couldn't locate her in the body. Mitz was in the voice, the brain, the rooms she inhabited.

After her transfer to the state school, Ona made acquaintances only. She told herself she liked it this way. She pretended she was from far away. When she spoke, she pressed the sound straight through her lips and tried not to bend her vowels. In the end they always guessed. Chicago? Detroit? Milwaukee?

"You can take the girl out of Wisconsin," Mitz would say. "But you can't get her to stop saying 'holy cow.'"

Mitz had taken Ona out of Wisconsin. That summer on the Vineyard, the two of them working as interns at a magazine called *Sailing Away*, Ona thought it might be that easy, she might just sail into a future of her own making. It would be a new beginning after too many nights partying, after academic probation and her advisor's warning about the permanence of records.

"Let me tell you something about permanent records," Mitz said. "I had a genius test at two. Psych evaluations at four. IQ tests. Rorschach. DSM-IV. Ennea-fucking-gram. Just wait until you meet my parents. They find out you're on probation and you'll be taking a learning-disorder test for dinner."

At *Sailing Away*, Mitz wrote unintelligible twenty-page manifestos and begged the editor to print them. The editor took Mitz off the events beat, sent her to the front desk to do menial tasks. Mitz stuck stamps on the wrong side of envelopes. She put people on hold and forgot them. She left for coffee and returned hours later with plastic bags filled with garbage from the bay.

Ona, on the other hand, was made for magazine work. No cheese factory, no foundry, no tending bar back home for her. The editor asked her to cover the Taste of the Vineyard festival. "Three hundred words, tops, please."

She shouldn't have brought Mitz.

Eight men and two women ripping apart bushels of crabs, a carnage of shells and flesh and butter.

College Girl Assaults Contestants. Charges Pending.

Mitz's father chose to call it "activism gone awry." He arranged for two weeks of community service doing what Mitz loved best, cleaning the beach, amassing more "evidence" for her theory of everything.

Those last weeks of break, they woke before dawn to pull crab traps out of the bay, to empty them into the water before Mitz's father could check them. Only sometimes a crab would get back in. Crawl right in, even when there wasn't any bait. Mitz called them suicide crabs. She couldn't watch her father lower them into the boiling water. She'd cover her ears. She'd refuse dinner. She believed crabs had a higher intelligence unrecognizable to humans. "You're blind," Simone said to her husband, "if you don't think it's happening all over again."

"You're overreacting," he said. "Mitz is fine." And to Ona, "She hasn't had any trouble at school, has she? You'd tell us if there was anything we should know?"

Sometimes the charcoal jerked sharply, the fingers refused to be polite, a figure's hands turned to claws. Sometimes she scurried into a corner and stared up at a fat, wholesome girl holding a bucket.

"The Crab Lady. I like it. You've got the beginning of a series for your senior thesis," her professor said. "You found a vein."

Unbridled one moment, perfectly functional the next, Mitz was a changeling. It was she who led Ona to her first art class, who hacked into Ona's student account and dropped Calculus I, Theories of Civil Society, and Intermediate Mandarin to enroll her in Two-Dimensional Design, Physics for Poets, and Healthy Living. She handed Ona her new schedule with the words "Remedy for Academic Probation" scrawled at the top.

"You've got to face facts, Wisconsin. You're no genius."

By then, the real genius's cheekbones protruded, her hips jutted from the tops of her baggy jeans. Everything Mitz wouldn't eat went into Ona's mouth or Ona's still lifes: sushi, Thai noodles with peanut sauce, Italian plums that sat on Mitz's desk until Ona had eaten every last one. The less Mitz ate, the hungrier Ona grew. She packed on ten pounds, then five more. She loaded her shelves with boxes of macaroni and cookies and jars of olives, and she drew. Mitz would stand back and pretend to be a critic. She would stroke her chin. She would raise an eyebrow. "So visceral! So sublime. The lines! The chiaroscuro! The sauce!"

*

The model before Ona had a scar down his chest. He should have aged out of the system. No twenty-year-old wanted to draw his soft belly, his thinning hair. But everyone drew the scar. Ona heard the long, hatched line. The model heard it too. He pressed his lips into a proud curl. She wouldn't draw him like that, holding a metal rod like a spear. She drew him in a hospital bed instead, a nurse handing him his heart swaddled like a baby. Mitz again, despite the white uniform. And look, there was Ona's father sitting in the corner with his newspaper, and there was Mitz's mother in her long dress, waves rushing under the door, and there was the wholesome model from blind drawing. No, that was Ona, balancing on feet as enormous as boats.

"Time to move out of the food phase, Peaches," Mitz had said. "Try a blue period. Everyone does." Ona's early still lifes made Mitz so dizzy she tore them down. She sat on Ona's bed and put her head between her knees.

Ona told her it was time to see a doctor, but they decided to go to a bar instead. They squeezed together in their favorite booth. Ona ordered a Manhattan.

"How gauche," Mitz said. She ordered a beer. She spotted their friends Bobcat and Charlie across the room and invited them over. She ate the cherry out of Ona's drink, ordered a pizza, and Ona thought it might be over. She might not have to call Mitz's parents, she might not have to listen to Mitz's pen scratching through the night.

Mitz said, "Let's smoke it under a blanket. Get the blanket, BobbieCat."

Mitz said, "Little Miss Peaches and Cream is high."

Mitz said, "Let's push the beds together. Let's go nighty-night."

Ona fell. Their beds were a raft. Now Mitz was making out with Bobcat. Ona was twisted around Charlie. Bobcat said, "Holy shit, Mitz. You're like a skeleton. What the fuck." Mitz toppled into Ona. She was laughing. She was laughing so hard she was crying. "Get out," she said. "Now! Get out! Get out! Get out!" Mitz threw out Bobcat. She threw out Charlie. She threw out Ona. Ona lay down in the hall next to the door and held onto the doorknob. "Mitz," she yelled. "Let me in!"

Hundreds upon hundreds of Post-it notes in perfect lines all over their walls. Mitz said she just needed to get them into the right sequence. She just needed a little more caffeine. She told Ona her scalp tingled. Her heart pounded. She stopped showering. At night, she rocked on her bed, talking through her theory, starting over and over again. She rearranged the notes. Where was it! Where was the one about the gold standard and pattern language? She slept with the pages of her notebook sticking to her face.

"I'm calling the RA," Ona said.

"Just a few more days," Mitz said. "I'm going to be all right. I know the drill. We just need the right recipe. See, you start with rice. Just white rice first, and then you build on that. I've got new pills. You're the only one who understands. Just let me get through finals."

Ona found reasons to stay out of the room. She started seeing Nate Elkins, a golden-haired geology major with a penchant for Dylan. He drove her out to the country for hikes and lectured about rivers and accumulation, about erosion and sedimentary rock. "Whatever you do, don't talk to Mitz about erosion," Ona warned. "She's got enough on her mind."

For her political science exam, Mitz wrote in tiny handwriting and needed two additional blue books.

"They never give you enough time. No one values intellectual curiosity anymore," she said, when the test was returned with a failing mark and the words "convoluted" and "Does not answer question." She took out another blue book and kneeled on the floor to finish.

Ona's father valued curiosity. When she told him she wanted to fly to the Southwest for winter break, he said, "You go right ahead, There's nothing to see around here. Live a little. Ticket's on me." She didn't tell him she was going with Nate Elkins, that it didn't matter who she was with or where, only that she was away. He said, "Is everything all right? You know, if there's anything you need."

Her mother said, "This might be his last Christmas. How could you, Ona?"

She'd never been west of the Mississippi. She'd never been on a plane. When she looked at the mountains below, she was free. When Nate squeezed her hand, she was free of Mitz. She wouldn't think of her, or of her father opening his presents, hanging the still life of plums Ona made for him above his new retractable bed.

Nate Elkins was so healthy he glowed. He called Ona his Girl from the North Country. She was pure, so lovely he could just about marry her. He brought Ona to his family's enormous winter "cottage" with its skylights and tiled veranda, and Ona thought, This must be what Mitz meant by new money.

"He's got that virgin/whore hang-up," Mitz said, when Ona returned. "Classic pastoral fantasy. Corn-fed-girl syndrome. It's in his DNA. He'll never get over it. Your mother keeps calling. It doesn't sound good."

"Things are going to be tight," her mother told her. "We maxed out your dad's insurance. You'll have to find a job."

If only Ona hadn't borrowed so much money from Mitz. She promised herself she would take Mitz to the counseling center. She would get a new roommate. She would pay Mitz back.

But first she loaded their shelves with groceries. She didn't feel well, no matter how much she ate. When she opened their medicine cabinet, she found half-full bottles of medications prescribed to Mitz and Mitz's mother and someone named Susan Kim. She found empty laxative boxes in the garbage. Bottles of herbal remedies for heavy metal contamination and teas for mental confusion. She found a nest of Mitz's hair on the floor. "Look at this," she said. "Whatever you're doing, it's not working. It's gone too far. You've got to talk to someone."

But then Ona missed her period again, and Mitz was so calm, so Mitz, so suddenly levelheaded. "But of course," she said, as she pulled the birth control packet out of Ona's purse and pointed to the uneven pattern of holes. "What did you expect? Did you think you were immune?"

At the clinic, Mitz held Ona's hand while the nurse took a sonogram. "I think you're having a fish," she said. "A rockfish. Definitely a rockheadfish."

The nurse stared at Mitz.

"Rockhead, get it?" Mitz said. "Her boyfriend is into geology?"

The nurse turned to Ona and pointed to a picture of a ten-week-old fetus on a chart. She lectured Ona on the importance of not drinking and staying out of hot tubs. "We'll need to see you in another four weeks," she said. "I can also give you a referral to a counselor, if you'd like."

"I told you we're both clichés," Mitz said on the way home. "You can't keep it, you know. Or you could, but either way it's no good. You'll be the tragic townie who fell for the rich boy. He'll freak. He only pretends to be progressive."

Then the bleeding began, in their room, the next night.

"I'm taking you to the hospital. You're running a fever. We should call your mother."

"I'm so stupid. Please, Mitz, I'll be all right. I promise, I won't call your parents about you if you don't call mine. We're both adults. Don't make me go."

Mitz helped Ona into bed. She gave her antibiotics from her arsenal in the medicine cabinet. She took Ona's temperature and helped her to the bathroom. She held her when she cried. She told Nate that Ona had the flu and he should keep away, and he must have known, because he did, for days and days.

When Ona woke from the fever, she was fired clean. There was no more turbulence in her mind, no more hunger. Then Nate came by with a milk shake. He kissed her forehead. He told her she would always be his Girl from the North Country, but they had to talk. "Things have changed."

So this is what it means to haunt a room. Ona and Mitz skipped classes. They fought about the mess. They pulled their beds to separate corners and put on headphones and ignored each other until the quiet erupted into slammed doors and windows opening and closing.

Then Ona left. She hung out in cafés and bars. She didn't come home for days. She brought men back to their room and asked Mitz to sleep in the lounge.

"This is ridiculous," Mitz said. "It's textbook, you know."

"You're just pissed because they don't come running to you anymore. Here, Mitz, have a cookie." She threw a carton from the nightstand.

She expected Mitz to lob the cookies back. She had witnessed

Mitz's most spectacular and regal tantrums, had watched her turn purple and listened as her voice reached terrifying octaves over nothing more than her parents' refusal to buy her a laptop. But Mitz didn't throw anything now. She just crumpled onto the bed and cried into her pillow.

"Who's the cliché now?" Ona said.

Mitz said, "Take a look in the mirror."

"A good man. He'd give you the shirt off his back," they told Ona and her mother and brother, one after another, in the church basement after the funeral.

The good man was buried in a silver casket the undertaker convinced Ona's mother to buy. Her father would have had a joke for this too, and she almost heard him whisper it into her ear. During the wake, he looked like he was sleeping in a metal canoe, and Ona thought how wrong it was that a man who spent his last years fighting for breath should be buried underground.

"We took out a second mortgage," her mother said. "There's nothing left. He didn't want you to know, but you're an adult now. I think you know what this means."

Everything was so intermingled. Mitz helped Ona sort her books and clothes from her own. They carried Ona's belongings to the parking lot and loaded her father's Buick. Mitz struggled with the boxes. She had been sick for months, first a cold and then pneumonia. She was seeing a therapist, but telling her little. Standing in the parking lot, in her ragged sweater and long skirt, the snow coming down like dust, she reminded Ona of a consumption patient from the nineteenth century.

"You know I'm going to let you go," Mitz said. "I'm not going to make a scene. I'm going to stand here and watch with no expression at all, and when you disappear down the road, I'll still be here.

"Please don't hug me," she said, when Ona reached out her arms.

"I'm sorry," Ona said. "About everything. You'll come and see me?"

Mitz raised her hand in a mock wave. "I'm going to pretend to smile. I'm going to pretend to wave. It will be very Lars von Trier."

When Ona called several months after her move, it was Mitz's new roommate who told her Mitz was gone. "She almost died, you know."

Mitz wouldn't leave the room, that's what the new roommate said. She smelled bad. She wouldn't turn off her lights at night. She covered the walls with Post-its!

"A stroke. Can you believe it? At twenty? She weighed ninety pounds. I don't know if she was anorexic or just crazy. All I know is I don't blame you for leaving. I don't care what people say."

Sometimes Mitz still talked to her, when Ona was alone and painting.

For instance, she might say, "Maybe all those times you think you see your father, it really is your father. Like, maybe he's just checking up on you."

"But what about you? I see you too. Just yesterday, that girl standing in line at the movies."

"Oh, that was your guilt. It's ridiculous, by the by. We make our own fortunes, our own beds. Sow what you reap and all. Isn't that funny? All those words for the same thing, but it mostly comes down to luck. And genetics."

Ona would call her senior exhibition "Mitz's Endless Theory

of Everything." She would cover the wall with small paintings, from ceiling to floor, just like Mitz's Post-it notes.

"It will be an inside joke though," Mitz said. "And no one likes those."

Ona called Simone again. "Will you call me as soon as you find her? I'm worried too, you know."

"You're worried too? You colluded with her! You lied to us when we could have helped her. I'm going to hang up. I can't do this now."

"Please. I just want to talk to her. You'll tell her, when she comes back?"

"I'm going to say something I shouldn't, Ona. I don't like you. I don't trust you. I know it's unfair. I know I'm not blameless, but I'll always associate you with this. You were supposed to be her friend."

From across the gallery, Ona spied Mitz wearing lipstick and a sleek trench coat, like this was a fancy Manhattan opening. Ona's heart pounded. Her mouth was dry. She was afraid Mitz would disappear if she looked away. She watched Mitz pass several student exhibits and stop before a gigantic painting of a purple vulva that reminded Ona of the entrance to a tourist trap in the Dells. Mitz raised an eyebrow at Ona and mouthed *Oh my god*.

Then she circled a tower fashioned entirely of illuminated X-rays, fishing wire, and bleached bones. Mitz turned to watch the crowd. She gazed at disoriented parents, mothers with too-wide smiles, fathers in uncomfortable suits. She watched a rural couple pose for a photo with their son as she made her way to Ona.

Ona knew she wouldn't really be there, but she reached out her arms anyway.

"You're seeing things again." Mitz gazed at Ona's paintings.

Ona had managed to cram seventeen canvases into her small allotment of space. "There's no focal point," Mitz said. "And don't tell me that was your intention." She read Ona's artist statement. "At least you didn't use the words palpable or enigmatic."

Several people glanced from Ona's work to Ona.

"Smile or something. You're scaring them," Mitz whispered. "By the by, I think I'm touched, but I'm not sure. You did a fine job of capturing the pathos, but next time I want boobs."

"Disturbing," a woman said, as she looked at Ona's sketch of two skeletal women tangled together on a doll-sized bed, men flat as rugs stacked to either side.

"You had to be there," Mitz told the woman. "It was a lot more fun than it looks."

Mitz stepped closer to the painting of a fat girl holding a bean-sized baby in her oversized palm. "It won't work, you know," she said to Ona. "You can't fall apart. Even if you try."

Then she was gone. She didn't slip into the crowd, or vanish through a wall. She was simply not there.

If Ona could just find Mitz, she'd tell her she finally understood the problems of relative distance and sampling from the whole. Mere arrangement would never suffice.

A few days before they parted, Mitz removed her notes from their walls. She told Ona she was "on the mend," though it was clear this was just another respite, and Ona knew if she opened Mitz's desk drawer the notes would be there, stacked and waiting.

That night, before bed, Mitz opened the window. "Smell that air!" she said. "Now we'll sleep." She didn't wrestle with her sheets or get up repeatedly to use the bathroom or wake Ona to tell her about a possible link between gray matter and the metric expansion of space.

"I can hear you thinking," she said. "Tell me about that night again. Tell me about the ice."

Once, when Ona was eight and she and her father couldn't sleep, he took her out to the river to skate. Mitz loved the story. She liked the idea of Ona's father shoveling to make a rink. She liked the detail of his sinking a Coleman lantern into a snowbank. But most of all, she liked to imagine the sound of ice cracking, like far-off gunshots coming close.

"My dad said it was the river breathing. But that made it worse. I kept thinking of a monster down there, trying to get out."

"The ice monster of Wisconsin. I love it. Do you think it wears a hat with earflaps?" They laughed and said goodnight. Several minutes later, Mitz said, "Probably forms in layers, like glaciers, or tectonic plates."

Toward morning, Ona woke convinced Mitz was at her desk writing. But when she sat up, she realized it was just Mitz's heavy coat hanging from her chair. Mitz was sleeping. Her back was to Ona, her knees pulled to her chest. She mumbled something. Ona could smell rotting leaves from the open window, new cardboard from her packed boxes. In that half-light, the cold blowing in, she could almost hear crabs scuttling across the ocean floor, rice growing in distant fields, the universe expanding around them.

Then Mitz turned toward Ona. Her eyes were open and staring, though she was still asleep. Her arm slipped over the edge of her bed and hung there. "Turn off the music," she said. "We're almost there."

THE SPEED OF SOUND

by Elizabeth Gonzalez

A NEW MOON AND A CLEAR, cold Michigan night, the sky dead black and loaded with stars, so clear you could see the tendrils in the Milky Way dust—things were aligning, and Arthur Reel was prepared. He called the two neighbors across the road, who were kind enough to turn off their automatic lights whenever Arthur said he would be skywatching. Three a.m. found him perched in his rooftop observatory, sitting in his padded folding chair next to a telescope that was almost as big around as a basketball, waiting. He was there to watch Leo rise, Leo with its telltale sickle, the backward question mark, although to Arthur it would always be Hook's hook—his son James had renamed it, along with most of the constellations. It had always puzzled James, made him indignant, in fact, how none of the constellations looked anything like the things they were named after, and who could argue? Even with the aid of an illustrated chart, it was hard to make out a lion in Leo, and as for Aquarius, forget it.

Hook was a far better name, Arthur thought.

He'd come up almost grudgingly, girding himself for disappointment because the Leonids were notorious, peaking for just one hour, almost too far north to catch, and yet so spectacular that few amateur skywatchers could resist the temptation to at least show up, just in case. It had already been a good year: he'd seen a nice Capricornid shower in July. Then in September in *Sky & Telescope*, some French astronomer had predicted "a chance for a brief Leonid outburst in 2006." A chance for people like Arthur, who missed the historic showers of 2001, when the meteors rained down at the incredible rate of 480 per hour. And as the date approached and the conditions fell in line one after another, he'd calmly made his plans to set his alarm and come up.

He'd just unscrewed the top of his Thermos when he saw something blaze straight out of Leo, a bright thing slipping almost too fast to follow across the sky. It left a trail, a pale streak with just the slightest arc, and Arthur stared, counting off seconds without meaning to—he'd heard the Leonids could hang in the air for minutes, they're so bright—when he felt hot coffee on his leg. He jerked his leg and tried to right the Thermos, but the more he turned it, the more it poured, and he realized the floor was rotating, tipping up from the right until it was vertical, then beyond, overturned.

He dropped the Thermos and tried to stand, but pitched over instantly, getting bungled up in the chair. He turned over on his knees, made for the open trap in the floor, which was also rising, rotating sickly counterclockwise like everything else. Later he remembered clinging to the stair rail, then a hard fall. After that, rolling. He would recall later it felt exactly like rolling a plane.

For four years before college Arthur had served as an Air Force pilot. In his last assignment, he flew F-89 Scorpion fighter jets out of Thule Air Force Base in Greenland, 700 miles north of the Arctic Circle. The base ran strategic air defense along the Canadian border, the DEW line, distant early warning, guarding against Russian planes. Any plane entering radar range of Thule was greeted by an F-89, lofted within three minutes of the first blip on the radar. If it was deemed hostile, which never happened on Arthur's watch, the orders were to come in at a ninety-degree angle and salvo the entire payload of 104 rockets at the target, because it was understood that if the F-89 missed the target on the first shot, she would never get a second. The newer planes were lighter, faster, more advanced; the F-89 was heavy, designed for a single purpose, no great maneuverer, not a plane you'd want in a dogfight. Unlike most planes, which lift off the runway when they reach a certain speed, the F-89 could make five hundred miles per hour on the ground and never bump a wheel. "You got to nudge her up," the instructor at Moody, a kid from Georgia, had told him. "Otherwise, Lieutenant, what you got here is basically a very big, very heavy, very fast automobile."

It was, in fact, an old bird even back then, but the F-89 was a fun plane to fly, Arthur would tell his kids, and perfectly good for the mission, as the odds of engaging anything were very low—particularly since any engagement was likely to set off World War III. The idea was deterrence, a visible presence, and for that the F-89 was well suited.

Usually after making contact and calling in the numbers, Arthur and his radop would fly over the mountains to burn off the fuel—it was that or dump it, since it wasn't safe to land fully loaded—and they would turn on the music, military radio KOLD out of Thule, and do Aileron rolls and Immelmans, sometimes buzz the tankers on the lonely road to the bay.

The Air Force limited duty at Thule to one year, for a reason. Thule tended to make people alcoholics, whether they were genetically predisposed or not. Six months of daylight, followed by six months of night, unshakable cold, and nothing to do off duty besides sit in the club and drink. At Thule you couldn't trust your own eyes: day was no longer day; night, no longer night. Even the compasses were wrong there, off by a full ninety degrees because the base was just west of magnetic north.

Arthur served an extra tour there, eighteen months in all.

When he remembered Thule, what he remembered first was not the cold or the hardship, but the sky. In Thule the sky and the water were both indigo, a shade of blue Arthur believed only existed in that place, the water just a shade darker, set off by white glaciers. You could always find Thule from the small lopsided one just east of the base in Baffin Bay. The sky was cloudless, and even in the heart of the dark season it never quite went black, but just turned darker blue, like ink. Arthur thought it must have been the snow, reflecting light from somewhere, maybe even the dim light from the stars.

Arthur awoke to a bright, empty room full of harsh sunlight. It poured in a solid block through a large window to his right, lighting up the sheets on his bed and the dingy white curtain hung alongside it. The sound of a television on low volume came from the other side of the curtain, some game show, people applauding, and he felt the uncomfortable sense of being intimate with a stranger, made worse when the stranger coughed and cleared his throat. Arthur noticed the coarseness of the sheets, the smell of his blue gown, something between petroleum and soap. A bad, metallic taste in his mouth. A curve of flesh under his right eye that wasn't usually there, pushing up from his cheek, moving back and forth as he turned his head to try to look at it.

He remembered falling and realized he'd survived. Some kind of attack.

He turned his head toward the window and felt painful stiffness all the way down his neck. The aqua curtains on either side of the window were pulled back, giving Arthur a view, made hazy by streaks of dried-up rain, of a neighboring brick wall. Susannah had been here. She would have opened the curtains, frowned at the dirt and the view, reconsidering, then left them open for the light. Susannah had to have sunlight. This was determined light, mid-morning, he guessed. The sun lit up each drop of fluid that gathered and fell from the IV bag next to his bed, making it look precious.

He heard a creak, a whoosh; the curtain swayed. His wife appeared, purse tucked under her arm, a magazine in her hand. They looked at each other, surprised.

"How do you feel?" she asked, coming to his side, leaning down to give him an awkward kiss, just making contact with his hairline.

"What happened?"

"It wasn't a stroke," Susannah said. "They're running tests but they don't think it was a stroke. The doctor said it could be a mini-heart attack."

"A what?"

"Sometimes you can have a slight blockage, I don't know. Let me call the nurse and tell them you're awake again." She pulled a pager from the side of his bed and pushed a button, giving Arthur the impression she'd been here for a while.

"Again?" he said. "What time is it?"

"Three-thirty."

Arthur sat forward instinctively—he'd lost an entire day. He needed something for his head, that was all. Some strong pill to kill the terrible ache radiating from behind his eyes, pushing on his teeth, his skull. "I'm fine," he said. "I need ibuprofen."

"You fell on concrete. Arthur, nobody said you could get up," Susannah said, taking his forearm anyway as he moved his legs over the side of the bed.

"I have to go to the bathroom," he said. He felt her watching him and was glad for the IV pole, which he used to steady himself. For a moment when his feet hit the clammy floor, it seemed like the room was shifting, and he was afraid it was happening again.

He breathed deeply, pushing the pole around the end of the bed just as the nurse came in. Arthur made an awkward introduction of sorts and nodded toward the bathroom.

When he was back in bed, lightly sweating, nauseated from the effort, he began to sort out what day it was. Friday, six days from Thanksgiving. "Did you hear anything from James?" he asked, while the nurse pumped up his blood pressure cuff.

Susannah shook her head, eyes on the nurse. The light flashed off her glasses, shone through her hair, fine as cobwebbing. It was a little flat. He could tell she hadn't showered, but she had carefully applied her makeup, here in the room, probably, using the makeup she always carried in her purse. Trying to keep things together.

The doctor came in shortly, a bit young and chipper for Arthur's taste, though Susannah seemed to trust him. He was thinking vertigo, he said, a little mix-up of the inner ear that makes the body temporarily lose its ability to tell up from down. Still, he would need more tests tomorrow, and Arthur had a low-grade fever. The upshot was, Arthur was stuck there for the night. Just for observation, the doctor added on his way out, as if that made it any better.

Susannah would have to drive the twenty-five minutes home, and another twenty-five back with his cholesterol medicine and the various supplies he needed to get through the night. Her entire evening would be eaten up in the car while he sat here being observed. Arthur apologized, urged her to take her time, eat dinner, call Carrie and Matthew and tell them he was fine. As she walked out, he thought to ask her to bring the *Scientific American* from his nightstand.

He watched the space she'd left, watched the curtain sway and settle, fighting down the frustration that welled up as soon as she left the room. A rush of tears, insistent as tiny fingers, prodded hidden spaces behind his eyes, deep in his head, spaces already tender and swollen. He blinked hard, took a slow, deliberate breath. Why now, of all times? He knew it was a childish impulse, knew that at his age, he should be grateful it wasn't something worse. But James was due in any day now, Wednesday night at the latest, for his first Thanksgiving home in six years, and that was where Arthur needed to be. Home.

James was nearing the end of his final tour as a Night Stalker, a special operations transport unit of the 160th Army Airborne Division out of Fort Campbell. His battalion flew specially configured MH-47E Chinooks equipped with long-range fuel tanks, multimode radar and infrared sensors—black, unmarked helicopters that could fly all but 150 miles per hour just a few feet off the ground or over the trees, in any conditions, dropping off and retrieving special ops troops on missions in Afghanistan and Iraq. He'd had mountain training, had done HALO jumps, had learned Arabic. Arthur and Susannah knew little more about their son's service than that. Because of the sensitivity of his work, he disappeared for six or eight months at a time. Arthur never knew specifically where he was, what he was doing, or when he would resurface. When he came home—long, scraggly hair, beard grown out—he never told them what he'd done. Painful as it was to go without word for these long stretches, Arthur pointed out to Susannah that James was probably safer in his unit than he would have been in most others. It was definitely safer than the infantry. Every month that went by without news meant almost certainly that James was still accounted for. The Army knew where he was from mission to mission. They had results to track.

During his time in the 160th, James had been home five times. Two were in the first year. The last time was eighteen months ago. So when he'd called in September to say he had leave for Thanksgiving, possibly through Christmas, Arthur and Susannah were elated in the measured way they'd learned over the years, knowing that there were good odds, at least even odds, that those plans might change. His leave might be withdrawn at the last minute, as it had before, maybe even suspended right through April, when his tour ended.

But then he'd called again two weeks ago to give them the number of a flight from New York to Detroit, arriving Wednesday. He would probably make it in earlier, but that flight would be his fallback, he said. Susannah had missed that call; she'd gone to the grocery store, which was probably why James said what he did. After he read off his flight information, he'd hesitated, then said, "Dad—just between us—if anything ever happens to me, if they say afterward I was spying, or doing anything other than working for the Army, don't believe it. OK? Everything I'm doing is under orders of the Army."

"Of course," Arthur had said.

"Everything's fine, I just—if anything happens, they're going to tell you whatever suits the unit and the Army. They're under no obligation to tell the truth, not even to you. You understand that, right, Dad?"

"Of course," Arthur had said again, of course he knew that. That's what they do. Still, it had unsettled him. Since that afternoon, he'd run many possible scenarios through his head, trying to imagine the set of circumstances that would lead James to tell him that at all, let alone then, when he was due home in two weeks. Stuck in bed, with nothing to do but watch the light creep across the wall, he ran through them again. Most likely, it was something James had been saving up to tell him, something they talked about in special ops, and he had just decided to say it then because Susannah wasn't on the phone.

Arthur had never minded James's secrecy. In fact, he found it almost comforting. He sensed that the details would prove more worrisome than the wondering, for one thing. And it was part of the Night Stalkers' pledge: *I guard my unit's mission with secrecy, for my only true ally is the night and the element of surprise.* And Arthur knew that following orders, following his training, gave James the best chance of making it home.

The next morning, after a bizarre test involving blurry glasses and a swivel chair that struck Arthur as disturbingly low-tech, his diagnosis was confirmed. A spell of vertigo, something Arthur could cure with a pill whenever he felt an attack coming on. Probably had something to do with the frostbite he'd suffered in his left ear at Thule. "I'd avoid roller coasters," the doctor said, giving Arthur's arm a little shake. Arthur accepted this gesture gamely—good news is good news, after all—and agreed to come back for some tests early the next week.

That afternoon, Arthur went back out to his observatory. He climbed the spiral stairs deliberately, his hand a little tighter than usual on the rail. Susannah hated those stairs, so steep and winding, and they struck Arthur as twisted now, narrower than before, the gaps between treads wider.

He'd purchased the observatory, a nine-foot, fully wired dome unit, as a kit over the Internet three years ago, after he got his new Celestron CPC 800. He designed the platform for it himself, and built it into his garage roof, just under the peak on the north side. The dome was generous by home observatory standards, but still quite small, just big enough for two chairs, a running ledge for the equipment, and his scope, which was mounted to a cinder block column that ran down to the garage floor. The stable mount allowed him to get deep space images, the kinds he saw in magazines. The dome had retractable roof segments that afforded a full 360-degree view. With all the vanes open, on a clear night, the sky seemed so vast and so close overhead it was disorienting, as if you could fall up.

The Celestron was an automated scope. It relied on global positioning systems to lock in targets, the same systems Arthur had worked on in his job with Syncrotek, which designed the GPS technology for General Motors in Detroit. The Celestron used global positioning only to locate itself. From there, it located everything in the heavens with astonishing precision, deducing the location of each space object in relation to that single orienting point. The CPC 800 was a technological leap; older scopes, without that absolute starting position, could only point to the neighborhood of an object. Even they were an advance over pushing the telescope around by hand.

He flipped a switch and a gray light filled the room, just enough to work by but not enough to feel lit, the sort of dull, inadequate light found inside a ship or a plane. He never liked the feel of the observatory by day, even with the dome opened wide. The daytime sky looked small in it, daffy, even, and the room felt smaller somehow, too. It was a room made for a purpose, made for night.

The last time James was home, Arthur had brought him up after dinner. It was James's first time in the observatory, and Arthur wanted to show him what the Celestron could do. It turned out to be a poor night for skywatching, cloudy and a waxing moon, and they weren't up there half an hour when Arthur turned around to say something to James and saw that he'd fallen asleep sitting up, the side of his head tilted against the metal base of the scope. Arthur put off waking him. He powered down the scope, straightened his papers, and then just sat, watching James sleep, watching the clouds make their slow progress across the opening overhead.

I pledge to maintain my body, mind and equipment in a constant state of readiness for I am a member of the fastest deployable Task Force in the world—ready to move at a moment's notice anytime, anywhere, arriving on target plus or minus thirty seconds. The pledge James took. Arthur wondered, not for the first time, whether he'd charmed James into the service with his stories about the scrambles, his tall tales of the planes. The F-22 Raptor: the pilot's dream to fly. The SR-71 Blackbird ramjet that broke Mach 3.2, so fast that the cockpit smelled like a self-cleaning oven in flight. So fast that it couldn't even be fueled up on the ground, because it leaked fuel all over the place until it reached speed, when it grew a full two inches and everything sealed. So fast that on its trial run, the tires exploded in their bays.

How many times—two, three?—he'd taken the family up to Wurtsmith in the years before it closed, eating picnic lunches in the parking lot, then standing by the fence, watching the F-16s come out of the hangars, shimmering in the fumes and the heat, the crews running through their checklists, the twenty-foot flames as the afterburners kicked in, the roar and the plane ascending, always rolling off to one side. The coordination, the precision timing. Arthur thought that the whole family enjoyed the trips, but James was always the last to leave the fence. And the last one awake on Arthur's skywatching vigils, the one who never tired of deciphering the charts, back when they used the Meade and they had to find everything by hand.

Arthur pulled up his files from the night of his attack. He stopped at a frame and, in spite of the tender stiffness in his face, smiled.

Sunday afternoon, Carrie came with her family. Arthur assured them that he felt better than he looked, which was good because Arthur looked pretty bad. The right side of his face was bruised from his eye down to his jaw. His eye was swollen; two spots on his cheekbone were bright red. Carrie's older daughter, Amanda, was afraid at first—she was only eight and very sensitive, Arthur thought. He let her touch his cheek, assured her it didn't hurt. And then said, "But look what I got for that shiner," and brought them all back to his study.

He showed them his photo, a bright fireball with a sky-long tail tracing all the way back to Leo. "The Hook," Carrie said, touching it with her finger.

"Hook's hook," Arthur said, smiling, and then showed it to Amanda. "See it? And that," he said proudly, "is one of the fastest meteors in the world. That meteor was traveling 44 miles per second," he added. Before long he'd opened his display case, and was passing around his collection of mail-order meteorites, specks of dirt in little plastic boxes with somber labels, Shergotty (AEUC) Achondrite, Shergottite SNC Signature Meteorite, Fell: September 10, 1935; Location: Gaya, India.

"Does anybody verify these?" Carrie's husband asked, frowning down at one of Arthur's specks. "What do they go by, the composition?"

"That's part of it," Arthur said. "Although often after a big shower they'll find scattered debris. Sometimes you can actually see them fall."

"It looks like dirt," Amanda said.

"That's a shooting star, honey," Carrie said.

"No, you're right, Amanda, that's just what it is," Arthur said. "Shooting stars aren't stars at all. They're just ordinary rocks. In fact, these are big ones, these made it to the ground—most shooting stars are no bigger than a grain of sand. And yet you can see them from hundreds of miles away. Know why? Because they're going so fast they blast the air into plasma and it phosphoresces. They're going so fast they make light."

Amanda looked puzzled, handed it back to him.

"How do you like that?" Arthur said, gazing at the bit of rock in his box. "A grain of sand."

*

Monday morning, Arthur returned to the hospital for scans and more blood work. It was after lunch before he sat down with his doctor. This time, no tousling, no roller coaster jokes. They'd found spots in his scans, several in the region of his left ear. He showed Arthur an image of his head, with little fuzzy areas like mothballs. "Here," he said, "and here."

"So, what do we do?" Arthur said, catching himself in the medical "we" he'd adopted from the doctor, shaking his head.

"I've asked an oncologist, Dr. Bodner, to join us. She should be here in a few minutes." Arthur blinked at him—first a kid, now a woman—not that he didn't think a woman could do the job, but just the intimacy of it. He'd rather take it from a guy his own age, preferably one who was falling apart at roughly the same rate as Arthur. But the kid was assuring him she was the best, and Arthur was trying to pay attention. "Surgery may not be possible, given the locations," the doctor said. "She'll discuss your options."

"Options," Arthur said, choices to make.

"Either way, you'll want to begin chemotherapy right away. I might expect as early as tomorrow. Unfortunately, Mr. Reel, this is a fast-moving cancer." Arthur watched him fiddle with the flap of his coat pocket, pull out a pen. "I'll let Dr. Bodner explain," the kid said uneasily, checking his watch.

"What happens if I do nothing?" Arthur asked.

There's one antidote to fear, and it's training. You do the right thing over and over in practice, Arthur liked to tell his grandkids. Then, when the time comes and you're in an emergency, you do the right thing without thinking.

By Wednesday afternoon, they'd had no word again from James, which was unusual even for him. Arthur and Susannah busied themselves through dinner—it was his last window, in New York, to make a call before boarding the commercial plane, his fallback flight. When the call didn't come, Arthur had a giddy sense that James might ring the doorbell instead, might appear with his bags on the porch, wave goodbye to some stranger in a pickup truck. James's plans had changed many times before, but he'd always called at some point to cancel or confirm.

"He probably lost his leave," Arthur told Susannah, who was chopping onions and mushrooms for the stuffing. "He probably didn't get a chance to tell us."

At seven-thirty, Arthur said he would go meet the plane James had reserved, even though he thought it unlikely James would be on it. Susannah agreed, reluctantly, to stay home. "He'll probably call while I'm on the road," Arthur told her. "Just call me and I'll turn around."

Sitting in a little plastic chair, bolted in a line before a large bank of windows, Arthur reconsidered their last conversation, what James said. He'd probably lost someone in his unit; maybe someone was killed and he'd heard rumors afterward about differing accounts of the death, the official report given to the family. Probably one of his buddies talked to a wife, something like that. Stuff like that got around. Arthur had read stories of body laundering in special ops, bodies doctored to match stories told to the families.

Once Moscow Molly had said in a broadcast, "To the boys at Thule—the lights at the end of your runway are out." And the guys in the tower looked out and they were. It was understood up there who the enemy was, where the boundaries were, what it meant if they were crossed. And it wasn't just the troops, back then, who were in a state of constant readiness—it was the country. People built bomb shelters, stored food, something the kids laughed about today. They couldn't fathom it, didn't realize there was a time when the cold war was very close to becoming a hot one.

James's war was different.

Often when Arthur told people, usually in answer to a direct question, where James was or what he did, they'd do a little check, then recover with something like, "Oh, yes, that's terrible, isn't it?" And Arthur would realize they forgot we were at war.

But there's no comparing then and now, Arthur often said. Things were slipping; he couldn't necessarily relate to them the peculiar smell of brown Fels Nap soap, the way Lynn Fontaine said "I love you" and it sounded like she meant it, the hot chocolate in little hockey pucks. Lucky Green has gone to war. The queer satisfaction of field dressing a cigarette, pressing the paper into the earth, invisible.

For a while when he was a boy, Arthur had believed that all the sound on earth traveled forever into space, the result of misunderstanding something his father told him about radio transmissions. Some years later he'd realized his error, the difference between electromagnetic waves and sound, which is a pure compression wave, a clumsy thing, stuff bumping into the stuff next to it, which bumps into the stuff next to it. Not like light, part particle, part wave, which could travel two paths at once, could travel through space for a hundred million years to bounce off a patch of snow. Much as Arthur enjoyed reading about the new physics—god particles and quantum uncertainty and multiple universes—he had to admit that most of it had very little to do with life on the planet, which tumbled along, day into day, and traveled only one path, and petered out.

A woman around Carrie's age walked toward him, took in his face, then looked hastily past him, trying to be polite. She sat in a row of chairs across from his, looking nonchalantly everywhere but at Arthur. He felt the need to explain his appearance, to tell her it's OK, I just fell.

In the black space beyond the windows, practically obscured

by the harsh airport lights, tiny blinking lights floated silently in the sky. Every so often a pair of them would line up with the runway, seeming to hover beyond it, then finally descend, the shadow of the plane spreading between them. There was a chance James was on his plane. He'd have a story to tell when he got off it, some crazy story about getting dropped on the tarmac, jumping out of an unmarked black Chinook. Something to explain where he was, why there wasn't time to call.

YOU ARE THE GREATEST LAKE

by Greg Schutz

WE ARE AT THE TIP of the thumb of Michigan. The sky threatens sun, so John has reluctantly left the water and run into town for groceries. His waders, latex and neoprene, hang in the mudroom. They smell sourly of rubber and sweat and still hold the shape of his legs. I put a pitcher of lemonade in the refrigerator to chill. The rental cottage is quiet. From the back porch, I can see Dot out in the bay, practicing the dead-man's float. Dot is John's daughter. She is eight years old. "I love you," I say.

Distantly, she stirs in the water, as if she's heard me.

The yard rolls down to the lake, grass giving way to pebbles and shells, pebbles and shells pouring smoothly into the water to form the firm, gravelly bottom that John says draws bass into the bay. I know nothing about smallmouth bass except what John has told me—a striped bronze fish, football-shaped with the slung jaw of a linebacker, that he wades for, casting, on cloudy mornings and afternoons. I know that in broken light they rise from the depths to prowl the bay for crayfish and leeches, mayfly larvae and minnows. I know the bay is broad and flat as a pan. A quarter-mile out, where Dot is floating, it's only two or three feet deep. Still, I worry. John makes allowances for her that I could never imagine for my own daughter. She is so small.

"Dot!" I call from the edge of the water. "Hello, Dot?"

Dot lifts her head.

I cup my hands around my mouth. "I made lemonade!"

Her voice comes back to me: "What?"

"Lemonade! Do you want some?"

No answer. She may not understand; she may not care. Out in the bay, her body looks exactly like a tiny, floating body. I wrap my arms around myself, though it's spring, and warm.

I climb the yard and pour a glass of lemonade. It hasn't chilled yet. "Too soon, too soon," I say, just to break the silence. On the porch, I lean against the railing, sipping lukewarm lemonade and watching Dot and waiting for John.

John would like to marry me, he thinks. I would like him to keep thinking this, and eventually to believe it. But of course it's not so simple as that. We're both divorced, John and I, and John more recently and acrimoniously than I. "How do you get over a person hating you?" he asked me once. "Real hate. Like you didn't know you could make a person feel."

I told him I didn't know, and I don't. I don't hate my ex-husband, and I hope he doesn't hate me. After a few good years and a few indifferent ones, we unclasped our hands and drifted apart. He met the woman he is living with now, and I met John. I took John away from his wife.

Tonight I lie atop the stiff mattress in the cottage's only bedroom. Dot is in her sleeping bag on the floor, sweetly snoring. John is curled like a comma, his back to me. It's not easy—he's a tall man—but I do my best to hold him. The back of his neck smells bluely of minerals, like the lake. I run my hand through his hair, fingers seeking his scar.

When John revealed our affair to his ex-wife, she hurled a cut-glass tumbler at him. He needed eleven stitches. A dull pink keloid, nearly an inch long, notches his hairline. In court, he was ruled at fault: his ex-wife won primary custody. For six months now, he has seen Dot only on the weekends.

"You are a good man," I whisper.

I still believe this, even if John does not.

He leans his dreaming body into mine. I am his only regret.

I practice the ugly side of estate law, the parts that get gnashed out in court. It's not so different from divorce, in a way. A central loss—of love, of a loved one—unglues a family, leaving each member to claw for advantage. Adrift, they take sides, cementing fierce new loyalties. I mouth Dot's name into the back of John's neck. An ellipsis: Dot, Dot, Dot. Below the foot of the bed, she growls sleep at the ceiling. I close my eyes and follow her down, arms open, sinking.

Near shore, the bay is the color of the spruces and pines it reflects. The open water is the depthless gray of the overcast sky. John is up before dawn. By the time I pour my half of the coffee he's brewed for us, he has already stepped into his waders and into the water. I can spot him only by the distant hint of patterned motion against the irregular surface of the bay as he casts. There is no opposite shore here and, for a little while this morning, not even a horizon. Sky and water mix. When I stare too long at the place where they should meet, I begin to feel ill. We are truly at the edge of something vast.

Dot pads into the kitchen, knuckling an eye.

"Good morning," I say.

She doesn't look at me. "Hello."

"Would you like some breakfast?"

"Huh," she says. She pulls a chair out from the table and climbs into it.

"Would you like cereal? Maybe an Eggo?"

Dot folds her arms atop the table and lays her head down, concealing her face. Her downy blonde hair will soon darken; John and his ex-wife are both brunettes. But her scalp is softly, pinkly visible through her hair, and I can't help but hope this never changes. My ex-husband and I didn't have any children. I never thought I wanted any.

"Eggo," she mutters at last.

So I place a frozen waffle in the toaster, heat the bottle of syrup in the microwave, spread a pat of margarine over the waffle once the toaster spits it out, douse everything in the warmed syrup, and set the plate in front of her, along with a glass of milk.

"Fork," Dot says.

I bring her a fork.

"You know," I say, "that looks so good, I think maybe I'd like an Eggo, too. Could I eat my Eggo with you?"

"Huh."

It's an all-purpose sound, the thing she says when she doesn't know what to say. Dot often finds she doesn't know what to say to me. Does she understand what I've done, and what her father has done for me? Does she hate me for it? I'm waiting to find out. And while I wait, I make myself an Eggo. We sit across the table from one another, eating our Eggos together.

At midday, John returns to the cottage, his body slowly growing as he crosses the bay. I watch from the kitchen; Dot watches from shore. She has been lying in the grass, reading *The Black Stallion*—a book I remember from my own childhood, about a boy and a wild horse marooned on a desert island together. I wonder if she has reached the part where the boy gathers moss to feed the horse, or where the horse first pushes its soft nose into the boy's waiting hand. But I cannot ask her; I wouldn't know how to begin. Dot's concentration—flat on her stomach, her bare feet swaying in the air like seaweed—is complete. She only tears her gaze from the book to look out across the water at the blur of distant motion that is her father, the man I love.

I have made sandwiches.

Ashore, John opens his arms. Dot leaps into them, her book forgotten in the grass. He carries her up to the cottage.

The fishing has been good: John is smiling, at ease, pleased with himself. "They move so silently," he says of the bass he has caught and released. "The big ones have this effortless gliding motion, like whales." He slides his broad hand across the table. It becomes a gliding bronze bass, swimming over to the plate of sandwiches, pausing to nip at a pickle spear. Dot giggles. The bass takes notice: John's hand tenses, fingers arching. Dot snorts, stifling laughter. John's hand darts out at her and she grabs it, squealing, and bites down on one of his fingers.

"Yowch," John says mildly. "Let me go, little fish."

Dot releases his hand and beams up at him.

I am amazed at the red toothmarks just behind John's cuticle, the saliva shining his nail.

"Do you like your book?" I ask.

Dot's face drains.

"*The Black Stallion*," I say, "was one of my favorite books when I was a little girl."

She studies the bubbles in her apple juice.

John takes my hand. His finger is wet. It burrows into my palm and I hold it there, squeezing tightly.

After lunch, Dot becomes a superhero. She drags the garden hose into the backyard, using the trigger nozzle to launch jets of water in all directions. "I am the Greatest Lake!" she announces. "I'm made entirely of water!"

John sits with me on the porch, placid and happy, his long pale legs splayed in front of him. "Time," he says, patting my knee. "Give her time."

John is good at patience. A carpenter, he has spent his life measuring twice to cut once. He told the doctor who stitched his head that he'd banged himself on an open cabinet door. Now his daughter disappears every Sunday night and he doesn't see her again until Friday afternoon, and he believes he deserves this. I want us to pool our lives together. Someday, he answers. I'm waiting, I say.

"I can communicate with fish!" Dot shouts, hosing a forsythia bush.

In her bright swimsuit bottom and drenched, billowing shirt, she appears costumed, streamlined, aquatic. I imagine her slicing through the water of the bay, easy and graceful, a little whale. The image brings an ache to my chest, as if she were swimming away from me. Dot fires water straight up into the air and does a stomping, stiff-limbed rain dance as it showers down.

"She hates me," I say.

"Hey." John brushes my chin with a rough finger, turning my face to his. I smell fish on his hands. We kiss. His lower lip leaves a rim of moisture beneath my own. "She's a little girl," he says. "She hates peas and carrots and fruits with pits in them. She hates bathtime and the boy at school who put paste in her hair. But not you. You she's just not sure about."

I want to believe him. But I remember driving to the emergency room to sit with him while he waited his turn in triage. "No," he kept saying, holding a bloody washcloth to his forehead, his voice miserable and low, "no, she was right to do it."

Soon, John rises to collect his fishing rod and slide his legs back into the waterproof skin of his waders. Instead of marching into the water, though, he joins Dot in the yard, clomping around in his felt-soled boots. "Fear not!" he cries. "It is I, the Master Angler!"

I stay where I am, happy to go unnoticed. I am not ready for Dot to make a supervillain of me, or else to grow suddenly silent in my presence, her face flat and still as the surface of the bay. Once their game has carried them around the side of the cottage, I step quietly into the yard and pick *The Black Stallion* out of the grass—miraculously, it is dry. I carry it inside. Dot has folded down the corner of the page she is on, and I am impressed by the attentiveness of the gesture. In the living room, I turn the armchair toward the window that overlooks the lake and arrange an end table and a floor lamp on either side. I set the book on the end table. This would be a comfortable place for Dot to read. She could look out the window and watch her father fish.

I understand that I am trying to trick her into staying inside, close to me.

At the heavy oak table in the mudroom, I shuffle some papers from the accordion file I have brought with me and remind myself that I will always have my work. Outside, the heroes are springing into action. "Dot," I say. Her name in my mouth is round at one end and pointed at the other, a raindrop. My pen, tapping paper, is a clock.

The next day is Sunday, the end of our long weekend on the shore, and Dot wants to fish. After breakfast, John finds a small rod for her and ties a golden hook to the end of the line. The knot he uses is a complicated, twisting thing, his fingers moving faster than my eyes can follow. He and Dot walk the edge of the yard, prying up rocks and rotten logs to gather angleworms and grubs. I watch from the kitchen window. Dot is fearless, plunging wrist-deep into the dirt.

Today, John heads out into the bay until he disappears from sight. I scan the horizon for him, but there is only the endless rolling of the waves. Dot is unconcerned. Fishing rod in hand, she walks the shore, catching tiny fish. The end of our visit has filled my head with muddy desperation, and so I steel myself and approach cautiously, as I might a wild animal.

Dot, however, is aglow with success.

She shows me a fish as round and flat as a little tea saucer. "This one's called a bluegill." This may be the first time she has ever spoken to me unbidden, offering the words like a gift.

"Bluegill," I say.

I learn that another fish, with the same round shape but prettier, speckled colors, is called a pumpkinseed. Dot pops the golden hook free from the fish's mouth and lowers the fish gently into the water. It darts away, pauses for a moment as if to catch its breath, and then flits farther into the green reflections of the trees where it cannot be seen.

"Pumpkinseed," I say, and Dot nods, very serious.

I follow her down the shore, my head empty as a sleepwalker's. I move like Dot, with fluid gliding steps so as not to frighten the fish, and keep my careful distance so as not to frighten her. The clouds feather open; a white sun appears. Dot's hair lights like a lamp. Frowning, she turns to the sky. Looking at her, I see John, chest-deep in the bay, squinting as the light burns his shadow onto the water. UV rays, he tells me, are the problem. They drive the bass out of the shallows and into the depths. Dot rubs the back of her neck. In her mind, I imagine, she follows the fish, sinking down and down. She is the Greatest Lake. Sweat glistens on her upper lip.

"I'm thirsty. Are you thirsty?" I am thinking of the lemonade in the refrigerator.

Dot blinks up at me, reminded of my presence. I might as well be the sun, spilling my dangerous heat.

"No," she says.

I smile at her. I do not want to press my luck. This has been a good morning, something to build upon. By the time I've reached the top of the yard, the clouds have knit together again.

For an hour, I try to work in the mudroom, but how can I concentrate on the boilerplate language of quitclaim deeds? The words drift away from me. "Pumpkinseed," I say, picturing Dot's face. I slide my papers back into the accordion file and cap my pen. I sit in the armchair by the window. Down below, Dot's toes are in the lake. "Pumpkinseed, I love you."

I am sitting there still, drowsy and warm and contemplating lunch, when Dot screams.

Something has happened. Her small rod bows sharply to the water. Out beyond the reflected pines, a small bright patch of the bay turns to froth. A heavy brown fish throws itself clear of the water, crashes down, throws itself tumbling into the air again: one of John's bass. The fish writhes across the surface. Dot, at the other end of the invisible line, is hooked to it.

I have never heard Dot scream before. There's no ragged tremble of adult emotion, only a high, pure tone that reaches through windows and walls to pluck me from my chair and carry me out the door and down the lawn without my feet ever touching the ground. Still, it takes me a very long time to arrive. "I'm here," I keep calling, "I'm here," but this is a lie. By the time I reach her, it is over: the bass has torn the fishing rod from Dot's hands. She stands open-palmed and shaking.

"I was pulling in a little fish," she says. "And then this bass came up and—he took it."

Her face bunches and purples. She bursts into tears.

John, I'm sure, good and patient as he is, a carpenter who builds things piece by piece until at last they stand complete, would know the right thing to say now. But I am not John. The bay is empty, and I am dry-mouthed with love. So I leave my sandals on the shore. The water is cold; my skin prickles. The pebbles are smooth beneath my feet, the broken shells sharp as teeth. My hands trail in the water. My skirt rises around my waist.

I find Dot's rod and draw it, dripping, from the bay. The bass is gone. At the end of the line there is only a tiny fish, its fins stripped and its body crushed, the golden hook fixed to its cheek like a pin. A pumpkinseed.

The red gills flex. I feel the little muscles pulling against my palm. The mouth opens and closes as if trying to speak.

"Let it go." Dot's voice is small. "Let it swim away."

"Dot," I say, "I can't."

I mean that it is too late now; the damage is done. I cannot stitch torn fins, affix lost scales. When I pop the golden hook free, it leaves a ragged pinhole I cannot close.

"No," Dot says as if I've misunderstood her. "It has to swim away now."

"I'm sorry," I say.

Her eyes wash over me, the dying fish in my hand. She pins elbows to ribs, fists to thighs, as if she were the one being squeezed.

"I'm sorry." Spoken at last, the words now bubble up unbidden. I am a primed pump, spilling stale, wet, mineral-scented regrets. "I'm sorry, Dot, I'm sorry, I'm so sorry."

Her reflection wavers in the water a moment.

"Huh," she says.

She boils up to the house.

The yard is empty; Dot is gone. The windows of the cottage are filled with the bay. I clutch the tiny body because I cannot bear to watch it float away from me. Against my palm the little muscles pull, and pull, and pull, and stop.

＊

I wait for John on the shore. Dot waits in the house.

"What is it?" The lake streams from his waders. "What happened?"

"Oh, boy. John, I don't even know."

I try to tell him about the pumpkinseed, but my breath keeps galloping, and it's hard for the rest of me to keep up. "If I could have saved it. If I could have made it better somehow." I shake my head. My hair hangs in my eyes. A rising wind blows waves up the beach. "'I'm so sorry,' I kept telling her. That was all I kept saying."

John takes my hands and tells me—calmly, reasonably, patiently—that there was nothing else I could have done. "You have nothing to be sorry for," he says.

"John," I say, "I am sorry."

I look at him until he understands.

"We," I say, "are the worst thing I've ever done."

The wind plucks the bay into curls. John raises my hands to his mouth. We must smell the same now—algae and mucus and minerals, the wet scent of fish. I feel his lips on my fingers. "I know," he says.

After a quiet lunch, we pack our bags and clean the cottage. It starts to rain. The wet lawn shivers. The lake steams, rising into the air.

"Better leave now." John has checked the weather report. "It's only going to get worse."

Dot turtles her heavy backpack out to the car. We have said exactly nothing to one another since our exchange on the shore. I straighten the living room, returning the armchair, end table, and lamp to their original positions. *The Black Stallion* is still where I left it yesterday, the same page folded down. I read: *The stallion's mane swept in the wind, his muscles twitched, his eyes moved restlessly, but he stood his ground as the boy approached.*

John leans inside. His car is idling in the driveway. "Ready?"

"Almost."

In the kitchen, I pour the lemonade down the sink.

Dot is asleep. Her mouth moves stickily, making big and little Os. Rain skins the windshield; John leans low over the wheel. "Pull over," I say. "We can wait it out." But John shakes his head. We both have work tomorrow, and he has to return Dot to his ex-wife tonight. He will drop me off at my condominium in Bloomfield Hills, and he and Dot will continue on to Ypsilanti. He will walk Dot to his ex-wife's door, which will open only wide enough for Dot to enter, and then he will stretch his long body across the Murphy bed in his basement efficiency downtown. Miles away, I will sleep alone, my legs swimming in the sheets, searching for his.

The storm brings early night. John squints into the gloom, driving slowly. The tires hiss. I begin to feel ill. It is the loss of horizon again, sky bleeding into water bleeding into sky. I have nowhere to fix my gaze.

"I think I need to get in back," I say.

After John pulls to the shoulder, I get out. The rain soaks me in an instant, cold through my clothes, as if I have plunged overboard. I breathe deeply. In the backseat I am sodden, dripping. "Try and get some sleep," John says. I look at the little girl snoring beside me and think that this is a good idea. As the heater breathes over me, my skin begins to steam. I close my eyes and sublimate, drifting up to the ceiling.

I touch Dot's hair. She is soft. The fine strands mat beneath my damp fingers, revealing delicate pink scalp. I slide my hand behind her head. My heart pops like a cork. John pilots a submarine through the rain. We are sinking deep. I cradle Dot's head as if she were my own. "Little fish," I say. And she turns to me now, recognizes my soaked and shining body costumed with water, and calls me by the name of her hero.

John touches my knee, waking me. The car has stopped. He says, "It's time."

NORTH COUNTRY

by Roxane Gay

I HAVE MOVED TO THE EDGE of the world for two years. If I am not careful, I will fall. After my first department meeting, my new colleagues encourage me to join them on a scenic cruise to meet more locals. *The Peninsula Star* will travel through the Portage Canal, up to Copper Harbor and then out onto Lake Superior. I am handed a glossy brochure with bright pictures of blue skies and calm lake waters. "You'll be able to enjoy the foliage," they tell me, shining with enthusiasm for the Upper Peninsula. "Do you know how to swim?" they ask.

I arm myself with a flask, a warm coat, and a book. At the dock, there's a long line of ruddy Michiganders chatting amiably about when they expect the first snow to fall. It is August. I have just moved to the Upper Peninsula to assume a post doc at the Michigan Institute of Technology. My colleagues, all civil engineers, wave to me. "You came," they shout. They've already started drinking. I take a nip from my flask. I need to catch up. "You're going to love this cruise," they say. "Are you single?" they ask.

We sit in a cramped booth drinking Rolling Rocks. Every few minutes one of my colleagues offers an interesting piece of Upper Peninsula trivia such as the high incidence of waterfalls in the area or the three hundred inches of snow the place receives annually. I take a long, hard swallow from my flask. I am flanked by a balding, overweight tunnel expert on my right and a dark-skinned hydrologist from India on my left. The hydrologist is lean and quiet and his knee presses uncomfortably against mine. He tells me he has a wife back in Chennai but that in Michigan, he's leaving his options open. I am the only woman in the department and as such, I am a double novelty. My new colleagues continue to buy me drinks and I continue to accept them until my ears are ringing and my cheeks are flushed. Sweat drips down my back. "I need some fresh air," I mumble, excusing myself. I make my way, slowly, to the upper deck, ignoring the stares and lulls in conversation.

Outside, the air is crisp and thin, the upper deck sparsely populated. Near the bow, a young couple makes out enthusiastically, loudly. A few feet away from them a group of teenagers stand in a huddle, snickering. I sit on a red plastic bench and hold my head in my hands. My flask sits comfortably and comfortingly against my rib cage.

"I saw you downstairs," a man with a deep voice says.

The sun is setting, casting that strange quality of light rendering everything white, nearly invisible. I squint and look up slowly at a tall man with shaggy hair hanging over his ears. I nod.

"Are you from Detroit?

I have been asked this question twenty-three times since moving to the area. In a month, I will stop counting, having reached a four-digit number. Shortly after that, I will begin telling people I have recently arrived from Africa. They will nod and exhale excitedly and ask about my tribe. I don't know that in this moment so there is little to comfort me. I shake my head.

"Do you talk?"

"I do," I say. "Are you from Detroit?

He smiles, slow and lazy. He's handsome in his own way—his

skin is tanned and weathered and his eyes are almost as blue gray as the lake we're cruising on. He sits down. I stare at his fingers, the largest fingers I've ever seen. The sweaty beer bottle in his hand looks miniature. "So where are you from?"

I shove my hands in my pocket and slide away from him. "Nebraska."

"I've never met anyone from Nebraska," he says.

I say, "I get that a lot."

The boat is now out of the portage canal and we're so far out on the lake I can't see land. I feel small. The world feels too big.

"I better get back to my colleagues," I say, standing up. As I walk away, he shouts, "My name is Magnus." I throw a hand in the air but don't look back.

In my lab, things make sense. As a structural engineer, I design concrete mixes, experiment with new aggregates like fly ash and other energy byproducts, artificial particulates, kinds of water that might make concrete not just stronger but unbreakable, permanent, perfect. I teach a section of Design of Concrete Structures and a section of Structural Dynamics. I have no female students in either class. The boys stare at me, and after class they linger in the hallway just outside of the classroom. They try to flirt. I remind them I will assess their final grades. They make inappropriate comments about extra credit.

At night, I sit in my apartment and watch TV and search for faculty positions and other career opportunities closer to the center of the world. There's a pizza restaurant across the street and above the restaurant, an apartment filled with loud white girls who play loud rap music into the middle of the night and have loud fights with their boyfriends who play basketball for the university. One of the girls has had an abortion and another isn't speaking to her father and the third roommate has athletic sex with her boyfriend even when the other two are awake; she has a child but the child lives with her father. I do not want to know any of these things.

Several unopened boxes are sitting in my new apartment. To unpack those boxes means I will stay. To stay means I will be trapped in this desolate place for two years, alone. I rented my new home over the phone—it is a former dry cleaner converted into an apartment. There are no windows save for one in the front door. The apartment, I thought, as I walked from room to room when I moved in, was like a jail cell. I had been sentenced. My new landlady, an octogenarian Italian who ran the dry cleaners for more than thirty years, gasped when she met me. "You didn't sound like a colored girl on the phone," she said. "I get that a lot," I replied.

The produce is always rotten at the local grocery store—we're too far north to receive timely food deliveries. I stand before a display of tomatoes, limp, covered in wrinkled skin, some dotted soft white craters ringed by some kind of black mold. I consider the cost to my dignity if I move in with my parents until I feel a heavy hand on my shoulder. When I spin around, struggling to maintain my balance, I recognize Magnus. I grab his wrist between two fingers and step away. "Do you always touch strangers?"

"We're not strangers."

I make quick work of selecting the least decomposed tomatoes and move on to the lettuce. Magnus follows. I say, "We have different understandings of the word stranger. You don't even know my name."

"I like the way you talk," he says.

"What is that supposed to mean?"

Magnus reddens. "Exactly what I said. Unless we have different understandings of the words I, like, the, way, you, and talk."

I bite the inside of my cheek to keep from smiling. I have a weakness for charming men who make witty comebacks.

"Can I buy you a drink?"

I look at the pathetic tomatoes in my basket, and maybe it's the overwhelming brightness of the fluorescent lighting or the Easy Listening being piped through the store speakers, but I nod. I say, "My name is Kate." Magnus says, "Meet me at the Thirsty Fish, Kate." On the drive there, I stare at my reflection in the rearview mirror and smooth my eyebrows. At the bar, Magnus entertains me with the silly things girls like to take seriously. He buys me lots of drinks and I drink them. He flatters me with words about my pretty eyes. He says he can tell I'm smart. I haven't had sex in more than two months. I haven't had a real conversation with anyone in more than two months. I'm not at my best.

In the parking lot, I stand next to my car, holding on to the door, trying to steady myself. Magnus says, "I can't let you drive home like this." I mutter something about the altitude affecting my tolerance. He says, "We're not in the mountains." He stands so close. The warmth from his chest fills the short distance between us. Magnus takes my keys and as I reach for them, I fall into him. He lifts my chin with one of his massive fingers and I say, "Fuck." I kiss him, softly. Our lips barely move but we don't pull apart. His hand is solid in the small of my back as he presses me against my car.

When I wake up, my mouth is thick and sour. I groan and sit up and hit my head against something unfamiliar. I wince. Everything in my head feels loose, lost.

"Be careful. It's a tight fit in here."

I rub my eyes, trying to swallow the panic bubbling at the base of my throat. I clutch at my chest.

"Relax. I didn't know where you lived so I brought you back to my place."

I take a deep breath, look around. I'm sitting on a narrow bed.

I see Magnus through a narrow doorway standing near a two-burner stove. My feet are bare. A cat jumps into my lap. I scream.

Magnus lives in a trailer, and not one of those fancy doublewides on a foundation with a well-kept garden in front, but rather, an old, rusty trailer that can be attached to a truck and driven away. It is the kind of trailer you see in sad, forgotten places that have surrendered to rust and overgrown weeds and cars on cinder blocks and sagging laundry lines. The trailer, on the outside, is in a fair amount of disrepair, but the inside is immaculate. Everything has its proper place. I appreciate that.

"You should eat something," he says.

I extricate myself from the cat and walk into the galley area. Magnus invites me to sit at the table and he sets a plate of dry, scrambled eggs and a mug of coffee in front of me. My stomach rolls wildly. I wrap my hands around the coffee mug and inhale deeply. I try to make sense of the trajectory between rotten tomatoes and this trailer. Magnus slides into the bench across from me. He explains that he lives in this trailer because it's free. It's free because his trailer sits on the corner of a parcel of land his sister Mira and her husband Peter farm. The farm is twenty minutes outside of town. There's no cell phone reception. I can't check my e-mail, he tells me as I wave my phone in different directions, desperate for a signal. I ask him why he lives this way. He says he has a room in his sister's house he rarely uses. He likes his privacy, he says.

"You took my shoes off."

Magnus nods. "You have nice feet."

"Can you take me to my car?"

Magnus sighs, quickly drains the rest of his coffee in the small sink. He is a patient man. I like that too.

On the drive back to town I sit as far away from Magnus as possible. I try to recreate the events between standing in the parking lot and waking up in a trailer with a cat in my lap. I refuse to ask Magnus to fill in the blanks. At my car, he grips the steering wheel tightly. I thank him for the ride and he hands me my keys. He says, "I'd love your phone number."

I force myself to smile. I say, "Thank you for not letting me drive last night." I say, "I don't normally drink much, but I just moved here." He says, "Yes, the altitude," and waits until I drive away before heading back to his trailer. My father would appreciate the gesture. I remember the pressure of Magnus's lips against mine, their texture and the smell of his bed sheets. I am in trouble.

In my lab, things make sense. The first snow falls in late September. It will continue to fall until May. I tell my mother I may not survive. I tell her this so many times she starts to worry. I test cement fitness. I fill molds with cylinders of concrete. I experiment with salt water and bottled water and lake water and tap water. I cure and condition specimens. I take detailed notes. I write an article. I turn down three dates with three separate colleagues. The hydrologist from Chennai reaffirms the openness of his options in the United States. I reaffirm my disinterest in his options or being one of his options. I administer an exam that compels my students to call me, "Battle Axe." I attend a campus social for single faculty. There are seven women in attendance and more than thirty men. The hydrologist is there too. He doesn't wear a wedding ring. I am asked thirty-four times if I am from Detroit, a new record for a single day. I try to remember where Magnus lives and all I recall is a blurry memory of being drunk, burying my face into his arm as we drove, and him, singing along to the Counting Crows. I love the Counting Crows.

*

There once was a man. There is always some man. We were together for six years. He was an engineer, too. Some people called him my dissertation advisor. When we got involved, he told me he would teach me things and mold me into a great scholar. He said I was the brightest girl he had ever known. Then he contradicted himself. He said we would marry and thought I believed him. A couple years passed and he said we would marry when he was promoted to full professor and then it was when I finished my degree. I got pregnant and he said we would marry when the baby was born. The baby was stillborn and he said we would marry when I recovered from the loss. I told him I was as recovered as I was ever going to be. He had no more excuses and I no longer cared to marry him. I spent most of my nights awake while he slept soundly, remembering what it felt like to rub my swollen belly and feel my baby kicking. He told me I was cold and distant. He told me I had no reason to mourn a child that never lived. He amused himself with a new lab assistant who consistently wore insensible shoes and short skirts even though we spent our days working with sand and cement and other dirty things. I found them fucking, the lab assistant bent over a stack of concrete bricks squealing like a debutante porn star, the man thrusting vigorously, literally fucking the lab assistant right out of her high heels, his fat face red and shiny. He gasped in short, repulsive bursts. The scene was so common I couldn't even get angry. I had long stopped feeling anything where he was concerned. I returned to my office, accepted the postdoc position and never looked back. I would have named our daughter Emma. She would have been beautiful despite her father. She would have been four months old when I left.

*

Snow has been falling incessantly. The locals are overjoyed. Every night, I hear the high-pitched whine of snowmobiles speeding past my apartment. There are things I will need to survive the winter—salt, a shovel, a new toilet seat, rope. I brave the weather and go to the hardware store. I am wearing boots laced high around my calves, a coat, gloves, hat and scarf, thermal underwear. I never remove these items unless I am home. It takes too much effort. I wonder how these people manage to reproduce. I see Magnus standing over a display of chainsaws. He is more handsome than I remember. I turn to walk away but then I don't. I stand still and hope he notices me. I realize that dressed as I am, my own family wouldn't recognize me. I tap his shoulder. I say, "What do you plan on massacring?"

He looks up slowly, shrugs. "Just looking," he says.

"For a victim?"

"Aren't you feeling neighborly?"

"I thought I would say hello."

Magnus nods again. "You've said hello."

I swallow, hard. My irritation tastes bitter. I quickly tell him my phone number and go to find a stronger kind of rope. As I pull away, I notice Magnus watching me from inside the store. I smile.

In my lab things make sense. I teach my students how to make perfect concrete cylinders, how to perform compression tests. They crush their perfect cylinders and roar with delight each time the concrete shatters and the air is filled with a fine dust. There's a lot to love about breaking things.

Everyone I meet dispenses a bit of wisdom on how to survive the "difficult" winters—embrace the outdoors, drinking, travel, drinking, sun lamps, drinking, sex, drinking. The hydrologist offers to prepare spicy curries to keep me warm, offers to give me a taste of his very special curry. I decline, tell him I have a delicate constitution. Nils, my department chair, stops by my office. He says, "How are you holding up?" I assure him all is well. He says, "The first year is always the hardest." He says, "You might want to take a trip to Detroit to see your family." I thank him for the support.

I am walking around the lab watching students work when Magnus calls. I excuse myself and take the call in the hallway, ignoring the students milling about with their aimless expressions.

My heart beats loudly. I can hardly hear Magnus. I say, "You didn't need to take so long to call me."

"Is this a lecture?"

"Would you like it to be?"

"Can I make you dinner?"

I ignore my natural impulse to say no. I am more excited than I would ever admit. He invites me back to his trailer where he prepares steak and green beans and baked potatoes. We drink beer. We talk, or rather, I talk, filling his trailer with all the words I've kept to myself since moving to the North Country, longer. I complain about the weather. At some point, he holds his hand open and I slide my hand in his. He traces my knuckles with his thumb. He is plainspoken and honest. His voice is strong and clear. He has a kind smile and a kind touch. He talks about his job as a logger and his band—he plays guitar. When we finally stop talking he says, "I like you," and then he stands and pulls me to my feet. A man has never told me he likes me. Like is more interesting than love. I stand on his boots and wrap my arms around him. He is thick and solid. When we kiss, he is gentle, too gentle. I say,

"You don't have to be soft with me," and he grunts. He clasps my neck with one of his giant hands, and kisses me harder, his lips forcing mine open. The flat softness of his tongue thrills me. He brushes his lips across my chin. He sinks his teeth into my neck and I grab his shirt between my fists. I try to remain standing. I say, "My neck is the secret password." He bites my neck harder and I forget about everything and all the noise in my head quiets.

I slip out of my shirt and step out of my jeans and Magnus lifts me up and sits me on the edge of his kitchen table. He places his large hands between my thighs and pulls them apart. I quickly unbuckle his belt, reach for him and he grabs my wrist. He says, "You don't get to be the boss of everything." I say a silent prayer. I close my eyes and he drags his hand from my chin, down the center of my chest, over the flat of my stomach. He kisses my shoulders, my breasts, my knees. He makes me tremble and whimper. "You don't have to be soft with me," I repeat. Magnus kisses the insides of my ankles and then my lips, his tongue rough and heavy against mine. I try to pull him into me by wrapping my legs around his waist. He laughs, low and deep. He says, "Say you want this." I bite my lower lip. I measure my pride against my desire. When he fucks me, he is slow, deliberate, rough in a terribly controlled way. I bury my face in his shoulder. When he asks why I'm crying, I say nothing. For a little while, he fills all the emptiness.

In the morning, I want to leave quickly even though I can still feel Magnus in my skin. As I sit on the edge of the bed and pull my pants on he says, "I want to see you again." I say, "yes" but explain we have to keep things casual, that we can't become a thing. He traces my naked spine with his fingers and I shiver. He says, "We're already a thing." I stand, shaking my head angrily. "That's not even possible." He says, "Sometimes, when I'm miles deep in the woods, looking for a new cutting site, it feels like I'm the first man who has ever been there. I look up and the trees are so thick I can hardly see the sky. I get so scared but the world somehow makes sense there. Being with you feels like that." I shake my head again, my fingers trembling as I finish getting dressed. I feel nauseous and dizzy. I say, "I'm allergic to cats." I say, "You shouldn't talk like that." I say, "I like you too." I recite his words over and over for the rest of the day, week, month.

Several weeks later, I'm at Magnus's trailer. We've seen each other almost every night, at his place, where he cooks and we talk and we have sex. We're lying naked in his narrow bed. I say, "If this continues much longer, we're going to have to sleep at my place. I have a real bed and actual rooms with doors." He smiles and nods. He says, "Whatever you want." After Magnus falls asleep, I stare up at the low ceiling, then out the small window at the clear winter sky. I wonder what he would think of Emma, if he could love her. I try to swallow the emptiness. I hold my stomach as hot tears slide down my face and trickle along my neck. Just as I'm falling asleep, his alarm goes off. Magnus sits up, rubbing his eyes. Even in the darkness I can see his hair standing on end. He says, "I want to show you something." We dress but he tells me I can leave my coat. Instead, he hands me a quilt. Outside, a fresh blanket of snow has fallen. The moon is still high. Everything is perfect and silent and still. The air hurts but feels clean. He cuts a trail to the barn and I follow in his footsteps. As Magnus walks, he stares up into the sky. I tell myself, "I feel nothing." It is a lie. When I am with him, I feel everything. Inside the barn, I shiver and dance from foot to foot trying to stay warm. He says, "We have to milk the cows." He nods to a small campstool next to a very large cow. I say, "There is absolutely no way." Magnus leads me to the stool and forces me onto it. He hunches down behind me and he pats the cow on her side. He hasn't shaved yet so the stubble from his beard tickles me. He kisses my neck softly. He places his hands over mine and I learn how to milk a cow. Nothing makes sense here.

Hunting season starts. Magnus shows me his rifle, long, polished, powerful. He refers to his rifle as a "she" and a "her." I tease him about his rifle and call her his mistress. He frowns, says he would never do that to me. I believe him. I tell him my father hunts and he gets excited. He says, "Maybe someday your father and I can hunt together." I explain that my father hunts pheasant and by hunt, I mean he rides around with his friends on a four-wheeler, but doesn't really kill much of anything and often gets injured in embarrassing accidents. I say, "You and he hunt differently." He says, "I still want to meet your father." "I only introduce serious boyfriends to my family," I say. Magnus holds my chin between two fingers and looks at me hard. It makes me shiver. This is the first time I've seen real anger from him. I wonder how far I can push. He says, "You won't see me for a few days but I'm going to kill a buck for you." Five days later, Magnus shows up at my apartment still wearing his camouflage and Carhartt overalls. His beard is long and unkempt. He smells rank. He is dirty. I only recognize his eyes. Magnus steps inside and pulls me into a muscular hug that makes me feel like he is rearranging my insides. I inhale deeply. I am surprised by the sharp twinge between my thighs. When he kisses me, he is possessive, controlling, salty. He moans into my mouth and turns me around, pinning my arms over my head. He fucks me against the front door. I smile. Afterward, we both sink to the floor. He says, "The buck is in the car." He says, "I missed you." I want to say something, the right thing, the kind thing. I slap his thigh. I push. I say, "Please take a shower." I don't shower though, not for hours.

*

I visit my parents in Florida for Thanksgiving and my mother asks why I don't call as often. I explain how work has gotten busy. I explain how snow has fallen every single day for more than a month and how everyone thinks I'm from Detroit. My mother says I look thin. She says I'm too quiet. We don't talk about the dead child or the father of the dead child. There is this life and that life. We pretend that life never happened. It is a mercy. Magnus calls every morning before he leaves for work and every night before he falls asleep. One afternoon he calls and my mother answers my phone. I hear her laughing as she says, "What an unusual name." When she hands me my phone, she asks, "Who is this Magnus? Such a nice young man." I push. I say he's no one important because I don't know how to explain him or who I am when I'm with him. I say it a little too loudly. When I put my phone to my ear I can only hear a dial tone. Magnus doesn't call for the rest of my trip. We won't speak until the end of January.

In my lab things make sense but they don't. I can't concentrate. I want to call Magnus but my repeated bad behavior overwhelms me. The weather has grown colder, sharper. The world grows and I shrink. My students work on final projects. I have a paper accepted at a major conference. The semester ends, I return to Florida for the holidays. My mother says I look thin. She says I'm too quiet. When she asks if I want to talk about my child I shake my head. I say, "Please don't ever mention her again, not ever." My mother holds the palm of one hand to my cheek and the palm of the other over my heart. I send Magnus a card and a letter and gift and another letter and another letter. He sends me a text message that says, "I'm still angry." I send more letters. He writes back once and I carry his letter with me everywhere. I try to acquire a taste for venison. The new semester starts. I have another paper accepted at a conference, this one in Europe. A new group of students tries to flirt with me while learning about the wonder of concrete. I get a research grant and my department chair offers me a tenure track faculty position with the department. He tells me to take as much time as I need to consider his offer. He says the department really needs someone like me. He says, "You kill two birds with one stone, Katie." I contemplate placing his head in the compression-testing machine and the sound it would make. I say, "I prefer to be called Kate."

The hydrologist corners me in my lab late at night and makes an inappropriate advance that leaves me unsettled. For weeks, I will feel his long, skinny fingers, how they grabbed at things that were not his to hold. Even though it's after midnight, I call Magnus. My voice is shaking. He says, "You hurt my feelings," and the simple honesty of his words hurts. I say, "I'm sorry. I never say what I really feel," and I cry. He asks, "What's wrong?" He knows me better than I care to admit. I tell him about the married hydrologist, a dirty man with a bright pink tongue who tried to lick my ear and who called me Black Beauty and who got aggressive when I tried to push him away and how I'm nervous about walking to my car. Magnus says, "I'm on my way." I wait for him by the main entrance and when I recognize his bulky frame trudging through the snow toward me, everything feels more bearable. Magnus doesn't say a word. He just holds me. After a long while, he punches the brick wall and says, "I'm going to kill that guy." I believe him. He walks me to my lab to get my things.

At my apartment, I hold a bag of frozen corn against Magnus's scraped knuckles. I say, "I shouldn't have called." He says, "Yes, you should have." He says, "You have to be nicer to me." I say, "I do." I straddle his lap and kiss his torn knuckles and pull his hands beneath my shirt and look into his beautiful blue-gray eyes and I don't say it, but I think, "I love you."

Magnus starts picking me up from work every night and if I have to work late, he sits with me, watching me work. There is an encounter with the hydrologist. Words are exchanged. Magnus clarifies for the hydrologist my disinterest in curries of any kind. He doesn't trouble me again. While I work, Magnus tells me about trees and everything a man could ever know from spending his days among them. He often smells like pine and sawdust.

In March, winter lingers. Magnus builds me an igloo and inside, he lights a small fire. He says, "Sometimes, I feel I don't know a thing about you." I am sitting between his legs, my back to his chest. Even though we're wearing layers of clothing, it feels like we're naked. I say, "You know I'm not very nice." He kisses my cheek. He says, "That's not true." He says, "Tell me something true." I tell him how I hold on to the idea of Emma even though I shouldn't, how she's all I really think about, how she might be trying to walk now or say her first words. I tell him I think I love him and I love how he likes me. He brings my cold fingers to his warm lips. He fills all the hollow spaces.

RAINBOW DOGS

by Justyn Harkin

Steve

WE HAVE A NURSE today whose name is Steve. Steve is a nurse but he is not a fag. Steve has sandy brown hair and it is short. Steve has a bristle brush mustache and it is serious. Steve wears dark blue trousers and a matching blue Dora the Explorer print scrub top. Steve has on a pair of Crocs. Steve is going gray about the temples. Steve keeps his emergency room ID on a North Park University Nursing Program lanyard. Steve writes left-handed. Steve looks like he could take care of himself in a scrap. The hair on Steve's forearms is darker than the hair on his head. Steve wants us to know that the doctors are coming. Steve sports a scar on his chin. Steve has muscles in his neck. Steve clamps a hemostat to his shirt. Steve calls my infant daughter "Princess" as he slides a needle up her arm.

Lumps

At a party at the in-laws, one of Karen's cousins, a nurse, noticed the baby had lumps under her jaw. "Those aren't supposed to be there," this cousin said. "You should take her to a doctor." We panicked. We cursed ourselves as unfit parents for not noticing the lumps on our own. We drove to the closest hospital and were seen at the emergency room as soon as we got there. The triage nurse weighed the baby, took her temperature, and escorted us to a private examination room reserved for children at the back of the E.R. The little room featured teddy bear wallpaper, a wooden rocking chair, and an angry metal crib that looked like it was designed for monster truck babies. We sat in the room alone for a long while and joked about the décor. Then came Nurse Shelly, a big girl with blonde hair, thick wrists. Said she didn't want to draw my daughter's blood. She could stick little kids all day long, she said, but babies were different. She hated sticking babies. Karen got upset and left the room. Shelly motioned that she was ready, and I leaned forward to give the baby a kiss. I pressed my lips to her head and she screamed and balled her fist in my beard. Shelly filled one, two, three vials with blood. Said again she hated sticking babies, then wrung those chubby hands of hers.

Bovary Was a Country Doc

Well, folks, I gotta tell you that I'm gonna have to go to the books on this one. See, your daughter's neck masses—hi, cutie—your daughter's neck masses are presenting bilaterally, here and here, along her parotid glands. The parotids are salivary glands. Salivary glands make saliva, or spit. We have three salivary glands on each side of our faces: here, here, and here, and the parotids are the biggest. Now the parotids aren't connected to each other in any way—oh, I know, sweetie. Who's this strange man, huh? Who's this strange man, and why does he keep poking me? They're not connected, so if something happens to the parotid on the left side, then the parotid on the right side should be unaffected. Oh, you're a cute one, yes. Yes, you're a cutie. Now I'm thinking she might have the mumps, because of the classic inflammation of the glands here, but that would be unusual because she's so young—oh, you're still a big girl, sweetheart, I see you holding your head up by yourself—because she's so young, and well, because there hasn't been a major outbreak of mumps in this country in over 30 years. I mean we're just a community hospital here. We get heart attacks, trauma, broken bones, drunks. Still, this looks an awful lot like mumps—a lot like mumps—so I'm going to leave you for a moment while I do some research. I'll do some double-checking. Then I'll be back, OK? I'll be right back.

Rubberneckers

When the doctor left, Karen and I tried to soothe the baby, who was starting to fuss. She was naked, so we diapered her, put back on her clothes, warmed a bottle of breast milk in the sink, and fed her. When she finished, I turned off the lights and tried to rock her to sleep in a sturdy old rocker in the corner. Just as I was starting to fall asleep myself, two men rapped on the wall outside our open examining room door. They wanted to examine my daughter, and because they introduced themselves as doctors, I let them. "Dr. Murphy is a fine physician," the one doctor said as he tilted my daughter's head to expose her swollen lumps to his colleague. "He'll give you excellent care." "Wow, would you look at that," the other doctor said. "It is presenting bilaterally." "You two haven't been out of the country recently, right?" the one doctor asked. "And when did you first notice the swelling?" the other one followed. The doctors, swift in their examination, were polite. Not until after they left did I realize they hadn't come to offer their expertise.

Discharge

The E.R. doctor sends us home. Tells us he's sending the baby's blood to a lab in Indianapolis. The lab in the hospital can't test for mumps, he says. We should just sit tight. Keep the baby away from other babies, and see our regular doctor if anything pops up. Something does pop up. The baby looks awful, like someone stuffed a pair of chicken eggs beneath her ears. We call our regular doctor and ask what to do. The regular doctor tells us to take the baby to the emergency room at the children's hospital. Don't come to me, she says. Go to Children's. If it were my kid, that's what I'd do.

Menagerie

The emergency room is not a room but many rooms. At an adult's hospital, the rooms might be numbered. Because we are at a children's hospital, they are named. We wait in Bumblebee. Burn babies wait in Bunny. Smash babies wait in Frog. Cough babies wait in Horse. Rape babies wait in Newt. Sniffle babies and ankle sprain babies wait with TV outside. NICU babies never have to wait because NICU babies are born here.

Flight of the Bumblebee: How It All Went Down

Triage
Nurse
Resident
Nurse
Rubbernecker

Rubbernecker
Rubbernecker
Nurse
Technician
Nurse
Attending
Nurse
Pack your things
Orderly
Rubbernecker
Nurse

Dirt Baby

Dirt Baby lives in the room next to ours. We can't yet tell if Dirt Baby is a girl or a boy. Dirt Baby has white-blonde hair and a bright red Kool-Aid goatee round its lips. Dirt Baby has a load in its pants. Dirt Baby can walk, it sure can. Dirt Baby walks and walks and walks and squeals like crazy when it's happy, which it is. Is it Dirt Baby who's sick? We don't know. Dirt Baby has countless brothers and sisters. Maybe it's one of them. Dirt Baby wears a diaper and a pacifier only. Dirt Momma calls it a plug. Where's that baby's plug, is what she says when Dirt Baby cries.

Ultrasound: I Can See Right Through You

An ultrasound technician named Tammy helps some doctor find out if our baby has cancer. If fluid fills the lumps on her neck, we should be OK. If they're solid, she's doomed. We get to watch. We accompany our 13-pound child, hold her hand, rub her chest. We sing to her. The room we're in is dark. We see what we see courtesy of the bluey white glow of Tammy's flickery blinking and blooping ultrasound monitor. The baby cries so hard she shakes. Tammy presses the probe against the baby's lumps, promising she's being as gentle as possible. Karen weeps. Sometimes she squeezes my hand. It's hard not to think the worst. If the baby has cancer and dies, what will happen to us? Can we survive? Will we be destroyed? How do people go on living after the death of a child? Do they try? Should we try? We won't make it, I decide. Karen will leave me. Maybe I will leave her. That'll be hard. I like our life. I like my in-laws. We'll leave each other. That's what we'll do. I'm pretty sure there won't be, but I'll have to check and see if there will be any money if the baby dies. I don't think so. How could there be money? Why would there be money? I'll be destroyed. Karen will leave me or I'll leave her. We'll sell the house. I'll get an apartment, a room or a loft. I'll live by myself, try to lose weight, try to look younger. Should I start drinking? Could I do that? How sexy, I wonder, is self-destruction? I mean, I'll be single. Karen will leave me. I'll leave her, both of us destroyed. I'll have nothing. A shell. I'll need something to remember. I should consider a monument to the baby. A tattoo. Many. Big ones. A full sleeve. I could cover my arm, my right arm, in tattoos for the baby. I'll hire an artist. I'm thinking maybe something in the traditional Japanese style. Something with a lot of color, a lot of flair. Something that tells the story. Something that honors her, the baby who died.

Rounds

OK, the meat is female, four months old. Initial complaint, irritability and swelling in the neck. Mom and Dad say they noticed lumps five days ago. Brought the meat to the E.R. at St.

Anthony's in Crown Point, Indiana. Initial diagnosis, mumps. Labs requested and the meat sent home and told to see the meat's pediatrician after the weekend. Pediatrician refers the meat to the E.R. at Children's. On 21 April 2007, meat is admitted. Meat has no medical history. Mom delivered vaginally without complications. Vaccinations up to date. No known allergies. No international travel. The household includes Mom and Dad. No siblings. Mom in advertising. Dad a journalist. Meat has been exposed to cats. Meat has no other complaints. Meat appears agitated. The masses are firm with limited mobility, tender to the touch. Initial CBC shows a high WBC count and low RBC count. We're waiting for the cultures to grow, and the ultrasounds indicate cystic rather than solid masses. In summary, the meat is a four-month-old female meat with blood and guts and bone and gore and meat and meat and meat.

America's Dog

Because she breastfeeds, Karen gets meal vouchers for the hospital's cafeteria. Every time the baby takes the teat, she gets five bucks. It's very big of the hospital to do this, I think, to reimburse us for the cost of breast milk. We don't take advantage of the vouchers at first. The cafeteria is a cafeteria. It sells cafeteria food. We don't eat there. Instead we dine at Chipotle, America's Dog, Noodles in a Pot, The Pasta Bowl, and The Spicy Pickle. We go out to get food or someone brings food to us. We eat together, Karen and me. We eat in our room when the baby sleeps. We eat with our parents and we eat with our friends and we eat by ourselves, we two. We bicker about what to eat and when. We no longer want to see another America's Dog. We liked Chipotle better when we were picking it up last-minute on the way home from work. Nothing good is open late. What would we cook with if we walked to the grocery? Sandwiches again, I see. They made it too spicy. The lettuce is wilted. The noodles are cold. I don't want the cookie. How can you eat that? How can you eat? Not right now. Not when she's under. Not that it matters, but the next one is free. Whatever you want. You chose the last time. You decide. You're taking forever. Make up your mind. I don't care. I just don't care. Pick up whatever. It's chicken or fish. It's lunch until three. It's Wednesday. It's pasta on Wednesdays. Here, use a voucher.

America's Cat

Papagena is going to cost us a fortune. The vet called today, and we are going to pay through the nose for good old Papagena. Papagena is sick. She has a bum thyroid, and we're going to pay fifteen hundred bucks for radioiodine therapy. Fifteen hundred bucks at a time like this! And we'll pay, yes we will. Papagena is Karen's first baby. They are tight, those two. Thick as thieves. They have a history. They go back, way back. Papagena goes further back with Karen than I do. Karen loves Papagena more than me. Karen saved Papagena's life. She pulled her out of a storm drain when she was a kitten. She was tiny back then—a little furry can of Coke, a cuddly avocado, a fuzzy wuzzy cell phone. She was a button, a doll. She was so very, very precious. She has never outgrown her squeaky, chirpy meow. She's still very kittenish. Cute as can be. Papagena saved Karen, too. Karen was lonely back then. She was homesick all by herself. She was miserable. Karen became Papagena's mommy, and she loved that baby up. Papagena is rambunctious, more so now than ever. She's been getting into everything. She tears up furniture and cries out at night. Before Karen made me take her to the vet, I told the old girl that I'd put her ass on the street. I picked her up and kissed her and squeezed her and said, "I love you, Papa, but you're too much kitty. You're too much, Papa. You're too much. It's not fair for this family to keep you all to ourselves. We need to share you with America, Papa. You need to get out among the people! Walk along the fence-tops and chirp hello to the people you meet." The vet says now that Papagena is sick. She needs a shot, a radioactive shot, and it's going to cost us a fortune. Fifteen hundred bucks! We're going to pay, all right. We're going to pay and pay and pay because Papagena was Karen's baby first. It's so important. I should know. I had a first baby, too. My first baby burned up long ago. My first baby is gone, baby, gone. Through a six millimeter Karman-type cannula went my baby. Suck, suck, suck! A Synevac Vacuum Curettage System sucked my baby all up. Into the collection bottle went my baby. Into the incinerator. Into the atmosphere! It was tiny back then, my baby—a precious suprême of tangerine, an adorable little diet pill, a red and yellow slimy dime. Oh, I paid for that baby, my baby, my baby-first-baby. I paid for the hotel and paid for the gas. I drove my girlfriend to the free clinic in Indianapolis even though the one in Chicago was closer. I paid for that baby. I used my mother's credit card. I told her I had an interview at Eli Lilly. That's what I said. I paid for that baby. I paid for that baby and I pay and I pay and I pay and I pay.

America's Birds

I spoke with my boss today. I needed to touch base with my previous life. Karen did, too. She went in to work to talk to some people and to pick up some things. Today I got to go to the paper. I caught up with coworkers. I checked my email and I made a few phone calls. I spoke with my boss. I described for him the hospital and I did my best to explain the baby's condition. I brought him up to speed. Because he is a writer, my boss asked what I had been reading. Because he is an asshole, he gave a few suggestions. There are a couple sick baby stories that I should be thinking about. There's one in particular that maybe I should read when I get a chance. Oh, it's a little ray of sunshine, that story. I bought it at the bookstore and I read it on the train. I'm glad I read it. It's super. It's the greatest thing. I am happy I got to read this story and not Karen. Karen's far too sensitive, and now is not the time. I am a lot more tough than she. I can take it. Of course, maybe I should go ahead and have her read it after all. It'd be something we could share together, something we could talk about. I could give her this story and say, "I think you should read this, honey," and because she loves me, she will. I'd be sure to give her some space, though. She won't want me watching over her shoulder when she reads, and besides, she'll need some room to crumple. She'll need a place to sob. I could watch her then. Wouldn't I feel powerful? Wouldn't I feel great? Maybe that's what I'll do. Maybe I can be the monster who writes about that.

The Angels of Mercy

Lydia talks like a baby around the baby.
Olivia is the rectal temperature queen.
Meghan will pull a double nine times out of ten.
Mary commutes all the way from Milwaukee!
Ludwika loves America.
Tina B. is a stitch.
Rachel does it by the book.
Janice is going to have a word with Dr. Modi's attending.
Tina J. went to high school with this guy on the Cubs.

Cora doesn't want to get married.

Dale started a squirt-gun war in room 719.

Jill is the best of the best but always leaves trash in the crib.

Wendy, sweet Wendy, can't believe we're still here.

Rainbow Dogs

They've been advertising the Rainbow Dogs on the walls by the elevators on every floor since Wednesday. The fliers say, "Don't Miss Rainbow Dogs! This Sunday from 10:00 to 11:00 a.m. in the Brown Family Life Center on the fifth floor. Come enjoy the therapy dogs visiting the hospital on Sunday. Play with them, watch them perform tricks, and get your picture taken with your furry friend!" Beneath the announcement is a clip art picture of a smiling boy in a baseball hat and another clip art picture of a big, happy dog that looks like it has stars and rainbows shooting out its ass. I see these little fliers all over the hospital all week long and I get excited. I start expecting a show. I mean, the kids in here are sick. They're bored. They need some excitement. I figure there's going to be like six or seven Rainbow Dogs. I figure they're going to walk on their hind legs. Jump through some hoops. Maybe form a pyramid. You're not even allowed to go to the Brown Family Life Center unless you're a patient or a family member of a patient, so I'm thinking these Rainbow Dogs must be pretty special. Those Rainbow Dogs are coming, and I just know that they have to be good.

Chart

C.B.C.

Ultrasound

M.R.I.

Labs

Ultrasound assisted fine-needle aspiration

Intravenous antibiotic therapy

Fever! Fever! Fever! Spike! Spike! Spike!

Emergency

Surgery

Penrose

Wait

Scar Tissue

At the conclusion of the baby's final surgery, we're summoned to the office of her surgeon, Dr. Modi, who explained that he was finishing his fellowship and would be moving to accept a faculty position at Cornell. Before he had to go, he'd like to take some pictures. Do we mind? This would be our last time seeing him, and he'd like to add the baby's case to his portfolio. We agreed. We liked Dr. Modi. He'd been good to us, and anyway he was nicer than his boss, an unctuous little weasel who always gave the same introduction and told the same jokes. We watched Modi unwind the dressings around the baby's neck. This seemed to make him happy. Pleased with his work, he explained that the matching sets of inch-long scallop-shaped railroad-track stitches would dissolve and the remaining scars would be inconspicuous. We wouldn't be able to see them from the front, and once the baby grew enough hair, we might not be able to see them from the side. As Modi took his snapshots, I tried to divert Karen's attention. I started talking, wanting her looking at me and not the fresh surgical wounds on our daughter's neck. I told Modi I hoped he enjoyed his time in Ithaca. I hear the country up there is lovely. Everybody raves about those gorges. Dr Modi looked up from his camera and said, "Thank you." He paused a moment, confused, and added, "Dad." I worked with this man every day for six weeks. He cut my baby open. He once consoled my wife by saying these things sometimes happen and you must understand that it's not your fault, and we are here to help you, and everything will be OK. Dr. Modi fussed with a button on his coat. He couldn't remember my name. We adults sat together in silence. Modi tapped his fingers along the edge of his desk. "Anyway," he murmured, "Cornell's hospital is in New York."

The Greatest Show on Earth

Sunday, Rainbow Dog Day, finally comes. We go down to the Brown Family Life Center, and when we get there, there's one dog. He's a big fellah—standard poodle—but still. It's just one dog. The Rainbow Dog's name is Bruno. He has an I.D. badge with his name and picture on it and everything. Bruno's trainer, Jill, has one just like it. Hers says, "Jill Witwiki, Child Life Volunteer." Bruno's badge says, "Bruno, Therapy Animal." Jill says that everybody that works for the hospital has to have a badge, including animals. They had to get Bruno to sit up in a chair in order for his face to show up in the badge maker's field of view. Bruno's not allowed to sit on furniture at home, so Jill was a little conflicted about permitting the shot. Dogs don't understand the concept of making exceptions to rules. Jill grew up with poodles. Loves the breed. She has another poodle at home, Dixie, who wasn't cut out to be a Rainbow Dog. She visits nursing homes instead. She does better with the elderly, Jill says. Little kids make her jumpy. Bruno is an angel, though. He is big and sweet and well tempered. Bruno wags his tail and the baby eats it up. She has never seen a dog before. She was born in January, and we couldn't take her outside much because of the cold. Anyway, the baby goes nuts. Karen helps put her tiny hands on Bruno's ringlet fur, and goes on and on about what a good boy Bruno is, and what a pretty boy Bruno is, and how Bruno can come and visit us any time, and when he does come and visit us, he can have a bone. Jill smiles and looks around the room for other kids. She excuses herself and walks over to the family center receptionist. I look to Karen and frown. "I thought there'd be more of them," I say. "I thought they'd form a pyramid." Karen laughs. "I'm sorry, baby." "The Rainbow Dogs are lame," I say. Karen gasps and covers her mouth. "Not in front of Bruno!" She kisses the top of the baby's head and says, "Daddy's going to hurt Bruno's feelings." "Bruno can take it," I say. Karen harrumphs and makes faces at the baby. Jill returns. She smiles at our little family and says, "Why don't you join us in the sun room? I found some other children, and we're going to get started." Jill pats the head of her big blonde dog and says, "Come on, dummy." Bruno jumps up and follows her to the other room. Karen hands me the baby while she gathers our things and places them into the stroller. "Come on," she says. "Let's get this show on the road." I smile and nod to let Karen know that I'll be right behind her. I kiss my baby. I whisper into her ear. "We both know that there is no show," I say. "There's no silly show here. No show." The baby tilts her head back into my chest and smiles at me because I am talking to her. She's old enough to smile now for real, and that's incredible. "Come on, kid," I say, standing up. "I'll show you some excitement, OK? We're going to get out of here, and when we do, I'll show you some excitement. We'll see a show then, huh? We'll have some fun. You just stick with me. I will blow your mind, OK? I will show you a show."

THE EVASIVE MAGNOLIO

by Mark Mayer

THE OLD PRIZE ELEPHANT DIED with his head in his trough one night in late November. Stony saw him there at sunup, foul water lapping against his open eyes.

Stony stood a long time staring at the dead elephant while the wind pressed at his back. Then he stared a long time at the blighted land and the cold light sifting dust, and when he looked again to where the blight showed curved and polished in the elephant's eye, the thought came to Stony that maybe the elephant wasn't fully dead. A little dead, but not the whole way through. He felt a flickering conviction.

Stony had waked that night unable to move, frozen in some presentiment of grief. He lay on his back, ear trapped to the pillow, and tried to lift his eyes from the dim jar of feathers on his stand. They were peacock, from the old days, the color all drained off by the dark. Their feelers were joggling, but his face couldn't feel the wind. With effort, he rolled his head away and watched the dim rafters of his farmshack cant as the storm made a rudder of his roof. He thought of Maggy, tall in the gale, dust lightening the creases in his hide. Stony sipped black air till the numbness faded and with the first shear of sunrise got up to check on Maggy, and Maggy was collapsed in his trough. The dust on the water nearly hid his trunk and chin.

The doctor, closest thing Goodland had to a vet, was in a straight back chair atop the cemetery rise. He'd been up there for weeks. A pair of field glasses hung around his neck and a junkheap of sardine tins shivered at his side.

"I hate," Stony said, gulping from the small climb, "to disrupt—"

"Easy, Elstone. Catch your breath." It was dry enough to make the doctor's glass eye chafe, and a scum of brown blood mudded its perimeter. "Rest," he said. "Emesis if you can. Nothing, unfortunately, to prescribe." A nail spun idly in the corner of his mouth.

"It's Maggy. I think Maggy's sick."

"Dead." The doctor picked up the lenses and peered into whatever shrunken image of the waste they delivered to his eye. Stony waited, looking out across their little town, the ring of farmhouses and the fallow gray fields, through a sky blown half black with dust. From horizon to horizon a new quiet held the air, a thing cold and diffuse as the fuming dirt. Nothing lumbered the single road; nothing had in weeks. The commerce the town survived on was the winter kind. They'd peddled to themselves from pantries and cellars since their last weak harvest, now a full year gone.

"There," the doctor gestured toward a ring of sunset around the risen sun. Spans of distant feathers formed small blots against the red. "They're coming," he said. Fish stunk up from his heap.

"What's it this time, watchman? Dragons? Wolves?" Doom mongering had been the doctor's sport for years. "Come look at Maggy. I don't think he's so well." Stony grinned it into a question, tried, but his face was numbed again.

"You saw some glint?" supposed the doctor. Dry blood fringed his own trinket eye.

Stony didn't know what polite thing he could say to that. "You can't call it from here. I got that much science," he said.

"Is his trunk blowing bubbles in the water?"

"No."

"Is his tail boffing off flies?"

Stony said he hadn't seen too many flies.

"But his bellows are pumping and his ears swinging and his eyes blinking like usual?"

Stony said they weren't.

"Well, I'm afraid you've got a lump of undertaking to do, Elstone. Now beg pardon, I've got a watch to keep." He adjusted his field glasses and regarded the rim of the world.

Down the rise a statue of Major Crabtree stared like the doctor across the wasting town. A parade of children wound through the town center, around the shuttered homes, around the dusty apparitions that rose from their own feet. Stony had watched their play these last weeks. It kept him well. It seemed anyone much over nine or ten just kept inside with their preserves. Goodland survived on its preserves—had before and would again—till the rain and loam returned. The children were as fevered as the doctor, but at least they were out. It seemed they'd taken up a kind of homemade witchcraft—staking the dirt with rings of clout nails, chewing rust flakes from the flagpole. They kept a basin boiling in the Halvers' yard and ate there as a clan. They'd skinned clean a stripe on the one tree and carved a register of made-up script into it. Stony had looked it over when they were through. It was strict nonsense, but it put some peace into him. Young folks found their fun, regardless.

"Look at that, doc," he said pointing at the kids. "Your troops are getting ready." Stony's laughter broke like an event within that quiet, and the doctor stared on as if to watch the effusion of the noise.

The doctor extracted a tin of sardines from a chapped valise and bent the ring with the nail. He lifted a skinny fish to watch the orange oils drip and bore the dirt. The little spine was showing.

"Your elephant spared himself," the doctor said, relishing this grand yet token ruination. He sucked down the fish and rubbed his oily fingers across his dry glass eye—a big production, Stony thought—blinking at whatever it was he thought he saw.

It had been a long time. If he'd toiled his brain to count them, it might have been fifty or it might have been four hundred years since the Major—Stony and the medic youngest among his company—had founded Goodland. It had been long enough for the famous soil to degrade into thin gray silt. The drought hadn't helped, but there was fatigue in the land itself after so many bumper years. It didn't matter. Every year, they tinned and jarred enough of that bounty to make it till the spring. When they weren't rich in peaches, they were rich in pickles, and Stony was glad to suffer a long winter if it would bring the soil back.

In the meantime, the dust was bad. It was hard to walk through. It got under your tongue. In the summer, it parched your sweat before the sweat could cool. As he worked down the cemetery pitch, Stony could feel it shawling him step by step. The dust was pretty when you watched it though, playful. It writhed within the stillness that it cast. Stony hobbled through the mothy air to the statue and rested a hand on a bronze riding boot.

Goodland was a circle of houses, arrayed to the Major's design. The Major had drawn the land into wedges, sixty homes, overseeing a vast circle of farmland from one town center. He had traced it out with a compass, right there where his statue stood, and walked off the bearings himself, his Yorkies trailing behind. A great flaxen wheel of blessed earth it had been. Now the sixty homes formed the inner circle of the blight, and the Major, bird-shat and tarnished, stared off blindly to where dead earth and dry air wafted into one.

The houses were humble whitewashed rectangles faced

in toward the commons. They'd freighted in the boards from Michigan by bulk. The stairs were mortared stone dredged up from the fields that narrowed to meet each structure at its back. It was a frustration, sometimes, tending a wedge of land, but the design allowed them a town, and neighbors, and a center square. There was the statue, the stage where the band shell had been, the public well, the picnic benches, and Goodland Hall, where the Major had had his office and the doctor had taught school.

Stony stood up straight as he could and gave the news of the day to the empty ring: "Hello? Listen now. Listen up. Everyone? I'm afraid I've got bad news. The Evasive Magnolio is dying. The doctor says he's on his final lap. If you want to pay your respects to Maggy come on by. Understood? Come soon."

The stale air drank the words right from his mouth. Shuttered houses and untracked dust. He waited for some few to come to listen from their doors. None came.

"I'm not sure just how one buries an elephant, but you can count on a memorial for Maggy. We may not have bagpipes and daffodils, times being what they are, but we'll give him a proper burial. I'll let you all know. I hope you'll all come out and wish him off."

"Could hear a corpse snoring," he muttered to himself. Even the doctor's back was turned. "Maggy is, was a prized and famous..." he began, but he stopped himself. Poor old elephant, he thought and turned home.

The Evasive Magnolio had been the grand-finale elephant for a tent circus long since bankrupt. Stony had never been to a circus, but he could picture it just the same: a caravan parading wonders nearly perished from man's earth. Dogs talking in Japanese, gals with knives sticking through their ribs, a Muscovite chewing on steel. The Major loved the circus, had wanted to be Boss Crabtree, leader of his own someday. Maggy was "evasive" on account of his part in a vanishing act the details of which Stony never comprehended. It must have been something great, no doubt—an elephant gone straight into air. "Could you ever look at the air the same after that?" Stony used to say to Maggy's visitors. "No," they'd all say back, "I suspect you couldn't."

When the show sank, the Major bought Maggy and drove him back to Goodland—"a land as lush as any jungle," he'd said. He rode him in the final mile, bugling all the way, the Major halfway hidden behind the elephant's skull. Everyone was out to greet them. He tromped him over to the tree and anyone who wanted to could reach up and have his hand shaken in that strong, nibbling grip. Stony had been shy.

He'd thought—forgive him—that a bull elephant might not adjust with kindness to farm life, but he saw right away that the beast's heart was sweet and tired. The elephant would droop his head and track you with those amber eyes. They could have done away with his feeble pen altogether, only he might have cleaned the orchards. The Major led him through town those first weeks, till he knew every housecat and everyone had had the chance to touch his hairy side. "He's big," Stony said when they first met, struck too dumb to know what else to say.

"That's the last thing about him," said the Major, beneath an ear the size and shape of a baby pram.

"He looks a hundred years old," Stony said. But the Major explained that they all looked that way.

"Would he like a peach?" he asked, and with the Major's permission Stony fed the giant his first Goodland peach.

"Well look at this," said the Major watching Maggy's face. "He likes you now." Maggy wasn't doing much, just gazing down at him and swinging his trunk at a damselfly, but if the Major said it, it was so. Who would ever have thought it? Stony was friends with an elephant.

It would be wrong to bury him in his pen. There ought to be pallbearers and trumpets, an artillery salute, a eulogy grave as a king's—those and a headstone equal to what would lie beneath. But it seemed unlikely. It would be task enough to get Maggy up the cemetery hill.

Begging a truck meant begging gas, and folks were tight on gas. He'd need a flatbed. There were two in town and probably he'd need them both. One belonged to Jonas Hames, the other to the Petersons. Stony had driven before, plenty of times, but things always ran a little herky-jerky under him and he'd been accused, he was sure it was true, of revving out too much gas, so with his toes still a little stiff from whatever had chilled him that night, Hames and one of the Petersons would need to pilot. Then he'd need at least six pallets for the base of a coffin and two pallet jacks to lift and to lower. He had some crate wood that would work for the sides and lid. He'd need to run planks across the pallets to strengthen and fit them. Roll Maggy onto the pallets. Dismantle the rusty pen first and roll him somehow with a truck and a few lines. He'd work it out. He bent his path toward the Hames cabin.

Every house in Goodland had been fitted in its day with a weathervane, each a different species of that land. The Major himself had drawn and cut the tin, and sixty unalike creatures crowned the sixty homes with a crowded local zodiac: a weathercock, a weatherpig, a weatherwolf, a weathersquirrel, all the way around the circle to the Major's home, where a weatherelephant pointed his nose with the breeze. Hames lived under a wild boar, but when he looked up to confirm the address, Stony saw that most of the vanes were gone, blown away or bent flat or vanished.

There was no answer to his knock.

"Mr. Hames? Jonas? Estelle? Hello?" He dragged his knuckles on the shutters. "Just Stony here. A favor to beg. Anybody home?"

Dumb question. There was no place other than home. If Jonas wasn't home, he'd be out there in the center where Stony would see him or around back on his smutted land, where he'd stand out like a steeple.

Well, no need to be a perturber, Stony thought.

But at the Peterson twins', a few porches down, it was the same. Folks must be in some kind of hibernation, he thought. A drought can do that. After a while all the preserves tasted the same, like tin and jar gaskets, the same two flavors, weeks in and out. But you had to keep sunny side up: he'd been squirrelly with the canned plums Lotte Billums brought around, but a few days back for some pick-me-up he'd opened all three jars, fed most of them to Maggy, right from his sticky palm. He listened to radio dramas, what he could catch of them, raked his pens, watered Maggy, watched the kids take their run of the town. There was no need to travel much past the pantry.

Goodland would turn up eventually. Maggy would bring out one last crowd. Stony tapped one last time on the Petersons' door and turned home, bending back through the center, his track a string of far-off birds.

The children went dancing by like a muster of gypsies. They stopped by the well and lowered one end of a tin-can phone. A boy—the name escaped him—listened close with one ear and mouthed to the others what he'd heard. They jackrabbited at the news.

Stony stumped back home and there the elephant lay inside the pen: an acre of their good dead ground balled up into a beast. There were no bubbles, no signs of breath. His tail hung plumb and still. The Evasive Magnolio rested on his rear knees in an outsized posture of prayer, as he might have in his heyday to let a lesser elephant climb his back. His head was sunk into his basin. Its rim dammed against his throat. His sawed tusks jousted blindly out. Stony stirred the floating grime off the water. Except for a worm of blood at the end of his trunk, Maggy seemed to be at ease.

Stony rested on the dung fork and stared again at Maggy's eyes and the frustrated water skeeters trying to skate into their amber. The elephant was armored in weariness. His wrinkles held him from the teeth of the world as if he had long ago cringed a safe inch inward. Maggy had been in his care since the Major died, and that was many years. Life brought some men families, made some rich and others handsome. Maggy had been gift enough for him, and that was not a thing he said for consolation. He'd been the biggest thing in Goodland, twice a chicken shed, taller when he reared up than any of their homes, the biggest living thing in the state and farther, until one reached the sea and giant squids and whales. Summers, Maggy used to haul around a swimming pool on two rows of tractor wheels, and kids would plop in from every side. They worked his trumpet into the Society Band, even if he only blew one braying note, and let him play in the Apple Day parade so long as he wore the same derby as the rest. Christmas, just one foolish time, they put wings on him and stood him in the pageant—the angel, annunciating a kingdom with no end. That was long ago, a dreamtime. With the cows and pigs all butchered, there was plenty of silage leftover for Maggy to eat, but he'd always preferred fresh feed—dry grass, corncobs, fruit of any kind. Stony had fetched every castoff husk, leaf, and root he could manage. Even so Maggy had had to live on sour silage, and you could watch the hunger in him.

Wind was gathering. It was cool and still and charred air sank from the sky as if storing up to squall. Small cold spidered about and bit at bare skin, but its sting wouldn't preserve an elephant for long. No truck meant no pallets. That made the job harder, but no question about it: Maggy would get a place on the hill.

Stony waited two hours on his back steps for the grievers, but none came. He ran his sweating thumbs over the stair until the gray stone was polished brown. Maggy lay there waiting too, wide eyes staring across the scum, his big hind in air. Stony would have waited longer, would've given death every chance to change its mind, but the rot wouldn't wait with him.

He went about it slowly. He got the wheelbarrow, oiled its axel, got his box crates and began prying off their short ends, using planks to join the crates in pairs. It went faster than he wanted. Eight crates in twos for limbs, three together for the head. He wasn't going to do it, it was just a way to waste time till he found a truck. He was bluffing Evasive Maggy back to life. He got his knives and rags, his stepladder and the handsaw from the shed. He stood the ladder at Maggy's shoulder and washed his neck with a cloth.

In Goodland, a stepladder was a vantage, and the dry land back of the house seemed to stretch too straight and flat to fit a rounding planet. The plain was centered here, at this cooling heap of beast. Stony felt unsteady. He sat a minute atop the ladder with the saw across his knees and leaned back into Maggy's hard-crusted dough.

Soon, he thought. Not yet.

There'd be eulogies tomorrow, but he needed something now, someone to force some poetry from this. "It's all right," he told Maggy, but Maggy was dead. Alone and embarrassed, he sang a dumb old song, though he couldn't feed it enough breath and had to hum through some forgotten stretches, an army-camp song, because he couldn't think what else to say. Then he rose and, steadying himself, turned toward it.

Stony pressed his buck knife into Maggy's throat, but sharp as it was, it only pushed the tough skin back. He tried to punk it quick and hard, but it made no difference. He lacked the strength. He washed the neck again with a rag and waited for the shame to pass.

It took a pickaxe to break through and some will to bring it overhead. Stony opened his eyes in time to see the head bob against its trough. A strong elephant smell escaped behind the spike, mud and crushed grasshoppers. He hadn't smelled mud—real mud, not mere wet dust—in a very long time, and it braced him some. He sunk the buck knife into the rip and tried, to no avail, to widen it, but the bread knife and with its small teeth chawed a line along the neck. The skin was a full inch thick, and the blade bent against its handle. He tried his skinning knife, but it was too short for the skin and he had to make a double pass. Twice he scored the neckline before any pink showed through, twice more before the grim line shined red. He turned his knife and traced a collar in the hide. It took some hard pulling, but the flaps unpeeled sickly from the meat. Beneath the skin, the bright lodes of fat seemed the cleanest things in the world.

Stony stepped down and moved the ladder to Maggy's other side. He repeated his cuts and tore down another wet collar of skin. He reached along the line and yanked the hide and shucked it back from the neck. His gummed hands were cold and the skin loosed in spits, quick bursts of radio static. He felt about in the meat and deliberated where through the titan spine to aim his cut. Then with his rusty handsaw, he began trenching through the elephant's neck.

"Maggy," he said, "You hang in there."

The blood had already set into ready-mix, as strong and thick as elephant blood should be. Dragon's meat could have run no redder. It was a red more densely hued than any black, richened from a lifetime of straining against that weight. The grease smeared along the toothy smile of the blade, and the blade dragged deep and bucked and hawked like a bog man clearing his raw throat.

The children dropped from the skinned-white trees and walked to the elephant's pen. They were short and tall and smudged with dirt and colored each a different shade of filth. One dragged by rope a clapperless bell that tolled briefly rock by rock. One walked on stilts and one chose to crawl and one dragged another on a sled of shredded tire. One wore a cat-hide sling and one a crown and one a swelled and shining growth beneath his eye. They had christened themselves with makeshift names and when they spoke they called to Nickel or Friar, to Blisters or Clips, but mostly they were silent. They bobbed in line like a snake over rails as they crossed the rutted paths. They spoke of signs and soothsays, of movements in the ground. Behind their procession the dust lifted up like a row of ghostly corn.

Raggle-taggle they paraded upon the elephant's pen and wound about the butchering like wasps before a bloom. Their eyes were wide as children's eyes, but clear of innocence, or guilt, wide only as the holes breached in their skulls.

Two held empty mason jars and gasket lids as if they'd come to make preserves.

Stony saw them coming but there was no way to shake them off or shield their eyes. He gasped and shook his blood-licked hands, not thinking of the stains or saw. He knuckled quickly at the teardrops on his cheeks. And when he felt the smears and looked at his hands, and at the children, and at the gaping neck, he felt an instant, boiling horror at what they saw and had already seen.

"Are you going to eat that?" the children said.

It was a Brangart boy who said it. He held a bladeless snath. At his sides, two girls, Caseys, spilled cups of sugar in the sand.

Stony fell across the elephant and tried to cover up the wound.

"You can't eat it all," said the Brangart. "It's too much for you."

He looked at the small trench widening at the back of Maggy's head then at the feral children. They were skinny and fly-bitten, more roughed than he'd have guessed, smocked in ash and badged with scabs. He knew these kids, or had known them, but their first names escaped him now. They watched him fixing the saw in the neck with weary, unjudgmental eyes. They seemed filthier even than the dust and drought accounted for, as if their grime had festered. The two with canning jars crouched and pinched some sugar for their cans.

"You're wasting that sugar," he said at last.

"Are you going to eat that?" asked the Brangart. He wore a straight, humorless look.

"Maggy?"

"The elephant. You should have cut underneath the neck."

"We've got enough tins still."

"They're bad," the Brangart said.

"They get a touch tiresome, but—"

"They're bad," he said again.

"We tried to tell them," said a Casey girl.

"We told them," said the other.

"No one listened."

"They wouldn't listen."

"It would go quicker from underneath."

Stony took in the circle—blankets chewed into ponchos, a bird skull on a string. Here were his mourners. "No one will be eating Maggy," Stony said. "We set enough aside." The words were clumsy on his lips.

"It's in his face," they said. "He has it."

"He has it in his face."

"No one will be eating Maggy," Stony said again.

They were looking at him now, not the elephant.

"You are forbidden to eat Maggy."

"We know," said the Brangart boy.

They were silent.

"Is he killed yet?" the Brangart said at length. "Or still frozen?"

"Is he dead? Yes, the doctor says he's gone."

"Did you keep his ghost?" the Brangart said moving quickly into the ring. "We need to keep the ghost."

"We're going to have a funeral as soon as I can get Maggy ready. You kids will be there, along with everyone, I hope."

The Brangart put his ear to the elephant's side, unflinching. "We need to save the ghosts," he said.

"It's very simple," said a girl with bark ribbons in her hair.

"Ghosts," said the Brangart, "can be preserved indefinitely."

There were large birds in the sky. One of the girls wore half a locket around her neck and the sun was red in its cold metal. The children sucked on their dead teeth and a few stepped forward to drag their hands along the sooty skin. Stony felt for them—weird crop though they were—inventing their own lamentations while their parents hid at home.

"Well, all right," he said, "have at it then. But take good care of our friend's ghost."

"Quick," the Brangart said, and he tapped the bladeless snath.

The children yowled out and clapped a beat against the ground. The two with jars spooned in pectin from a rusty box and a third poured doses from a jug of browning wine. Stony smiled and hurt for them, the strange little souls, who weren't too scared of death to pay their own half-mad respects.

Caught on his ladder, Stony tried imagining the older ones recalling fond times with the elephant—primping him up in his old headdresses for the Fourth of July, taking sleigh rides, drawing him on old pillowslips with stolen bricks of coal—but all that seemed a distant past, another Goodland, centuries gone. These weathered young ones had never known those days, the elephant dressed up to beat the cold, his winter robes pinned beneath his tiny chin, "EM" monogrammed in faded gold, a felted hood pointing over his dome, another generation of children planting snow angels around his pen.

When their clapping had mounted and fallen, a famished cherub girl in a rose-pink dress stepped forth and held a mason jar to the elephant's collapsing underthroat.

"What was his name?" she asked. She held a case knife in her hand.

"The Evasive Magnolio," Stony said.

"Evasive Magnolio," she repeated, the words slowly forming from her cherry voice. And with a jerk she stabbed the knife into Maggy's throat.

The ladder shuddered under him—but it must have been his own nerves that made the shivers that he felt.

The Brangart repeated the charm. He took the knife and fixed the other jar to the elephant's neck. "The Evasive Magnolio," he said and made another fatal strike into the skin. His held out the jar with his birdly arm to catch a few slow drops of blood.

"Mr. Golten?" said the Brangart.

"Elstone—Stony if you like me."

"Stony. What's left is only meat."

Their yellow eyes set on him and they said nothing else. They curtsied or bowed and lipped at their gums and mounted their stilts and were gone. Stony watched them go, wondering if he was just too old to understand. One by one, they wound past the barns and out through wreckage to the Halvers' yard, a parade of ragged dollies strung along the ground.

The bone had cooled and pinched the saw. Stony gripped a steadying ear and yanked the grim blade free. Its sides were oddly polished from its work. He tried climbing his knee onto the head to press down and widen his cut, but the skull sprung eerily back and almost bucked him to the dirt. He thought to tie a rope around the hump of the skull and bind it down, but that seemed wrong, so he let the trench pinch the blade and burn his arm, and he pulled and pushed till the meat was warm again.

The work came along. All told, it was three hours leaching the neck brawn through. He knew which stroke would free the head, but when it loosed and fell he still gasped, unprepared. The head bobbed and spilled water from the basin. The trunk swung ungoverned through the murk. It was no simple labor hefting the head out and into a ply-board crate.

The work strained his heart a little less once the head was off. The saw teeth found easier passage through the haunches. By dusk, he'd severed four legs and the head from the bulk of the elephant. The rest was a lavish mass of common gore. Sad white bones, wide as ladies' necks, craned from the meat. Thick yellow fat spoiled in the cold. Tomorrow, with some help, he'd roll the torso onto a few pallets and cask it in from there. He laid the crates in a row beside the pen. His fingers were numb from the cold blood, and the crates stained wherever he touched, but it only took a few clean swings to nail them closed.

When Stony climbed back up the cemetery rise to scout out a patch of earth, the doctor was still in his chair, watching the self-similar distance, the splay in the field glasses identical to the splay of their fields, governed on all scales by an endlessness that everywhere gestured toward its end. A high sunset leered back at them. Stony looked west and east across the ring of homes. What behemoth earth must be to make these horizons join. It took believing in.

"Rest," the doctor said without turning. "Emesis if you can. Nothing, unfortunately, to prescribe."

"It's me," Stony said.

The doctor glanced. "You're one mess of giblets."

"We'll have a little burial service up here tomorrow. I just need to pick a spot. I hope you won't mind the company."

Another sardine tin balanced on his knee. "Give your elephant my apologies. I won't be able to make it tomorrow."

"Oh? And where's our doc off to?"

"I don't know, Elstone. Elsewhere. A frenzy's mounting."

"Dragons, is it?"

The doctor pointed down to his heap of sardine tins. The lids quivered in a subtle wind. "Foot beats," he said. "The glower's rising. Dust is drawing up like smoke."

"Giants on the march, I see. We're in for a little more wind tonight—that's all."

The doctor pulled on his canteen and gestured. "You'll see. You're carving ancient meat for an ancient purpose, cadet. I'm going to do what I can to spare myself. If I were a friend of yours, I might advise you to do the same."

Stony smiled at the old goat. You just mistake a bloody eye for a bloody world, he thought. But he wished him luck. He'd sighted a plot for the elephant, and now he let himself feel tired. Breathing was coming hard.

"How long you been living on fish?" he asked the doctor, but the doctor only laughed.

The wind came on that night, sinking out of the cold gray sky and rising up from the cold gray ground. It drummed the pail within the well and made the orchards crackle. It fleshed itself in dead husks and dust and the scrap feathers of long-dead chickens, but the breaching mass they shaped sprayed them out to gather again, like the whale drinking back his boiling column of breath. The storm drew a voice from every solid thing it scratched, but it was the catgut. It hastened its own notes through the air. When the wind sucked its breath and for a moment fell, Stony could feel the confusion of things displaced: a raving cat in his floorboards, the tin hog squealing on his roof. But soon that tidal peace was spent, and the wind roared forth with its rage renewed, foul enough to flint a fire on the night. Stony clung to his bed on this ocean floor and paced the storm's passing with the unmourning clang of the Evasive Magnolio's pen.

He lay sheathed in layers: his union suit clamming to his thighs, his rag blankets and the old rug on top. Then the room, the roof, the storm, the night, the unreasoned space beyond. He did his best to keep his thoughts there beneath the sheets.

Tomorrow was Thanksgiving Day. He would announce the burial as he'd announced the death, from beside the Major. If no one showed, he'd have to make five trips with the wheelbarrow—no millionaire hearse, but it would manage—and find some answer to the gore left in his pen.

Whatever eeriness had overtaken Goodland, Stony had had about enough. They'd weathered droughts and famines before, but hiding out inside wasn't how they'd done it. He would say something to that effect. Here was Thanksgiving, and no, there was no harvest and there wasn't a turkey in all of Goodland. But they could throw together a Beggar's Feast, just like they'd done in hard times past. A little bring-what-you-can. It might just amount to a meal. A service for Maggy—then a bite. Lotte Billums's plums were gone now, but Stony had a bag of almonds he'd been saving for an occasion.

He thought about what he would say when they lowered the elephant down. He had some ticklish notion of elephant heaven. Wide grassy plains, of course. Not in the clouds, but on a good, solid tramping ground. Long mucky rivers. Banana meat sunning on every rock. And, more than anything, the numbers of them—hundreds, thousands of elephants, called to herd by instinct. It seemed a sufficient view of heaven. But of course Maggy wasn't there anymore than in some mason jar.

Stony thought of old Goodland, and his ribbon pigs and the airshows and the barnstormers who kept their goggles hanging around their necks and illustrated their stories with the ruby ends of their cigars. And the Major, when he was still alive, planted on the bandstand, telling his same story every Apple Day and hailing the households: "Mr. Billums, how're the plum trees? Mrs. Gelder, any luck with your strawberries? Who's growing beets this year? Almanac says it's a year for beets." And Stony thought of the corn crop they sent a man out from New York City to photograph. And how the man's hat had held its shape, all day in their sun, had kept its perfect dimples and hadn't let a patch of sweat seep through, and the fellow saw Stony staring and let him hold it and try it on and took his picture—"a real guapo" the fellow had said. And then they'd got to talking, and the fellow said Stony was a lucky man because the prettiest women in the world were right there in Goodland. In Goodland! How about that? But Stony wasn't as stupid as sometimes folks liked to assume, and he knew the man was only aiming to be overheard. He'd seen the magazines, and there was not one woman in Goodland qualified to smoke a Lucky Strike in her beachwear. There had never even been any beachwear.

In fact, Stony thought, the greatest authority they had on such matters was dead now. Some of them had been as far as St. Louis, and the Major had been to Washington D.C., but an elephant never forgets and theirs had traveled to Geneva and Rio de Janeiro and farther, to say nothing of having been born in Africa. Maggy had seen prettier women than any Goodlander ever would. And that was nothing, Stony thought. Maggy had walked in the shade of jungle trees with fruits the size of possums hanging down. Stony saw him there now, saw him blinking under Christmas lights in Boston and shaking the soft hands of United States Senators with his trunk. He saw him wandering bone-white beaches with his old circus friends, the talking dogs, and drinking from high mountain streams. He imagined the fireworks, the dagger dancers, the ladies singing through all their paint. Every wonder of the world.

He thought of the parceled elephant in his pen and of the memories, never forgotten, in the elephant's brain and of the bright world held in those memories and lost with them into a spaceless dark. He saw that the world, having lost some ballast greater even than an elephant's mass, was drifting from him. The room was dark and distant, and again Stony couldn't move. His limbs were frozen, his face was fixed, his lungs could barely breathe. He felt himself wearily cringing inward, toward a numbness in which he was alone. The winds thrashed and there was a sob inside of Stony that his body couldn't muscle out. It gurgled thinly through him to his lips.

The room blazed with children's song.

He could hear their cheeping witch-caw voices, the feral weave of their footbeat, but he couldn't sit up and see them. A nightstand fell; a glass of peacock feathers crashed into the ground. Feet pounded up on the bed slats underneath.

"What's the matter?" Stony tried to say, but his lips were numb. His eyes wouldn't open or even flinch as if the dark itself had sealed them closed.

The tip of a case knife landed on his neck. He could feel its single point of cold against his skin. The wind scraped against the roof.

They ripped the blankets from him. The point hovered heavily on the sink of his neck.

Stony choked and feared for his heart and tried to feel at it, only his hands refused to lift, but he was OK and his heart was OK, and all kids are good kids, he thought.

"Elstone Golten," said a cherry voice.

"Stony Golten," said the Brangart boy.

They were graceful, efficient, and unhesitating. He heard the pillowcase puncture behind his ears. He knew the hot taste that sopped his palette—a familiar, rusted taste, sweet and warm as bedtime milk. He heard a slow warm loss and then heard nothing more. No music but his own fading thrum. A cold without malice—the still brace of ruin—clasped him in itself, and he felt nothing more.

The children preserved him in a mason jar and carried him through the coiling dust. They walked over the empty ditches and the flattened trees, across the spinning circle of their town. Short and tall and strung of bones, little things in the night, small and brave and certain.

A memorial was held. It had begun before the knives and saws came out. A fly landed on the elephant's scalp and hopped into a floating nostril. She climbed past the chaff of oat and hay, holding her stained wings above the ooze, which dried into crystal as she climbed. Deep within the passage, she found a nub of fertile flesh and set upon it with thin claws. Some enduring outpost of the Evasive Magnolio's nervous system fired a signal of warning, but it went unheeded: no trumpeting sneeze was summoned and no water drawn up the sluice. The fly turned around with dainty steps and deposited some hundred eggs in the blooded nest. Then she toddled on.

One, a hundred, a thousand hundreds. Maggy drew a crowd. A vanguard of carpenter ants traced the steps of a gravid fly, beckoning with their antennae and yipping in their language at the meat. Leagues into the dark, they dislodged a gram of elephant flesh and returned to their kingdom bearing the news, soliciting volunteers. A neighboring colony spied their frenzy and mounted a campaign of its own. Soon a stream of ancient blood, red as any metal of the earth, spilled down the cold trunk, like a banquet carpet unfurled. The blowflies flittering on the elephant's corneas sensed the tremble beneath them, vast and fecund and dead, and stirred they shot their helpless eggs into the beast's dark lunar eyes. Larvae wormed their way into the elephant's brain, chewing rows through uncalled memory.

Now, on Thanksgiving morning, the dismantled mass quaked with the traffic of maggots—impatient, hook-toothed, and enraged with inborn hunger. Blind in the dark of the meat, the newborn creatures bowed and ate and bowed and ate again until grown fat and strong. Maggots combed highways through the ropy muscle, churned it to a froth, and, nested deep within its cover, sheathed themselves and waited to be born anew. It was a new frontier, planetary with promise: plenty in absolute, a plenty comprehensible only to an insect mind. A golden age. Centipedes chased maggots with wild forceps. Roaches shingled wounds. Mites bored into the wasted bones, mined wood deposits in the creature's gut. The kings and queens of that order—the carrion beetles and burying bugs, the rose chafers and dung rollers—moved in clicking formation across the rot, dragging processions of lesser bugs behind them. It was carnival beyond proportion or hope, a ceaseless feast meant for ceaseless hunger, a feast that wasted into further feast—prosperous decay, ruin preserving ruin.

And within a tiny faceless race laid a conquest of its own. Its spores had slipped undetected into the very middle of the meat and grown to toxic millions that clove through membranes, sporulated deeper through the dark, paralyzing every nerve they met to preserve these proteins for themselves. This secret clostridial dust, risen from the soil, waited now to infect even the insect kings.

The children wrote the names of their dead on the mason jars and carved them into the one tree's flesh. They took good care of their ghosts, as Stony had said. They remembered what they could of Goodland. Their memories were mostly dark, but they held them firmly, as if morsels by which they would survive.

The children told different stories of what had swept their town. Some said it was all part of a cycle—that anything that happened once had happened twice before and would again. The one called Shelf said they should plant the ghosts into the ground and the town would grow anew. Others said it was only what happened everywhere, in every town: pantries spoiled and the parents fell into a wakeless frozen sleep, and the task of children everywhere was to free their fathers from their meat. The one called Blisters, who had searched the doctor's shelves, said it was a Botulinus. The Botulinus, he read before their fire, lives in the airless dark of jars and cans and sickens what was meant to be preserved.

They ate well in their circle that Thanksgiving, around the boiling basin in the Halvers' yard, meat they had preserved, and each in turn told the tale of how Goodland perished and how Goodland had survived. And when they were full, they spilled their songs and prayed their thanks and let the sun go down.

And so in Goodland a civilization writhed. Beetles rejoiced and dug with spiny legs. Worms fed on rare and precious meats. Maggots bloomed wings and flight was born and an elephant, by atoms, took to air.

Was it over? Had it just begun? The doctor, fleeing east, looked back and up and tried to watch for talons sweeping down. But the dust that rose was thick and fine and far too fast encroaching.

MULLIGAN

by Steve De Jarnatt

THEY ARE DRAWN NOW from all directions—families down to their last drop of hope, coming through the gauntlet of a gathering storm to the dead center of America. They have until midnight to cross the border here in the Cornhusker State, before the music stops.

Arabelle Tunney drives a rusted Ford camper exactly the posted limit, heading east out on Highway 70—the comforting drone of engine and wind pierced by a shrill wave of young laughter.

"Simmer down back there. Simmer down!" she shouts to her children in the rear.

Arabelle buried her husband Earl under the turnips out in the truck patch late Tuesday night. His kidneys gave out at long last. Earl had a well-documented history of renal trouble, but the warfarin-laced stews she fed him the last few days probably helped the reaper do his work.

The bastard Earl kept Arabelle knocked up without mercy, seeding her womb, his "property," with seven children in six years. Because the Lord told him to. She hid away inside her ample girth—only her ornery toes would betray feelings sometimes, making the sounds of animals scuffling under a rug, clicking and squirming down in the fortress of her hard shoes.

She's leaving hell back in the Beehive State, en route to the high plains of freedom and a second chance at everything. It's not just mouths to feed with no option but for charity that has her in distress; it's the six-year sum of all that's been inflicted on a child bride thrown into such a cruel arrangement. Arabelle longs to know so much: Google, travel, and tender love. But she's known only Pampers, breastfeeding, and the sting of a backhand slap.

Five girls and two boys. Now the eldest, Dora, can help some with the toddlers. These angels of hers should bring joy, but they reflect only some blank, engulfing sorrow. Sometimes when Arabelle looks their way they have no faces. Sometimes their voices scree like wounded birds and their eyes swirl like fun-house pinwheels. She craves a week of narcotic sleep, maybe a year of it—craves, for goddamn once, not to have something leeching off her blood, her milk, her time.

The children look out windows greased with noseprints, searching the lateral flow of countryside for white horses and old barns, a contest to pass the time. As they sing an old hymn, their off-key harmonies reach deep into Arabelle's brain and begin to turn the red-hot screws again.

Ned Laporte drives his yellow Saab north from the Land of Enchantment. No need to rush; he left with time to kill. Headphones protrude from either side of his narrow, shiny pate. Spinning the crackling dial through a spectrum of fading stations, Ned smiles at the road ahead as tears crust on his cheeks. The confluence of three major fronts is birthing a statewide electrical storm. Lightning flashes somewhere, and speckles of a drought-ending rain begin to pelt evenly across a thousand acres, air spiced with a bouquet of fresh-dampened soil.

Ned's seven-year-old, Byrd, strapped in a booster seat in back, squirms, face eclipsed by a bowl of black hair, hanging wet. The boy's hands are tethered together, on each a soft leather mitt. He wears goggles to save his eyes from mashing; a bike helmet protects his head, which bobs like a sports souvenir. Byrd screams at the top of his lungs.

"You know I can't hear you when I have these on. And you know your throat will bleed when you yell like that," father calmly shouts to son. Ned beholds the perpetual fidget his boy is stricken with. He has always done the calm, correct thing with Byrd. Until this day. The boy's tantrum melts to a passive slouch, and his eyes meet Ned's in the rearview. A precious thing, such connection.

"It's not your fault," says Ned, and Byrd looks away.

Ned met his wife, Lenore, through Mensa personals, and it seemed perfect—two sensible, solvent academics on the fast track to tenure. Lenore's fragile beauty was beyond any the average-looking Ned could ever really hope for, yet after two months there she was, agreeing to be his wife. The hooks went deep.

They both had a great wish for children, which proved difficult, then impossible. In their third year of marriage, after enduring a lengthy and humiliating process, they were finally blessed with a year-old orphan from Moldova. They kept his given name, Bogdan, meaning gift of God, nicked that down to Bog, then to Byrd for the way he would sometimes tilt his head back begging for food.

All babies cry, but Byrd never stopped. They knew at the moment of his first seizure that rearing him would not be the bliss they'd imagined.

"He's defective," Lenore had said. "He's our son," Ned had told her.

Ned stayed home with Byrd, putting his career on hold to provide the constant nurturing the difficult boy required as Lenore traveled more and more on the university lecture circuit. She withdrew, seldom even touching the child. For years the couple maintained the façade of what was expected of decent people, but in the end it came down to this—Lenore or Byrd. He still cannot believe the choice his heart is making.

Byrd lifts a plastic bottle from his lap, holding it with force between the awkward mitts. He sucks on the teat until a mouthful is ready, then spits the soy-milk concoction across the back of his father's head. Ned does not flinch. He was expecting this. White glop swirled with blood hangs a moment, then slips down his neck across an already caked and drying mess. Byrd laughs, and then the sound—growing louder—turns back into a scream.

Coach Ike Pisapia floors his Dodge Ram balls out, racing up from the Lone Star State to beat the deadline. A large man, slumped in pain—his jaw tight and bothered, eyes red and watering. Mack and Jack, his corpulent fourteen-year-old twins, are ensconced in the quad cab playing World of Warcraft, one of many games that have usurped their young lives.

"We hungry yet?" Coach asks, and as if to answer, *Nope, we're fine*, Mack rattles a half bag of Cheetos, not bothering to look up.

Coach had been an always-picked-last chubby teen, just like them, but he willed himself into becoming a lettered athlete at Texas A&M. The summer after high-school graduation he was a new boy, eating only raw eggs and vegetables and doing his own killer two-a-days. He read *The Power of Positive Thinking* endlessly, then walked on varsity football with a different body and a ferocious new spirit, making the special teams squad freshman year.

Coach has taken the twins to athletic contests since they could walk, tried to fuel them with healthy food and dreams. He's played tapes of Larry Bird, Billy Mills, and a hundred others, encouraging them to choose whatever sport they wished, as long as they busted their asses at something. Anything. But Mack and Jack are bereft of willpower. All they do is gorge on processed crap, twitch their thumbs to kill imaginary monsters, shit, sleep, masturbate, and do it all again—day after day.

Last year Coach arranged to take the boys to a Galveston morgue. Four dead bangers on the slabs after a gang shootout.

"You look long and hard at these fools," Coach told them. "Full of life yesterday; now they all torn up with their purple guts leakin' out. This is your cost of real violence."

The twins seemed mildly bored with the corpses, muttered that the bodies smelled, then went back to finger-fucking their little boxes.

Why are his little men so damn soft—so lost? That estrogen in all the food people talk about? Because he spared the razor strop his daddy used to mold him? Has he failed them with kindness? Does he blame them for breaking her open, for taking his one true love away? Marie and Coach were inseparable, never a day apart. If she hadn't made that road trip with him—miles from nowhere on the way back from league quarterfinals—her breech could have been attended to, so it's as much on Coach's soul what happened that night.

Loose skin hangs from sinew near a constellation of bruises where he keeps an IV flowing. He has only months left, the doctors say. He wants to live them fully and, if he can, get another liver and live a little more. Coach knows he's a stone-cold shit weasel for what he is set to do, but he's claiming his own precious time— he can do no more as a bad father.

*

Every state has its Haven Law granting amnesty for leaving a newborn at any hospital, law enforcement office, or fire station. Thirty days is par for the course, up to a year in the Flickertail State. But here in Nebraska, the last to enact, no specific age was set, and the gesture of mercy has spawned a fiasco of unintended consequence, deluging the social-service network with an overflow of humanity, or lack thereof. Tonight, lawmakers toil in a special session in Lincoln, called back from fishing trips and mistress trysts to undo the gaffe they signed into law only months ago. Tomorrow it comes to an end.

Though Omaha, Lincoln, and the east have borne the brunt, southwest Nebraska was ill-prepared for any onslaught of urchins. The abandoned youth in outskirt counties from Red Willow to Keith have been rounded up and temporarily corralled at the Sleepee Teepee Motor Court—a kitschy roadside wonder boarded up for years and scaly with pentimento, just a stone's throw from the county fire station on 61. The rooms reek of Lysol and old bodily fluids; bedbugs lurk in half the mattresses—so the eleven youngsters run wild outside, playing games until the evening comes, milking the gift of an Indian summer. They camp out behind the motel in the castles and volcanoes on what's left of a once-glorious miniature golf course, now rotting in the elements.

Yesterday Del Manners, an apprentice fireman from the station, was helping out. He strapped a makeshift blade onto a miniature windmill as a hubbub of youthful noise orbited around him. Shirley Hempstead, the veteran DHHS liaison sent out by the state, handed him another section of baling wire and a pair of needle-nose.

"You hear about that couple from Saginaw flew into Eppley last week to dump eight kids with the TSA?" Del asked. "Drew straws—then took just one back home again."

Shirley clucked her tongue. "Headin' up to the Sand Hills tonight," she said, walking a circle around him. "Five more come down from the Dakotas, 'nother meth family. Back tomorrow. Soon as the governor signs, I'm off to Lincoln with the load. Booked a charter; should be en route about now. Sure you're OK to spell me?"

"We thawed our freezers. Least none goes hungry," Del said, then stepped down and stood awkwardly in front of her. "About last night—"

"You're married, Del. And I'm not quite divorced."

"Another time then."

"Was just the once."

Del held the sheepish pout of a chastised pet, whimpering for a head-pat. The older Shirley sighed, itching a ruddy splotch on the back of her calf, then something fragile shattered nearby and broke their moment too.

"Augie!" Shirley shouted over at a grimy towhead, stark naked but for his mismatched cowboy boots. He stood atop a giant tire leaned up against the building, smashing in motel windows with a length of pipe, trying to sing like T-Pain. She hurried off to disarm and dress the little demon, and Del moved on to brace a lighthouse that was tilting like the Tower of Pisa.

You could quickly see reasons for some being given up, Del thought. Like Augie from the Show-Me State—put on the train to Lincoln, but stowed away until McCook. He tore holy hell out of all things Amtrak, biting and kicking whatever was in his path. Damn near feral.

Some broke your heart. A tiny girl, Xiang Lee, the product of a night of errant groping between code monkeys out in the Golden State. Her father was yanked back to Bangalore when his H1 expired. Her mom, a timid programmer from south China, kept the child mainly in the bathroom until she was three, slept her in the tub, afraid to let another soul know she even walked the earth. Two ancient lineages should handsomely mix, but by some curse of the helix, Xiang was born with clawlike appendages—and was further cursed to be unloved. When the mom got wind of the new Nebraska law, she drove all night, dumped her daughter with the Chase County Sheriff's Office in Imperial, and hightailed it back to Guangzhou. Xiang has been near invisible at the Sleepee Teepee, hiding wherever she can.

Wild tantrums were contagious for a time. The madness of sudden change. But bled of tears and sleep, the tykes have found a strange solace and community—making up the way of the world for themselves.

Still in early training as a ladder-truck driver, Del would love to have a manual to help guide him. He makes sure the children are warm and well fed, keeps them occupied with hand-me-down toys, but generally fails to answer the impossible question of where their parents have gone. Tomorrow they'll be packed off back east, to disappear into the cold maw of the foster-care system.

Molly Swisher twists the key in an old Crown Coach school bus, sixty miles over the border in the Centennial State. She sips Irish joe from a paper cup, flints a butt she found in the ashtray. Molly bought the pink slip with twelve hundred dollars won at craps a year ago. The bus sits mainly in the driveway of her "dream home," a four-bedroom in the mid-three hundreds, part of a new development tract gone belly up. The engine mule kicks, finally churning over, choking out a black fart of oily wind.

"Attagirl, Delilah." She pats the blistered dash of the yellow beast.

Molly checks her morning face in the pulldown mirror, the sun-worked skin just like her mother's, teeth she rarely shows until she knows you well—midthirties mistook for late forties more often than not. She was all set to drive for the new school district here, but like everything in this mirage community, the job was a promise unkept. She wills the bus into gear, and it rolls off down the way.

Molly has pulled her own weight in this world since being run off a Pentecostal home just shy of fifteen back in the Tar Heel State. Bus driver was to be her latest bid for plying a trade—on a long and varied list including playing bass in an L7 tribute band and crewing in Alaska during salmon season. She's managed to book a few field trips up to Rushmore for some smaller schools in the area, but it's been piecemeal at best. Now she's been hired to transport the children from the Sleepee Teepee back to Lincoln, some on to Omaha and God knows where. "How the hell could anyone give up their own flesh?" she'd asked on the phone, but clammed up quick and took the job. To miscarry as many times as Molly and hear such tales made her come half-unglued.

She squints out across the ruby dawn above her aborted cul-de-sac as the bus lumbers down a blank avenue. Only thirty-six of the planned six hundred homes were ever built; the rest of the lots lie fallow along curbed streets and sidewalks gently curving nowhere.

Molly bought here nothing down—in on the ground floor of a good thing, roots for once, a place to raise family. She enjoyed pretending it was a cabin in the woods when she first moved in, helping the workers complete the interiors. The day their pay was stiffed again, the drywalleros shoved the Sheetrock from the truck to rot in a ditch, leaving her with skeleton walls and dangling wires where appliances should be. What had been a din of round-the-clock construction fell to silence. The developer's phones rang endlessly. Molly's four months in arrears on her albatross loan, living off the leavings of other abandoned homes, but she has steeled herself to make a stand here, homesteading in the half-formed landscape of the modern dream.

The bus chugs on through the pedestrian square, where the theater and state-of-the-art gym were to be, coming upon a slumbering herd of buffalo blocking the way. They must not have got the memo—this is no longer open range. Molly eases through them, heading east through the last shoulders of the Rockies toward the Nebraska state line.

Toes cramped and aching, Arabelle shifts her heel up to the pedal, keeping a steady sixty-five. She reaches deep in her bag for another clot of yellow diet pills, long past expiration. You can't change your mind so easy if you keep yourself in motion. If you slow or stop, you might wake up from one nightmare into another—his breath upon you, a magazine rolled and ready, his ghost screaming, *Why?*

Arabelle lowers the window and sniffs the metal tang of ozone in the air, remembering electric motors and fish tanks her daddy kept. The brood sleeps soundly in back as the distant sky begins to crack open. In the hush between thunders, she listens as seven little out-of-phase snores come gently into alignment, holding unison for several magic seconds.

Arabelle can feel a world of change just around the corner. Her hamster wheel is finally coming to a stop—the cage door will open soon, and she can slip out and hide somewhere.

Byrd screams for another twenty miles, seizes, and passes out. Ned pulls to the shoulder, cleans them both as best he can, then moves the boy into the passenger seat. Byrd has calmed upon waking, happy to be riding shotgun. He hangs his face out in the wind, canine style. This late afternoon a massive static charge sizzles above the parched rolling hills, and Byrd seems touched by it, as if his nervous system craves some of the building amperage.

"We're driving over the world's biggest aquifer—the Ogallala. It stretches from South Dakota all down through the Panhandle to the caves of Carlsbad. Been so depleted by drought and irrigation, it was on the brink. Quite the godsend, this rain. The storm will really help replenish."

Byrd nibbles a corndog with the stick removed as they motor through the Sunflower State. The first flash of lightning spider-cracks the sky—singeing their retinas, leaving bright ghosts drifting through the mind's eye. Ned counts until the thunder comes.

"Ten miles off," he says as a low rumble bowls across the land. "Looks like they jolt down from the sky to earth, but actually it's the reverse. Too quick for the eye to see."

"Tin mi," mimics the boy who rarely speaks, turning to his father with wonder in his eyes.

"What, son?"

"Amm lectreec!"

For the first time in a hundred miles, Ned's PDA finds a network out in the troubled ethers. He texts Lenore, who swore she would fly back from the Garden State and meet them for this last good-bye.

You en route?

Plane delayed. Nothing I could do. Is it over?

It?

You know what I mean.

Trips done Byrd a world of good. You wont believe it.

Thats great. Im glad. Does not factor in.

Lenore you have to see him.

He waits for a return, but there is nothing more to come.

Ned agreed to follow Lenore to her new department-head position at Rutgers. A clean start—they would cut off their old friends, make new ones, and never mention any son. There was a narrow window of opportunity, and it was a chance to save their marriage. Lenore could be persuasive.

Jagged bolts scratch the sky, and Ned times the lag of every thunderclap. Tumbleweeds wheel in the staccato brightness. Jackrabbits and nimble fowl dart every which way through the chaparral. It seems every able creature is stampeding across Kansas.

Coach stops to swallow pills, and medicines spill from his trembling hand. The twins remain oblivious, glued to Level 70, their games twinkling tinnily whenever the rumbles quiet. He's made a long list, nothing on it sports related. Coach is done with wholesome life lessons and personal growth. He seeks some new, wanton path, a hedonistic spree. He'll change his name, keep driving, and never look back. The Dodge Ram has 54,000 miles. He hopes to pass 200,000 before he dies.

The next coruscation erupts into a roiling ball of angry blue-and-yellow light, miles away in the low northern sky. The expected thunder does not peal; instead comes the slap of a significant shock wave. Devil smoke and mad flickering climb heavenward as more explosions nearly blind the eye.

As the yellow bus coasts down onto the endless expanse of the high plains, Molly glimpses snippets of the same disturbing light-show off to the east. She ponders if it's even worth the drive back to her development. She could sell the bus, take what she gets, and look for something out in Omaha. In the spring she could work concessions at the College World Series and root for some scrappy team. There might be a good life there.

Walk away! Abandon your mortgage! Molly had heard a man on TV say. Her ex, Tim Gentry, would surely hate such a coward's thought. One should make good on a hard promise, even if it was cajoled with brokers' lies. You gave your word, and your word is your bond, he'd say. Quite a thing to be judged so harshly by a man you met in a prison chat room, but Tim was sent up for shooting at an assessor. He claims the government never had the right to tax—so he holds himself above a lot of things.

Molly knew since she was a little girl that it was her destiny to be a good mother, and she and Tim tried hard each conjugal they were allowed. Every time, it took just like that—the strip turned blue, there would be the heartbeat, then the snowy shape. First two were boys, Henry and Louis. Named for kings. But the template of creation was not within her, and each perished before the third trimester. Had it been a jinx to give names? The next child was left without, just in case.

Tim escaped his work farm down in the Pelican State, stole a car, and drove north to be there for the birth of this child, the only one to make it out into the light. The doctor knew from the stillness and the empty heft—it was only so much organic matter now, not anyone's daughter. Tim got another six years tacked on and cut her off. He wanted someone who'd breed his legacy, and he moved on, trolling the incarceration chats again.

A dull chime rings deep within her good ear, pressure built from altitude and barometric drop. Atmospheric machinations are afoot, and Molly can feel a shadow cross the land. She drives on—smack dab into the eye of it all.

Across the Nebraska state line Ned crests a knoll, heading toward the lights of the next small town, Byrd peaceful in seizureless sleep. Ned observes the verdant hue of the furious cluster of cumulonimbi boiling low above them. Far off something like gunfire comes closing fast—crack-crack-crack—so loud it shakes bones. A shattering, then again, then too many to count. Ned cranks up the wavering classical station to drown the frightful sound, only making it all seem some blasting movie trailer. The windshield gets bashed again and again as the Saab pulls beneath a narrow train trestle for some small cover. Byrd wakes, showing not a shred of fear, and Ned hugs him, praying a funnel hasn't formed that could snatch them skyward at any second.

As the din weakens, Ned realizes it's only the ass end of the maelstrom, voiding its burden in fist-sized shards of hail. Out in the headlights, as far as they can see, glass meteors streak and dash to pieces. Some bounce and dance themselves to a stop. Ned and Byrd grin ear to ear, rapt in transcendental awe—then the heavenly spigot shuts off as suddenly as it began, leaving the road crystal-strewn, faint crackling all around them.

Coach pulls over outside the county firehouse on Highway 61 as sirens scream up to pitch inside.

"Pretty damn cool, huh?" he says, getting out to assess his cratered hood. "Like being bombarded out in the asteroid belt in your starcraft or something." The twins exchange an eye-roll.

Firemen scramble to pull on gear and ready engines as Del Manners comes running up the road from the Sleepee Teepee, riled and winded. He's the last to dress and climb aboard as trucks race off toward the violent light in the next county, where a grain silo has been struck, sparking an explosion of sugar-beet dust and setting off a daisy chain of mayhem.

As sirens fade, Arabelle parks the camper opposite the firehouse, slapping her numb leg back to feeling. Making sure each youngster has his or her bundled clothes as the brood disembarks, she leads them like ducklings toward the open door.

We got hellacious engulfment out here—worse than Scottsbluff. Three dead and God knows how many set to join 'em.

Gonna need every able man or gal out here—ten more silos on the verge, barks a harried voice from the station squawk box.

The building is empty, the air thick with diesel. Arabelle gives the kids quarters for the soda machines in the back, then hurries off toward the camper.

"I'll go get us more change," she calls out.

Arabelle opens the driver's door, glancing back for one last look at her children, who open drinks and explore the world around them. Something shifts above, and her hand reaches out by reflex to catch a hailstone tumbling from the roof.

Driving west, Arabelle guns the camper up to eighty-five—wild at last. She licks the frozen orb as if it were a popsicle.

Sirens doppler past the motor court, and children come out to watch the red beacons whip through twilight. The little demon Augie blinks at the distant sky, unwrapping his king-size Kit Kat bar as the others collect around him. It would be in his nature to gobble it all just to spite them, but this time he hands a chunk to the larger boy he beat down yesterday, then breaks the rest in two, then in two again and again and gives up all the pieces. As if he's heard a beckoning, Augie sets off in a brisk walk toward the firehouse a quarter-mile away. The others follow him like he is Moses leading them into the desert.

Ned, cruising past, sees the march of children. Byrd waves, and some wave back.

"Last pit stop for a long patch now," Coach tells his boys as they walk into the mouth of the firehouse.

"Where're we goin' anyhow?" one of them mumbles.

"Don't know, son, but when we get there, I guess we will."

The twins disappear into the head, and Coach retreats, avoiding the eyes of Arabelle's curious tots, as if one look from them might skewer him like a spear. Near the door, he hustles to a wastebasket, urping out his lunch. He undulates and makes a wounded sound until there is nothing left but clear liquid. Young Dora stands in front of him as he pulls his head away. She offers him a napkin and her Cherry Coke. He takes the napkin, then hurries back to his truck—his life—his death.

Molly parks Delilah at the Sleepee Teepee. No one answers her knocks on any of the doors. Shirley from DHHS was to meet Molly here to help chaperone the forsaken back to Lincoln, but a washed-out bridge in the Sand Hills has left Shirley stranded in the north.

Molly reads a framed article on the wall about an old fort that once stood on these same grounds. When the settlers' smallpox massacred the local Pawnee, their warpath returned the favor, leaving the surviving sodbusters holed up here, nearly starved out during a long winter's siege. Fragments of families stitched themselves together into new bloodlines, and those fresh clans bullheaded on after the peace was made, at least until the fort and everything around it got flattened by a tornado, the rebuilding abandoned the following year during a locust plague.

"Times ain't tough today, no matter what they tell you," she mutters to no one.

Walking around the bleached Astroturf and peeling iconic structures out back, Molly drifts toward a feeble cry on the breeze and finds tiny Xiang Lee weeping inside a giant conch shell of crumpled fiberglass. She has woken from a dream to find herself alone. Molly swaddles the girl in a coat and carries her to the bus. Xiang tries to hide her clawed hands, but Molly makes a point of kissing each of them.

"You're a mermaid, aren't you? Oh, yes you are," Molly says, and Xiang gives up the sliver of a smile.

Ned lays a frayed woolen blanket, chock full of hailstones, across the firehouse kitchen table. He removes the mitts from Byrd so the boy might feel the frigid, rough perfection of them.

"Three of the largest hailstones on record fell right here in southwest Nebraska," he tells the nearby children. "It's a vortex for such things." Dora and the rest of Arabelle's brood come round as if Ned were Mr. Wizard, watching him crack the largest ice ball in two.

"See the layers? Like an onion. To make one of these little devils, a tiny speck, just a kernel of dirty nothingness, must get sucked into the updraft of a powerful thunderhead. More water freezes around the graupel at the top of the angry cloud. It's buffeted around up there but gets so heavy it falls back down to earth, melting on the way from friction, gathering more dust and water, then rising and falling again and again." The children each take one to hold. Some stretch tongues to taste the residue of storm still embedded in the ice. Dora sneaks three cold balls into her pockets, to save for later.

"You could call them the pearls of the sky," says Ned.

A water-stone crumbles to mush in Byrd's hand. He laughs, and this time it does not turn to a scream. As he squashes another one down to sleet, Arabelle's young boys do the same. Molly Swisher walks in carrying Xiang and gravitates to Ned, the only adult in sight.

"You in charge here?" she asks.

"They all ran off to put out a silo fire, I think," he tells her as Augie and the others from the motel run over, joining in the hail-ball crushfest.

"You're not with Health and Human? I'm supposed to drive

some kids back east tomorrow."

"We—my son and I—we were just driving past. Came in to get out of the storm," Ned says as Molly, on the cusp of tears, looks at all the children.

"You heard about this—this law? What they let you do here?"

"I heard," says Ned, blushing halfway to crimson.

"Fuckers oughta all be strung up by their balls. Tits too. Man and wife! You're spittin' right in God's eye, giving up your own," she whispers.

"Yes, they should. Bastards," he whispers back.

In a booth at a greasy spoon in the next town, Arabelle pours gravy across the food mountain on her plate, counting out the dollars to her name as Coach Pisapia devours his second Monte Cristo sandwich at the counter. Their eyes meet and, with no reason not to, stay locked a moment. If he squints, she could be the spitting image of his young Marie. He twitches a good minute before getting up the gumption.

"Hey over there—how's that gravy, anyway?" Coach asks Arabelle.

"Well, I make better from scratch."

"You cook, then?"

"All the time."

"For who?"

Arabelle lowers her gaze. "Just myself now." "Sounds a little lonely."

They kill two bottles of Mateus and a whole pecan pie. Coach picks up both checks, and they ride east in his hail-dented Dodge, leaving her camper on the shoulder, Earl's loaded Colt under the seat.

"Think you ever might want kids?" he asks her down the road a ways.

"Not if you paid me a million in gold," she replies, unlacing her well-worn boots and tossing them out the window. Coach smiles, knowing that this life, whatever time he has left, will be better than before.

Children squeal and tease, scuff knees and pee their pants on into the night. More reports from the silo explosions pour in—word that a young ladder-truck driver was paralyzed by flying debris, with triage underway for six more wounded.

Byrd, who has always avoided those his age, joins the play—hide and seek, kick the can. When the batteries die in their game device, Mack and Jack watch the others a while, then jump in as well, telling Xiang Lee she has awesome weaponry for hands and picking her for their side in king of the hill. Later, the older children take turns sliding down the pole, with Molly and Ned spotting down below.

"Kids say the motel up there has the chiggers somethin' fierce, so maybe best we all stick around here tonight," Molly tells Ned.

They raid the cupboards and make a mulligan stew to remember, then children begin to wilt like flowers and are tucked, two by two, into the firehouse bunks.

"Think these firemen'd miss some Costco cans if I took a few?" Molly asks Ned.

"If they did, they'd get over it."

"Wards of the state now."

"Breaks your heart."

"Boys Town'll take in some. Foster for the rest, and that's both a good thing and a bad. But every last one scarred for sure."

"Hell of a thing."

Molly falls asleep with her head in Ned's lap. When a text from Lenore comes in at 5 a.m., he pries the batteries from the device and, without looking, gently drops it in the trash.

QUEEN OF THE HEAVENS

by Susan Power

I WAS BORN IN MINIGIZIS, when the blueberries are ripe, the month you know as July. It was 1935, the big Depression when everybody was scared and hungry. My grandfather said I came along to cheer people up, put the smile back on their faces. I got my name because of the way I came into the world. I was early, you know, I took my mother by surprise. She was all alone in our little shack, doing quillwork, when her water broke. And then, so soon after that, I came tumbling out. She said it felt like I did all the work, swam and pushed and tore away from her because I was ready to get started. I didn't cry. I sighed with satisfaction the way the Creator must have when He set this world in motion. I approved of my birth and was pleased. So they called me "Ogimangeezhigikwe"—Chief Woman of the Sky—because I was bossy from the first minute.

I was raised by my grandparents since I was the last baby out of ten in my family. Sometimes the older ones need a little sweetness in their life, someone to spoil, someone to make them laugh, so they had me. And they did spoil me, they fussed over me the way parents do today, treating their children like little kings and queens. They made me dolls and toy snares, miniature woven mats for my babies to sleep on, and a cradleboard to carry them in, perfect little canoes, snowshoes I could fit on my fingers. In this way it was as if they gave me the whole world. But more than that, they gave me stories, told me all about the people who came before me, a long line of very special healers—the consolation singers. When someone lost a young husband or wife, or a beloved child, any loss that seemed particularly cruel because it came too early, the singers would be asked to stay with the family and sing them funny songs, story songs, anything to distract their sad hearts. They might labor for days or weeks to cheer these grieving people, but they would keep at their work until they believed the survivors had remembered how good it is to be alive, and smell the air, and be with your relatives. So I guess that's how I came to have a pleasant nature, and to see the good patch of light that's always waiting on the other side of a bad experience. Oh, I had nightmares, like anyone else, both sleeping and awake. But deep down I always knew there would be an end to the bad dream, every bad dream, so I let myself just live through the sorrow. Angry people can be jealous when they meet someone like that, someone who seems to own all the hope in the world. What they don't understand, these bitter ones, is that hope isn't anything like money, there is always plenty to go around, and anyone can be rich.

I think my first husband was one of those angry lost people. He had a bad heart, and I don't just mean the one in his body. I mean his spirit. He must have watched me for a long time, saw me living so pleased with the world, as if the sun was my personal lamp, and grass a carpet just for my feet, and stars a messy scatter of beads I could scoop into my hand and sew on my skirt. He was greedy for that happiness he must have thought I captured and hoarded, when in truth it was always out there, around me, a warm blanket draped across my shoulders.

You might notice that as I'm telling you this I haven't used his name. I say, "My first husband," or "him," because if I speak his name, now that he is gone, it's like calling his spirit and I don't want to do that. I want his spirit to stay wherever it is. But I can tell you that he was ten years older than me, and handsome, I think, on the outside. He wore his black hair in a mean crew cut that looked knife sharp, though his skin was light—yellow pale as wood pulp—and his eyes were the dull green of paper money. He was well-formed and strong, but he walked funny, with a jerky motion, like those puppets I've seen at fairs. Something was wrong with him from birth and it made him angry at the Creator, mistrustful of everyone he met, thinking they were laughing at him behind his back.

My grandparents didn't want me to go with him when he chased after me. I was just seventeen, and so different form him we were like two people sitting across from each other on one of those seesaws, and I was always drifting up, pie in the sky, expecting miracles and grace and good news, and he was forever plunging down, down, harder and harder, the more I floated above him. But he got me, snagged me, even though deep down I didn't really want to be with him or have him touch me.

"Why? Why?" my family asked, and my curious girlfriends, and me, I asked myself that question a hundred times a day. I couldn't explain it to anyone, my love trap. I lived like that for three years, a good wife, though he wouldn't have said it. We had one little boy in that time, smaller than some of my dolls. He came out skinny and starved, furious, scratching his face. I tried to make my body a good home for him before he was born, but maybe he had his father's ways? His fears and temperament? And so he couldn't grow the right way inside me, make any use of love. He screamed at every one of us, and then he died.

My boy's father died a week later. His heart stopped while he was eating his supper, glaring at me because there wasn't any meat, just fish, trash fish, nothing tasty. He spat out the piece he had just forked into his mouth and it could be he spat out his soul, too. Because after that he tipped backward in his chair and stayed down, empty and heavy at the same time, the slug of his spirit crawling the floor, leaving. I finally discovered where my three years had gone when we were washing his body and dressing him in his last clothes. I was able to peek inside the medicine bag he always wore around his neck, even when he bathed. I choked when I saw what was in there—two tiny people, the size of my fingernail, crudely carved from wood. A man with his bump at the waist, and a woman with two bumps near the top. A long brown-black hair bound them together, secured in place by sticky sap. My hair. My husband was a thief, you see; he used magic to steal me, to make him his family. But even now I can see the good side of all this. He never robbed me of my heart. He was an obligation to me, not someone I cherished, and so for all that sneaky work he ended up poorer than me because the Creator made things right by taking away what he had coveted. He lost his heart.

I was twenty-one years old when I fell in love the right way, my heart free and choosy. Maybe because it had no practice in the past, my heart didn't fly ahead in search of anyone, but stumbled over him instead, like he was a rock in the path. My Abraham was always there in our community, like the sun and the moon and Misi-zaaga'igan, our lake that is noisy with a hundred young woman emotions. The first time I saw one of those armrest pillows you can lean on to prop you up in bed, I thought of Abraham. "That's him!" I said to myself, fingering the soft corduroy. "That's my sweet man."

My heart noticed him one winter at a memorial feast—my husband's. I was the young widow dressed in all my layers of clothes to keep out the chill, cold wind outside the tribal hall, colder wind inside me, freezing my blood. I was not made to pretend, and that is all I'd been doing for one year, pretending to miss the one who trapped me until sometimes I felt more dead than he was. Then, my mind switched on like the twist of a lantern, flames leaped, awareness. Abraham sat with the other old uncles and grandfathers, all of them teasing and boasting, reminiscing. The others had children and grandchildren they could have reached for, summoned from across the room. Only Abraham was a tree without branches beyond the square tips of his fingers. I saw him as if for the first time, in a bubble of light, soft, hazy. His smooth skin was dark as a muddy river but unlike the other Ojibwe men, he was near bald, his silver-black hair no more than the soft fuzz of a newborn. His cheekbones were bright polished knobs his smile seemed latched on. All his wrinkles framed that smile, the one that touched a match to his soul and lit him up until he shone. My fingers were laced together in my lap, but I lifted them to peek at Abraham through their design, become a net. "I will go fishing soon," I said to myself quietly, a promise.

A few days later I brought him a present, maple candy I'd made just for him, thinking sweet thoughts as I did the work.

"Uncle," I rapped on the door of his small shed of a house.

"Yes?" He opened the door and heat from his stove and his smile blasted into me, through me; a fire ghost lit me like a candle.

His world smelled delicious, a wood smoke incense that swirled around my head, making me dizzy. He helped me sit at his table, took the parcel of candy from me and removed my gloves. He held my hands then between his own, concern showing on his face. Oh, those hands weren't skin, crude flesh. My Abraham was softer than velvet suede, smooth as satin but warmer—satin with a heartbeat.

"I want to glide you," was the only ridiculous thing I could say. And instead of laughing or pushing me out of his house, he pulled a chair beside me and sat with me, holding my hand, my new clumsy bear of love sprawling over us both. He waited. He let things develop. When I could finally speak and explain my crazy quilt of feelings, beg to look after him, be with him, he listened respectfully and didn't let my words wash him away, though they were a dangerous, unexpected flood, like a rising creek. When I was done, not finished, neat with conclusion, but tipped empty, he sighed.

"You know, I had a dream when I was little that I would be everyone's uncle, their counselor and friend, their old tree that is always there for shelter and support, no matter what else changes. But near the end of the dream it all flipped over, and instead of my arms cradling the world, the world was cradling me, and I woke up so happy I thought I must have died. Ogimangeezhigikwe, I don't know why you look at me with love eyes when you are Queen of the Sky, but I think my dream was telling me to wait for you. And I did. I listened. I am seventy years old by the chimookoman calendar, and I have never touched a woman in a way that said, 'I am a man.' I saved my touches for you."

My girlfriends snickered behind my back, looked at me cross-eyed, when they heard the news that Abraham was my new husband. I didn't care. I laughed into my hands, rich with delicious secrets, love snacks. When a man has waited for you since before you were born, and then finds you in his bed, in his lap, wound so snug and perfect against his body you are two strands of yarn become one stitch, his desire is more than a pond or a creek or even a great lake, more than an ocean. He is the flood that kept Noah paddling the globe in his crowded boat, he is the rain poured heavy from every cloud, morning tears squeezed from every flower. His love juice is shocking, limitless, you begin to think he will populate a new planet if you give him half the chance. You forget that he is old because his manly parts have had a lifetime of rest, without recreation, and so he is a soldier down there, trained not by practice but by years of imagining. Think of it. When my Abraham touched me, he worked a magic of opposites. How could he be so gentle, the pressure of a thumb wisp-soft as the nap of a butterfly wing, and still, at the same time, so warmly focused, intent, packed dense with delight, that touch penetrating as if I was no more than warm butter? Oh, he melted my shoulder with his hot mouth and busy, swiping tongue, and the brown acorns of my nipples, and the deep swirl of my navel, and the dark roses that led inside me. Was I burning wax pooling in our bed, sliding off the sheets? Was I still a woman beneath his hands and lips? He helped me lose myself, my edges, so that I opened up into him, and through him I opened to the world.

And what about Abraham, you might be wondering? Was he happy, too? Every time I kissed a section of his land, the country of his flesh, I was whispering in my head, "I love you, I love you." My thoughts worked their way into his trusting form, he heard me, all of me, and so our bodies learned to speak the same language. We created poetry good enough to last the ages. Whenever I led him to the burst-open dam of pleasure, danced and sang him there with love and vigor, he roared with laughter, showing all his teeth. Does everyone know such moments of joy? I hope so. I hope they have a treasure like mine, two fistfuls of my man's laugh, each one a diamond.

We were together for eighteen years and had two happy daughters, wine dark and round as chokecherries, spicy and sweet as those coiled sticky buns my man favored. Why do I speak of them as food? Because that's all we seemed to do together—feed each other tasty meals and stories, jokes and old songs, new songs. Our girls brought us Elvis Presley and The Beatles, live before us, wiggling and shaking, howling out of tune. They confused us with their New Math, and we puzzled them with all the layers of spirits that populate our world, our Minnesota woods, more even than those ancient Greeks and greedy Romans worshipped.

Abraham died in 1974 while he was carving out the stone bowl of a pipe and humming "Yellow Submarine." In all our years together I was the one who curled to him, against him, held in work-strong arms. But that final day he left his tools and pipe, nodded toward our oatmeal-lumpy couch. This time he climbed into my lap, hardly any weight at all for me to handle, twig thin as he was by then. He rested his mirror-smooth head against my chest and breathed out a long, contented sigh.

"Megwetch." His final whisper. I didn't answer until I knew I could speak without spoiling my words with tears. "No, thank you," I told his retreating spirit.

Then I gave up on men altogether because what's the use of chasing tickly champagne with a cheap can of Schlitz? I'd had eighteen years of the froth cream of life, skimmed right into my eager mouth. I had been given enough small miracles to pave a stone road to Venus. I traveled down to the Cities more often, for powwows and week-long visits with family and friends. Years passed that way until, at the big Minneapolis powwow they put on around Thanksgiving, I met my third husband. It was 1984 and I was almost fifty, my girls in their twenties, not yet married. I was content to be an older lady, proud of every silver hair that sprouted from my brown half braids—just long enough to point like arrows at my sleepy breasts. I danced traditional, in an old-time calico tear dress a cousin gave me, not for contests but for pleasure. There was a graceful straight dancer in simple old-style bustles, his body so stitched to the music, I fancied he worked a sly magic and could direct the drum, the singers' pounding sticks, from a distance, with each movement. He started falling into step with me during intertribal numbers, so we circled the arena together like that, a tie already formed between us. He didn't speak as he danced though, and I was glad. I taught my daughters not to do that, because when you jabber and gossip over the music it is like telling those songs to be quiet and go away.

"If you're going to dance, dance," I'd been scolding them

forever. "If you want to run around with your friends, then go take off your jingles." Old-fashioned, I know.

The straight dancer turned out to be Dakota, Rudy Gates. I teased him during a break: "Where's your red nose?"

He rolled his eyes at me, dark mink eyes, shadowed. "Not the reindeer," he said. "I'm named for an old time star of the silent screen—Rudolph Valentino, the Sheikh of Araby." He spread his arms for drama.

I fluttered my fan, waved wings of hair off my temples. "Oh, the sex object," I said. "The dead one."

"Jeez," was all Rudy said, grinning, embarrassed. That was the best he could do, you see, because he was Dakota, and while I'm the first to admit they are an intelligent people (possibly from living alongside us for so long), they are not as quick-witted when it comes to insults. I decided to show off my verbal sparring skills. I teased him more.

"Rudolph Valentino. He sure sparked a lot of hearts in his day, ladies who are dead by now, or the grandmas of grandmas. So, do you have success with the white-haired gals?"

Rudy poked out his bottom lip in a pout that really was seductive. "You tell me," he finally answered.

Oh, he got me then. He didn't know it at the time because I stalked away, my thick back doing all the talking. But he'd won, he'd fished me out of the pond. For a while I pretended I wasn't interested. I called him "nephew" to point out the difference in our ages, his thirty-five years to my forty-nine. But he had fish luck, laughed about it all the time.

"Fish line up to seize my hook. I don't even need any bait. 'What an honor,' they say to one another, 'to be eaten by Rudy Gates, snagged for his supper.'"

I hated when he bragged like that, though it is a man's custom I'm used to, because fishing is the talent, the divine gift of my people; we are so clever with our lines and bait, our secret places in the lake, it annoyed me that one of the Bwaan would excel at our passion. But he did, and with that effortless touch hauled me in as well, over his dark gunwales.

My Rudy kept his black hair longer than mine, and it flowed down his back or was tied with a rubberband, formed into a thick horse's tail. His eyes were a black so impossibly full of light I thought of them as black candles, strange dark flames that lit up every room he entered, every space of me he devoured with a long hot look. His face was handsome in an old-time way, dignified, but behind closed doors he could work that modest mouth in roguish, daredevil ways, like that skinny grasshopper, Mick Jagger. Kissing Rudy reminded me of my girls' favorite book they read me when they were in grade school, *Alice in Wonderland*, the passage where she falls down waboos's hole, falls and falls, because this English waboos is from a deep upside-down part of the world. Boy, my stomach would drop and my feet wouldn't feel the ground anymore, and I was so absorbed in that lovers' greedy clinch, for all I knew I might've sprouted long scarves of blonde hair, a pinafore, and shiny patent leather shoes. You could call me "Alice" and I wouldn't care, not when Rudy sucked on my lower lip as if it was a sweet bone he nursed to extract its final subtle taste, a memory of flavor.

We lived in his apartment in Minneapolis, just blocks away from the Indian Center and from the storefront office where he worked. He counseled troubled teenagers who appeared to be headed for prison if he didn't show them all the other roads they could travel if they stopped staring at the only one they knew.

"Do you have a mother fixation?" I asked him once, after I'd been learning a lot of the psychology lingo from his textbooks. "Are you with me because of a Mama complex?"

Rudy laughed so hard he choked on a forkful of chicken, and

I almost had to Heimlich him. "God, no," he finally said when he could breathe easy again. "Look, there are a thousand complicated reasons why I'm with you, having to do with all the ways you're so specifically necessary to my life, and there are two plain ones. First, I'm surrounded by youth all day—young spirits, minds, and bodies. But, as you well know, it's a smashed-up world, full of the pain of beginnings. So I find it easier to be myself and relax with someone I know has already discovered her good road. Second, when I saw you for the first time, I kept blinking at you like an owl because I saw everything in you, more than you, and that's a vision I've never experienced before. You wear your spirit outside your body and your clothes, and it was so strong I couldn't look away. I'll never look away."

And he didn't. We were together for fifteen years, in that same apartment, content, occupied with family and rescues and powwows, busy with pleasure. Then Rudy tried to break up a fight on the street outside his youth center, his small oasis, and someone shot him accidentally, aiming for one of his kids. He didn't come home. When we buried him I told his spirit to look out for Abraham because I thought the two of them could be friends, the kind of relative you have a joking relationship with to avoid any tension. I imagined them competing for my attention in a teasing way, once I'd joined them. Won't I be the lucky one? With two husbands, old and young, to warm my front and my back at the same time.

"I won't get married anymore," I promised them, since where would I fit another? Down by my feet where he'd have to curl like a dog? No, that's enough, I said. I'm done. So I haven't married anymore.

That doesn't mean I've given up on love, the romantic kind. Just a few years back, the spring of 2004, I found myself a boyfriend at the University of Minnesota Powwow. Rudy had been gone for a few years but I could still feel his presence, especially at powwows. I sensed that he was dancing beside me, quiet, as was his way, solemn. I noticed an old whiskered man, watching our doings with a fierce fascination. He sat forward in his chair, leaning onto a cane he held with both his hands. He rapped that cane in time to the music, matching every drum-stroke if it was a slow number, and just the heavy downbeat if the song was fast. He wasn't simply an audience member settled on the edge of our celebration, our performance. He was a participant without ever rising to his feet. I came to learn that this was how Yuri lived in the world; his eyes and mouth and hands, large and hungry, latched onto everything. I don't mean to say he was greedy, just willing to eat whatever life set in front of him.

I presented myself to him at the dinner break, shook his hand, welcomed him to our gathering. Only then did I notice the young man seated beside him, pale as skim milk, his eyes as dark with rings as a raccoon's. Thin blond hair was pasted like loose threads to his skull.

"This is my grandfather," the young man explained. "He's from Russia, Saint Petersburg. He doesn't speak any English. His name is Yuri. Mine is Sergei."

The grandson turned out to be a scholarship student at the University of Saint Thomas, a cleric in training. He'd found a family to sponsor his grandfather, bring him to the States, because the two men had only each other in the world. Yuri had worked most of his life in a bottle factory, but his true vocation, the art God gave him, was blowing glass. Sergei talked and talked, about the miracle of things that were both liquid and solid, about the deaths of their relatives, about loneliness and God. I half-listened, nodding at his large sunken eyes every now and then, but noticing Yuri the whole time, how he cocked his head to the side during his grandson's speech as if he understood. I later learned that Yuri did understand what people said. Not always the words, seldom the words, but the fruit pit, the marrow of their meaning. After I while I shooed Sergei off so I could sit with Yuri and talk to him in our private way that worked so well for us. I didn't tell him my chimookoman name, Gladys, but my real one, Ogimangeezhigikwe. To share the meaning I made the sign, with my hands, of a shapely woman, the hourglass curves. Then I pointed to the sky and opened my arms wide to indicate the vault of heaven. He nodded, growled his own words in a raw, burned voice.

Yuri was all silver hair and big teeth like those polar bears I've seen on television. He had that same quality of suspended power, terrific energy stored up and waiting for release. We became friends, we became lovers. He would speak to me with his hands and his zigzag Russian words, I would answer him with my own dramatic fingers and vivid Ojibwemowin. He was born in the Revolution year, I came to understand, and had lived a life that was like climbing, and then sliding down, the faces of great mountains; up and down, loving people, losing people, sharing stories, keeping secrets. Sometimes we pressed our foreheads together and spoke with our eyes, our thoughts. I never knew people could communicate in so many ways when they couldn't rely on words.

Sergei would drop Yuri off at my apartment for however long we'd arranged. I'd feed him, and we'd talk our more-than-talk. Then we'd let our bodies bring us even closer. I never actually shared my bed with Yuri. Arthritis worked on him, turning him to stone, so it was easier to leave him sitting in an old ladder-back chair, empty of arms. And when he rested his cane on the floor and held out his hands to me, I would arrange us so that I straddled his lap and we were joined, still clothed, underwear askew to give us access. Because my plain grandma dress hid our activity, covered our yin and yang, it made our love even more exciting. We were like two kids hiding in a closet or the stall of a barn, desperate to do our business but having to be quick and sneaky. Yuri's arms were so strong, he could lift me up and down, bounce me like a baby. "Hoopa, hoopa, hoopa," was his happy, rhythmic noise. And after our joyous, bumpy ride, better than any I'd ever tested at the fair, we would collapse against one another, breathless but smiling, locked together on that chair. We became one round body with all those arms and legs—a big love bug in my kitchen!

We relished the minutes we were able to stay connected if we held still, very still. Our old bodies merged continents, we were a testament to how much people can live through without giving up. Yuri entered me stiff with hope, I accepted him generous with need, and together we made survivor's love, smiled on by our ancestors, those tough, enduring people who had swallowed black oceans of tears and been clubbed by history.

Yuri died just eight months after we met, fiercely alive until the last minute—watching the news with his grandson and shouting at Donald Rumsfeld. Sergei brought me a gift he said his grandfather wanted me to have after his death. He handed me a small wooden box.

"Careful," he warned, as I lifted the lid and dug through old-time excelsior to find the object. My hand closed on a smooth globe, the size of my fist. I gently lifted it from its nest. The gift was a bubble of clear glass that tinkled softly, faint as the ring of spirit bells. I held up the globe to the light and saw that there were seven in all, one inside another, inside another, each smaller, just like those Russian nesting dolls. They were seven glass pearls without any flaw that I could see, no seams or bubbles.

"This was his life's work," Sergei explained. "It took him years to get it right, manage to fit them all together without breaking a single orb."

I hadn't cried when I learned my friend had died because

there was nothing to grieve or regret, but now I felt tears burning my eyes, saw the glass planets as his honest spirit resting in my palm. He had somehow captured the likeness of all our spirits, the miracle artwork that is our soul, both fragile and strong, perfect and beautiful, and beautiful, and beautiful.

"Imagine," Sergei interrupted my tears and my thoughts. "Imagine a life's work being something that just exists, that can't be worn or properly exhibited or put to any use." He shook his thin skull.

What I didn't tell Sergei because he was so young and already so tired is that he had just perfectly described how it is with pure love, the kind the Creator wants us to learn. This truest feeling lives deep and is quiet, patient, so modest it has no need to be shown off, no requirements that it be used or returned or even recognized. But all I told that old young man was, "This is a good gift from a good man. Megwetch."

I have lived my life with open hands. When you live like that you will lose things, people and money and pretty objects, which you would probably lose anyway, according to the Creator's plan. But when they're open like that, new things come and fill them up, too. The world sees your need and so the next thing comes, and then the next. When I was little my Grandpa noticed this quality in me and he said, "Noozis, look at how fearless you are, even though you can't make a fist. That is good. That is good."

ALIVE

by Sharon Solwitz

SNOW WAS COMING DOWN in fuzzed, aimless clots. He was ten, it was Saturday, Ethan was mad at him. If something good didn't happen he would burst out of his skin.

He opened the door of his brother's room. Nate sat, bent over his desk. From across the room his head looked a hundred percent bald. Up close, hairs could be seen, transparent like ghost hairs.

He drifted toward Nate's bureau, on which perched a large Lego pirate ship. He pulled off the skull-and-bones. "Nate-ster?" he said with more force than he felt. Force he wanted to feel. "Let's have a snowball fight?"

"Later. This math is a bitch."

"When's later?"

Nate shrugged.

He considered snapping the slender plastic flagpole then stuck it onto the 4-blade tail rotor of Nate's Lego Apache attack helicopter. On the shelf below was a box of Day-glo markers that Nate had gotten in the hospital. In Day-glo orange he wrote ETHAN on the back of his hand, noting aimlessly that ETHAN backward was NATE, if you lost the H.

He was trapped in a world without joy and the possibility of joy.

＊

His mother sat at the kitchen table drinking coffee from a mug that read around the rim: *Well Behaved Women Rarely Make History.* Her laptop was open but the screen was dark. Her hand covered her eyes. "Where's Dad?" he said.

She sat straight up. "Why Dad?" she said. "Isn't Mom good enough?"

It was her merry, acting voice. She was in theater before she went back to school and met Dad. He looked out the window. The snow had stopped. The sky was bright blue, taunting. "I have nothing to do," he said.

"Don't whine, Dylan."

He smacked the counter. Not as hard as he could have, daring her to overlook it.

"Why don't you call Ethan?" she said.

"I hate Ethan."

"So call another friend."

He opened the refrigerator thinking of other friends, but their homes required driving. He raised the lid of the Tupperware container of last night's dinner, greasy yellow islands floating on brown water. Prison food. Beyond the kitchen window the snow sparked and glistened. The hedge along the backyard fence could have been made out of sugar. "Drive me?"

"Close the fridge."

He did so then threw his arms around his mother's neck, a gesture that had served on other occasions. "Come outside and throw snowballs at me!"

She laughed. "What, are you four years old? What's the matter with you?"

"Nothing!" he almost shrieked.

She set the mug down; he hunched against her reprimand: If he didn't learn to keep his temper he would lose all his friends and hurt the people closest to him. "I've got an idea," she said. "How would you like to go skiing?"

He was filled, suddenly, with love for his mother so vast and profound that he was struck silent. They had skied last year once, all four of them and their cousin. Blur of white. Wind in his face. He kissed her shoulder under the cottony fabric.

"If Nate's feeling well enough," she said.

"He's well enough!"

He ran up to Nate's room, hopped up and down behind his brother, who was still, inexplicably, at his desk. "We're going skiing, Nate-ster!" He repeated the news, hopping on one foot, counting the hops, till their mother appeared. "What do you think?" she said to Nate. "Pay attention to your body."

Nate's hand went automatically to the bulge under his collarbone where a small box lay right under the skin. Dylan looked at the rug. "I'm not sure your father would think this is a good idea," she said.

"It's a good idea!" The cry burst out like a bird taking flight. Their father, more cautious than their mother, said no to the most harmless of ventures. In the realm of "fun for the children" the boys and their mother kept secrets from their father. "It's a great idea!" He eyeballed Nate till he closed the book. Not without bookmarking the page: Nate the good, Nate the nerd. But he forgave Nate for everything.

Alpine Valley was 75 or 90 minutes away from Evanston, depending on traffic and weather. They'd ski for two or three hours, grab a snack, be back by dinnertime. "You go nuts in the winter around here if you stay in the house! And Nate's doing so well!"

That was what their mother said into the phone, to her sister or a girlfriend. Their mother liked to talk and drive; had to, in fact. If I'm not doing two things at once I feel like I'm wasting time, she would say. She called their father: "Monday he's going back in—let him have fun for a change!" Clicking off, she said to Nate in the passenger seat, "Your father." Like he was a burden she had to bear, though both boys felt in their separate ways that she admired him. Their father was slow to express pleasure but even slower to anger; his pleasure in their existence, in the entity of family, discharged clouds of tenderness. *He's a sage, your father*, Nana had said, and on another occasion, *Nate takes after him.* Now, alert to his place in the family hierarchy Dylan had to counter such remarks. Who did he take after, Osama Bin Laden?

Would they laugh if he said that?

Soon the car picked up speed and self-love returned. The whitened streets slid by in silence, marked by stop signs with their faces blanked, the ghosts of stop signs. Sometimes on a turn, the back of the car spun out. "Go faster!" he cried, not that he expected his instructions to be followed. But he liked the feeling of things not being quite under his mother's control.

He sat in the back-seat tranquility of motion he had no control over until roused by animated voices. Up front, his mother and brother were discussing a movie. "It's the best film of the century," Nate said, and she: "Film?" mockingly. "So, Roger Ebert. Where did you get all that movie perspective?"

"It totally sucked," he offered, which was funny, he thought, because he had no idea what movie they were talking about (and why was he in the back?). He tried to follow up with fabricated facts about the unidentified movie. He tried to think of a movie he'd seen that he had an opinion about. His tongue felt tired. Roger Ebert? Louder, he said, "I wish I had cancer."

Nate laughed. Their mother: "What did you say?"

He repeated the statement aggressively. The car skidded to

stop. She turned and nailed him with her eyes. "Do you know what you're saying?"

He nodded in support of himself, of his pride of a ten-year-old. Then he felt enfeebled. He knew what he'd said, the string of words that had bubbled up (not from his brain but from a spot close to his stomach). But they had floated away like balloons he'd inadvertently let go of. He maintained his ferocity for another moment or two but there was nothing behind it. Her eyes flashed what looked like hatred for him.

"He didn't mean it," said Nate. "Give him a break, Thea."

"It's mother to you, boy. Say it!" Laughing, she whacked at Nate then with a cry drew her hand back. "Oh God, your port."

"Chill," said Nate. "Mother dear."

Three teenagers and their jackets, caps, scarves and gloves occupied the single bench in the Rental Hut. They were two boys and a girl; an electric current flowed among them, barring outsiders. Dylan, who had arrived before his brother and mother, toed off his galoshes, slid his feet into newly rented ski boots—quickly, a man who knew his business. "Where are these so-called Alps?" said the girl to her friends. "I don't see any Alps."

"There's an Expert run here. A thousand yards." One of the boys pointed to a map on the wall behind them on which different colored trails ran like veins up the mountainside. The girl bent backward on the bench and regarded the map upside down. Her hair, long, brown, straight, shining, spread out on the floor. "Ya-ards? Try feet. And it's just Advanced."

"You're a cunt, Lindsey," said the other boy.

She pulled herself upright in a single swift motion like a wave smacking the beach. Like a whip. "Watch your mouth, bitch."

Dylan cast a covert glance at the girl—Lindsey!—who didn't

need to think before she spoke. Words rolled out of her the same way her hair whipped behind her. "It's called Big Thunder," she said nasally. "Let's hit Big Thunder." Yawning, she dug into her pocket and pulled out a tube of lip balm. The back of her red parka glowed in the block of light coming in the doorway. Then Nate arrived, and their mother, regarding the scene like she wanted to improve on it.

"Uh, guys?"

It wasn't Dylan and Nate that she was addressing. Her face shone with a sour smelling light. Dylan squirmed down inside his parka. "Would you mind," she said to the three teenagers, "moving over a little? There are other people in here who might want a seat."

Without actually acknowledging anything outside their compass, the three drifted closer to one another, leaving a small space at the end of the bench. Dylan's mother and brother regarded the space, each commanding the other to sit. Dylan edged back into a corner, as far as possible from so-called Family. His mother had a regrettable habit of not knowing the limits of her domain. Before Nate got sick, they used to joke about it. He looked toward the door; the light was blinding. With unbuckled boots he ran out into the gorgeous strangeness of not being able to see.

This was it, what he had dreamed of. The smell of wood smoke, the icy packed snow under his feet, the broad white face of the mountain. He buckled up, snapped his boots onto his skis, and moved back and forth in front of the Hut, picking up each ski and slapping it down on the snow as if leg and ski were one thing; he was born to wear these things. Last year in Minnesota he and Nate and Cousin Jenna took a ski lesson. He remembered everything. Schuss. To ski straight down the face of the mountain.

When Nate and their mother emerged at last, Dylan pushed off with his poles, knees bent as the instructor had said, to impress upon anyone who was looking the pointlessness of more instruction. His mother skied toward him, steady and quick. He admired that.

Then he saw what she had under her arm. "No way," he said.

"Oh yes."

It was a helmet, clunky and moronic like the top of a trashcan. "You aren't wearing one."

"Check out your big brother."

He didn't have to look. "He's a nerd!" Trouble started in her face but he went on, "They aren't wearing helmets." She knew who he meant.

"They could break their necks. Wind up in a wheelchair. In a hospital bed being fed through a tube."

"Mom," said Nate, "you're overdoing it."

Dylan felt he'd won the argument, with Nate's help, but in his mother's court of law being right counted for nothing. Her ski came down upon the front of his skis, and he was glued in place while she situated the helmet and snapped it under his chin with a merry grin on her face. He was boxed in, cut off from the possibilities that so recently had stretched before him. No wind in his ears, and this protrusion, this shelf, to peer out from under. He thought of a movie (all of a sudden!) where the hero's entire head, front and back, was padlocked inside an iron mask, slits for the eyes and mouth. He tried to release the helmet's clasp, couldn't manipulate the tiny plastic pieces, and in the consolidating organ of his psyche, something came loose. It was a small glitch in the system, activated when an impulse of his was checked, not invariably but once in a while. A wild dog that lived inside him had yanked free of its chain.

As if for his life he fought the thing on his head. The strap was tight, his hands felt dead inside his fat-fingered gloves, he couldn't even feel the buckle. The poles on their wrist straps swung against his legs as if they had it in for him: Dylan against Things. With a heave of strength and will he pulled off his gloves with his teeth, he flung off his poles. "Stupid buckle!" People cast glances. His mother shouted, "Dylan, get hold of yourself," but she seemed frightened of him, and then he too was frightened. To restore himself, he tried to turn around, turn his back on her. His skis crossed, he teetered and fell, legs entwined, at the mercy of his uncontrollable skis, and all he could do was roll onto his back, skis flailing like the broken blades of a helicopter or the legs of some mutant insect. He squeezed back tears of shame.

Then Nate was leaning over him. "Yo. Little bro." The words went by without touching him but Nate's eyes found him. Nate clicked their helmets together. "Chill, man?"

His mother on one side, Nate on the other, Dylan was raised to his feet. "I ought to knock your two heads together," she said, reclaiming maternal control of a wry, amused sort. "Now listen to me. On the slopes I want us all to stay together. Promise, wild man?"

For a while it was as if a fever had passed. They lined up at the rope tow like ducklings, mom in front, and let the thick rope run through their gloved hands, then one-two-three squeeze—yank!—they were moving. Last year Dylan's skis kept sliding out of the ruts, and several times he fell and they had to stop the rope and wait for him to take his place again, but he was good now. At the turnstile he let go just a little late and managed to stay upright, so pleased with his mastery that he didn't mind that the tow ended barely a third of the way up the mountain or that he remained last in the family line. Stoic in the shade of his helmet, he followed the other two down the gentle slope, veering slowly from side to side as they did, bending forward just a little to decrease wind resistance. The next time down he straightened his skis, tucked his useless poles under his arms and swiftly reached the base of the hill. There he raised his poles in a Victory Salute, for his mother and brother still mid-slope, traversing at snail speed, skis clumsily splayed. Nate fell; Dylan turned away in shame, thinking of yesterday at Ethan's. They were wrestling and it was starting to be fun when Ethan went limp and rolled out from under him: It was wrong when the enemy didn't even try. *You're a pussy*, he said to Ethan, which is exactly what the dude was and is—for quitting and for being a liar, because he had fought (he swore!) fair; there was no reason for Ethan's mother to send him home.

When the other two reached the bottom—finally!—his mother showed him the snowplow, as if he'd forgotten it. "I was racing," he started to say then comprehension dawned. He, again, was competing with nobody. "At least I didn't fall," he muttered.

"I fell on purpose," Nate said mildly. "To slow myself down."

If you went any slower, you'd've gone backward, Dylan said to himself but not to Nate. He fought his frustration, tilting his face up to the wind as he grasped the tow rope, snowplowing down the wide, gentle slope, back and forth, back and forth, like it didn't matter how fast he went or even where.

During lunch their mother commended Dylan's self-control. "You showed real maturity," she said. "You deserve a medal," Nate said, raising an elbow to ward off Dylan's punch. Nate didn't want to eat, though their mother coaxed him. Dylan ate his burger and most of Nate's. Snow was falling again, slanting at the picture window.

Outside the restaurant it looked like time had passed faster than inside. The swarm of skiers had thinned, though it might have been the blowing snow, into which people took a step and disappeared. It was hard to see where the tow lift ended and, farther up, where the slope of the mountain melded with the dirty white sky. Flakes were small and almost hard against his face. Fearful of being steered back to the car, Dylan grabbed his skis and poles and ran toward the tow rope. He was almost there when Nate passed him on skis, quick and strong as he had been last year. Nate swiveled, stopping dead in front of him, in a spray of stinging snow. The move looked classy. Dylan felt as always the impulse to best him; he stomped back into his bindings, stared his brother down; he was almost Nate's height. Then, maybe it was the mist thickening around them, snow settling on their twin helmets, or maybe he finally saw how futile it was to contest the advantages of age, but suddenly Nate's skills no longer agitated him. It was like losing a heavy book from his backpack. Of course Nate had skills. "Now we'll do a real hill," he said to Nate. "Right?"

Their mother approached. Dylan urged his brother toward the trails to their left, where a chair lift climbed the mountain and vanished into white. Beyond it were other lifts and trails that promised keener pleasures. "We're going there, Nate and me," he informed their mother, with a nod toward the white wilderness. "Want to come?"

She spoke drily. "I'm no Expert. Are you?"

"It's just Advanced."

"Just? Do you know how to parallel?"

"Yes!"

"In your dreams."

He pulled his skis together, pressed his knees together, and hopped to one side like an Olympic skier, following up with a withering look at his mother, who would never get over her need to impede him.

"I wouldn't mind us trying a long slope," she said, "but we're not going to be daredevils. Nate, how are you holding up?"

"He's fine."

"The man speaks," said Nate.

She had a trail map; she spread it out and pointed to a trail in green that was called, embarrassingly, First Adventure. According to the key, Green stood for Beginner. Big Thunder, three trails over, was black for Advanced. "Do you think we're babies?" he said, but she wouldn't budge. "Tell her, Nate," he said but Nate only grinned. He gave Nate a shove, Nate shoved him back, and it was like always, Nate's gloved hands against his hands, a stalemate, with Dylan suspecting he wasn't fighting his hardest.

The First Adventure lift had benches like porch swings, a substantial improvement upon the rope tow. Dylan and his mother and brother stood side by side till the seat hit the back of their knees and swooped them up, quicker and higher than Dylan expected. He sat in the middle, and inside his helmet he had to turn all the way around to see, but all his thoughts, good and bad, blew away in the gusty wind. The vista kept widening. Behind them, smaller and smaller, the bunny skiers went down the baby hill, or was it babies down the bunny hill, lurching, falling like dolls. On both sides of the lift silvery trails snaked up the mountain through pine woods, half-hidden and glimmering. Involuntarily he kicked out with his skis. The bench started swinging; he crowed with the thrill of it. "Don't do that!" said his mother. *Bitch*, he said, under his breath, almost dreamily. Heaven seemed close. And angels. Ahead, emptied of passengers, a bench clanked around the turnstile and started downward.

As soon as they reached the disembarking point he slid down off the bench, landed squarely, and poled himself toward the ridge, where a right turn led to First Adventure and a left toward the more rigorous trails he had seen on the map, hidden in the blowing snow. He had plans. After the beginner trail, he would go right back up—no Mom, just him and Nate speeding down the silver slope as fast as thought. He opened his mouth to catch a few flakes while his heart thumped with the force of his imagining.

Wind blew at him, front and back, but couldn't get inside his parka. There was wind and squeaking, crunching snow and the creaking lift and dimly audible human voices. They enclosed him, a thicket of well-meaning sounds.

Then under the rush of wind he became aware that one of the layers of sound was gone. He was inclined to overlook it—hardly an absence, just a thinning out, a barely perceptible dilution of the forces around him. Besides, going back to check on something, retracing his steps for any reason, subverted the proper order of things. But the silence seeped into his mind like fumes, and after a minute or two he was poling back to the lift—where he found a scattering of people stalled in confusion, and above them, perversely halted, the benches of the lift swaying a little in the wind, and below, seated in the snow, his mother and brother. Nate leaned against her, his head on her shoulder, while she regarded the onlookers with a stiff smile. "He'll be fine!" she kept saying. "He has to rest a few minutes."

Dylan stood on the edge of the gathering, remembering talk between his parents at the kitchen table, with him outside the door unable not to overhear: We have to keep it normal for them. As much as we possibly can. At which he had turned and fled, from everything beyond the bounds of his parents' vision of normality for him and Nate, expanses he still had no wish to explore. He wanted to flee again, and he might have if his legs weren't so spongy. Then his mother was beckoning. "He's just tired, honey. It comes on quick sometimes. I think his count is low."

He didn't want to look at Nate but it was hard not to. His helmet was off, their mother's plaid scarf around his head and neck. He had no eyebrows. Was this normal? Nate opened his eyes and smiled apologetically. Dylan wanted to punch him.

He punched his mother's shoulder. "Dylan, what's wrong with you!" she said sharply, then softened her voice. The Ski Patrol would ride Nate down on their sleigh easy as pie, like lying in bed. It was almost time to go anyway. She seemed to be talking to herself though her words were directed at him. Could he ski down and meet them by that rental place? Go in, take off his equipment and return it? He could do that by himself, couldn't he?

"Of course! Do you think I'm retarded?"

He moved slowly, in no willed direction, just out of his mother's sight, while snow blew at her and Nate, and people's hats and hoods and helmets and the boughs of evergreens. The lift creaked and started moving again though many chairs were empty. The few people getting off barely paused to look around before pushing off toward their chosen slopes. The wind seemed to have intentions that weren't kind. The word "evil" came to his mind but he didn't know what to do with it.

The sky had darkened toward the gray of night when the red parka appeared on high, and the girl, Lindsey, solitary on the long bench and helmetless, hatless. She slid down onto the icy packed snow like she didn't even have to think about it, her hair bouncing behind her. For a moment their eyes met; she grinned. Then, passing, she thrust a pole in his direction as if spearing a fish, and clicked open the binding of his left ski, crowing as she flitted by.

For a moment he flailed for balance. His freed ski was sliding off though it remained clipped to his boot by a short cord. He captured it with the sole of his boot. If she were a boy, he'd have been enraged—he'd have felt engorged with impotent hatred. But now, hearing in his mind the sound of her hilarity, he simply snapped his boot back into place and poled himself toward where she had vanished. Snow blew inside his helmet and down his neck unprotected by a scarf but he hardly felt it, passing the turn-offs to two or three unmarked trails (there were no signs, or else the signs were covered in snow) till he arrived at the top of a hill so steep he couldn't see where it went. A shiver climbed the knobs of his spine. He had dreamed this, riding a brakeless bike down a blind hill, trying to wake before the crash while simultaneously willing himself back inside the dream, into the pure speed of the drop. Digging his poles into the feathery new snow, he crept toward the edge. He felt Lindsey here and everywhere, her skier's soul joined with his, two Experts on unworthy slopes.

Then he was moving, slowly at first then faster than he had ever gone without the shell of a vehicle around him, bent over like skiers on TV twisting through the bendy yellow flags, except that he was going straight down, past skiers traversing—no time to see faces—faster than images could be processed, faster at last than his mind could think. This was schussing. This was riding the wind. He wondered for a second if he should try to slow down. A voice said in his ear, *Make yourself fall!* But falling was what Ethan would do. Falling was Nate. Dylan leaned forward into the whoosh of his skis, the wind of his descent, as if thereby he would rise into the air like a kite.

It was his last thought before he hit. There was a crack, a flash of red. He flew backward in slow time, like the moment on Nate's sled, in the circle of his brother's arms, when, swerving around another sled he saw a tree looming before them, and he had all the time in the world to think, *Turn, Nate! Swerve!* and to picture the aftermath of breakage and pain, though there was no time to say it aloud. Nate had miraculously managed to turn them; they'd missed the tree.

When Dylan opens his eyes he is sprawled in deep snow. The world returns bit by bit. He tips his head back, takes a cautious sip of air. There are things to do and things he mustn't do, so it seems. He raises his head then sets it down. His head, inconceivably, is lower than his feet. He's on his back, tries to turn; pain makes him gasp and the gasp hurts the top of his belly. From somewhere comes an outraged, teary female voice: "I'll kill him!" A chunk of time seems gone from his brain.

Then people are bending over him as they had bent over Nate.

"It's a kid. Oh my."

"Trying to set a record, are you?"

"Kids his age don't belong here."

"Little cocksucker. I'd like to wallop him!"

"Don't move, kiddo. He shouldn't move, should he? Are you OK?"

"Hey, bomber, what's up? Can you move your legs?"

"Let him lie still. Wait for Ski Patrol."

"I'm fine," he cries, raising his arms to prove it.

Someone taps his helmet. "Good thing you had this on. Protect those brain cells."

Was someone making fun of him? "Just help me up!" he cries.

While people are unhooking his skis, unlooping the pole straps from around his wrists, he wonders what he hit. If it was a person, and that person was Lindsey, he doesn't want to know. Someone takes one of his arms, someone else the other; they pull him upright. Then he tries to stand, and the pain is so vast and deep he has to scream.

That night in the hospital where Nate was being transfused, Dylan lay on an examining table while the doctor wound his leg in sticky white gauze from his knee to the bottom of his foot. It was cool at first then started heating up. He was lucky, the doctor said. It was a greenstick fracture. He should keep it elevated when possible. He had broken some ribs, too, but they would heal on their own, quickly because he was young. In six weeks after moderate physiotherapy, he'd be back on the slopes.

His mother stood on the other side of the table, and he looked up at her to see how he was supposed to take the news. She had tears in her eyes. He felt his own tears welling, though with his pain medication he was so relaxed he could barely imagine pain. "Mom," he said tenderly, "you don't have to cry!"

"He was down to nine," she said. "It's a wonder he could keep his head up."

The doctor signed a sheet of paper and left. They sat, Dylan on the table, his mother in a plastic chair in a tiny bright curtained-off room in the E.R., where they were obliged to stay till a wheelchair came to roll him out to the car where his father was waiting. His crutches stood in a corner; he wanted to try them but not enough to say anything. Footsteps passed but didn't enter. He was alone with his mother, which he liked though he'd never have admitted it. He liked the word greenstick. He didn't want to know what nine meant.

"It's so hard," she said.

"He's getting better," he said sternly. He sat up, kicked his good leg. "He'll be fine!"

His words sounded lame, but to his surprise her tears ceased. She put her arms around him. "Dylan," she said, "do you know how amazing you are?"

Despite himself he grinned shyly. She could stop now.

But she didn't stop. She held onto him tight. "You're alive. Alive. Alive." She sang the word against his forehead.

Of course he was alive. She smelled of sweat and deodorant. He sat breathing her in, with a combination of joy and terror that overrode his medication. His heart thudded savagely. At her trust in him that he had to live up to—from now on, it seemed, and for the boundless rest of his life.

DOMESTIQUE

by Ian Stansel

THE CORN TURNED TO TREES and we entered the Shawnee National Forest, the shadows cooling us, the air now moist and carrying with it the clean smell of dark plantlife. We'd made it just in time. It would be the height of the day soon and through the morning and early afternoon the sun had begun to take its toll on our skin and our spirits. But this was one of the parts my wife and I had been looking forward to. The trees seemed as high as skyscrapers and the road felt good. I'd found my stroke. Even, on the down and the up. I was in that sweet spot, those hours after the first couple when your legs just keep going. Dory and I were side by side, matching up the wheels of our bikes and staying close. We played at taking off, only to slow, coasting back to the other and then picking up an identical stride. *Whoosh* and *whoosh* and *whoosh*. We looked at each other.

We were riding the height of Illinois, tip to top, Cairo to Chicago. Myself, Dory, and our friend Terry, who rode a Schwinn Le Tour III that had to be twenty, twenty-five years old. I have no idea when he'd picked it up. Sometime between his inviting himself along and the time we all hit the road, I guess.

Terry squeezed between us and called to Dory, "D'you see that woodchuck?"

"What?" Dory said.

"Woodchuck!" he shouted.

"I imagine there are a few of those around."

"D'you ever read *Walden*?"

She looked at him and then back at the road. "I think so."

"That part where he sees a woodchuck? And he wants to grab it and eat it right there, all raw."

"Yeah?" Dory called.

"It's the nature and the wildness he wants!" Terry yelled. "He just wants to eat it all!"

A trio of cars came up on us quickly and I dropped back so that Dory could get over. She did, but not before the guy in the third car laid on his horn good and long and I could see my wife's shoulders hunch in alarm. Her front wheel wavered just ever so little.

"Motherfucker!" Terry yelled at the car. He got up out of the saddle and pounded a couple strides ahead of us, making a show for the guy's rear-view. He held up a fist and shook it cartoon-style. *Why, you...* I caught up to Dory once again and she tried to smile at me.

We stopped at the next picnicking area and ate some of what we brought: energy bars, smashed cheese sandwiches, apples.

"What was the name of that little dude?" Terry said, lighting an American Spirit.

"What little dude?" I said.

"That little dude a couple years behind us. Little dude who disappeared."

I knew the person Terry was referring to. A boy who went missing while we were in high school. He was on his way home, middle of the afternoon. "Matt," I said. They found his body a couple weeks later. "Matt something."

"Matt something, yeah," Terry said.

I waited a few beats for him to continue, but knew it was just

Terry's brain and Terry's mouth doing what they do.

He took a serious drag on his cigarette and blew the smoke in my direction.

I waved a hand in front of my face and said, "Come on."

"What? Don't be that guy." One of those ex-smokers, he meant. A hypocrite, he meant. Terry knows how to get to me.

Dory and I had been clean for three years by the time the summer of our trip rolled around. We'd been off everything: the booze, the pot, the coke, the x, the acid and mushrooms, the party-time whippits. Even cigarettes. One day we were Dory and Miro, that couple apt to take just about anything handed to them, and the next day—nothing. We gave up caffeine. We made a plan to quit and stuck to it even though our last night of indulgence we were both tired and only smoked a few bowls and cranked open a couple bottles of wine. It was a Saturday night and we passed out curled into each other on the couch. In comparison to how we felt most Sunday mornings, this next one was bright and sunshiney, this one was bluebirds on our shoulders, this one we walked outside onto our back porch and breathed in the city and it didn't feel polluted or hateful.

"You must have lungs of steel," Dory said to Terry.

"I'm still thinking about those woodchucks," Terry said. "That's the only part of the book I remember."

"Is that how you fancy yourself?" Dory asked. "Guy eating the woodchuck whole."

"Oh, man," Terry said. He lay back on the dirt, one hand under his head. He smoked his cigarette and made no signal that he had anything else to say on the subject.

Dory walked across a field of thick grass. All around the perimeter of the field were gathering areas, metal roofs over concrete foundations and picnic tables. There were no people anywhere. Where were they? Was it not summer? There should at the very least have been some teenagers hanging around taking care of their teenage business: smoking cigarettes and pot, shotgunning cans of Natty Light. Where have all the burnouts gone?

I asked Dory, "How are your legs?"

"Good," she said. "They feel strong."

"We're making good time."

"I'm not worried about time," she said. A small group of birds fluttered out of one tree and perched in another.

"I think he'll calm down soon," I said. "Maybe tomorrow. He's just excited. You know how he gets. I guess that's the reason I couldn't tell him no."

"Miro, it's done," she said.

"He was so goddamn psyched about it."

I ran a hand over Dory's back. I took her hand and we lay on our backs watching the sky. I had to keep in mind these small moments with my wife. I knew she was telling the truth: it wasn't that she didn't want Terry there with us. The problem was that I allowed the meaning of the trip to be altered. The whole point was to do this alone, Dory and Miro, just us. To be alone while we still could. The plan, you see, was that when we got back to Chicago, we were going to start trying for a kid.

After five minutes, we got up and walked back to the shelter where we found Terry asleep on the ground, his limbs flung out into starpoints. His cigarette had burned down to the filter by where his hand lay palm up. His mouth hung open with his lower lip drooping, like someone still-framed a video of him getting decked with a doozy of a right.

A few hours later, we decided to camp just inside the Shawnee National Forest, only a half mile from where the woods end and the area gets back to the business of agriculture. From inside our tent, Dory and I heard the repeated clicking of a lighter and then smelled the pot smoke wafting from Terry's own nylon housing. Dory turned over in her bag. I whispered, "You know we can't ask people to change for us." We had to accept the fact that the world is full of temptation and that it is up to us to resist. Then I said, "It's just some pot anyway." In the morning, as we ate our breakfasts, Terry smoked up again, this time right in front of us. I said, "Can we keep that to a minimum?"

"Dude, I am," Terry said and sucked on his bowl. He made a half-hearted effort to blow the smoke away from us, but the little wind there was brought it back. "I know you two are sensitive or whatever," he said. He put his stash back into his pack.

"You should come ride with us in the city," Dory said.

"I don't know," Terry said, yawning. "My asshole is killing me."

As we left the forest, we saw a small plane dusting the corn crops. It was sleek and modern looking, not the old bi-plane we all remember from *North by Northwest*. But old-fashioned or not, it was completely charming to a city kid like me. I pointed and smiled and waved at the unseen pilot. Terry seemed to take no notice of it. Dory tried to share in my enthusiasm, but she had fallen into a mood. The plane flew off and we continued down the road, inching toward the city.

Terry is my only friend—our only friend—from before we cleaned up. He and I went back to junior high. We played basketball together on the division's worst team three years in a row. We slept over at each other's houses and knew each other's parents as well, it seemed sometimes, as our own. We made out with girls for the first time on the same night, at a party in Terry's basement, sixth grade. Terry was with me, in fact, the night I met Dory.

We were twenty-three and looped on ephedrine and Mad Dog 20/20, coming in late to the California Clipper, watching some psychobilly outfit give bad medicine to the ghost of Hank Williams. Terry started dancing spastically (the only way he knew and the only style suitable for that music, really) and Dory, a stranger to us, joined him, matching his flailing arms and jerking legs. Of course I was attracted to her. I was twenty-three and fucked-up and Dory's a hell of a good looking woman. I've always thought so, though there have been periods when she looked less beautiful—a bit too much weight, or not enough, a little sallow in her face. I have no doubt she could say the same of me. There are pictures that make me cringe. But that night we were young and as beautiful as we ever were or ever would be. I figured if she was going home with anybody that night (she didn't) it would be Terry. He's handsomer than anybody realizes. If he could keep his mouth from falling slack or his eyes from going bloodshot, you'd see. The band finished up at quarter of two and Dory asked us to join her and her friends, who were not impressed by us or, it seemed, the larger world. The feeling was mutual. This was, in fact, the only time I would meet Dory's group of eye-rolling, cranberry-and-vodka high school chums. They didn't thank me when I bought a round of drinks I couldn't afford. They looked away while speaking to me in clipped, one-word responses. Dory, though, she looked me straight in my double vision. After a while, she and I were bringing each other drinks from the bar and it became clear that we'd hit upon something, she and I.

This is the only story I'll tell from those days, the only one I ever tell. Unfortunately, people want to hear the other ones: humorous tales of good nights gone bad, of near-misses, of bizarre cross-town cab rides and kooky dealers. We know, though, all too well, what's on the flip side of these anecdotes: the men and women playing chicken with a world of broken minds and tainted dope and unemployment and untold loss. We cannot tell these stories anymore.

When it comes down to it, we quit because we had to. Individually, sure, we could have kept on with the lifestyle a few more years, another decade—hell, maybe more. Maybe until we were gray and the damn stuff started to blow out our organs and then, eventually, put us down in the ground. But us? We were quickly hurtling toward the end. As wonderful as it was over the first few months, as much as we felt we'd found an extraordinary adoration in the space between us, we also found a capacity for meanness, the sort of cruelty you reserve for the ones you love the most. It was getting to where every night we would find some reason to turn on each other. Screaming matches neither could fully remember in the morning. Cheating. Who cheated first I couldn't tell you. There's no thought happening in the moment, no concept of ramifications. Once I hit her. She had fucked so-and-so or I thought she wanted to fuck so-and-so. A slap, really. And in my very weak defense, she had taken to hitting me quite often (the first time was shocking, but after that it just became a part of the sad routine). That, as memory serves, was the loudest alarm. She stood there with a hand on her cheek and we both knew that it was either the booze and the drugs, or us.

But I will say this: the chances of a couple staying together after cleaning up are slim. People are just too different after rehabbing. The world is utterly changed. And this is the thing I am proud of, that Dory and I survived and changed together, that from the get-go we were more than people who liked to get wrecked together. Despite the horror of those last months of partying, we had indeed fallen in love as deeply as either of us ever could.

It was turning into a beautiful day, the sun high and bright, but the air cool. Perfect. I came alongside my wife on the road and handed her a gel pack. She hadn't eaten much that morning and I knew she would run out of steam soon. Most people don't understand how a cycling team works. They think each rider is out there on his or her own, but there is careful coordination at work. Riders offer themselves as windbreaks for their teammates, taking turns drafting. And there's a member of every team who only supports the other riders. He's referred to as the domestique. This is the guy who fetches water and bars and gels from the team car and darts up through the crowded peloton to deliver them to the riders who have a chance to take the jersey. It's a necessary, if less than glorious, position. This is the role I find I naturally move to in awkward group circumstances, so over the next two days as we meandered in a general northward direction, switching from rough country roads to the shoulders of small highways, I gave myself to the team. I waved down cars to ask for directions when we became confused by the vast, unmarked intersections. I paid for more than my share when we stopped in small towns to eat and camped in KOAs. I filled up our water bottles at gas stations, leaving my teammates to relax outside. On the road, I offered food from my pack.

People in restaurants and shops were impressed by our trip, looking at our bikes and our gear and nodding their heads in some sort of appreciation. Terry was drinking and smoking each night, passing out and snoring clear through until morning, when he would wake and hack and spit into the grass outside his tent. Dory and I avoided each other's eyes.

Drying out was tough, I'm not going to kid you. On the last day, in the hours leading up to our breakup with all things altering, I had dreadful images of us in opposite corners of our shithole apartment, sweating and trembling, sucking down mouthwash or combing through the carpet for any stray sliver off a pill. It wasn't like that. In reality, except for our meetings and work we basically just stayed home. We watched a lot of movies and syndicated reruns. It was incredibly boring. There were moments I was at the door, hand on the knob, ready to find one of our dear, fucked-up friends, anyone who was holding anything. Or just hit the bar and toss back one whiskey after another. I didn't. We were miserable and we snapped at each other. We blamed one another, claiming the other's weakness to be more desperate than our own. We brought up the times prior to our meeting, mentioned how fine everything had been, how well we could handle ourselves. All bullshit, of course. We'd never been OK, neither of us.

But somehow we rode it out. After a few weeks my hands were still and my eyes clear.

Dory bought us the bikes as wedding gifts. "We need something to focus on," she said. She was right. Since quitting drugs Dory finished her degree in counseling and was interning at a clinic. I had somehow fallen into computers and took an IT position at AT&T. We bought a two-bedroom condo in Bucktown. We went to bed at ten-thirty, made love or read, and were deep in REM by eleven-fifteen, eleven-thirty.

Cycling became what we looked forward to. We rode up and down the lakefront. We participated in monthly Critical Mass gatherings, hundreds of riders taking over Friday rush hours on the streets of Chicago. From early spring to the near-dead of winter we rode every chance we got. And when we weren't riding we were looking through cycling magazines, reading the glut of biographies of LeMond, Obree, Lance. We got cable so we could watch the major races in Europe and California. We discussed the doping scandals, so many people feigning disbelief and tsk-tsking the latest poor, stupid sap to get caught.

*

So much of that trip was spent watching the gray road blur by just beyond my front wheel, and life rarely tells you that something special is about to happen. "Get ready," it does not say. "You're going to want to remember this." So all I can report is a mixture of memory flashes and information I've received since. I do know that on that fourth morning Dory had taken the lead and I was behind her with Terry bringing up the rear. We were on a bigger road than we'd have liked, but you can't always demand the most perfect conditions. It was a four-lane with a decent shoulder and a wide, grassy median between the directions. There was a little traffic, mostly long haul trucks that had the good graces to merge left as best they could when passing us. For about a half hour I'd been having trouble switching between gears. Not that I needed to change all that often; the landscape of central Illinois is famously pancake flat, just excellent for cycling in my opinion, but I can be a stubborn son of a bitch and something of a fiddler and instead of leaving it alone, I was clicking back and forth, looking down at the chain as it unstuck itself and changed up and down the gears. I was about to ask Dory and Terry if they'd mind stopping so I could have a look at my derailleur when Dory said, "Hey." She said it quite calmly, though loud enough for us to hear above the wind of our movement.

By then the presence of those small, yellow crop dusters had become old hat and none of us were very impressed with that sign of country life that had so delighted me only a couple days before. But I looked up just in time to see, not fifty yards from us, a duster coming in low over the road, getting lower. It angled itself and then smashed into the trailer of a semi-truck coming in our direction on the other side of the highway. A miracle of chance. The collision made an awful noise, explosive and ear-twisting. Dory screamed and we both crashed to the road. Much of the body of the plane went straight through the trailer, landing in a fiery crash on the other side. The impact pushed the truck on to its side and into the deep ditch lining the road. The wings of the plane sheared off and jagged hunks of fiberglass were sent hurtling across the area, slamming into the ground all around us. One of those pieces hit Terry squarely in the legs, flipping him and his bike over, landing him on his shoulder and smacking his head against the hot, black pavement.

For a moment there was deep silence, like the darkness past a flame. Then the sound came back, cars screeching, voices yelling. Metal on fire.

I couldn't say how long the ambulances and police cars and fire trucks took. Maybe a while, given that we seemed to be a fair distance from any sort of decently sized town. I crawled to Dory, whose legs were good and tangled in her bike. I might have asked her if she was OK, or I might have just known by her expression. I looked back at Terry. He and the bike were twisted at gruesome angles. We got to him slowly—I'd find out at the hospital that my wrist was sprained and both Dory and I were patched with scrapes and cuts and bruises. But Terry was unconscious. There was blood on the ground, not much, just a thin spot, but it was enough to hold my focus for a long half-second. Dory said, "Don't move him." Cars stopped and strangers' faces moved in close to ours. Soon the road was as crowded as a backyard gathering, with folks in pairs and trios, many of them talking on phones or taking pictures with them. The police were there a few minutes before coming to us. We must have blended in with the onlookers—just three cyclists down the road a bit watching the action. A man standing near to us waved his arms and yelled toward the cops. Soon Dory and I were being helped into the back of an ambulance while paramedics were carefully separating Terry from his machine.

Dory and I were treated quickly. The police took our statements in the Emergency Room waiting area.

"Is there a family member you know of that we should

contact?" the police officer asked. Terry's family was small: no brothers or sisters, no aunts or uncles that I ever met or heard of. His parents were always old—the must have been nearing forty when they had him, compared with mine who had me when they were barely into their twenties. His father passed away a few years before. His mother had a stroke shortly after and was living in assisted living. I didn't know where this was, but told the cop that I'd try to find out.

Then, finally, they let us speak to a doctor. He was a frail looking old man, about sixty, sixty-five. Too old for an Emergency Room, that's for damn sure. I worried about what kind of treatment our friend was getting in this tiny hospital in this nothing burg. "Should he be, I don't know, airlifted somewhere?" I asked. "Cook County?" The doctor looked at me over his reading glasses.

"Your friend has a broken ankle, a fractured femur, fractured collarbone, and a fairly serious concussion," he said. "That sounds like a lot, and it is. But each injury is independent and each one we are more than capable of treating here. You can arrange for whatever you like, but I have serious doubts about anyone's insurance covering an unnecessary air transport." He paused to let his point make its way into my understanding of the situation. I was then stuck wondering what the chances were that Terry had any insurance at all. "He'll have to stay here for at least a day, probably two. His legs have been reset. There's little we can do about the collarbone. Just have to wait for it to re-fuse on its own. He is under sedation right now, and on a good deal of pain medication." He said we'd be able to see him the next day, but that for now what he needed was rest.

A nurse appeared and said, "You folks can take his things and bring them back when he's ready to be discharged." She pushed his raggedy pack, even more raggedy now—broken straps, a rip in the outside pocket—out from behind the counter of her station and directed us to a motel about a mile up the road. Outside, Dory and I found our bikes leaning near the Emergency Room entrance. I sat Terry's bag on my crossbar and tied the straps to the handlebars. Dory and I slowly walked the bikes in the direction of the motel. It was dusk then, the sun setting on the west side of the flat, corn-and-soy horizon. I loved this landscape, still do. Even at that moment, with the pain of my own minor injuries finally finding the surface of my consciousness, I found it devastatingly beautiful.

It was dark by the time we got to the motel, a decent-looking place just off a highway overpass, surrounded by gas stations and fast food joints and liquor stores. We checked in and were happy to find a Mexican restaurant attached to the lobby. The clerk at the front desk said, "You two look like you've had a day. Where you headed?"

"Chicago," I said.

"Not the whole way on bikes." And there was that look—the dropped jaw, the tilted head, that expression of approval, even some sort of pride. But then that changed and she said, "You all the ones out there on the road?"

"Yeah," Dory said.

The woman held a hand to her mouth. "How is your friend?"

Whatever this town was, it was small. "He's OK," I said. "They're keeping an eye on him."

We took the elevator up and dropped our bags onto the floor of our room. My wrist throbbed. I laid down on the bed. It was the softest thing I'd ever felt. Dory turned the light on by the sink and, wincing in front of the mirror, carefully removed her jersey and shorts. Dory's limbs are long and thin. A cyclist's body. She pulled her hair back into a ponytail, revealing her neck to me. Because of her position by the mirror, I could see almost all of her at once. Both of us had crashed our bikes before. Anyone who rides as much as we do has stories of car doors flung open, of indecisive squirrels, of cell phone drivers turning without checking their mirrors. We've crashed together even, a few times, both of us limping home, taking turns sitting on the side of the tub while the other stung our scrapes with Bactine and covered them with gauze. We're used to seeing each other banged up. But this was different. Terry was perhaps ten yards behind me, maybe fifteen from my wife. Dory's bruised back and scratched arms and legs only made me think of how it could have so easily been her or me.

Still undressed, Dory turned to me, leaned against the sink counter. "We're going to have a baby, right?" she said.

"That's the plan, isn't it?" I said.

"Yeah," she said "Have you really thought about it, though? Do you know that that's what you want?"

"Of course I have," I said. "Yes, of course it's what I want." I don't know if this was true or not. Looking back now I think that this was an unfair question. Until the actual experience comes you can think of it in only the vaguest hypotheticals. You cannot know what it is to have a child, your child. You cannot really understand the hours and the worry. And the joy. Had I thought about it? Yes. Did I know what it would be like enough to make a fully rational decision, to weigh the pros and cons, to be sure? Not even fucking close. Neither had she and neither has any first-time parent in the history of the world. This is my firm belief. We have babies on instinct. We have babies because we have babies because we have babies. So we can all keep going.

Dory moved away from the bathroom, toward me, and for a second I thought that she wanted to start the baby-making process right then, and though normally I would have been all for it (there's something about the familiar anonymity of hotel rooms that has always urged us to be a little more adventurous in bed), my body was feeling sore and increasingly stiff. But she did not come to me.

Instead, she walked to where the packs and panniers were piled on the floor. She crouched down, unzipped the front pocket of Terry's pack, and pulled out his knitted Guatemalan stash bag.

"I'm going to smoke Terry's pot," she said. She came and sat by me on the bed and went about packing a bowl.

"Babe," I began, but didn't continue. I was too tired to think. I couldn't think anymore about babies or Terry or meetings or the utter nonsense of seeing a plane fly into a truck. Three years since we'd indulged in anything, but Dory did not hesitate before lifting the pipe and Terry's Bic lighter to her face and taking a good-sized hit. She was resolute. She held the smoke in her healthy lungs for five seconds and then coughed it out. She took another drag and then put the pipe down on the bedside table and stood the lighter up next to it. The earthy cloud of smoke hung in the air like an old song.

I picked up the bowl and took a deep hit and then another. "It's good," I said. Dory lay next to me and then reached across my body for the bowl. She got a small drag and said, "Cashed." I reloaded it and we did a couple more rounds. We fell further into the bed. I put my good arm around Dory's shoulder, careful not to touch any of her sores. After a few minutes, she said, "It just became very apparent that we haven't eaten anything today."

I splashed cold water on my face and we each got dressed. All we had with us were running pants and t-shirts. Hers was from a 5K run she did for breast cancer. Mine said "Circuit City" on it. I got it when we signed up for a credit card. Dory looked at me and then herself in the mirror. "Jesus," she said.

The host at the Mexican restaurant sat us in a booth, and we ordered plates of enchiladas, chips and salsa and guacamole, and large glasses of water. "And a margarita," Dory said to the waitress.

"Little or big?"

"Big."

"Extra shot of Cuervo for two dollars."

"Yeah," Dory said, a sort of amused resignation in her voice. "All right."

I held up two fingers at the waitress. When they came, the drinks were comically enormous. They were fish bowls. They were aquariums. God, what a world.

We could have said that we were doing this because of the stress of the day, because we were worried about Terry. We could have said that it was all just a pile of bad luck: the plane and us being there in a hotel room with a sack of weed. What were we supposed to do? We could have said that it was because we'd never had a proper send-off for our wild past, that we'd fallen asleep too early that last night (something that I had, in fact, come back to in memory, a regret for not having gone out in some great firework of consumption). We could have told ourselves and each other that we were high and getting drunk because we were going to have a baby someday soon and we were frightened as hell of that. And we would have been right about all of those, each one. But to be honest, we would have also had to admit that we were doing this because we both love the feeling of it. We love the fluid change from one state to another. We love the way the drugs and the booze cradle us in their chemical arms. We would've had to, for what surely would have been the thousandth time or more, admit our helplessness. But we did not want to admit that, not this night. So we shut up and drank.

After dinner, without discussion, we moved from our table to the dark wood bar with piñatas hanging above it. Dory spotted a jukebox and while she punched in some tunes I ordered beers and two shots of tequila from the bartender, a woman in her forties, early fifties. There were three other drinkers there: to the right of us was an old man in jeans and flannel and a mesh-backed cap that said Jefferson Elementary; and to the left was a couple, a little older than Dory and me. They were clean-cut in chinos and blue polo and white shorts and red blouse. A good, healthy flag of America. The two men were both drinking beers. The woman sipped at a tall, wet glass of white wine. "Midnight Rider" drowned out the mumbling TV newscaster in the corner. Dory got back and we ceremoniously did our shots and sucked on lime and each had a slug of beer. Dory sang along to the lyrics she knew from the song ("I've got one mooore silver dollar") and then laughed.

"Did you know," she said, "that two members of the Allman Brothers died in separate motorcycle accidents in almost exactly the same spot, almost exactly a year apart? Isn't that nuts? What are the chances? Both of them, riding along…the second Allman must have thought, 'Well, it's not gonna happen twice' and then wham!" She clapped her hands together. "Crash!"

"You talking about the plane?" the old man in the cap asked us. We looked over. "Duster that went down?"

"Oh, we heard about that," the woman on the other side of us said, leaning into the bar to see the old man past Dory and me. Her husband turned toward us slowly, looking like he'd just been left in mid-sentence.

"Something," the old man said, as in *Isn't life some kind of something?*

"You two heard about this, right?" the husband said to us.

Dory squinted her eyes toward the bottles behind the bar. "I think so," she said.

"You'd know it if you did," he said. "Goddamn plane flew into a truck. Right up the road. Exploded all over the place. Knocked the truck ass over tit."

"God," his wife said in a plaintive tone. "You know what it reminds me of."

"I know, I know," her husband said, putting an arm around her.

"The plane," she said, "and it's like, whoa, flashback. As soon as I heard about it, I just couldn't help thinking about that morning, what we were seeing on TV. We were watching the second plane live," she said toward us and the old man, then turned back to her husband. "I mean, not like we were the only ones, but still."

"This must have been much, much smaller, though," the husband said.

"Well, of course I know that." His wife gave him a playful smack on the arm. "But still. Similar."

I have to admit that I'd had the same thought. Not at the moment of impact, but sometime in the hospital or in the ambulance on the way over. Specifically, I'd thought of that field in Pennsylvania and I was struck by the weight that it still puts on my heart. To imagine the experience.

We drank and more songs came on: Bob Seger and Fleetwood Mac. Cat Stevens.

"Do we know what happened to the driver?" Dory said to the others at the bar.

"Going to have a mess of hospital bills, that's for sure," the old man said. "They said he got his arm stuck under something, all twisted out of sorts. Took a shot to the head when the damn thing went over. Man's gonna have a hell of a time with the insurance companies, too, on top of it all. Cocksuckers."

The word entered the conversation like a flung knife. Dory looked back and forth between the old man and the couple. I kept my eyes on her. My tolerance was on the floor and I was fairly drunk. That gorgeous feeling. My beautiful friend.

"That man can use some praying for, I'd say," the woman said, mending the breach of etiquette in our small community.

"You have to wonder what happened," the husband said. "Mechanical error or what. What was going on in that plane?"

"McIntire says he didn't see anything wrong with Grady this

morning." The old man held up his beer bottle and the bartender brought him a fresh one.

The husband ordered another and I made a circling gesture around our bottles and shot glasses.

"Sorry," the husband said, getting back to the conversation. "Who's this you're saying?"

"Grady," the old man said, a bit annoyed. "The pilot. McIntire said he seemed fine, not looking ready to keel over or anything."

"Did he seem…distraught?" the woman said.

"Didn't say anything about that."

"And this McIntire?" the husband asked.

The old man looked past Dory and I at the husband, square in the face. "Guy whose fields Grady was doing," he said, tired of all these nonsense questions. "Just over across 20." I liked this old man. He was a real asshole.

"We're from Dayton," the husband said after a moment. The old man turned his eyes to the television.

"Cheers," Dory said, and we did our fresh shots.

"Heading up to Minneapolis to see our boy. Going to be a sophomore there. Thought we'd stop halfway, take it easy a little."

"You have a kid in college?" I said.

"Hard for us to believe, too," the husband said. "But there he is, living in a dorm with another boy, doing whatever they do on the weekends, getting into trouble."

His wife tapped him on the arm. "He's no troublemaker, you know that." She said to us, "He's a quiet boy, really."

"Ah, well, that's going to change," her husband said, irritated. "It's college. For Christ's sake, you get out there. You learn how to navigate the world. You build social skills. Go out and see what you can get off some co-ed. Not—"

"Phil," his wife said.

"Not stay in all day playing video games."

"Do you two have children?" the woman asked us, moving the focus of the conversation.

Dory leaned back and put a hand on her stomach. "Expecting our first right now."

The woman and her husband both looked at the beer bottle in Dory's hand, the empty shot glasses on the bar, their faces dropped in confusion.

"I'm just kidding," Dory said, placing a hand on the woman's shoulder.

"Oh," the woman said, feigning a small laugh.

"Good," her husband said. "I thought this was about to be one of those 'what would you do' moments." Then his face took on an expression of recognition. "Hell," he said. "Oh hell, you're the ones that were out there at the accident. Aren't you? Remember," he said to his wife, gesturing toward the front desk of the motel, "she said that there were three people out there. They're the people on bikes."

"Is that true?" the woman asked us. The old man turned away from the TV to look our way also.

Dory ordered another round of shots. The husband said, "You deserve that. Day you've had."

"You should have told us," the woman said, perhaps a bit more seriously than she wanted. She finished her glass of wine and then made a smile appear.

"What were you people doing riding bicycles out there?" the old man said.

"Just heading home," Dory said.

The old man and the couple all left the bar soon after it became clear that we weren't going to reveal any details about the strange incident on the road. Also, Dory and I were getting to a point of inebriation that is uncomfortable for most people to look at. I continued to be nearly completely silent and Dory started singing the wrong lyrics to songs. When they were gone we ordered another round and the bartender told us that this would be the last, that she was closing up.

That might have been the night we conceived our son. For a while leading up to his birth I'd hoped it hadn't been—sloppy, blurry, drunk sex, a little aggressive, me taking forever to finish—but when he arrived all those worries drifted away, as he was perfect as far as I could see and he had a good set of lungs to holler at the world. It could have been any of the next few nights, though.

We woke up in a headachy fog. I stumbled naked to the bathroom and made myself throw up and felt a little better for it. I then remembered hearing Dory do the same in the middle of the night, though whether hers was self-induced I can't be sure. Aside from the physical symptoms, we were both feeling the blues that used to only follow a good, long drunk. We said little that morning, showered, and got dressed. I brought glasses of water from the bathroom and we slowly drank as much as we could. Outside, we hung the panniers on our bikes, strapped on our packs, and headed down toward the hospital to see Terry. Trucks rushed by us, loud and close. It occurred to me that this was the first time I'd ever ridden with a hangover. Two sides of my life came together with queasy and heart-palpitating results.

The hospital, now in the daytime, was a squat, yellow brick trio of buildings, acres of corn surrounding it. We signed in at the nurses' station and spoke with the old doctor who told us that the concussion was not as bad as they'd feared, that Terry could be released the next day.

"He'll need help for a while," the doctor said. "Eating, bathing."

"Yeah, yeah," I said, "of course."

The doctor looked untrustingly at my beat-up, bedraggled ass.

In his room, Terry was propped slightly in the bed, an IV drip in his arm. There was a bandage over his forehead and squares of gauze on his face and chest. Both legs were casted and suspended. His right shoulder was wrapped. The sight was terrifying. His face was stubbled with beard. Beneath that his skin was gaunt. He looked like he was coming off one of our old lost weekends. There in the hospital room I realized how valuable Terry had been to us. All these years, as I judged and clucked my tongue at my old cohorts who had kept at the game of indulgence, I saved Terry for myself. Dory and I both did. We'd kept him and ignored all of his behavior, excusing it as some joke, everything that made Terry Terry. We lived through him, forgetting our ten-thirty bedtimes and flirtations with veganism, forgetting the goddamn bikes. We could once again, for our moments with him, mix drinks and snort lines, slip cigarettes from hardpacks and joints from pouches and light them, taking in big, harsh lungfuls of smoke. This was what he did for us. And after he was gone, we could sit for a moment and say, "Boy, that Terry sure needs to clean himself up," before turning to the news or talking about what to name our children.

Terry raised his left hand about three inches off the bed and made something like a circular motion. "I'm all fucked up," he slurred.

"You'll be all right," I said.

"It's just the drugs," Dory said.

"Yeah," Terry said. Without moving his head, he looked over toward the window. "Is it today still?"

"No," I said. "It's tomorrow. You have to stay one more day."

"Ah, that's OK," he said, flopping his hand down to the mattress. "I'm all fucked up."

His food came and we helped him eat three spoons of applesauce, and then watched him fall asleep.

At the nurses' station, we borrowed a phone book and called a rental car company and booked a wagon big enough for our bikes. I hung up and the nurse said to us, "Police are saying suicide." She looked up from her computer screen. "The pilot. They made an announcement earlier this morning. Said he wrote a letter. His wife left him and he couldn't make his mortgage."

So it wasn't chance. It wasn't an improbably freak occurrence. There was, instead, according to this nurse, a mind behind the act. There was no accident at all. It was meant and purposeful. It felt like this news was supposed to change how we understood the incident, but, I thought, what could the difference possibly be to us? We, who happened into the situation, who had no idea who the players were, who didn't even know where we were—what did it matter to us whether it was a mechanical disaster or the will of a devastated man? Either way it left no control in our useless hands.

The nurse smacked the clipboard on the counter and I jumped. "Sign out," she said.

"We're coming back," I said defensively. "We're coming back tomorrow to get him."

"It's fine," Dory said, and wrote our names next to our names.

The rental car people came, and we loaded our bags and bikes and began driving northeast. Soon we were on I-55, cruising at 70, 75 miles per hour, the radio nattering on, neither of us speaking. It was another hot one, and getting hotter. We rolled up the windows and put on the AC and I had trouble seeing the world outside as real. It was as if I was passing through an imaginary landscape that neither touched nor affected me. I sat back into the cushy driver's seat, my right foot barely pressing on the gas pedal.

We got to the city in no time, but I wasn't ready to be back. I didn't want to see our apartment, our furniture, the way I knew the light would be coming in the kitchen window. I was about to head north on 90, toward our place off Fullerton, but Dory said, "No, keep going. Go on up to Lake Shore."

Relieved, I did so without questioning. Dory directed me, with slow movements of her hand or a whispered word, down Lake Shore Drive all the way to Hyde Park. We stopped at Promontory Point and looked out at the lake. There were few people out: a couple homeless-looking men, joggers going by, mothers in yoga pants pushing strollers.

"There's a meeting at eight," I said. "The place near Belmont."

"Yeah," Dory said, and nodded her head. Then she grabbed her bag from the back and there in the passenger seat she tugged off her pants and shirt and wriggled into her kit. "All right," I said and did the same. Neither of us had checked our bikes since we hit the deck the day before, so we flipped them over and went to work. We checked our cranks and cables, spun the wheels and tested that the derailleurs were doing their job, that the brakes weren't rubbing. The chains were good. Out on the trail the fresh lake waters slapped and smacked against the rocks, tossing up a fine spray. The moisture on the air woke me up. It was a Thursday afternoon, but the notion of days and times of day felt somewhat silly just then, the way an earlier argument can seem ridiculous after making love.

We rode north past the museums and the aquarium, the old Meigs Field, then Navy Pier with its Ferris wheel turning joyfully, mindlessly. The skyline came more into focus, gaining detail with each push on our pedals. It's a beautiful path along the lakefront, smooth and wide. As we got further north and passed the big beaches, the trail became crowded with joggers, skaters, other cyclists; Dory and I slowed and let our legs move in languid circles. Everyone looked to be in love with the city and the summer. To our right, the water was green-brown, as it always is, and I thought of how many animals and plants lived below the surface, how teeming with little bitty creatures it was. I'd read an article that said we only understand about half of what's in the ocean. There are hundreds of thousands of fish and plants and microbes that we haven't imagined yet. But they're there, living and eating and reproducing. I thought about the small, motivated little things crawling through the sand. I thought about the dirt of the cornfields we'd ridden past, about all the systems of life happening invisibly, food chains and splitting cells. And inside of us—all the blood and veins and specialized organs. I thought about how little I understood of my own body: how many bones I had, what my spleen does, how smell works. What I had done to my body through all the years of chemical abuse. I thought about the night before and my sperm and genetic dispositions, about traits passed on from one generation of animal to another.

When we got to Montrose Harbor, Dory stopped. I pulled beside her and saw she was crying. "It was a plane and a truck," she said. "What the fuck are we supposed to do about that?" She pulled the collar of her jersey up and wiped her eyes. "We'll have to take care of him," she said. "He'll be helpless."

She was talking about Terry. And of course she wasn't.

We rode back to the car and then drove to our place. We slept and then woke and made love. We ordered in food from the corner and ate on the couch, watching the evening news. Later that night, we went into the all-purpose room at an Episcopal church and looked at our watches and announced how long it had been since our last drinks.

We picked up Terry from the hospital the next day and set him up on our sofa, where he stayed for four weeks, seeming to enjoy the attention and care we gave him. He fell into our routine, minus the cycling of course. Surprisingly, he never said a word about wanting a drink or even a cigarette. I caught a faint whiff of vodka coming off him a few times and wondered who might be visiting in the hours Dory and I were at work, but mostly he lived soberly and uncomplaining. When Dory and I had gotten married, Terry showed up late to the wedding, obviously drunk. Our new friends, ones we had met at meetings, tried to talk to him about control and powerlessness, but he only laughed and clapped them on the back and walked away. Now with him on our couch, I came back to this and wondered if there was something he knew that I never would. He was the first person we told about the baby, when it was just nestled in Dory's womb.

One night Dory had gone to bed and Terry and I were watching TV and he said, "I wish I had gotten to keep that piece of wing."

"Yeah?" I said. "Souvenir?"

"Oh, man," he said.

A headlight swung in from the street and someone on the TV said something and I realized that after he left on his own two legs, we would probably never see Terry again. There in our living room I felt a sort of mourning weight on my chest over how much I would miss him, how much Dory and I both would, and how hard it was going to be adjusting to a life without him.

OFF THE MAP

by Mary Stone Dockery

In late July, Kansas moans beneath the weight of its sun. Plants crinkle like paper, leaves crunching green as they curl into jagged tongues. In my Kansas, it's always summer. Always sweat. Always bottle rockets zipping out of fingers. Wheat beer. Always hangovers on beds without sheets, open windows, mosquitoes slapping against our thighs and sticking. Everything sticks to everything else. Your hand sticks to my hand, my hand sticks to your shoulder. When we sit on the porch, drinking our beer, imagining the lives of those driving by, moisture drips from my wrist to the floorboards, and we swear to each other it hisses and a drop of steam rises for us. Kansas is in that drop of steam, Kansas with its muddy rivers, its dry hills, red sand. There's a sway of guitars, this sense of emptiness, the rhythm of flicking cigarettes into the charred grass. Kansas with its wind. In your Kansas, summer is a weapon of opportunity, and you use it against me. You crawl with your tongue over my body in prayer, your teeth hot, you claim me, saying this is how love is supposed to be—as if each melting finger and each swollen sigh might somehow help us ignore this Kansas, this heat, this death. Yet my Kansas sips cool drinks, looks up at the empty stars, and lets your fingers dig and dig.

*

We go to parties, coolers filled with cheap beer and kegs. It's as if beer is the only thing in the world worth attaining. At Burn-Out Bridge, we build a small fire because we can, because the gravel road has emptied for the night and we want shadows to flicker over us like soft tongues. The others drive in, sit on quilts and lie back staring at the space above them, swinging their hands to smack away bugs that only they can see. We stare into the fire, its warmth uneasy, purposeful, as if it might reach out and claw ashes from my skin.

You reach for me again, like you always do. Something about Kansas draws you toward me. You tell me it's all the stars moving in the sky, how when you are around me the scent of lilacs and burning novas pulls you to the twang in my skin, how my fingers reach with wheat and soybeans, your childhood memories.

Each time you touch me, something inside breaks into glass fragments piercing the inside of my lungs. It isn't my breathing I worry about. It's the way your hands knead me, work me into soft shapes.

I tell you about my dreams. Dark shadows twisting over my body. The way trees move as if spiders, bark aching over ground. How I dream of large hands lifting me by the neck and swinging me like a twig, tossing me across into muddy water. Suddenly there is quicksand. I tell you this is my Kansas, this quicksand dream, where my limbs are always moving, and you tell me I'm wrong, that no Kansas looks like this, even a Kansas in a dream, even though through our eyes it's always scorched and dreary, you tell me that Kansas has its own oceans, that all we have to do is find them.

We drink beer into the night and stare into empty spaces until someone starts snoring. I follow you to the other road, where we hide by a wall of corn, by now it has grown taller than us both.

I am drunk and swaying. You touch my hip and push a finger against it. Kiss my neck. The world sways. A Kansas breeze sighs around us. We find Kansas in your hands on my hip, in the wind that lifts my hair around my face, in the scent of smoke rising and rising, in me pushing you away.

The spaces we stare into start to overlap. Everything is empty now. We decide that we need to make noise, that this summer's silence has invaded our breath.

We hop in your Bronco and head through your neighborhood, driving over mailboxes. Each crash sounds like a sudden moment of panic, then fades into sounds of cicadas, into wind. At each house we leave a mangled box, sometimes a wooden one, sometimes a metal one, but all of them fall, revealing their instability, their flaws. We love the sound, and this is our new Kansas, mailboxes crunching against your hood. The sound of tires spinning out of yards. Our laughter, and the silence after as we smoke.

We build up to stealing roadwork signs and street signs. One night we steal enough orange and red signs to block a friend's driveway. Another night, we climb the street sign out by the Platte River and saw for hours. We want tangible things to take with us, to shove under beds.

Your Kansas fades into a deep black color, sadness, brown, burning leaves. The flood has taken most of your family's land and we row a boat to the farm where your grandfather built a hill before building a house on top of it. When we get there the house has become its own island. Around, the Missouri River has danced and spread, licking out across the land. We see this Kansas as infested with sleep. With heat. Mosquitoes the size of fists squirm through the air. When we anchor the boat, we find that frogs and toads have infested the island, and most of them have died belly-up where they wither and crinkle beneath the sun. We spend the day kicking frogs back into the river, watching their bodies float off in currents that seem to spread into every direction. If only we had a proper way to bury them, you say. You imagine pearls and Sunday morning church with your grandma, but we both know that this may be the last summer your grandparents live through, that this flood could push them into places beyond the Catholic scent of sidewalks, that what will be left is rust and corrosion bleeding from tractors and old barns into the cracked land. For now, we count frogs like they are stars, watch them drift into blurred constellations, and we fall against the porch weary, waiting for the water to become new again.

Someone told me once that Kansas was the center of the world.

On maps, it's close to the center of the United States, yet my eyes always pull toward the Missouri River. It slits the country down the middle, hardly even a squiggle. Hardly even a cut. And yet, from the surface, the Missouri is a carotid artery that bleeds and bleeds. Every few years, it opens again, hemorrhaging into Kansas and Missouri, not worried about borders. During summer, we worry about borders because alcohol is more available in Missouri. We can buy beer in gas stations. Because we are close to the border, we don't worry about liquor stores closing early in Kansas. In our Kansas, alcohol is only a state line away.

When we drive to Missouri, it's always after eleven and we take the roads our parents used to take, the old twisting highways and gravel roads. We drive with all the windows down. Sometimes we stop to take turns riding on the hood of the car, stretched flat on our stomachs, holding on to what we can with our thin fingers.

You swerve on purpose and I drive too slow. We love the wind, the air. The openness. We drive because we want to move. Moving is like living. We have not yet learned what lies out there, beyond this middle earth. Our Kansas is stagnant, hot. Kansas is flat plains, not the center of everything. When we bring our Kansases together, we can smell the greens of tornadoes, sawdust, 100-year-old barns falling and falling.

When we stop long enough to feel sober, Kansas is sideways. We can feel ourselves sliding right off this map. We feel as though our feet are filled with water. It's muddy in here. The walls are like chalk. The fingernails brittle enough to break against thighs.

In Kansas, things are always inevitable. It's the word we always use to talk about our future. We can predict parts of the future, know that Kansas is there, even if it waves before us like a gloomy mirage, we can see it, the Kansas sky doming over us blue then black, an open bruise. It's unavoidable. It's expected. You tell me I will have babies and eat lots of meat. I will gain weight and my Kansas summers will weigh more and more with each child that slips from my body.

We enjoy the routine of our Kansas summer. We lay up at the moon tower, drinking booze, toasting the inevitability of our dreams and colors fading. This old shirt you wear, it will fade from blue to gray. The sandals I wear will splinter beneath my feet until one day I walk out of my own shoes onto molten asphalt.

The moon hangs in the sky as if from a noose. Sideways, you say. We talk about what is expected. In our Kansas we party, and tonight another one happens to turn on down the lane. When we show up at the party, the lights are so bright you stand in a corner in the living room and face the wall. You are used to being looked at, to being called weird. It's inevitable. Otherwise, you'll start a fight, just to feel a fist against something soft. In the presence of others, it's inevitable for me to talk and smile and feel like a ghost inside myself. Boys flirt with me. I am wearing a shirt that glitters in the light.

Somehow, you and I end up outside, alone.

We drink faster when we talk about this inevitability. You are fated to me. My hip bones are fated to yours. We are meant to be found here at the side of a house, you pushing into me beneath the dark before I can tell you no, pushing me against the peeling paint. Flecks of paint stick to my back, my neck. You smell like gasoline and matches. You are bound to take me like this, quickly, before anyone walks around the corner, covering my yelps with aching kisses. I am fated to fall to the grass, my panties torn at the side, dangling from my body like a hangnail, like nothing, until someone turns the corner and laughs at us, the light falling just right on the pointing finger. This is my Kansas, this wet grass sticking to my wrists like stitches. My Kansas is you adjusting your belt in the soft glow of moonlight and tossing an empty beer bottle onto the gravel drive next to us; you brace for it to shatter, glass blooms spearing the ground, then leave me to clean up our mess.

They begin adding mansions to a nearby neighborhood. Someone goes on television claiming us as an All-American City. On television, our Kansas is suddenly colorful, filled with sidewalks that wind from one neighborhood to another, beneath oak leaves, sidewalks that bend and give, where bodies disappear and reappear different somehow, changed, overwhelmed with sweat.

The mansions are a sharp contrast to the photos of your grandparents' farm. We stopped looking over the photos when your aunt sent one of a dead fawn floating near the flagpole at the house, one leg clutching grass still water-free. Its eyes gray swirls, reflective gauze, all mirage. The Missouri muddy and smoldering around it. We burned the photos a couple days later at Burn-Out Bridge, tossing each one into the bonfire. We watched the photos crinkle, blacken, and wilt like bruised flowers, the burned train bridge like a blackened door in the backdrop.

The mansions they build are empty at night, so that's when we go to them. We are like ghosts inside the half-built frames. We imagine what lives will live in them, what dark silhouettes will slink along the halls. We build the houses. Bamboo floors in the living room. Floating bookshelves. A secret door from one bedroom to the next. A glass wall that glows purple in the bathroom. Canopy beds like your grandmother used to have, to remind you of your childhood. Lots of wood and ceramic pottery and quilts. Lots of dangling lights and soft blue paint. The mansions we build are rustic and expensive, part Kansas, part something we have never seen. Part of us wants to live in each mansion we build, and part of us wants to mark the unfinished walls with our names using black paint, erasing the lives we've created in one big sweep of an arm, their future, someone else's inevitable.

We sit on coolers and drink beer, playing a radio into the dark. These songs will always remind of sawdust and summer, remind me of your arm around my shoulder, your fingers pinching my nipple too hard. A shriek. You sing into my ear with the windows rolled down, tell me I am stellar. The mansions remind us how small our Kansas is, how far away we are from the rest of the world. Yet we break in to build, becoming architects, idealists. Your breath is always cutting the air around my neck.

In our Kansas, it's always summer. You are there, sweating over me. You move in slow circles and I think sometimes that I can't touch you, that you are too far above me. Are you moving toward the moon? Are you lifting me with you or am I falling? I don't let you hear, because you would laugh at me and the slow motion would stop and the quicksand would swirl back in.

In your Kansas, it's all booze and bellies rubbing.

In my Kansas, it's about inevitability. It's about listening to the sound of the wind. It's about forgetting where I am for a moment or many moments. About pain. Ache. Fingers circling the air. Bottle rockets. Whistles. The sound of your breath. Crawling through your window. It's being outside and smelling like leaves and sap. My Kansas is us opening and closing our fists at night just to keep moving. It's spinning in a dress. Sunflowers. Blue. Islands. Muddy water and rust. Floods repeating. It's the pictures that linger when your eyes close. Blink and only green remains.

ZERO GAINS

by Bonnie Nadzam

YOU SAY YOU'D LIKE A STORY for the ages, but you should know we live a little outside of time out here. Out here is the Nebraska panhandle, leveled as immaculately by wind and the spin of the planet as if it'd been planed by a master carpenter. As if the raw materials of the earth had yet to be assembled into their most perfect arrangement of signs. We is me and my boy Avery. Will Grover and his girl Jenny are the nearest neighbors, in the last standing two-story sod house in the state, about a half-mile beyond our tree line to the west. This concerns them as well.

Myself, I never much took stories at face value. There's the one about the hand of God interrupting the feast of Belshazzar— the one Laura and I argued about in the unbearably hot days of early July. Palace of sand-colored stone in the midst of a fertile alluvial plain, dark sky, glassless windows lit up by firelight. It's early on the night Babylon falls to the Persians and everybody's drunk, having a swinging old time when suddenly in the great hall five bluish-white fingers shape themselves out of nothing, horrifying all the company, profaned goblets lifted halfway to their purple mouths as the hand writes across the wall, above the light of the candles so that everyone can see. The king trembles, his beard stained with wine. The gates of hell are opening before him, the next hour paved as neat and straight as a boulevard of ancient stones.

A story like this was easy for Laura to follow. It all happened years ago, she'd said. She turned to the globe on the bookshelf behind her and pointed to the exact place—these days just a tell of dust and human debris in the Iraqi desert between the Tigris and Euphrates rivers. See, she'd said, there was a king, his palace wall, all of his guests, the hand of God, and the wise man—Daniel—to translate what the hand had written: doom was at hand and the days of glory and riot were numbered. Before midnight, the city had fallen and the skull of the irreverent king had been smashed to bits by his own subjects.

"The writing on the wall, Ben." She sat on the edge of her desk. "That's what they say." It was the hottest summer on record in Box Butte County, and Avery's eighth birthday. The earth shimmered in every distance. Crabapples baked on their branches and fell like green stones. The meadowlarks had disappeared and there were strange, low, whooping birdcalls. Grasshoppers collected by the hundreds in the bristling dead wheatgrass, blinking and trembling like a single body. Scarab beetles drew thin cuneiform inscriptions in dirt as fine and dry as mustard powder. Yellow dishes of lawn circled the base of each tree. At night we sucked on ice cubes on the porch and watched heat-lightning fan out behind the distant black cutouts of yellow western pine.

Laura held the Bible open in her lap. I looked out the window and across the road at a flat pan of dirt so hard and sere it glittered in the violent light. The tidiness with which she read made it easy to see how every person, word, and act in the Book of Daniel corresponded to something in our lives. The ancient barricaded city was our sleepy peeling white farmhouse tucked behind soft green bands of grassy fields. The quick and humiliating fall of the empire was the birth of our son. In both her biblical and Nebraskan versions, God was the same: an angry yet benevolent self living outside of us, whose messages we were to read in the wind and in the scattered wreckage of our lives so that we might navigate our miserable earthly days guided by the certain promise of something better. Of a new life. One we would all live later. Some other time.

"But what if this is the hand of God?" I'd said. "The house. The katydid in the pickle jar. Avery. You."

"Avery the hand of God? Avery who can't speak or think or remember to breathe is your hand of God?"

But Avery does speak. When from the bed he reaches up to touch the ends of his mother's bright hair, that is a word. When he throws back his beautiful white-blond head and looks up at the stars that I tell him are his cousins, that too is a word. His breath on the window glass. His fingerprints in the yellow grease in a pan of cold chicken broth. But I don't say any of this. Instead I tell Laura the boy is as pure as children come. And that she knows it. And that he loves her.

She was dark around the eyes and in the hollows of her cheeks. "He doesn't know what love is. He doesn't know what his own hands are." I looked down at my hands, turned them over before me.

No words on the matter were going to change her feeling that a judgment had been passed upon us—one that meant our lives would continue to diminish in happiness as Avery grew, eventually ending in the same deteriorating house on the same eroded and fruitless farm to which we'd moved with our books and notepads when we were young enough to believe that a hundred pages of verse a year were all we owed the world. We'd asked for nothing more in return than the space and time to write them. But in her mind Laura was an insulated woman, a complete system that took suffering as a warning that she should adjust her circumstances.

"It's not as if we've accumulated so much wealth and live so riotously that we have to be humbled," I told her.

"This is supposed to make me feel better?"

"What exactly is it you think we're being punished for?"

She closed the Bible carefully, set it beside her and stood up. "For this," she said. She threw all the drafts and paper on her desk toward me. The space between us erupted in white. She threw Emily Dickinson's collected works and they spat a powder of dried flowers when they hit the wall beyond which Avery was napping. "And for this," she said, throwing John Crowe Ransom, the sonnets of Shakespeare and Donne.

I left to check on Avery, as clean and pretty as a boy carved out of freckled marble in his little blue bed. I kissed his forehead. I kissed his chin. I found Laura in the kitchen, crying in a heap on the cracked linoleum. "You can quit," I told her. "You can do something else."

Her breaking point came the next day. It was 106 degrees. Ragged cowbirds perched on the rusting spools of fence wire like harbingers of a slow brown death. The house windows and metal gutters blazed with white light. Laura and I were out near the road spraying shipping containers with the ceramic coating they needed before they'd be ready to resell. In the back, in the shade, Avery peeled off all his clothes and underwear and sat on a huge pile of sand, liquid with red ants. He must have simply sensed that Being—if you took your clothes off in the daylight—burned from the inside out. We found him riveted to the earth, howling. Laura was furious. By the middle of the month the heat broke. Cool rains restored the grasses and iridescent blue prairie violets. All the familiar birds came back, and Laura left.

There was a place in Lincoln where Avery could go, she said. She might return—though never geographically, never to Nebraska—if we sent him there. Avery, who was to be our shining little cowboy, in a complex of urban hospital buildings and tended by strangers and swallowed up by a sad little envelope of mute and pale-faced children. They'd schedule his playtime. They'd give him TV.

*

The mistake in this story, the one I'm telling you now, began when I stopped my car out where all our mailboxes line up on a single block of the boundless west Nebraskan grid. Wayne and Millie Hargraves were giving away mutt pups out of the back of their station wagon, and I took two of them—free as rain—for Avery. Something to fill the space his mother left when she went to seek her fortune, as it were. Every night since she'd gone I'd checked the boy in his sleep—checked him for breath—at ten p.m. and four in the morning. Too often I found him awake, bewildered, blankets kicked off as though he'd been betrayed by their softness and comfort, as though in his sleep he suddenly realized they were no help at all. On the wall beside him shadows of leaves rising and falling with the slow pulsing breeze. The little case of his ribs rising and falling with the shadows of the leaves.

The puppies' bellies were slick and pink and radiated heat, their little teeth razor sharp. They cried like baby seals and their breath stank softly of warm skunk spray. They climbed all over the boy. They puked on his skinny Wranglers. He stared at them with rapt joy, fondling them and pulling them back again and again into his lap. Because we weren't expecting puppies, I unloaded the groceries and tore up a few slices of white bread and pieces of bologna for Avery to hand feed them under the hickory tree. He was all teeth and gums, his stone-blue eyes rolling up into the tree leaves and to one puppy, then the next, then up again. Eyelashes thick and white as caked sand. I joined him there, with cold chicken and early garden cucumbers. Lemonade for him, a can of beer for me. It was—all things considered—a day full and perfect. Avery laughed and laughed. I was thinking we'd make a summer of picnics and the weaselly pups. Tomatoes in a few weeks. Corn when that came up.

The mistake completed itself when I set up the puppies in the old punched-in potato barn for the night, walled them in with wood crates and old fence boards and loose field stones. Sometime around eleven the coyotes found them. I will not describe to you what I heard. By the time I got out there barefoot in my pajama pants and swinging a rake, it was over. I cleaned up what was left, the full moon pouring its watery sheets of light through the broken boards. The world was warm and thick and soft. The grass was lavender green and the trees were blue, finely calligraphed with shadow. The million-noted crickets lit up the ten thousand corners of the yard. It was the most beautiful night of the summer. For the first time in weeks, Avery slept like the dead. So now, I thought, laying myself down alone in my marriage bed, now the boy will make his headlong spin into loss. And I'll tell you something: I hoped for it. If it was terrible enough, it might register in him some sense of his own suffering. It might wake him up. By ten he'd have the mind of a toddler. By thirty he'd be reading in earnest. These terrible pictures we dream.

Of course the potato barn was the first place he ran after I dressed him in the morning. I set myself in an aluminum lawn chair at the rotten mouth of the long skinny barn and he went in. It's a narrow building, like a tiny house stretched improbably backward in space, designed so trucks could back way into it, dump a load of potatoes, and continue filling it from the rear, one load at a time. The roof is mostly fallen in and weeds and grass have cracked apart the stone foundation. The clapboard is split and whitened by sun and wind, nails orange with rust. It's hard to imagine it clean-lined and filled to the blonde rafters with fat white potatoes. The last of its vertebrae are cracked and separating slowly into a rubbish of metal, stone, and wood. I probably ought to have it razed. Avery came out minutes later, face blank, and stood before me.

"Coyotes," I told him. "I'm sorry." I lifted my empty hands

and my eyes filled with heat. I took his hands, his wrists, elbows, shoulders, head. I held his ears and kissed his mouth. "It's the price we pay for being in these bodies." He stared at me. "They're gone," I said.

He smiled.

"Gone," I said again.

He went back into the barn and I went into the basement for my old hard hat and leather gloves from road crew when Avery was a baby. I found the boy in the barn on his hands and knees, his pale hair in a shaft of light. He was feeling around in the shadows for puppies. I gave him the hard hat and helped him pull on the gloves for sifting through the splintered wood and rusted nails. He would have to wear himself out to understand that what had once been puppies had become looking for puppies, which wasn't nearly as glorious or interesting a way to spend the last weeks of summer.

We spent the whole day out there, my boy alone in the ruins of the weird, elongated nightmare house and me in the lawn chair staring into its grainy blue shadows. I wanted to be right outside the door when he came out, when he gave up. I wanted to check his face for some glimmer of recognition, for surrender, for grief, for confusion. For any sign at all. Plovers and black-throated sparrows circled the dirt around my chair looking for millet, leaving faint patterns of interlocking feet in the dust. Four dozen times Avery approached me and raised up his gloves, palms out, and spread his legs to mirror his hands in a nonsense rhyme. A meaningless gesture. A capital X. Then he ducked back into the dark. Did he even remember what he was looking for?

I should have stopped him. Hauled him out of there. Put a hot dog in his hand. Put him in the car and taken him out for an ice cream. But I sat in that chair, still as wood, eyes pointed at the doorway. In the morning, we'd stop. I'd drive him into Alliance. We'd spend the day on the highway, eat cheeseburgers, walk across the derelict farms. Stop at the pawn store in the tiny town pinned to the prairie by lampposts and a Shell station sign. But I didn't move from the chair. The sun made a low arc across the sky. The planet spun. We ate nothing. Drank nothing. Found nothing in the barn. Avery wet his pants. A cold breeze washed through the trees in late afternoon and by evening gentle fingers of rain were brushing through the wooly fabric of dry earth and grass. We took baths and Avery slept in the hard hat.

I was prepared to spend another day, the rest of the month, the next forty years of my life waiting in the lawn chair for Avery, but the following morning I watched, baffled, as he emerged carrying a shining red apple, cupped like an egg in the big dirty work gloves. His face broke open as wide and as happy as if he'd found his puppies, or as if it'd been an apple he was seeking all along. It kept him busy all morning. He set it on the windowsill.

"Yes," I said. "Balance."

He set it on the ground.

"Earth," I said.

He pressed it to his cheek, rubbed his lips over it, licked it, pushed it into his pants.

"I know," I told him. "I know." We drove to Alliance anyway and he held the apple out the window, turning it in the rushing wind. "Speed," I said. He handed it to me. "Father," I said. "I'm your father." We sat outside at the burger stand that had been Laura's favorite and I ordered vanilla malts and double-hand-battered onion rings—her favorite—but Avery wanted the apple. He gnawed on it. Held it out before his face to examine. Gnawed on it. "You're consuming it," I told him. "You're turning yourself into a bright little apple."

In the morning Avery came out of the potato barn with a big silver hubcap in his hands. It was a hubcap I recognized. I started keeping an eye out in the rising tide of slough grass, but there was no one.

It was a day of hubcap and light, Avery's new discovery flashing like a heliograph in the sun, like an unblinking metal eye, a miniature UFO. He threw the hubcap and it rolled and spun like a giant coin. "Geometry," I told him. "Circles. Wheels. Rotation. Silver. Daylight. Mirror. Spin." He didn't even look up.

The hickory trees, the wild petunias and the den of kit foxes across the road and the hollow dripping music of the mourning doves. The down of tall grasses and green bursts of dropseed. On a bad day they are symbols. The puddled rain, my boy and our filthy sneakers and the splintered ribs of the hay barn exist someplace else—in a parallel world of pure insight—as lines on a page. They are a tissue of poetic fragments to be collected, read, and finally understood. On such days I look upon my presence here with Avery and I look upon forgiving Laura as private possessions, with real weight and a certain heat and which I keep in my front shirt pocket beside my bit of pencil. I take the shape of an expectant man who will be rewarded in this life or the next for decoding this confusion of languages. In leaves of dying pin oaks that rust and cling to their iron-limbed branches, in the script of tire tracks pressed into mud, in earthworms dried and flattened into hieroglyphs on the flagstone patio when sudden sun follows hard rain, in every detail of the natural world I discover a cipher, a temporarily insoluble riddle, and so I must memorize them and store them away for the moment when some Being who has been observing my life as if it really were a story finally asks me the consummative question about...what? The maps of raised green veins on the backs of new leaves? The fine white roots of dead hostas that run through garden soil like human nerves? Because of a lifetime of dutiful cataloging, the answer will rise to the surface of my brain, and because of a lifetime of dutiful reading, I will have only the most exquisite language with which to explain myself.

Thus have I sometimes considered the world. It's a much trickier business, expecting nothing. Glimpsing then sustaining the awesome recognition that there is no one and nothing out there keeping track of accumulated merit. That there is nothing to read. That Avery's words—the hubcap pressed to his bare belly in the sun, the apple deliberately carried out and set in the rain— have the quickness and heat for which my imagination is always reaching, reaching, reaching but which is forever set a hairsbreadth out of imagination's grasp.

I went out early to watch the fields, to see who'd come. What they might bring. The last of the white stars faded and the day slowly absorbed the paper face of the moon like a soft blue cloth soaking up a small white spill. The potato barn was half silver in wet grass and dew. Barn swallows shifted in their cupped nests of mud. I watched Grover's girl coming from a quarter mile away, straight through the soaking grass and through the collapsing rail fence. She's a head shorter than Avery and perhaps not quite so beautiful. Smart. A year or two older. She was carrying a lump in her arms. I crept through the last film of dark toward the house and left her to her business.

I woke and dressed Avery and in the kitchen I fried bananas and toasted bread and poured cold milk and we ate. I helped him with his gloves and hard hat and got to the dishes, watching from the window as he carried his next discovery out of the potato barn and into the daylight: an exhaust manifold from the same 1964 Ford Galaxy as the hubcap. The old parts car had been corroding in the weeds beside Grover's shop since before Laura and I had discovered our little hermitage. Avery set the exhaust manifold beside the hubcap and howled until I figured out he wanted his apple. I brought him one from the refrigerator, but it was green and he refused it. He sat blank-faced between the exhaust manifold and the hubcap in the dirt beneath the hickory tree as if he could sense they were all a part of something. As if he knew he was missing something essential. The apple would reoccur to him and he would start in howling all over again. Why the apple and not his mother? The apple and not the puppies? At noon, I called Grover.

"She's going to clear my yard of this rubbish once and for all," he laughed. "Long as she has incentive."

"I'll give that some thought."

"I'll tell her to bring over another apple."

I thanked him. I didn't think Avery would understand that he was an apple behind.

On a stump beside the door to the potato barn the next morning I left Laura's old illustrated copy of *Huck Finn*. It was gone before breakfast, after which Avery came out with a new apple and a small black cone. It was the ignition coil from the Galaxy. He set his loot in the dirt with the hubcap and the exhaust manifold and tipped his head back, mouth hanging open, gulping the morning. Inside the coil, in a car that works, electricity pulses through spiraling copper wire. The circuit is broken again and again between points in the distributor as the coil's electromagnetic field collapses and surges through a mile's worth of infinitely fine wire. Twenty-five thousand turns of it. Enough to keep a Ford Galaxy running. From the outside the coil is only a little black cylinder, four inches long, an inch and a half wide and tapered down into a nozzle. In Avery's world beneath the hickory tree, it rests on the middle of the hubcap, the apple balanced on top of it. "Center," I told him, and stopped. Electricity. Distance. Heat. Metal. Varnish. Restore. Rainstorm. Heartache. Innermost. Worms. He picked up the apple and set it down again thirty, forty, fifty times in an hour. He circled the little pile with the exhaust manifold in his hands, uncertain.

On the stump I left *The Odyssey* and one of the bookmarks Laura made with a dozen skinny braided ribbons—a long-term investment for Jenny Grover. I left a thin gold bracelet Laura forgot beneath the bathroom sink, strung with clear blue beads. The day Jenny delivered the entire—and heavy—driver's seat from the Galaxy, Avery and I drove into town and I bought a liter of brown whiskey for Grover, left it on the stump beside a cowgirl hat pinned with an artificial sunflower which Laura used to wear when she gardened. In the basement I found the spade she used to turn over earth, the hand claw she used to aerate, a handful of bulbs she never planted—they'd be appropriate for Grover's girl in September and perhaps a forgotten surprise the following spring. I found a broken kite with a rainbow-striped tail and a needle and spool of poultry thread that would fix it. I made a little pile, and as it shrank, Avery's grew.

By the middle of August Avery had assembled a tower of car parts facing the driver's seat. I watched him from the front where I was sanding steel siding to prep another container for paint, Avery's bright head as soft and white as whorled milkweed against the grass. He would sit in the seat, gaze upon the tower, stand, move the muffler out an inch from behind the steering column, and seat himself again. He had favorites, I could tell. He set the exhaust manifold on its metal legs and stroked it like a giant rust-bitten spider. Tenderness, I didn't say. Contact.

The rocker arms went to bed with him every night, no matter what place they took in the tower at the end of the day. He would carefully disassemble until he could get to them. Every evening I watched him carry this beloved part over the lawn, over the long bars of tree shadows pointing nowhere. In a car that runs as it should, the rocker arms—lifted by pushrods pushed by lifters—open valves that allow fuel into the cylinders. Sparkplugs ignite the fuel and the explosion forces the pistons to move, which rotates the crankshaft, which turns the camshaft, which pushes the lifters, which lifts the pushrods, which allow the rocker arms to open the valve....Though most of these parts are unattached, they gently propel each other in a perfect mechanical circle of power and motion. In our life the rocker arms were—analogous to something? Synonymous? Anagogical? They looked like a dozen giant finger bones—or more vertebrae—all lined up in a row. They looked like the smooth mettle of a huge piano. In my ridiculousness and in my despair I'm sure I gave them every consideration, saw them in every possible light except the last light of day. On his way up the stairs one evening Avery played them like a soft clicking instrument, as if he were the fire that makes engines run, tires spin, matter drive itself over the earth at ten and forty and eighty and a hundred miles per hour. That puts wind in girls' hair. I selected a dead silver wristwatch from Laura's pile and brought it to the stump. It only needed a battery. Jenny could wear it to school.

*

We had a terrific thunderstorm the last Sunday afternoon in August. It came in on a cold wind and rent open the sky, stripped the smaller trees of their leaves and loosed boards from the barn that lifted and spun away in the distance like helicopter seeds. As fast as the storm came it disappeared, trailing a gauze of clouds. Avery and I went outside among the puddles and earthworms and I could see beyond Grover's tree line a colored speck of kite whipping in the blown light.

There is no new matter in our game, only new arrangements. The book on the girl's nightstand instead of in Laura's old office. The rocker arms supporting a dead field mouse in a small cloth sack on Monday, the apple on Tuesday, and set clumsily beneath the hubcap on Wednesday. The weight of our story in your hands.

THE GARDEN OF
EARTHLY DELIGHTS

by Gina Frangello

THE MISTRESS WATCHES JAMES APPROACH her car, his fur-collared vintage coat flapping around him in a way that reminds her of England. Back when she was a girl, the word "metrosexual" did not exist, but the boys she knew in her youth were often this way: lithe and effete, with a ruined, decadent air battling a watery bookishness that usually won out by middle-age. In her formative years, though—the late 1980s—androgyny helped get you laid, so she is hardwired to find it sexy. James gets into the car, cigarette still ablaze, and she thinks of Ethan's asthma and wants to bat the burning stick from his hand. Then, "Hello, darling," he says, affecting a British accent, his strange ESP at work. He hugs her, smelling of cold and smoke and faded cologne that may have come with the coat. "God, you're so tiny," he says pulling away. "You feel like you could snap in two. I love it."

And this is how desperate she is these days: this is all it takes for her to sell her son's lungs down the river. She takes the cigarette from James' fingers, but instead of dying it out, fills her car with still more secondhand smoke, taking a hungry drag.

*

The Boy likes Emerson's dress. Sophie's dress is pink, too, but Emerson's is a different pink the kind called hot pink hot pink is his favorite one. There are a lot of pinks. Pink like Mommy's fingernails and pink like the cat's nose. Those pinks you don't have to look at if you don't want to. Hot pink fills you up like when you look at the sun but close your eyes and the color is still there inside your shut eyes. Hot pink is like your eyes are on fire. Mommy has a shirt this color too but she doesn't wear it. When he gets home from school he can take off his clothes and wear Mommy's pink shirt as a dress but he can't do that at school Mommy says it's not allowed. She says the shirt is too big for him and falls down too low and shows his chest. Showing chests is not allowed. Emerson's pink dress does not show her chest but Mommy does not buy him a pink dress that does not show his chest because Ethan is a boy. Ethan has to wear boy clothes to school. Miss Illya can wear girl clothes at home but even when she does Mommy still calls her Ethan. Mommy lets him wear the pink shirt like a dress if they are in the house. She hangs it in her closet too high for him to reach and when he asks her she says, "Let's dress up like doctors!" or "Don't you want to wear your Woody hat?" but when he says no she will get the shirt.

Ms. Oak claps her hands. "OK, everybody!" she says loudly. "One, two, three, eyes on me!" The class claps two times and yells back, "One, two, eyes on you!" The Boy forgot to clap from looking at Emerson's dress. He has to pee all of a sudden. He looks at Ms. Oak, but she is smiling and looking at something else; she didn't see him forget about the clapping. Everything is OK! Fast, he trots to the carpet to sit on his square. He doesn't even have to pee anymore.

*

The Alcoholic needs to urinate. She has pressed the call button four times, but the nurse has not come. In the hospital, you are at the mercy of nurses: a prisoner in a jail cell is less dependent on his guards and warden. A prisoner can use his own toilet, even if he has no privacy—a prisoner is not prodded in the middle of the night for taking heart rate and blood pressure. A prisoner can stand in his own crowded shower and soap his own body. The Alcoholic does not own her body anymore. Her body is a thing handled by other people, but people who cannot feel its urges, to whom her skin and wasted muscles are so much dead meat.

Nurses tell her when she should eat and drink. They say this ceaselessly, though she is nauseated and cannot keep the food down; they say it even as they mop up her sick. They cannot feel her stomach's waves as her body rejects the nourishment, spasming it out again, foul-tasting now and mixed with bodily acids, back through her mouth. The nurses give her potassium tablets to prevent dehydration, to prevent her heart giving out, and refuse to crush the horse-like pills because they are "time release," so she throws these up too. Every way you look, the outcome is the same, but in the interim still they insist on the food and the pills and the IVs to rehydrate her; still they persist in keeping her here, the third time this month.

This is what you come to, then. Her liver is no longer functioning enough to rid her body of toxins, so her body itself has become a toxin. Though she has been too nauseated to take a drink for weeks now, still she is being poisoned to death by herself. Five years ago they diagnosed her cirrhosis, and she had not thought she would last this long. Her preparations for the end, then, had felt surprisingly easy, surprisingly clean. Her daughter,

Imogen, was thriving—a circuit court judge, which was both trivial and prestigious in its way—and still married to her Upstanding American. The two had seemed a muted-but-complete painting, hung safely (if sanctimoniously) above the hearth of a distant shore. But these doctors, playing at their Brave New World, had managed things otherwise. They'd suspended her dying just long enough for matters to complicate: the birth of a grandson; Imogen's divorce. For desires to complicate.

The Alcoholic has to urinate, which must show her liver is still filtering something. She presses the call button again but the nurse does not come. Fine. The world is full of incompetent people, so full of them that now they seem to run things. She will get out of bed, then, and do it herself.

"So last night," James says, "I'm driving home after the show, and she calls me no less than eight times while I'm on I-94. Can you fucking believe it?" He holds his hands up in surrender. "I know, I know, it was my own fault for calling her when I left the bar. I should have called two minutes from the goddamn house and said, 'Hi honey we just wrapped,' then by the time she hung up I'd be walking through the door and everybody's happy."

The Mistress laughs. She does not find James' marital dramas particularly amusing, but laughing at his wife is her role—it is what he is here for, she sometimes suspects, as much as sex.

"It's the twins," he explains, shrugging. "They're demons. They've turned her into a crazy person."

"From the stories you've told me," the Mistress stipulates, "she was always a little nuts."

James gets up from the sectional sofa to get them a beer. The Mistress is annoyed because you are not really allowed to move when reclining on the sofa in James' studio or the entire contrapment comes apart, sliding away from itself under your ass. The sofa is red faux leather and supposed to be kitsch, she assumes, but really it is just some kind of furniture abortion, ugly and incomplete. They cannot even fuck on it because of the way it will not stay put, so they have to rut around on the hardwood floor like teenagers, though James has a bad back and the Mistress is going to be headed for knee replacement if she spends any more time on all fours on this floor. Lately, she has been bringing her yoga mat, claiming to have just come from the gym, so they won't slip and slide around the floor like pratts too. This has been going on three months, but if James were to buy furniture to accommodate comfortable middle-aged copulation, it would be a commitment of some sort that neither is eager to make, so for now the yoga mat, the metrosexual coat spread atop it, will have to do.

"Sure," he says from the mini-fridge. Naked in the afternoon sun that streams through the tall windows of his art studio, he doesn't look like the boys of her youth anymore. Those boys had not an ounce of spare flesh on them, like feral animals. James' middle is not fat, but it is loose. There is a smattering of gray in his pubic hair. "She was nuts, but she used to be crazy in a sexy way," he explains. "Like thinking I looked at some other woman and freaking out. She was territorial, she was a drama queen, sure, but it was because she was obsessed with me. Now she doesn't give a shit who I look at—she just calls eight times cause she wants me to get my ass home and help with the twins."

"She may not care who you look at," the Mistress says. "But she probably cares where your dick has been."

"I doubt it," James snorts. He hands her a beer, though she does not drink. She has been playing a little game with herself, a game of not touching the beers or glasses of wine he casually hands her in this place, not even one sip, to see if he will notice, if he will ask, but so far nothing.

"I wish I had someone to harass to come home and help me with Ethan," the Mistress says wistfully.

"See?" James says, nodding as though she has taken his side. "You're a mother too, but you haven't turned into a screaming shrew who doesn't care about anything except your kid. Some women just aren't built that way."

The Mistress' head feels cloudy, despite her lack of beer. "No," she says. "I didn't mean it like that. I was being sincere. Being a single mother can be incredibly..." She does not want to say "lonely," does not want to give him that power. "Isolating," she decides on. "I often feel isolated, especially when Ethan's asleep." She thinks of her mother, who remedied this problem with endless bottles of wine until she passed out on the couch, rendering the prospect of facing another lonely night moot. She thinks of her childhood, spent wandering rooms while her mother was passed out, sometimes not going to bed until long past midnight because there was no one there, and the feeling of being shipwrecked. "At night, sometimes I feel like I'm trapped on a desert island," she tells James. "I wish I had someone to call eight times in the car."

"You can call me," he quips. "We'll have phone sex on the highway. Live fast, die young, right?"

The Mistress suddenly feels incredibly tired. Sometimes this happens when she is at home with Ethan: if they play a game that involves lying down, she will fall asleep right while he is talking to her or sitting on her legs or brushing her hair. She can sleep even while he is banging on a frying pan with a metal spoon. Sometimes, she is simply too tired for Ethan's games. For the games of boys in general.

"Too late, honey," she tells her lover, turning her face away so she will not even have to smile to soften the blow. "We left young a decade ago. If we die now, it's not tragic anymore, it's not poetic. We're just dead."

*

They are learning about the rain forest. The Boy draws the howler monkey's eyes in red because school markers don't have the right kind of pink. Miss Illya walks up to the howler monkey and says, "A howler monkey." Then Mommy comes over and says, "Do you want a band-aid?" The Boy is not sure how to spell "band-aid," so he writes it SICWA, which is how you spell things you don't know how to spell. Miss Illya's name was spelled that way for a long time until Mommy taught him how to spell it right. She said he was spelling it so it sounded like Sic-wa, but that wasn't right: SICWA doesn't sound like Sic-wa, it sounds like whatever you need it to sound like.

Ms. Oak comes over to the table to see what he is doing. Since he started going to speech, she writes down things he says. She does it so she can tell Mommy if he is talking enough. Mommy says he is supposed to talk at preschool like he does at home because Ms. Oak thinks he doesn't know how to talk he is so quiet. It is loud at school so it's easy to forget not to be quiet because there is already so much noise you forget you're not making any of it. There are so many things to look at that if you say things it takes away from the things you are looking at and you have to think about your mouth and what it is saying. Ms. Oak says to him, "What is your picture about, Ethan?" Ms. Oak is pretty with black eyelashes. Ms. Oak's hair is honey with colors in it—Ms. Oak has a honey face. The Boy feels so happy it is hard to know what to do with all the happy. "The howler monkey's eyes are on fire!" he says, proudly.

Ms. Oak frowns. "On fire?" she asks, making a sad face. "That's too bad. How did that happen?"

"From the pink," Ethan explains. The happy is gone already though, it can go so fast, it can go and now he wants to cry. He didn't mean to make Ms. Oak sad. "It's only from the pink," he assures her.

"Oh," she says, looking at him in a careful way. She writes something down on her paper. "Ethan, do you know what color this is?" she asks, pointing at the howler monkey's eyes. "This color is red. Remember we learned about red?"

The Boy has to be careful. He knows about red. He does not remember learning about red in preschool, but he learned about red in other times. There was powder from the inside of a flower and it made red on Mommy's hands. There was paint in the art cabinet and he made it into a hermit crab on the wall and Mommy said no, no red on the walls, but what she meant was no hermit crabs on the walls, no paint on the walls, Mommy was sad about the walls. He does not want to make Ms. Oak more sad about the howler monkey's eyes on fire, so he points at the picture and says, "Mommy fixes it, look! She puts a band-aid on the sun so it can't make pink anymore. The pink is all gone now!"

"Ohhh," Ms. Oak says, but her voice is far away and she is not looking at the picture anymore; she is writing something else down about him, something to tell Mommy, and Mommy will tell him to talk at school but he did talk at school, he did and Ms. Oak is still writing something down. Ms. Oak's hair is not like honey. The Boy thinks about the pink teacup at home that Mommy lets him drink tea with honey out of. If Ms. Oak keeps telling Mommy he does not talk, maybe Mommy will not let him use the teacup anymore.

"I don't like you when you do that!" he yells abruptly at Ms. Oak. "You make me very frustrated! Your hair is poo-poo now!"

But even though they read a book called *The Feelings Book* and Ms. Oak told them to talk about their feelings, and Mommy told him to talk at school, still the Boy has to spend five minutes in the naughty chair.

*

The Alcoholic lugs her body toward the toilet. Her body weighs less than one hundred pounds now, but it feels leaden as she leans on the table with wheels that normally hovers over her hospital bed, trying to use it now as a walker to get to the bathroom. She leans and pushes, so that the table wheels away from her, and she hangs on to it so that it pulls her along, her feet stumbling leadenly to keep up. The pressure in her bladder makes it hard to move her legs. Everything feels focused down to that one area, swollen and full. She pushes the table but it sticks and will not roll. Harder, she leans on it with her torso, trying to propel it forward, but some wire is in its path and it sticks there like a car run into a guardrail; she cannot push the table over the small protuberance of the wire. "Please," she murmurs, "please." Who is she talking to? There is no god here. Her Uncle Owen was a vicar, and that taught her all she needed to know about that. There is nothing after this life. This is what we come to, then: a skeletal body unable to best a small lump of wire on ugly hospital tiles. The fullness of a bladder like an ocean tide, uncontrollable and following its own rhythms. The Alcoholic pushes herself off the table with a violent jerk, but the motion is too much for her and she vomits into her hands, which automatically rise. Her legs collapse beneath her, her body banging like a sandbag into the wheeled table so that it falls and her body on top of it, its sharp angles colliding with her sharp bones. Somewhere on the way down she has pissed herself: she did not even feel it happen until she hit the floor and found it wet. At first she took it for blood; at first she prayed for blood, prayed to the god in whom she does not believe: Make it fast. But no, it is only her own waste: urine on the shoe-scuffed tiles and the tang of vomit in her hair.

She had feared so much, during those long hours in the car,

that her mother would thrash her for wetting herself, for being sick on her new dress, that she can remember the spanking even though it never took place. She must have confused it with some other time. She knows only that when she woke after the long drive from her Uncle Owen's country home, her parents were no longer in the car. She must have been three—maybe younger? Her father left for good when she was four, so it was before that. Her parents had quarreled on the drive home, as they did nearly continuously, so continuously that their quarreling did not prevent her from dropping to sleep on the backseat. Her father was threatening to leave again, but at that time she did not realize it was not just something fathers said. At that time she knew no fathers who had left and did not think it permitted, so the movement of the car lulled her into sleep.

When she came to, the road was dark and the car no longer moving. Her house was outside the window—they were home—but her parents must have forgotten she was back there, so carried away by their quarrel, because they were gone and she was in the car alone. She tried the door but it didn't open. She did not know how to open the car door. It seemed a complex matter beyond her. How was it to be accomplished? This was something her mother always did. Her small hands slipped, slick on the door lock. She was not sure whether or not she was locked in, or even if she was setting out to open the door in the proper manner. She knew nothing of it. The road was dark. Her parents had forgotten her. Noticing that she needed to use the toilet, she began to cry. Her voice cried out for her mother but nothing happened except the echo of herself inside the locked car. The house was far from the road. It seemed a great distance. She yelled again but no one was on the road. She tried again the way she thought you might open a car door. She beat on the windows with her fists and wept some more—in her mind the Alcoholic can see herself, as though on the other side of the car window: a pitiful little nearsighted girl sobbing and banging on the glass in a panic, glasses askew. The vision sickens her. She thinks the little girl deserved to be thrashed. Something was the matter with her, clearly. She was simply in a car, that was all. Did she think her parents would forget her forever? That she would starve and die out there, as she is starving and dying now in this hospital? Yes, yes of course she thought that, or something like it. She pounded her small, sweating fists on the glass crying, "Mummy! Mummy!" like a fool. Maybe her parents had not forgotten her at all, but had decided purposefully to leave her there. They fought about her often, and her father said he would leave. He said he did not like the way her mother treated her, and that he would go away if she continued. He did not like the way her mother struck her and shouted at her and would not stand for it, he said. He would leave. He never mentioned taking the Girl with him, even though he said he did not like her mother hurting her and this was why he would go. It seemed clearly nonsense, even to someone who could not open a car door. It seemed nothing but silliness to threaten to leave your child alone with the woman whose treatment of said child you could not abide. It seemed only words. But maybe it was more. Maybe her mother had said, Don't go, we'll just leave her here and then I won't treat her in a way you don't like anymore. Maybe her mother had said, She's the thing we always fight about, so if we just put her out we'll be happy again. Perhaps they had not forgotten her in their quarrel, but walked to the house hand in hand, delighted with their plan. Perhaps the car door was locked in some magical way known only to adults, so that she would never get out again, would never eat again. She soiled her underpants, and if it was at all possible her parents were coming back for her, her mother would thrash her for that. She would use the hairbrush or possibly her father's strap, when her father wasn't looking. She would take the Girl's wet underpants and for them she would give her a proper thrashing until the Girl did not cry anymore. Her mother was driven mad by her crying, so the Girl tried to be strong when thrashed and not to cry, but the crying didn't stop until you were too weak to continue it, that was the bad part of it all. But that made no difference because they weren't coming back. The Girl cried and smelled her own waste and thought of the spanking she would never get again because this was her home now until she died, which had happened to their cat, the dying, which meant you went to God, and God was terrifying, more terrifying than her mother. She wanted her mother—she remembers this, that it was her mother's name she called, never Father's. She vomited into her hands, and sick clung to the ends of her hair.

When the Girl woke, she was in her own bed. What passes for sun in Wales shone in through her lace-curtained window. Her clothing had been changed, including her underpants, and her nightgown smelled fresh. At breakfast, her father was already at work and her mother acted like nothing had happened, so the Girl believed for a moment that she had dreamt it all, about the car. But although they had changed her clothes and wiped her down, they had not bathed her properly in her sleep, and so she knew it was not a dream, for she could still smell the sick in her hair.

The Boy sits with Mommy in the car. Mommy is driving so he is in the backseat by himself: this is his seat and that is Mommy's seat. Often he calls to her, "I want to sit on your lap," while she is driving, even though he knows she will say no. He can't stop his mouth from saying it anyway, because sometimes things you don't expect happen and maybe she will say yes, but if he doesn't ask how will he know? Something funny is going on in his belly, like it does sometimes when Mommy drives him home from school. He is getting too excited because he knows he can be Miss Illya soon. Mommy has told him he can't call himself Miss Illya at school, though he does not understand this because he gets to pretend other things at school. Today in the garden he and Emerson played pigs because of her pink dress. He said, "Pretend I have pink too and we're pigs" and she said, "Oink, oink," and they ran through the garden shouting oink and telling everybody they were pigs and nobody was upset. Nobody said he could not be a pig. The Boy understands that he can be a pig but not a girl, but he does not know why. It is OK to dress like a dog on Halloween, or like Woody if he is going to a Toy Story birthday party, but it is not OK to dress like a girl anywhere because Ethan is a boy. Ethan is not a pig or a toy any more than he is a girl—Ethan is more like a girl than he is like a pig or a dog or a toy because the only difference between Ethan and a girl is that Ethan has a penis. So the Boy is not sure what this means. Mommy does not want him to be a girl but she does not mind if he is a pig. Mommy does not want Ms. Oak to know he wants to be a girl. He feels nervous in his belly because the pink shirt is up high on the hanger and he will have to ask Mommy for it and even though she will give it to him she will say other things first and she will not like it about the dress and Miss Illya and the Boy wants to make Mommy happy. He thinks maybe he will not ask about the dress right away. Maybe he will play a puzzle with Mommy first and be Ethan. Mommy likes Ethan better than Miss Illya. She says Ethan is her baby and Miss Illya is just pretend. She calls Ethan "My little man," and the Boy likes it when she does this and the way she hugs him and the way her eyes look shiny and happy. Mommy smells like Mommy and her boobies are soft for his head. She is even prettier than Ms. Oak. Mommy is the prettiest one in the world. When he gets to his home, he will tell Mommy he wants to do the planet puzzle, the one where Pluto is crying because he's not a planet. Pluto can't be a planet anymore just like Ethan cannot be a girl. Mommy likes how fast he can do the planet puzzle. She always says, "I'm so proud of you!" and lets him sleep with the Pluto piece, still crying inside his hand.

Clybourn is bumper-to-bumper, their car barely moving. Already, James is texting. *Great time*, he writes. *You are a marvel. Off to conquer the world now, eh?*

Since James' wife sits at home all day while her twins are in preschool, and then harasses James to help her every evening when he would like to be out playing unpaying gigs with his band like a slacker teenager, James apparently believes that the Mistress' ability to hold down a job and raise a child simultaneously is tantamount to conquering the world. The Mistress finds this both flattering and idiotic. In fact, she feels capable of conquering little of late. At one point, prior to Ethan's birth, she was actually a circuit court judge and believed herself on her way "up," though now "up" seems a less clear destination than it did at that time. Now, however, she trains other attorneys, because training other people to do things permits more time flexibility and less dedication than actually doing the thing herself. The work is not particularly exciting, but it pays well enough that the Mistress can afford a fancy preschool for Ethan, and a real house rather than a condo, and other things that children with fathers might have. She is determined to provide Ethan with everything a father might offer, excepting, of course, the father himself. She is the third in a matriarchal line of Divorcees. The Mistress had not wanted to get divorced, but her inability to keep her legs shut for other men had seemed to indicate otherwise to her husband, Ethan's father. After he left, he became prone to saying things like, "You're like a black widow" and "A woman like you should never have tried to have a normal relationship with a man."

But what did it mean, a woman like her? She is not any particular type of woman that she can see. She is a type of person—that she will consent—a member of a club with wide membership, including many famous men like Bill Clinton and Tiger Woods. In some circles, she could claim sex addiction and make scads of new friends at Twelve Step meetings, but she lives in Chicago, a large but provincial city, not Los Angeles, and nonsense like that does not fly here. It is not the sex itself she is addicted to, of course. She cannot speak for Tiger Woods, but on the whole she doubts it is the sex that motivates most members of her club. There is, in her, simply the clawing, craving need to be desired, to be paid attention to, to be held and complimented, to be the center of a drama. Knowing this is so makes it no less so. Since Ethan, she has tried to be pragmatic about her needs. Married men fit well within her current perimeters, because they are high intensity and full of mad desire when you're with them, but usually unavailable which—like training attorneys—allows more time flexibility for a working mother.

The Mistress has never gotten on particularly well with other women, so the wives do not bother her much. Lately, though, she increasingly finds herself empathizing with them rather than with her lovers when her lovers regale her with some story or other of the way their wives fail to understand them. Increasingly, she has started to view her lovers as silly children with whom their wives have to put up, and to covertly hope she may be helping their wives out by sharing the load. Increasingly, she can understand the concept of polygamy, and the kinship of women saddled with one man's nonsense for the long haul. Lately, she has found herself closing her eyes during sex, so as to lose herself in the physical sensations without having to actually look at the man involved. When she first met James at the annual fundraiser for the preschool his twins and Ethan both attend, James reminded her of a fresher, cleaner time in her life, when everything about the male body was magic and desire to her—when she could not get enough of men. But although she likes James, his informality and harsh wit and inappropriate-to-private-school-fatherhood chain smoking; his studio where he records music as though it has entirely escaped him that he is forty-five with gray pubic hair, still she finds her eyes closing when he pumps into her so that she will not have to see the intent look on his face, like a little boy building a tower or trying out his new, fast sneakers. If she looks at him too long, the mystique of him seems to evaporate and he seems a child trapped in an aging body, and any tenderness she feels toward him is less to do with sex than pity, and this seems a dire state of affairs, worse even than the prospect that her own desirability and beauty will soon dry up and render her unfuckable to most men. The prospect of a life of unrequited desire seems bearable to her, but a life without desire altogether sounds like death.

Can I see you tomorrow? James texts. *Can you get away?*

Tomorrow is Saturday. She does not like to leave Ethan on the weekends, but maybe she should give it another try, and if James is just not doing it for her, she will have to move on, find someone else who can bring her back to life. She pushes the texting icon of her iPhone—

The noise! Worse than the garbage disposer, when Mommy says "Run and cover your ears" because she knows he doesn't like loud things. Loud everywhere inside him so he can't run away from it. Hurting in his neck and the window gets closer to him, rushing at his face until it splits, a hundred pieces flying like when the Boy's project for the hundreth day of school—he brought in one hundred pieces of pasta—all fell out of his bag and splattered on the floor. The glass splatters like that, like he is the floor, spraying across him, biting his face. Glass bugs flying through his hair and he screams, brings up his hands, Mommy! Mommy calling his name, "Ethan, Ethan, baby;" Mommy throwing her body over the seat and pulling the glass off him, her hands bleeding. "You're OK, you're all right, Mommy's here, I'm getting you out, you're all right." He stares at her. He is crying though he does not feel sad. His face is hot and wet, and Mommy puts her blood hand to his cheek, presses her face and hair into him; the boy notices his pants are wet too, that he pee-peed without knowing it. Mommy's hair against his wet face, unbuckling the straps of his seat and pulling him toward her, "Oh, my little man," she sobs. Ethan clings to her neck. He holds on to her and breathes her and breathes the still air now around them, no glass bugs anymore. People are outside the car calling to them, but Mommy doesn't answer and Ethan doesn't answer and nothing happens for a minute they just hold on.

"Why are you out of bed?" the nurse snaps from the doorway. Soundless rubber shoes approaching. "Well, look at this. Now look what you've done. You know you can't get out of that bed yourself. Just look at yourself, lying there. You've made a fine mess, haven't you? Well, no matter, it's not like you've got to clean it up, is it? I'm here to serve you, isn't that right?"

The Alcoholic lies on the floor. "I pressed the call button," she says. "I pressed it five times."

"Oh, rubbish," the nurse insists. "You pressed it one time, but I was busy with someone else. You're not the only one round here with problems, you know." The nurse hoists her up under her arms, yanking her to her feet.

"Ow," the Alcoholic says softly. "You're hurting me."

The nurse flops her back down onto the bed and pushes her legs center. "Some people do everything to take proper care of themselves and they're even sicker than you—what do you think about that?"

The Alcoholic begins to cry. She stammers, shamed by her crying, "You're a nurse! You've come on to help the sick—not to berate us. You're a nurse—this is your job."

The nurse stares down at her. She is a pretty woman, though her face bears the shapeless doughy quality of a working class lifestyle of pints, chips, and take-away curry. "I know your sort," she whispers. "I was cleaning me dad's nappies when the cirrhosis got him, wasn't I? You did it to yourself and now we're all cleaning up after you." She yanks the blanket over the Alcoholic's skeletal legs and leaves the room, this time her rubber heels oddly loud on the tile.

The Alcoholic sits in her bed weeping. She can only presume the nurse has gone to get a clean gown, that she will be back soon to change her, give her a sponge bath, and the horrible helplessness of it makes the crying come harder. She would rather rot here in her own sick than have that smug, hateful young girl surveying her sagging, empty breasts and soaping between her legs. If only she could die right now. If only she had someone, someone to come in and complain about this nurse to a superior; someone to quietly slip her just enough sleeping pills to call it a day. These days, you cannot go to hospital without an advocate: without someone to protect you from this sort of abuse.

The Alcoholic thinks briefly of Imogen, off in the States for more than twenty years now, raising little Ethan, whom the Alcoholic has met only twice. Her daughter does not like her. Her daughter never comes to England, and now that the Alcoholic is so ill she cannot travel to visit her grandson anymore. Her daughter is set to arrive next week on a visit, now that the cirrhosis has advanced to the stage that the Alcoholic is an object to be pitied (except, apparently, by the smug young nurse), but even then, Imogen is not bringing the boy with her. "He's four," she explained glibly. "What would I do with him, stuck in a hospital all day?" Ethan will remain in Chicago at a friend's home, someone the Alcoholic has never even heard of, some shadowy figure in her daughter's inaccessible life. Once, her daughter wrote her angry letters from boarding school, demanding that she needed to "admit your addiction" and "go into recovery," but the words seemed like some strange childish code. One simply didn't do things like that, or if one did, it was folly to think it would yield any result other than a wider net of noisy people with whom to make a mess of things. There were things Imogen could not understand, things she could not grasp because she had never been thrashed until she was too weak to cry by the same hand that fed her; could not feel because she had never been told she'd ruined her own mother's entire life and was too ugly to ever find a man herself—that she was worthless and to blame for driving away the man her mother had. The Alcoholic's daughter thinks it such a terrible calamity to have a mother who drank, who sometimes became vitriolic and did not word things in a polite, appropriate manner—but her daughter does not understand from the spectacular range of calamities possible when it comes to mothers, does not understand the heroic efforts it takes to merely love badly when you yourself have never been loved at all.

Perhaps she should have answered those boarding school letters. She could have tried to explain. But there is nothing to be done for it now. Now, her daughter is a middle-aged woman, an American, a refugee from all the Alcoholic has wrought. Maybe if Imogen could see the little Girl on the other side of the window, maybe then she could find forgiveness in her, but that Girl is gone now, long buried under the weight of denials and excuses and justifications, entombed somewhere under the flesh and bones and toxic liver of the Alcoholic's skin, still trapped, still abandoned, biding her time for the poison to win out so she can finally escape that car.

And her daughter will have to live and die by her own mistakes.

The Mistress' iPhone keeps vibrating with James' texts. She turned the sound off back in the ER while Ethan was being checked out, but there is no way spare smashing it to keep it from buzzing silently to signal the world trying to reach her, wanting a piece of her. Now, Ethan has a large bandage under one eye. Had that shard of glass hit one inch higher, he could have lost the eye, the doctor said. Her son, her beautiful son without an eye! She feels a tight sickness in her chest, as though the world would dim immeasurably without Ethan's eye to witness it. Now, he sits on the floor with his planet puzzle, doing pieces quietly and swiftly, a thirty-seven-and-a-half pound package of precarious breath. Anything could get him at any time. When the Mistress was young, her best friend from boarding school died of an asthma attack at the age of thirteen. When Ethan was first diagnosed with asthma, she could not sleep for a week, though the doctor and her friends kept assuring her that times had changed and that Ethan's asthma was not severe. Still, she had not done enough to keep him safe. She had not even seen the car approaching, she was so busy fiddling with her iPhone. By the time she knew what had happened, the shattered window was already laying claim to her son's face.

He may have a scar now, the doctor said. "Thankfully he's a boy," he added. "It will look tough. Tell him he looks like a pirate." But Ethan does not want to be a pirate, his mother knows. Maybe it is her fault for not fighting harder when his father decided to join the firm in San Diego—maybe it is her fault for thinking Ethan was more hers anyway. But Ethan does not care about pirates. He wants to be Lady Gaga, or Princess Jasmine, or pretty young Ms. Oak. Ethan wants to be her.

In five days, she will get on a plane for England. In five days, she will visit her mother, who is finally dying after trying a passive-aggressive hand at self-destruction for more than forty years. She had thought not to take Ethan with her, but maybe this was a mistake. What if something were to happen to him while she is gone? Maybe better to keep him near. What if something were to happen to one of them only a week or two after she got back? She would not want to have relinquished that time with him then. Soon her own mother will be dead. Already it has seemed as though she could be dead, living as far away as she does, but while her mother has lived, the Mistress has been able to interact with her by not interacting with her—by choosing to avoid her, she speaks to her daily loud and clear. Twenty-odd years have passed in this fashion, in this constant state of (non)communication. Soon, however, the Mistress will be on her stage of silence alone, the audience having left the building. Soon, her mother will be dead, and it will be too late for anything to ever be other than what it was.

She stands in the doorway to the kitchen, watching Ethan. It is late—they spent hours in the ER—and she needs to prepare dinner, but she cannot seem to take her eyes off him. When she picked him up from school, Ms. Oak said, "He's still having some trouble with his colors," but Ethan has known his colors since before he could talk. Ethan has gravitated toward certain colors, holding objects in his preferred shades for hours at times just to look at them: she remembers things falling out of his Baby Björn if he fell asleep and loosened his grasp on a pink hair clasp or plastic block—how the object would clack against the floor and startle her. "He had a little outburst today," Ms. Oak said, "but I think that may be a good thing. He was a bit more talkative. It just concerns me that he seems to speak out of context a lot of the time—I can't always follow what he means. I'll say one thing, and the answer he gives has nothing to do with my question. With your permission, I'd like to bring this up with the speech teacher." And the Mistress had nodded. Her hand in her coat pocket had fingered her iPhone, waiting for the text from James that she knew would come, waiting even though she does not love him and never has, because he was something to do, something to fill the silence and the void, and Ethan is only four years old, and she is lonely in a way a child cannot solve.

"Mommy," Ethan says. "I want to drink something."

That funny formality of his, that stiff little way of speaking brings a lump to her throat. Her son, who owns two good eyes—her son who is alive for her to bring to England. If only she could hold on to this—to now being the only moment, to today being the only thing that counts—then maybe he would be enough forever. "Of course," she says, her voice cracking, faltering. "What do you want, honey? Do you want some chocolate milk?"

"Uh, OK," Ethan says politely. "Only, can you make tea with honey instead?"

One day, when she was a little older than Ethan, she had fallen outside and was bleeding, and when she ran into the house to tell her mother, her mother was sprawled out on the couch, unresponsive. She shook her mother and shook her but couldn't rouse her. She shook so hard and shouted "Mum!" over and over again so loudly that it only seemed possible her mother was dead. At that time, passing out had not yet become a nightly occurrence. At that time, the Girl lay sprawled across what she believed to be the dead body of her mother. She sobbed for a long time, and when her mother did not wake she went out to tell a neighbor, who of course said her mother was not dead at all, and called her a poor lamb after that whenever she saw her.

Soon, her mother will be dead. Someday, in the best of all

possible scenarios, her child will grow up healthy enough to leave her. Someday, her body will move beyond desire, will enter, too, its final stage of decline. All we have is today, she thinks. Puzzle pieces of todays will make up her son's life to form a whole picture in his memory. The Day We Crashed The Car, he may call this one in his mind. He will never know his mother was texting her lover when it happened. So much he will never know. So much we never understand about each other. Everything lost to the color and noise of time, trapped behind our own eyes.

The Mother enters the kitchen to get the kettle. This is it, you understand, she says inside her head. To whom is she speaking? Perhaps her ex-husband. Perhaps herself. Perhaps (oh, how her mother would laugh), she is speaking to god. This is all I have to give him—this is what he will remember. Right now.

Quickly, the Boy pulls out his paper. Mommy is in the kitchen, and fast, before she comes back—she will have to make the water hot, for tea, so he has time—he can write her the note. He wants it to say, *I want to play with the pink dress now please thank you.* But he does not know how to write all those words. Ms. Oak says he is a good writer, that his writing is very good for preschool, but his writing makes him frustrated because there are so many words and he wants to know them all but he doesn't even know how to write this letter. He writes, *I want to SICWA SICWA the pink SICWA now peas thank you.* He looks at it. He thinks maybe Mommy does not know how to read this note. He wants to leave the note for her on top of the planet puzzle and then hide while she reads it so he can see what she does but without her seeing him see her. He wants to see if her face looks sad. He wants to not be there so she can't ask him about playing doctors or firefighters or Woody instead. He feels again like the howler monkey's eyes on fire only not in a good way like the color, in a bad way like when Ms. Oak was poo-poo. He crumbles up his note. His note is poo-poo! His face hurts a little bit and he wants to take off the big bandage but Mommy and the doctor said no. Maybe he wants to play doctor. He can give shots to all his animals. Maybe he will play doctor instead. He will pretend like he is giving Mommy a shot and make her say "Ow!" and pretend like he gives her a lollipop. In the car, when Mommy called his name it was his name. Ethan was his name. He was not anybody else. When the glass flew at his face and cut him and the noise was loud, Ethan was behind his own eyes. He did not think about Miss Illya then. He still wants to wear the pink dress and to pretend about Miss Illya, but Mommy is right that Miss Illya is pretend. Miss Illya was not in the car with them. This makes him sad, but happy too. He does not know where Miss Illya was, but she was not inside his eyes.

The kettle is whistling, but instead of going to get it Mommy stands at the kitchen doorway again. For a second, Ethan thinks he is imagining it, but the pink dress is in her hands. Mommy's pink shirt that she never wears, there, dangling from one of her hands like a present, and he jumps to his feet fast, though then he remembers that maybe the present is not for him. Mommy got the shirt as a present from Nain and maybe she is going to put it in her suitcase to bring it to visit Nain to pretend like she likes the shirt, the way she made Ethan wear his Transformers shirt to school because it was a birthday present from Max; even though Ethan didn't like the shirt he had to pretend so Max would be happy. Maybe Mommy is going to pretend about her shirt to make Nain happy too, and she will bring it with her because he is not allowed to bring it to Emerson's house when Emerson's mommy babysits him anyway, so Mommy will take it with her, will take it away, and he won't have it anymore or Mommy either.

"Well, hello," Mommy says, still from the doorway. Her

voice is like make-believe, like when she reads him a book. "I was looking for Miss Illya," she says. "I thought she might want to have a tea party with me. Do you know where she might be?"

Ethan's hand goes up, like people do at school when they want Ms. Oak to call on them, though Ethan never does that at school—he forgets that he should want to be called on. "I'm here!" he says, like it is attendance, too excited. "I can come to the tea party!"

"Great!" Mommy says. "But you'd better change your outfit first. Your clothes are messy from the accident, and this is going to be a fancy tea party, Miss Illya. We're going to put extra honey in the tea."

Ethan's body is humming. His face doesn't hurt anymore. If he were a howler monkey, he would howl. If he were a rainforest toucan, he would fly. If he were a color, he would be so pink the sun would hide. He runs to Mommy and snatches the dress from her hand, kicking off his shoes and yanking down his pants. Mommy has to help him with his shirt; it feels hard and crumbly from the blood. Soon he is standing in nothing but his underpants, and Mommy slips the pink shirt over his head so that it is a dress that comes almost to his ankles. She ties the sash in the back in a big bow and turns him around. Her eyes are bright like marbles, like stars. Ethan thinks about telling her that he is still Ethan under the dress—that Miss Illya is just pretend—but he doesn't want to spoil the game, he is too happy. He jumps up and down in place. "I'm Miss Illya now!" he says. "I'm ready for the party! Can I put the honey in the tea?"

And Mommy smiles, and steps back from the kitchen door to let him in.

TRACKS

by Kate Blakinger

ALL THAT WINTER THEY DROVE into storms. Rex steered them through snow and hail to Lake Erie, while Angela smoked his cigarettes one after another until she was dizzy. She always felt a little lightheaded sitting next to Rex. Smoking just buoyed her up faster, floating her through the drive toward the moment of arrival, when his hands would hold her instead of the wheel.

Even with a storm coming on, their car was never the only one on the road. Other drivers would honk at them at stoplights, laughing at Rex's surfboard, which was tied to the roof with rope.

You could surf on Lake Erie when a winter storm churned it up—otherwise there were no waves worth catching. The water was the color of milky coffee, and a chemical tang hung in the air around it. After surfing, sometimes Rex would get ear infections or pink eye, and once he got a rash that started at his hands and neck and spread up his arms and down his chest for days, like a slow-moving parade of tiny red ants. Angela remembered how he'd clawed at himself. She'd spread calamine lotion all over him and it stained his clothes. She still let him touch her with those red-spotted hands.

Her mother told her Rex was trouble. "You better open up your eyes, Angela," her mother said. "Take a good look at what you're getting into." That made the girl laugh. It was what she liked about him: all the trouble he stirred up. Her mother told her a sixteen-year-old girl belonged in school. She sure didn't know what to say to change a person's mind.

Rex had a fancy dry suit he propped up in the backseat like a third passenger. He had to wriggle into it through the zippered slit that ran from shoulder to shoulder across the back. That day in January, as he wriggled, he told Angela that divers peed in their dry suits.

"Liar," she said. "They'd be wet inside then and what would be the point."

"I'm serious. There's this condom thingy you wear with a tube on the end of it and the tube attaches to a valve at your knee." He told her it was called the P-valve.

"What about girl divers?" Angela asked, but she was thinking about condoms, how they hadn't used one that time in the backseat, her sweaty butt sticking to the vinyl. She hadn't made him stop.

Rex shrugged at her question. "Diapers maybe," he said.

It wasn't snowing too hard yet, so she got out of the car and walked with him through the drifts from an earlier storm, which gave way to sand as they approached the water.

There were a couple surfers already out on the lake; probably people they'd seen around before, but it was impossible to tell from the beach. Not a lot of folks surfed Lake Erie; you had to be a little crazy to get into that water. The waves were highest right before a blizzard, pushed up by the wind. Icicles formed on the surfers' suits, and their goggles froze to their faces. They had to watch each other for the glazed eyes and slurred speech of hypothermia.

Snowflakes caught in Rex's eyelashes as he leaned down to kiss Angela. She frowned and he asked, "What's with you?"

"Nothing."

"You'd tell me if something was up, right?" Rex's hands were huge. He cupped one around her cheek.

She wanted to tell him that she felt sick and scared, that lately each time she pulled down her underwear she looked for blood that was never there, but all she said was: "There's nothing, really. Go surf before the snow gets too thick."

Rex waded into the water, slid onto his board, and paddled through the whitewater to beyond the breaker line. Angela listened to the lick of the waves against the shore. When she closed her eyes, it was easy to mistake that sound for the ocean. She'd never seen the ocean, except in movies, but her mother had a tape of ocean waves that she listened to as she lay in bed, trying to sleep. When Angela was little, sometimes she'd sneak into her mother's bedroom, crawl under the covers, and snuggle up to her big warm body, listening to the waves crash again and again. Her mother would scold her, tell her not to touch her legs with those cold toes. She'd ask Angela why she always went barefoot in winter, did she want to catch her death?

Angela walked a little further up the beach, the wind whipping her hair into snarls. She wished there were shells to collect, but all she found was a used Band-Aid by the edge of the water. She nudged sand over the Band-Aid with the toe of her boot.

That morning, she'd lifted her shirt, unbuttoned her jeans and looked at the pale dough of her belly in the cracked mirror hanging in the gas station restroom, trying to detect changes. She touched her breasts and they were tender. Her period was late by three weeks, maybe more. She almost wanted to talk to her mother, but she'd stopped buying new minutes for her cell phone long ago, and Rex's needed to be charged. Besides, she could just hear her mother. "That boy's a rotten apple," she'd say, "and you went ahead and took a bite."

Angela retraced her steps across the beach, returning to the car to read her magazine, but she couldn't concentrate, not even on the pictures. Wrapped in a t-shirt at the bottom of her backpack was a home pregnancy test she'd bought at the drug store next to the gas station. She'd purchased several candy bars, too, setting everything down in a pile as if chocolate could camouflage what she was really there for.

She hadn't had the guts to use the test while she was in the restroom. She'd stood there, dancing back and forth on her toes, her bladder bursting, trying to work up the courage, but finally she just sat and peed, unable to hold it any longer. She pulled the box out now and stared at the pictures on the back: a plus sign would appear if you were pregnant and a minus sign if you weren't. As if bringing another person into the world was a simple matter of arithmetic.

She didn't want a baby; she didn't want anything growing inside of her. She could picture her belly ballooning outward, stretching her belly button wide. Rex wouldn't dump her and tell all his friends she was a big slut—the fate of Angela's lab partner sophomore year, a Chicana girl who'd stopped coming to chemistry when the baggy overalls she wore no longer disguised the round push of her pregnancy. Rex would never do that, but she wasn't sure what he would do. She wasn't even sure what she'd do. She'd need her mother's consent to get rid of the baby. There was some kind of law.

She shoved the test deep into her backpack when Rex returned. He retied his board to the roof with the knots he'd learned in Boy Scouts and eased into the backseat, where he proceeded to strip off his dry suit, dripping lake water everywhere. Some night when it wasn't so cold they'd end up sleeping back there. She'd stretch herself out and the smell of the lake would push into her nose, taste like car exhaust in her mouth.

"Couldn't you change outside?" Angela asked.

"It's like negative degrees out there."

"You're getting the seats wet."

He shrugged. "It's just water."

Angela balled her hands into fists and stared at them in her lap, curled and small, as Rex climbed into the driver's seat. She'd already started the ignition and heat was pumping from the vents. He held his hands in the streams of hot air, his fingers white and pruned, the skin shrunk close to the bone with cold. Then he patted a hand around under the driver's seat, looking for the film canister he kept his pot in. Once his fingers were thawed and nimble, he rolled a joint.

"We should go," she said. She didn't want to get stuck on the road in the storm. She imagined snow piling so high around them that they couldn't open the car doors. Someone would find them during the spring melt. They'd be naked, maybe. Angela had heard that freezing people ripped off their clothes near the end because they felt so warm, like their skin was burning.

Rex nodded but lit the joint. When he passed it to her, the end was soft and wet with his spit. She hesitated for a second, then put it to her lips. They smoked with the windows closed, letting the car get foggy and pungent, the scent of the pot overwhelming the lake smell on Rex's skin. He put a tape of The Ramones into the tape player. The snow was really coming down now and the wind rocked the car. "If you squint a little," Angela said, "the flakes look like flower petals." They squinted at the snow together.

"You want to go to Tino's tonight?" Rex slurred his words just a touch, holding each one in his mouth a fraction of a second too long.

"OK," she said. Tino was a friend of Rex's who had a studio apartment that was a straight shot up Route 90, a fifty-minute drive in good weather. Everything in that apartment was all piled up in one room: the bed, the fridge, the rickety kitchen table with its sticky stains and the folded napkins slipped under one leg. Tino was a slob. When the garbage can started to overflow he'd pull out the bag, tie it, and set it on a chair. Sometimes all the chairs were taken and there was no place to sit but the bed, which was just a twin mattress in the middle of the room. But Tino was also a gentleman. He let Angela sleep on the mattress when they crashed there, and in the mornings he'd get her a coffee from the mini-mart on the corner, done up hot and sweet how she liked it, with six sugar packets. Once he showed her his wrestling trophies, a cluster of plastic towers on a shelf in the closet, a tiny gold man shining astride each one. He'd flushed when she touched the tallest. Tino had been state champion.

Rex drove slowly into the snow.

"You ever think about what you're going to be?" Angela asked.

"Be?"

"When you grow up."

"I am grown up, Ange." Rex was three years older than her, and he liked to point that out.

"So this is it? This is what you're going to be?"

"What?"

"Just some surfer who's never been in the ocean?"

He laughed and reached over to burrow his hand under her shirt, but Angela pushed him away, saying she felt carsick.

The night she'd met Rex, he'd taken her to the 24-hour Kroger. She waited in his car until he came back with a chocolate cake. He'd gotten someone from the bakery to write her name across it in neat, blue letters, the name he'd learned only an hour earlier. Slipping into the driver's seat, he started unzipping his pants. He reached into his jeans and, as though he were doing a magic trick, pulled out two bottles of shoplifted beer. That night, for the first time ever, she missed her curfew. They ate the cake with their hands, licking icing off their fingers, and she couldn't stop smiling. She smiled so hard her face hurt and Rex smiled back, dimples popping up in his cheeks.

The first time they slept together, Angela thought about all the things she should have been doing instead. Rex fumbled with her bra clasp and pressed his weight on top of her, and she thought about how she should be reading *Madame Bovary* for English class, or picking the dirty clothes off her floor, like her mother was always after her to do, or even gossiping on the telephone with her friends. But soon Rex was the only thing she thought about, Rex and his hands on her.

The snowflakes looked like angry white insects now, attacking the windows.

They drove past a warehouse. Except for the sharp tips of the 'A's, each block letter of the MATTRESS GIANT sign was peaked with snow. They must have missed the entrance to the highway. She didn't say anything, though. Rex hated it when she tried to direct him.

"Are we moving?" she asked, after what seemed like hours had passed in silence. "I can't tell if we're moving."

Rex laughed. He pointed to the speedometer, which showed they were going 27 miles per hour.

"That's fast."

He didn't answer. He was staring out the window again, getting hypnotized by the snow.

Angela saw the lights first, headlights cutting through the white air straight ahead of them. The collision vibrated through her an instant later. Her head jerked forward then back, and she was thrown against the door. The car spun. Then stillness.

"Are you OK?" Rex asked, gripping her arm. She nodded.

"What the hell was that?" he said. He rubbed his head gingerly. A lump swelled by his temple, the skin going purple with blood. Angela touched the sandpaper of his cheek, but he was already turning away, getting out of the car.

Outside, the snow fell in thick curtains. She could just make out the glow cast by the headlights of the car they'd hit.

Rex knelt by his old Volvo, cursing. The whole front was crumpled up, like a wad of tinfoil. He tried to lever the hood free with his palms, but the metal was twisted and stuck. "Are we in the middle of the road?" he asked, suddenly agitated. "We have to get out of the road."

Angela couldn't tell where they were. She walked through the snow to the other car. The battered hood had been pushed back, exposing the car's engine, and the bumper dangled. The impact had pushed the car's back tires up over the curb. Rex must have let their own car drift across the road into the wrong lane.

She brushed snow off the windshield and saw a web of cracks, the glass green where it was broken. She ran her fingers over the glass and chips fell away under that slight pressure. Through the jagged gap, Angela could see the driver: a woman, all twisted around backward, her long black hair falling over her shoulders, her face buried in the back of her seat. "Ma'am? You OK?" Angela realized she was whispering. She jerked the car door open and reached out to touch the woman's shoulder, her hand trembling violently. The woman's shoulder was damp. That's when Angela noticed the blood. Matted in the woman's hair, soaked into the fleece she was wearing, and there on the fingertip of Angela's glove, a red smear. She took a step back, air hissing out of her mouth, her tongue pressed against the back of her teeth.

At first, Angela thought she was making that sound, that howl. But the howl came from inside the car. In the back, strapped into a car seat, was a baby. His eyes were squeezed into little slits, and his round face reddened as he cried.

The back door wouldn't open, though it didn't look damaged. Angela went around the car. The doors on the other side were locked. She walked back to the woman's side and stared in at her, glad she couldn't see her face. Maybe the woman had pulled over to tend to the baby in the backseat; maybe that's why she was facing backward with her seatbelt undone. Angela tried to lean over her and unlock the opposite door without letting their bodies touch, but she didn't have enough reach. She had to get close to the woman, intimate. Her breasts pressed against the woman's back, her nose near that dark hair, inhaling the wet-metal smell of blood.

Finally, Angela unbuckled the straps and lifted the baby awkwardly, careful to support the head. He flailed his tiny fists, still wailing. She couldn't imagine something like this coming out of her.

She looked the baby over for scratches or bruises, but he seemed fine. He smelled like baby powder and warm skin. His poof of black hair was the softest thing.

"Maybe your mommy's sleeping," she whispered to the baby. "Let's find out." With the baby balanced against her shoulder, she slid into the passenger seat and reached toward the woman again, lifting her limp wrist. The woman was wearing a wedding ring. Thinking of a husband waiting for her, worrying, Angela's stomach flip-flopped. She couldn't tell if she felt a pulse or not, her hands were shaking so badly. She got out and backed away from the mangled car.

Rex materialized out of the snow, dragging his surfboard by the leash. His face was white, and he swayed slightly as he stood there, looking at the car and the woman inside. "Is she OK?" he asked.

"I don't think so."

Rex pressed his fingers against the woman's wrist. "No pulse," he said. "I don't feel anything." His voice wavered.

"I can't believe it," Angela said.

Rex dropped the dead woman's wrist. His breath fogged the air in quick puffs. Angela could hear him panting. Embarrassed, she glanced away from his frightened face and looked down at the child she held.

Fine, translucent lashes lined the baby's tiny lids. "Look what I found," she said, but Rex's gaze was fixed on the woman and her bloody hair. Angela touched his arm and he jumped.

"We have to get walking," he said.

"How old do you think he is?"

Rex didn't even look at the baby. "How would I know?" he said. He kicked at the snow with one foot and muttered about how the car wouldn't start and they had to move quickly, before the cold got to them. "Maybe you should put the baby back. Maybe it would be better off in the car."

"I'm not leaving him here."

"The police will come. We'll call them from a convenience store or a restaurant."

"No," she said. "You're not making sense." Who knew how long it would take the police to show up. They weren't on the highway, where the state troopers patrolled.

"That baby's going to be too heavy for you to carry very far," Rex said. "It's going to slow you down."

"What's wrong with you?" Angela could hear the rise in her voice. "You're taking your surfboard, but you want to me to leave behind a baby? The baby is alive, Rex. Your surfboard is just some foam and fiberglass."

Rex threw up his arms in a gesture of surrender. "OK, chill out. Lug the damn thing around if you want to."

"It's not a thing."

"I'm just saying that it's freezing out here, and we don't know where we're going." Rex stared past her as he spoke, twisting the leash of his surfboard around his fingers. His eyes were glassy and strange.

Angela turned and started to walk, slinging the diaper bag she'd found in the car over her shoulder and hugging the baby to her chest. Rex just stood there at first, but then he stumbled after her.

She should have been scared, walking into the blizzard with a baby that wasn't hers, the wreckage of two cars collecting snow behind her. Thinking of the woman made her feel sick inside, but some other feeling was there too, smoothing the edges off that sorrow. Lifting her feet high over the accumulating snow, she strode forward, following the chainlink fence that ran alongside the road, a nothingness of snow yawning open beyond it. They might be headed back toward Cleveland, or they might be headed toward nothing at all. They could be walking in the exact wrong direction; it was impossible to tell. She wondered at how this didn't trouble her, how her feet didn't falter. She let the snow fill in her tracks and erase where she'd been, and she made her way into the storm.

THE MOVE

by Debbie Urbanski

THEY MOVED TO CHICAGO because of their son and what their son did to that girl. Their new house looked like anybody else's, only it was emptier, and without family photographs, because Alice threw out their pictures before the move. Alice's friend Judy said the Midwest was supposed to have big and honest people in it who didn't go nosing around in others' lives. Judy said, "You have moved to a place that has a large and healing heart." *Has she ever been here?* Michael asked. *Does she even know where Chicago is?* Neither Alice nor Michael needed jobs right away. Their savings would be enough for a while, based on their inexpensive tastes and also on the lack of Jake, who was their only son. Without a child, life was a bargain. Everything seemed on sale. Michael said other people dreamed of living like this.

A month after the move, Alice signed up to be a role model to an inner-city youth. "Since when do you care about black kids?" Michael asked. But she needed something to do with her time, something more than gardening, and she had seen the advertisement in the paper, a woman of Alice's age looking satisfied as she clutched a dark-skinned girl to her, while the girl looked up at the woman with an enormous love. Alice remembered Jake, too young to speak, looking at her like that— his clear eyes speaking to her. "I believe in your love," his eyes said. Her hand cupped his head. A tired caseworker sat in their kitchen and passed Alice a picture of a skinny twelve-year-old in tight braids, laughing at something outside of the photograph. "She's too old," Alice said. The caseworker said everybody wanted a younger child so they were all taken. "Her name is Alissa and she needs you," the caseworker said. Alice pictured the girl with the eyes of an infant. She pictured the girl looking up with love in her eyes. It was August by this point, the sky hard and blue, and squirrels had begun chewing through the wood of their garage. "Let them," Alice told Michael, feeling kind-hearted, saving this, saving that, until she spotted Michael, in the backyard, chasing down the squirrels with a fierce and focused intensity, an iron rod in his hands.

In this new life, Alice thought her son would become an afterthought, hardly worth the mention, but even on the drives away from the city, where the landscape became obvious, a flat obvious surface, with nothing to hide, and nowhere to hide things, there Jake was, hiding. His hands over his eyes. "Can you find me?" he said. "Find me, find me!" They were driving west to someplace, the sun in their eyes, and Michael was talking to her again. *Alice, listen*, he said. Michael was saying shit happened to everybody. And did she think everybody walked around like she was, like a sad clown with shit all over her face? "People are more than their tragedies," Michael said. He was full of big talk that year.

Michael said all along he would not set a foot in jail to visit their son, so, in their old life, Alice had gone alone three weeks after the arrest. Jake already looked different, paler, and his hands—had they always been like that? How they appeared stronger than necessary now. She asked what he ate for breakfast. How he slept. "How do you think I sleep?" Jake said. The new and sterilized smell of him, the smell of disinfectant covering a gray and possibly rotting thing underneath. "Are you all right?" she asked. According to police reports, Jake had done what he did, and then he packed his linen shirts and swimming trunks and joined Alice and Michael in the Caribbean, their first family vacation in years, to celebrate the new year, where they all had a fine time, eating bowls of shellfish in the sun. Things had been more beautiful there. Everything. Paradise? Alice asked, and Jake leaned over to place a shrill red flower in her hair. He was shirtless and young and people turned to watch him. I made him! she remembered thinking. There is my son and I made him, I made this radiant person!

"Listen to me," Jake said to Alice, his voice an unnatural whisper. "I've heard about people having sex here."

"What? Where?" Alice asked. She forced herself to touch her son. She put her hand on his arm.

"In the visiting rooms. Right here."

"How? Why would you say something like that?"

"I'm telling you because it's true," Jake said. He leaned back in his chair and covered his eyes with his hands. In Alice's wallet was a folded picture of the girl. The photo was cut from a newspaper article that called Jake a monster. She meant to show her son the photograph. She wanted to watch her son as he studied the girl's picture. She wanted him to cry as he gently—gently!—touched the girl's face. Jake said, "I'm telling you because maybe someone here is having sex right now and we don't even know it." He was not crying. Why was he not crying? Alice told her son he would be OK. "I promise you'll be OK," she said. Her mouth pressed to Jake's infant ear, inhaling the milky smell of him, which was also her smell. "What are you talking about?" Jake said. "You'll be OK," Alice repeated. She remembered he had drifted to sleep in her arms and she promised him all sorts of things.

＊

When they first arrived to Chicago, just the two of them, Michael said *Doesn't this feel like it used to?* They were to start over here. "Let bygones be bygones," Michael explained. "It was a necessary free for all. I understand that. We did what was needed to survive." "But what did you do?" Alice asked. "Other than sleeping in our guest bedroom, what did you do?" There was supposed to be forgiveness. As if to prove this, before they finished their unpacking, boxes stacked in the hallway, bare mattresses in the bedrooms, Michael organized a romantic getaway, the sort of thing, he assured Alice, that childless people do all the time. He held her hand during the drive north to Wisconsin until they arrived. "Michael, this place is amazing," Alice said, though the woods looked as expected, they looked like any woods. That first night in their lodge suite, Alice dreamed of Jake. He stood beside the kitchen sink, wiping down the unbroken dishes with a tea towel. It was a boring dream. Ordinary light. Shadows and dark and so on. There he was. There.

The following morning, Michael busied himself at the fireplace, stacking logs into a teepee, like this was the Boy Scouts, stuffing outdated newspapers between the logs, lighting a match, blowing until the fire took hold. He told Alice to lie down. "I brought something for you," he said. He held out a black zippered bag and inside the bag were straps, handcuffs, a gag, clothespins, a lighter, and some latex things she had never seen before. "What is this, Michael?" Alice asked. He piled the objects in the center of the bed. "You don't know how hard it is to find some of this stuff," he said, not looking at her.

"You thought I couldn't do this but I can do this, if this is what you want. Show me what to do." Alice reached for Michael's hand. How much must two people go through together? What were the requirements?

"I told you. I was trying to make sense of something then," she began.

"Do you want me to hit you?" Michael said. "Do you think that guy was the only one who could leave a mark on you?"

Judy called Alice and said a door never closed without another door opening. She said when she thought of Alice—"and I've been thinking about you, I have"—all she could think of was this Oprah show where a newborn baby boy had only a few weeks to live, so the parents videotaped the baby every day that he was alive, an hour each day, or two hours, knowing each day was a gift. "I think it would help if you watched that show," Judy said. "It was so joyful, how they did it. It was not about grief. It was about appreciating what you still have."

Their son had, on the day after Christmas, in a Days Inn off the New York Thruway, murdered a call girl. Not the expensive type that politicians apparently used, but a girl with bargain rates, a not even pretty girl, somewhat overweight, who advertised in the back of the free weeklies. She looked—in the photograph the newspaper kept running—like a kid who had been awake for too long, with blown-out hair and exhausted eyes.

The motive of the murder remained unknown. Shooting the call girl with the gun pressed to her cheek was not enough. Shots in the knees and the ankles and the stomach. Knife marks along her inner thighs. The broken ribs and teeth marks and the bruises. "Did you?" Alice asked. Images of Jake as a child crowded her mind: her son, two years old, in tears, because the cars in the picture book had crashed again, apples and oranges and the rabbit drivers suspended in the air. "That is a stupid question," Jake said.

His semen down the girl's throat. Pictures of the ruined girl on his phone. Because of the girl's black mother, the question of race was considered. Did Jake hate black people? Or people of mixed race? Or did he simply hate all women? Alice had no idea. "Fix it," two-year-old Jake demanded, so Alice took the book and turned back to the beginning.

They called her son a monster on the news. "Mom, get me out of here," Jake said. But she had no idea how. She had not been given the resources. The correct resources must have been given to other mothers. More women came forth. It appeared Jake had wide and varied sexual tastes. It appeared Jake had a habit of going too far. When pressed for details by a reporter, one of the sex workers cried, remembering the things Jake made her do. What had Alice forgotten to teach her son? She closed her eyes. There Jake was, rubbing his pudgy fingers against the sad rabbit's face, as if it were a real rabbit and not a picture of a rabbit. Petting the page like she had shown him, his little hand careful and cupped. "Good," Alice told him. Another call girl said, "I guess I'm lucky to be alive."

Alice took the girl to a working farm that smelled like animal shit. The smell embarrassed Alissa, who barely spoke the whole outing, despite the constant questions Alice asked, the conversation starters suggested by the volunteer agency. The girl did not answer any of them. How did one speak to a child again? But when Alice asked should they do something the next weekend, Alissa nodded. So the following Saturday, they canoed across a lake with nothing visible in it. Alissa asked what the point of a lake was without fish in it. She had hoped to see fish. Alice had told her there would be fish. Wherever they went, there were rarely other black people around, but Alice was not sure what could be done about that.

Along the piers, men cast out fishing lines into the water then tugged their bare lines back. Alice paddled the canoe to the lake's center, where she eased the oars out of the water, allowing the boat to rock, and then, to her surprise, Alissa began to sing. Her voice was steady and hopeful; it sounded like someone else's voice, though the song itself was an odd choice—it was a song for grownups, popular years ago. The song was about a person viewed from a great distance, far enough away so no one could see the details of this person, but they were luminous somehow anyway. If I dreamed about you, would you become true? At night, in bed, Alice pictured a protective light in her hands, like she was a god or something, shining warmth and light all around the girl. She pictured herself cradling Alissa and singing quiet but powerful promises into the girl. That was the summer: the blank and dry wind, the urine in their yard from the strays, the daffodils with their yellow heads knocked off.

The man's name had been Adam, a produce clerk at the grocery store back in their old neighborhood out east. Alice liked how he watched her, like he did not care who she was but he was watching her because he cared about something else outside of her, something fantastical and garish flashing around her head. After Jake's arrest, Alice finally agreed to meet him at a motel in the afternoon, the room lit by a thin but direct sunlight. Adam's eyes moved from her breasts to the television then back to her breasts. "You need to be rough with me," Alice said. Or else she would leave. That was the whole point of it. She expected him to protest, though he didn't. He pressed his mouth hard against her ear. "You remember what you asked for when we're done here," he told her, and his voice sounded like a public alarm, controlled yet capable of causing panic.

Every few days, Adam chose the motel and paid cash for a room that looked identical to the room before. His hands near her neck, teasing at her collarbone, her windpipe. "I wish I could see the inside of your throat," he said. His hand crushed her mouth if she made a sound at certain times. "No sounds now," he said. Alice pictured a black bull on an inadequate leash. A lot of fraying ropes holding down something that could not be roped. The wrecked sheets, and the sounds of the sheets, ripping. All her life she had been told violence of such sorts should have looked rotted out, an old cellar with a busted light that no one wanted to descend into or admit, the sort of thing you turned away from, but it wasn't like that. It looked like any other place. It looked like any other thing. Not shoved into the shadows but crowing. There was something good here, she was sure of it, something understandable and human amid all that force. Then he used his teeth on her, she did not know where, she felt only her skin giving in to the edges of his teeth, and she was elsewhere, in an overwhelmed place made of rabid color.

Once, in the middle of it, she opened her eyes, and in the corner of the motel room, in a mirror, she glimpsed her son. Jake had dressed up for this. He was wearing a button-down shirt and a tie. His hair was smoothed down and side parted. He was holding his hands very still. He was holding his hands like they wanted to be doing something else but he needed to keep them still. It wasn't as simple as the light and the dark. Jake watched her and nodded, with a look of sad approval, with sympathy, at what went on there.

Alice was supposed to be her son's character witness in court. This was in their old life, of course. In their new life, Alice barely had a son, while in their old life, their son had a public defender, because of his credit card debt and Michael's refusal to pay legal fees. The defender's name was Jill and she said, "Alice, I need you to come to court and talk about your son's integrity." Jill needed Alice to keep three specific examples in mind. "Do you understand me? I need you to talk about him now, as an adult. Convince me and everyone else how he is a kind and loving man. Why he is good. Can you do that? Listen," Jill said, "I think you, as the mother of the accused, speaking honestly from the heart about your son, it will really help here." It was nearing dusk, the outside falling into the dark. Good riddance. Alice preferred the house when she could see nothing out of it. "Do you understand? Or else you can go ahead and give up on him," Jill said. "You can give your son up to the wolves if that's what you prefer."

Alissa lived with a cousin now. She and her mother were evicted from their apartment, they had spent a few nights in a homeless shelter, and now Alissa slept on the floor, in a closet. "Can I come stay with you?" Alissa asked, and Alice had to explain, uncomfortably, "Now is not a good time. There are a lot of things going on and it's not a good time." Alissa said her cousin wouldn't let her sleep with a pillow. If she went to sleep with a pillow, then her cousin came over in the dark and pulled the pillow from under her head. "Honey, it's OK to be frightened," Alice said. "But I'm not," Alissa said. "I'm not frightened."

When Judy called that week, she told Alice to stop worrying about other people. She said worrying about other people's problems was the number one way to avoid dealing with your own problems. "You need to care for yourself now," Judy said. She told Alice how every single event in your life is an opportunity to choose love over fear.

Michael found out about the affair eventually. When, in her old life, Alice allowed herself to be led upstairs, to their old bedroom,

Michael said, "I promise we'll be enough for each other." He said, "Jesus, Alice, I've missed you." For the last month he had slept in the guest bedroom, since that phone call from Jake had come in the middle of the night. They had barely looked at each other since. Michael said, "Look at me," holding her face between his hands so she either had to look at him or close her eyes. She closed her eyes. He smelled of a floral and pale soap. He touched her with such gentleness it was like he wasn't touching her. Eventually Michael noticed the bruises, of course he did. He kissed the first bruise he saw on her, and the second. "What have you done to yourself?" he said, laughing, until he saw how many there were. Dozens of them, of varying colors and sizes, starting above her knees and trailing up to her hips. A look of surprise and something else on Michael's face. The look of a person waking up from a dark dream into the dark. She struggled to pull up her skirt, but Michael had moved on, unbuttoning her shirt as she turned from him, so he saw more of them, the dark bruises on her abdomen and, beneath her bra, the marks across her right breast. Alice shoved his hand away. He yanked her underwear down. The sun's insistence of brightness in the room. The lack of shadows and the lack of the dark. When Jake was an infant, she walked around holding him in her arms, believing everyone must be filled with this buoyant kindness, everyone must be brimming with this warm generic light. But people had all sorts of things inside of them. "Go ahead," Alice said to Michael. Around them, cracking, the heat of something sharper-scented. Michael didn't look at her, he looked at his hands. He broke several things from the dresser, things of no apparent value, before leaving the room and slamming the bedroom door. When Alice tried to follow him, she found the door barricaded from the hallway. She sat on the bed, it must have been an hour or two, until she grew hungry, and then she pounded on the door until her fists stung from pounding the door. Whose forgiveness was needed here, and for what? She tried the door again, and this time it opened without resistance.

When they moved to Chicago, she wrote her son a letter. "We are in a new place now!" she wrote. "We are in a place of promise and wonderment. Anything can happen here. I wake up in the morning every day and I think to myself, today will be different." She was trying to give her son hope. She was trying to teach him something. She did not inform her son of their new address, but she included other personal details in her letter. "Our new house is yellow. You would find it funny because all the other houses on our block are brown or white and then here we are, the bright yellow house. Don't you think that must mean something?" She wrote how she was a mentor to an African American pre-teen ("would you believe it, Jake? But I am doing a good job of it"). And how her husband, "your father," she wrote, now snored at night, loudly, like something oddly shaped had lodged in his chest, something that would not come out, so Alice had started sleeping in the spare bedroom, "on your old mattress," she wrote. They had gotten rid of almost everything that belonged to their son, but the mattress—it was organic. They had paid a lot of money for it. Nothing had started to sag on it yet. So they had dragged it across the country with them. Instead of their son, she had a mattress, where she lay in the evening, face down, without sheets, her face against the pillow top, remembering her son. She remembered how Jake had surprised her once, pursing his lips to give her the first of one hundred small kisses. One! Two! Three! Four! Five! Six! Seven! Eight! "Enough!" Alice had laughed, pushing him away, as if the flawless kisses would go on.

"You sound like you need a good fuck," Judy said over the phone.

"Oh, we're fine," Alice said. "All of us here are just fine." They weren't in the movies for God's sake. Nobody was radiant anymore.

But larger problems appeared all around Alissa like gnats, like tiny viscous bugs. Problems that Alice had no idea about. "There's a gang of white boys," Alissa said in the car, on the way home from a modeling call she begged to attend. "They follow me home after school. They threw mud on me." The audition had been a scam, a way to entrap poor black kids into expensive classes that promised you nothing. Alissa wanted to sign up anyway, though Alice talked instead about focusing one's energy on reality, on what's possible. "What, like basketball?" Alissa said. "All you white people keep telling me I should play basketball." Alice stopped listening. She nodded as if she was listening, but she wasn't. What were you thinking, Michael asked, lying again when Alissa called.

Room #27. The Rest Haven Motel. It was not a pretty place but she did not need it to be. The room was dark and they left it dark. This was the day of Jake's court hearing. Certain people expected her to be there on the stand, in a suit, testifying to her son's good character. She said this out loud and Adam laughed at her, sprawled naked on the bed, the old bruises on her legs mixed with the new marks he had left. "Oh you mothers," Adam said, laughing.

She told Adam to tie the blindfold around her eyes again and, as he pulled the cloth tight, she thought—I am handing Jake to the wolves. What an odd old expression, though she could see herself doing so: knotting the coarse rope around her son's waist, gagging his mouth with a clean rag, the final glimpse of his face—

how he always looked like her!—before she lowered the hood around his head. Wondering, can't we all forget what happened and start over? Can't we all chop off our hands and be done with it? However, it was not done. Alice lowered the hood on her son ("Is this what you wanted?" Adam asked her. "Is this what you wanted me to do?") in the blunt light, in a plaza of direct light, so everyone could watch if they wanted. She understood what she did, and there was some relief in this. No more trying to do one thing but actually doing another. No loving and years of attentive loving to find out she raised a thing she didn't want—a thing no one in their right mind would want—but she had to want it, and find it beautiful, though no one in their right mind would find it beautiful. Alice let her son stumble and fall onto the road because people thought he deserved this. She helped him up then let him stumble again until his trousers tore, his left knee exposed, bruised and bloodied, parading him past all the houses, all the windows with the cracks in the drapes and the people looking through the cracks, her love for her son dragging after her, like a smashed-up cat shackled to her left ankle, attracting flies and the titters of the neighbors. She was glad people were watching, so they saw she did what was expected ("I bet your husband wants to know the kind of things you like," Adam whispered. "I bet you don't do this stuff with him, do you. I bet he has no idea"), how she led her son into the darkening forest, where she chose a rotted tree and she tied him to that tree with additional lengths of rope. From his mouth came a suffocated sound, but she did not remove the cloth from his mouth. He looked like her son. He looked like a child again. She kissed every finger of his right hand. She kissed his palm ("What kind of noise is that?" Adam said, laughing. "Shut up. Someone will think I'm raping you, Jesus, shut up"), then she left him, as the dusk and the dark and the cold came. She left her son hooded, gagged, and tied to a rotting tree, as the howls of the wolves began at the near borders. Because she was not one of those mothers who could change the course of things. She wished she was but she wasn't. ("I want to keep seeing you, Alice," Adam whispered into her hair. "I want to see you for a long time.") Everybody is supposed to get a second chance, someone older and wrong once told her.

Michael said he never had pretensions about the challenges of a long-term marriage. He was not one to sugarcoat. If the glass was half empty, then let's call it that, he said. And he understood the statistics, which allowed very few a hope in hell to create a lasting and permanent relationship. But hadn't they had raised a son together? Hadn't they known each other for years before raising that child? "How long have we known each other by this point, Alice?" he asked. They had years ahead of them, and those things that were done? He didn't want to talk about those things anymore, other than to say they should view those things as being done by other people. "You have no idea what's inside a person," Alice said. Michael ignored her. He said he believed in their strong foundation. He believed if a foundation was strong enough, it didn't matter what it covered up. He said this as if quoting a wise man, as if preaching from some holy book to a large and accepting crowd, though there was just Alice in front of him. He knelt beside her, and as if offering her a gift, he opened his hands, though there was nothing in them. He looked ridiculous and exposed like that, with his sadness and his empty hands. "Look, I am grieving here," he said to her. He said this as if his grief should have been an object she could see. As if it were a bright dust, settling onto his shoulders and his face, and onto Alice now too, onto her lips and her neck, and her feet too, and elsewhere.

*

The previous spring, Alissa hadn't wanted to go, but Alice took her anyway, to an Easter Egg hunt held in a puny forest south of the city, Alissa complaining she was too old for such shit. "If you're too old, then what about me?" Alice asked. Alissa rolled her eyes but she was laughing, her face open and attentive, as they joined the colorful crowd of children. There were streamers in the trees, and a musician who played shrill songs on his flute. The sun illuminated the forest. "This is a magical place," a volunteer said to them, to welcome them, and Alice felt welcomed. She felt Jake at her side, his small hand lost in her hand.

Were Jake still a child, and beside her, Alice would have told him look, pointing here, and here, and here. Look, the trees are budding. It's spring, she would have said, lifting him so she could carry his weight and he could feel the tight hard green buds of a maple tree. She had tried to create the perfect world for her son. If anyone needed proof of her love, if anyone questioned did she love her son enough, this was her proof. Of course she would have chosen some kinder place, a place with better lighting, but she worked with what she was given, and if, in the distance, there had been a glittering edge? If she heard snarls of certain animals, the red smear at the far grass, the shadows dancing suggestively with mock violence? Who wouldn't have turned away, to pretend such things could not belong there. She remembered, once, kneeling close to Jake, at his level. She knelt behind him and held him, and faced the same direction he faced, and she watched him. She could not see what he saw, but she wanted to see. She wanted to see a world overwhelmed and protected by her love. Jake's look was delicate, but certain too, and full of faith. What was he believing in then? She assumed he was watching something with goodness in it, though perhaps she was mistaken.

The eggs were not particularly well hidden. They were on the path, or right beside the path, unnaturally colored pinks and blues and yellows. Alissa picked up one egg and placed it in her pocket. She took another, then a third, causing the volunteer to frown. "Is this your child?" the volunteer asked. "Of course not," Alice said. From a hidden place, a bird repeated the same penetrating note and something about the sound, the pure sameness of the note, made Alice recall Jake, asleep in her arms, his head tipped back against her breast, his little mouth still sucking, with peaceful certainty. She had felt then like she was holding herself, the best parts of herself.

Alissa was talking to her now. "Tell me again," Alice asked, straining to pay attention, and Alissa told of a dream of her mother's, about a house sent to them by God. "My mom said the house has a fence so we can get a dog. My mom's been praying and then God told her everything," Alissa said. "It sounds like a nice house," Alice said. And why not? She could picture the mother and girl in a devastated place, where nothing they needed was there, so the mother handed her child imaginary things, because this was what mothers did when there was nothing else to be done. The girl held each imagined thing as if it were real, and why not? "We are in a magical place, Alissa. Did you know that? You are in a magical and shining place," Alice said to the girl. The world looked as it always did, but she repeated herself, hoping Alissa would believe her. Alissa waved her hands as if swatting away flies. She said, "OK, I get it, OK." The signs pointed deeper into the woods. "This way to the Easter Bunny!" the signs read. It was ridiculous, of course it was—a man in a rabbit costume, asking each child what she wanted, then offering in return a bag of six jelly beans—but something needed to be believed in here. There Jake was, beside her in the warm light of her love, believing in things. The girl led the way, and Alice continued to follow.

THE SOUND OF CRYING SHEEP

by Sarah Elizabeth Schantz

— For my mother, Enid Schantz

"EVERY DAY IS A NEAR-DEATH experience," Mama says, exhaling a cloud of smoke. She's not talking to us, but that doesn't keep me from listening. I always listen to Mama. This might be all she says this week. Daddy grips the steering wheel, driving the smooth blacktop that stretches across Kansas, the state I've never left. He hates cigarettes. His eyes are bloodshot from the smoke. I still live at home. I don't know where to go or who to be. I'm waiting for a path to take me. Living on the farm with Daddy means I'm there when Mama visits. Gran says I need to quit calling them Daddy and Mama, but I don't know what else to call them. I go to church with Gran to make her happy. Adam and Eve get stuck in my mind, though no one discusses them. I think about Eve and how she was fashioned from Adam's rib. I want to ask Mama about that, but it's Monday again, and we're taking her back to the hospital. Just like every week. Like Eve, I was cut out, too. Emergency Cesarean. Nineteen years ago, come next week.

I go to a therapist. In her waiting room, I sit on the sleek leather couch. I have a habit of reading everything, like shampoo bottles in other people's bathrooms. I scan the magazine covers, the pamphlets displayed on the walls. When it's my turn, I go into her office and sit in the overstuffed armchair. She shakes my hand and tells me to call her Carla. She explains what paranoid schizophrenia is. Tells me it's hereditary. She tells me how Mama first struggled with hers when she was a teen. But Mama took her medication and learned to manage the disease. The therapist is the first to explain that when Mama went off her meds to have me, she never went back on them. She says the C-section had nothing to do with Mama coming undone, but that's where she's wrong. I've seen the long scar that runs vertically down Mama's belly. Mama used to talk to me about the birth. Unlike everyone else, Mama told me things as if I understood her, and I did. "They put me to sleep," she said. "One moment you were inside me, and the next, when I woke up, you were gone."

I hate the interstate: the rush, and the passing—the complicated loops of highways all coming together like a complex nervous system right there in the heart of Lawrence. We're still in the rural outskirts. Not there yet. I close my book, feeling carsick, and watch the oil rigs. They dip back and forth and look like grasshoppers. Every time a semi passes, I'm sure this is it. On the news it's this stretch of interstate where all the catastrophes happen: "Entire family killed," "Semi full of hazardous chemicals overturned."

Mama's right. Every day is a near-death experience.

The medication has made Mama fat. In the winter they dress her in shapeless sweats and in the summer wrinkled muumuus. Framed by the side mirror, I watch her face. She smokes her Salem, counting under her breath with each exhale. I find myself counting with her sometimes. Every once in a while, from behind her bloated face, I see how she used to look, used to be.

*

I'm in the third grade. We're supposed to choose a fairy tale and make our own book at home. It's my first homework assignment, and Mama is excited. Mama decides on "Little Red Riding Hood"—I don't tell her I want to do "Rapunzel." Mama took a multi-media art class as an undergraduate at Cornell before she met Daddy and tells me she learned how to make pop-up books. She thinks it'll be fun to make one for the assignment and laughs, telling me, "You'll be the only kid in the class to make one." She buys tubes of paint and a variety pack of Sharpies from Hobby Lobby. And two new scissors, a pair for me and a pair for her. Back home before we begin, she takes all of the boxes of cereal we have outside. She dumps each one, even the ones that were unopened. Laughing, she throws the contents of box after box into the yard. The crows that Daddy tries to keep away with his faceless straw men come, and will for days, to peck the dead grass for cornflakes and Cheerios. We go inside and start the book at the kitchen table.

My scissors are meant for paper, but Mama's are for cloth—they're expensive, stainless steel. The shine is dangerous. She does most of the cutting because mine won't make it through the thin cereal box cardboard. I make the ax for the woodcutter. I use a toothpick for the handle and a scrap of cardboard for the blade. It starts out silver, but Mama says, "Add more red." I'm using a red paint pen. It's leaky and hard to control.

Mama forgets to have us write anything in the pop-up book, but the pictures tell enough. There is red paint all over the table, all over me, on Mama too. Daddy comes in for dinner and studies Mama's face. She talks to him in a shrill voice that doesn't sound like Mama. Daddy takes Mama to another room. I'm left alone with my spaghetti. It's left over from the night before, still cold. Instead of eating, I carefully separate the red-soaked pages and don't tear a single one. The woods pop up, then the wolf, the house, the grandmother herself, and finally the woodcutter, his ax springing upward. I look at the wolf's belly, the damage already done, and little Red's head just poking out of the slit Mama cut.

I can hear them talking through the heating vent in the floor, their voices tinny. Daddy says, "You have to try and let go." A pause. "Try to be happy that she made it out alive." A longer pause. "Is that even what's bothering you?" he asks. "Are you having any of those other thoughts?" Then Mama yells, telling him that she's perfectly fine. "Stifled," I hear her say once she's done screaming; she says it like it's Daddy's fault. Then Mama leaves. I can tell because of the sound the front door makes when she slams it behind her.

The next morning, the pop-up book is gone and so is Mama. Daddy keeps me out of school for the day. He needs my help on the farm. They are weaning all the baby lambs by taking them away from their mothers. The world is loud with the sound of crying sheep. Mama comes home in time to make dinner, and everything returns to normal. I go to school the next day, and Mrs. Jefferson takes me aside during free time. She says not to worry, that she's talked to my Daddy, and she understands everything. Not to worry about the assignment. But I don't understand.

Mama lights another cigarette. We're approaching Lawrence now. A silver station wagon drives beside us, and I don't feel as anxious as I would if it were a semi. The car is full: father driving, mother riding up front next to him with a map folded in her lap. There are three kids buckled up in the backseat, and I can tell they're singing by the way their mouths move and their heads sway back and forth. In the far back I see a red and white cooler, pillows, and suitcases. As they pass us, I see the Colorado license plate, the outline of green and white mountains. There's a bumper sticker, too. It reads, "What if the hokey pokey really is what it's all about?"

Mama started smoking after she was committed to St. John's. Then her weight came on. Daddy explains that she smokes to keep track of time. Most schizophrenics, like her, chain smoke. With each cigarette, I watch Mama drift away with the gray smoke, and I don't understand.

Mama and Daddy meet in college, fall in love, and are married—just the two of them, at the courthouse, both in blue jeans. When they graduate, they decide to leave the rat race behind. They come to Kansas, to the family farm where Daddy grew up. They begin the long process of converting the farm to all organic. I'm conceived, and Daddy tells Mama that she glows. Mama joins a homebirth group and goes off her medication so she can have me all natural. She picks out a midwife and begins to grow me while Daddy plants corn and sweet potatoes. Mama starts a sunflower patch, tall and yellow. I grow bigger and bigger, take up all of Mama, and when I'm supposed to turn like all babies do, I don't have enough room. The midwife has Mama do exercises to encourage me to turn. Carefully, Mama does headstands against the wall with Daddy spotting her. They laugh at the absurdity of a fully pregnant woman doing such a thing. Mama shines a flashlight into her vagina. I'm supposed to move toward the light, but I stay in the darkness and don't turn. The midwife has delivered other breech babies, but none as big as she thinks I'll be. She presses her fingers on Mama's belly. "There's her head," she says. "And her feet, down toward your cervix." The midwife measures Mama's belly from navel to pubis. "Nine pounds if not over." But she agrees to try the homebirth.

Mama nests. She buys and gathers all of the equipment on

the list the midwife gives her. The other women in her homebirth group have babies one by one, all at home. One woman gave birth outside at sunrise. Another delivered her child right into her husband's hands. They all describe birth as empowering. Empowering. Mama has no doubt that I'll turn when the time comes, and if not, she'll push me into life backward.

Mama's contractions come on fast and hard. She says it felt like she was being split into two. The midwife comes but refuses to do the homebirth, tells Daddy Mama must be taken to the hospital. Mama agrees to go but can't stop crying. She tells them she can still do it, deliver me breech, but the nurses and doctors ignore her and prep her for surgery instead. Like how God put Adam to sleep, the anesthesiologist does the same to Mama. I'm born from a dream as though I'm not real.

When I enter the fourth grade, Mama joins a support group for women who also had unplanned C-sections. Mama tells me no one realizes how much it hurts some women. But Mama's disappointed right away with the group. She's the only one with a child older than two. She can't concentrate with all the babies fussing, all those distracted mothers. I hear Gran on the phone saying the other women must be scared of Mama because it's been nine years since I was born, that Mama needs to get on with life. Gran stops the conversation short when she sees me in the doorway.

Mama comes and goes lately. Even if she hasn't left the house all day or changed out of her nightgown. She comes and goes. Mama goes to the group until she meets Theresa and Florence, therapists specializing in C-section grief. Daddy says they're just the same as ambulance chasers. Mama doesn't tell Daddy she started doing private sessions over at Florence's home office. After a month,

Mama brings me for my first session. She tells Daddy we're doing a mother/daughter craft class together at the Rec Center. Daddy ruffles my hair. I think he knows how much I've been missing Mama. Then he kisses Mama on the mouth—he hardly ever does that anymore. I decide it's best to keep Mama's secret. Not tell him. Together we drive to Florence's ranch house in the suburbs. Mama stops at the Dairy Queen, and we get strawberry milkshakes and suck them through straws as she drives.

What Florence calls the "Recovery Room" is the basement of her house. She leads Mama and me down the stairs. Theresa's already there, straddling a big purple yoga ball. There is no furniture in the room except a pile of red sleeping bags and a couple of bed pillows. Mama starts crying. Florence wraps her arms around Mama, and I stand there not knowing what to do. Theresa smiles at me as she gently rocks back and forth on her yoga ball. Florence talks to my mother like she's a little girl. "You deserved a real birth experience," she says, looking Mama in the eye, framing Mama's face with her palms. "The patriarchy robbed you of that. All those doctors..." she says, and she and Theresa exchange a knowing look. Florence even blames my father, and I feel mad when Mama doesn't correct her. Florence tells my mother, "Now it's time for you to have your baby on your terms."

We go to Florence's house a lot. I learn to take deep breaths before they wrap me up in sleeping bags. That way I don't run out of air as fast as I did the first few times. It's hard to breathe in there, but I love the warm, smothering feeling. I feel their hands all over me, massaging me, unfolding me. Florence tells my mother that they're manually turning me, that I'm not breech anymore, that she should push. Mama's moaning now, and both Florence and Theresa coach her. "You're doing such a good job!" they tell her, and then they yell for her to push. "Push. Push harder!" All hands are on me, pushing me and rolling me. From the dark heart of those sleeping bags I am delivered, again and again, gasping to breathe and surrounded by wide-eyed women. I feel embarrassed when one of them says, "Here's your beautiful baby girl." But then Mama takes my little girl body in her arms, holds me tight. She kisses me gently, and there is no better place to be.

Mama lights another cigarette, and Daddy rolls down his window. The sound of the interstate rushes in, and I take deep breaths, one after the other. We're going awfully fast. Another weekend with Mama home, over. I never seem to get any time alone with her. I think that if I ever do, then maybe I'll move out, go to college, go far away. Gran always comes to help out when Mama's home and Daddy overloads me with chores. This weekend he had me split wood. I chopped all the wood we'll need for November. I think Daddy's afraid I'll be disappointed with Mama. I think Daddy's afraid I'll end up just like her. Gran, who is his mother, has always said that Mama and I are like paper dolls cut from the same paper. Looking at Mama now, I see why they're afraid. My eyes are in her eyes. My slouch is in her shoulders.

When Mama comes home, she sits out on the day porch in her rocking chair. She doesn't look out at the fields or the old apple orchard. She sits there because it's the only place Daddy lets her smoke. She even sleeps like that, through the night, with an old quilt wrapped around her. She rocks back and forth, nervous, smoking her Salems, and stares at the fake wood paneling that runs beneath the windows. When she's gone I clean that spot she stares at, polish it with Murphy's oil as if it were real wood. When she comes home, I wait for her to notice. She never says anything. Daddy says I'm going to wear away the surface until it's just cardboard. Gran tells him to leave me be.

I wish the frontage road could get us to the hospital, but it can't. I feel trapped on I-70, and everyone drives so fast. Every Monday, Daddy drives Mama back on the interstate. He pulls in at the drop-off area in front of the hospital, and Mama gets out of the truck as soon as a nurse comes to fetch her. Every Monday, Mama leaves us as if she was never with us. No hugs, no goodbyes. Daddy hands her two cartons of cigarettes to help her through the week, and Mama takes them like he's a clerk at the store. She shuffles off, a nurse hooked to her arm. The nurse smiles like I never do, asking Mama how her visit was. But Mama just looks at her feet and walks where the nurse leads her.

Florence and Theresa's practice gets closed down, and somehow Daddy finds out me and Mama have been going. I hear Gran on the phone telling someone how Mama is disintegrating. I remember when Mama told Daddy that Gran was nothing but a gossip. Now Mama leaves the burners on a lot, and one day the tea kettle explodes. I ask Mama questions—simple ones, like where the bath towels are, but she won't answer me. It's like she can't see me.

It's more than just the engine or the rain that wakes me. It's a bad feeling. I've been dreaming, but the dream runs away fast. From my window, I watch Daddy in the dark rain, throwing stuff into the back of the truck. I grab my robe and go downstairs. Gran is in the kitchen. She looks at me, surprised.

"Why are you here?" I ask. She says Daddy called her to come stay the night with me. All the hogs got out, and he needs to get them back. I tell her I'm thirteen years old, that I don't need a babysitter. Besides, I think, Mama is here. I slip on my rubber boots and rain slicker and ignore Gran's protests as I rush outside into the wet night. Daddy doesn't see me slide into the truck, not until he gets in, too. For a second he stops, looks at me. His eyelids droop because he's tired. His eyes are sad. He nods and shifts the truck into gear, and we slip out onto the county road that runs past our house.

Daddy has the brights on, and they highlight long strips of rain and road. All of a sudden, the headlights pick up the hogs. They're snorting at the sky, awkward and miserable under the hard rain. Daddy pulls over to the side of the road, and that's when I see Mama. She's in one of her white linen nightgowns, and she glows against the black night. She's soaked through, and even from here I can see her breasts and dark pubic hair through the wet white fabric. She's just standing there with her arms raised, smiling. She stands there like she's being spotlighted on a stage. She doesn't pay attention to us. Daddy gets out of the truck, pulling his hood over his head. He starts leading the hogs back through the gate and doesn't tend to Mama until he's finished with the livestock. That's when I understand that he's done.

Without Mama the house sounds different. At night I still suck my thumb. I'm embarrassed because I'll be fourteen soon, but I just can't stop. I fall asleep afraid I'll be caught and jump at every little noise. At first we go visit her a lot. The visiting room is noisy and full of stale smoke. Mama won't look at me or Daddy. She just counts each drag she takes and lights one cigarette off the other. Her complexion begins to blend in with the hospital walls.

We sit in silence for a long time. Daddy goes to get a cup of coffee. There's a television on and people talking and one group is playing a board game, but no one laughs here. Mama looks at me. "You're not mine, you know?" she says as she lights another cigarette, smiling at me like it's not my fault or anything.

*

By the time I'm fifteen, Daddy's sold off the livestock and leases the fields to other farmers. His heart isn't in it anymore. I stay with Gran a lot. She makes me take cotillion classes. She tells me how blessed she was to only have sons to raise, that girls are nothing but trouble. I don't like my grandmother and wish that my mother's mother was still alive. I want a soft grandmother. Gran tries to be nice, but it comes off fake. Like when she says I'm a poor dear and I don't deserve any of this, but then she looks at me the way she does, searching for something wrong.

"What do you guys do, as a family, when your mother visits?" Carla, my therapist asks. She looks relaxed, her tortoise-shell eyeglasses low on her nose. She sits in her chair with her legs tucked under her. I look at her shoes on the floor where she kicked them off—brown suede, practical soles.

I look at Carla long enough to shrug my shoulders.

"How is your father doing?" Carla asks, waiting with her pad of paper and pen.

On the wall above Carla is a painting. An abstract, rendered in runny grays and blues, the painting is of a naked woman with a bird's head; she has an aura of messy white and a yolk-yellow beak. I think about the little bird that's taken to sitting on the roof outside my bedroom window every morning. The bird is quiet with blue-black feathers, bigger than a swallow. I wonder what kind of bird it is.

"He's OK, I guess."

"I see. How about you? How are you doing?" Carla never shows her impatience. "How have your anxiety levels been? Tell me about the last time you and your father drove your mother back to the hospital."

*

Daddy exits the interstate. The Dodge Ram seems so large on the side streets. I feel safe again. Mama lights another cigarette. We're three blocks away from the hospital. The houses are old in this part of town. Some have remnants of gingerbread architecture, but mostly they're just run down. Red and yellow leaves gather in the gutters, wet, beginning to rot. Daddy signals, turns right. Mama ashes her cigarette, counts under her breath. Daddy turns again and pulls up in front of the hospital. The American flag and the Kansas flag turn lazily in the wind. A guy in blue coveralls uses a leaf blower to clear the wide sidewalk in front. It's still early, and the nurse hasn't come down to gather Mama. Daddy puts the truck in idle; the engine eases. We sit quiet. The smoke from Mama's cigarette, without the outside wind to suck it out, fills the cab, and Daddy leans his head out the window. My throat is dry.

The nurse appears from the revolving doors and comes to our truck in her rubber shoes. She's very young. I feel older than she is although I'm not. The nurse is sure to smile at me and tells Daddy good morning. Still smiling, she helps Mama out of the truck. Mama has the cartons of cigarettes under her other arm. When they get to the door, Mama drops them. The nurse stoops down to pick them up, and while she does, Mama stands there. I watch Mama wait for the nurse. For a second I can see the woman Mama was supposed to be. Somewhere inside all that flesh. I think about those scissors of hers from so long ago. I think that if only I had those, maybe I could cut my mother out of this stranger. The nurse stands and takes Mama by the arm again. They slip into the building, and both Daddy and I stare after Mama, looking at where she was, as if there's something to see.

ALL THEIR RICHES

by David Yost

MY ENGLISH WASN'T ALWAYS this good. Once, I stood before an impatient pharmacist, touching my son's throat and saying "Sick" and "Help." I stuttered in fear buying a bus pass or a sack of oranges. I set a microwave dinner afire on the stovetop because I couldn't read the four sentences of instructions.

Now I've crossed the mountain: I've battled my way through night school, learned to understand the swift English of Jay Leno and Conan O'Brien, and bought a dozen used books, the first I've ever owned. They wait on a shelf in my son's room for the day that Gay Htoo is old enough for us to read them together. Some days, when he's at school, I go in and say the titles aloud for practice: *Dracula. A Tale of Two Cities. To Kill a Mockingbird. The Bourne Ultimatum.* I buy chicken and pumpkins using crisp, clean consonants. I'm still a foreigner, but at least people don't revolve their eyes when I speak.

Today there are hundreds of resettled Karen refugees from Burma here in Milwaukee, but you can imagine what life was like for us, the first twenty, sprinkled across the city like the seeds of a careless farmer. Picture me following Derek, our startlingly obese caseworker, through the new apartment, trying to concentrate on his English with all of my mind. Picture me flipping a light switch for the first time and seeing the lamps blossom into electric life. Picture me flinching at the scream of the smoke alarm and the rush of water in the toilet and the wintry blast of the freezer, the coldest air I'd ever felt. My new apartment was full of traps, it seemed.

Derek demonstrated the telephone, the gas oven, and the toilet paper. (Put it only in the toilet, he instructed, never in the trash.) Finally he moved to the door, and his hand engulfed mine like a catfish eating a minnow.

"Congratulations, Naw Me Me," he said, shaking my hand. "You made it."

After he left, I held the card with his phone number and read it. I picked up the phone and practiced pointing my finger at the numbers. I sank into the couch with Gay Htoo, but its softness unnerved me, and we moved to the carpet instead.

"When will we see the Statue of Liberty?" he asked me in Karen.

"Say it in English," I told him, and when his face sank, I added, "Maybe soon."

For all I knew, it could even have been true.

When we finally ventured to the supermarket, we walked every aisle, marveling. I hefted onions as big as my fist and an eggplant the size of Gay Htoo's head. I stared at boxes for manicotti noodles, Hamburger Helper, and frozen blueberry waffles, trying to imagine what foods they might contain. We watched carts go by full to the top with potato chips, frozen pizzas, and bottles of juice and soda.

I wanted to try one of everything, but I was still confused by American money and its decimals, and I didn't know what I could afford. In the end I took two five-pound bags of rice and an orange for Gay Htoo, and I got in line to pay.

"Hello," I said to the tall boy behind the counter as he dragged my food across the sensor. I held out a pair of bills, careful to touch my left hand to my elbow in respect. "Please, thank you," I said. He had a faint blond mustache, like the hairs you scrape from a hog before its butchering. *It's not my fault*, I wanted to tell him. In my country I could speak just like you. Alone in my apartment I knew hundreds of English words—I could walk through, pointing for Gay Htoo, and say, "Microwave, ceiling fan, electrical socket," with him repeating after me—but whenever I actually faced a white person, the words faded like ghosts, and all I wanted to do was run.

"Please, thank you," I said again, pushing the bills toward the boy. Finally he took one. I picked up my rice and my orange, grabbed Gay Htoo's hand, and hurried toward the sliding doors.

"Miss!" the tall boy called behind me. "Miss, wait!"

I hadn't paid enough, I feared. I thought of the police, of the stories I'd heard in Thailand of beatings and gropings of the women unlucky enough to be caught outside the refugee camp. Two days in America, I thought, and already I have one foot on the prison wall.

The tall boy caught up to me, his face flushed.

"Jeez, Miss," he said, "don't forget your change." He held out two bills and a handful of silver coins.

"Please, thank you," I said, taking the money, and I meant it.

After that, I hid in my apartment, afraid to leave, afraid to stay, watching the television and eating rice, my son trapped beside me. This is how the Pritchards found us a week later. When I heard the three sharp bangs on the door, I reached for the phone, thinking, *Nine-one-one, nine-one-one,* as I'd rehearsed so many times, but then a woman called my name.

"Hello?" I called back, gesturing for Gay Htoo to silence the television. "Who, please?"

"I'm Belle Pritchard," the woman said through the door. "I'm here with my husband, Alex. We're from the First Lutheran Church?" She said it as a question, as if I were expected to confirm.

"We're here to help," a male voice added.

I stood on my toes to look through the peephole and saw two smiling white faces: Belle's slender and well made-up, and Alex's bearded and fat as a pineapple. I was relieved. In those days, it shames me to say, I was still terrified of my black neighbors; a friend who'd resettled in Dallas had written to us that it was the dark-skinned Americans you had to be careful of, and seeing the angry slouches of my building's teenagers, I foolishly believed her.

"Enter, please," I said to Alex and Belle now, opening the door. I motioned to the couch as they stepped inside. Gay Htoo stood quiet, awed at our first white guests. With her church-mother's instincts, Belle noticed him immediately.

"And who's this?" she cried in exaggerated delight, crouching and clapping her hands to her thighs.

Gay Htoo's eyes went big with fear.

"Please," I said. "This is my son, Gay Htoo. You are very welcome." I motioned again to the couch.

"I'm Alex Pritchard," Alex said. Before I could react, he grabbed my hand and shook.

"Yes," I said, touching my other hand to my elbow. "Thank you."

"Hey there, little buddy," he said, crouching beside his wife to look at Gay Htoo, who now ran to my side and grabbed hold of my longyi.

"Please," I said, "sit," finally finding the word, and they did.

Their church was partnered with Derek's refugee agency,

Alex explained; he and Belle had come to see if there was any way they could help me adjust to America. As he talked, I could see Belle assessing my apartment: the carpets littered with rice grains that I couldn't seem to sweep away; the greasy coffee table where we'd just eaten; the nose-smudged windows where Gay Htoo and I perched to watch our new world of brick, concrete, and streetlamps.

"How do you like Milwaukee?" Alex asked.

"Oh," I said, "very good city," as if, had I given any other answer, they would have sent me home.

Belle stood and wandered into my kitchen.

Alex continued asking questions. "Is your apartment satisfactory?"

"Oh," I said, "very good apartment."

Belle opened the refrigerator and furrowed her plucked eyebrows. Inside I had four boxes of light bulbs and nothing else; they'd seemed so delicate that I hadn't known what else to do with them.

"Is there anything we can bring you?" Alex asked. "Anything that you need, or that your son needs?"

Fish paste and curry, I wanted to tell him. Tea-leaf salad and mohinga. A plastic floor mat for eating. Pumpkins and tofu. A job, so I could pay the first installment of my airfare debt. A way to leave my apartment without watching for tripwires. A way for my son to live a better life than his father's.

"No," I said. "Everything, very good."

Then Belle opened a cabinet in the kitchen and gave a shriek. Alex jumped to his feet, but already Belle was shaking her head and trying to make herself laugh.

"Just a roach," she said. But I knew my cabinets, and I knew that she hadn't seen just one. Alex moved to Belle, squeezed her shoulder, and gave her a look that even I understood. We're helping this one whether she likes it or not, his look said, and her look back said, I love you, and then she turned to see me watching them like a beggar outside a wedding feast.

"If it's OK to ask," she said, "are you married?"

"Honey," Alex murmured, but I said quickly, "Oh, yes. Very happy."

Belle smiled, relieved. "Is your husband still in Burma?"

"He will come," I said. "Later."

But Saw Isaac had left with the Karen National Liberation Army five years before, and I had not seen him since.

On their second visit Alex and Belle brought bananas and rice and, though I had no can opener, dozens of cans of vegetables, beans, and fruit. They brought milk, which I dutifully put in my refrigerator, too shy and word-clumsy to explain what I'd learned in the camps: that both Gay Htoo and I were lactose intolerant from our Karen diets. They brought carrots, tomatoes, and asparagus and showed me how to store them in the crisper drawer. They brought lamps for my apartment's shadowed corners, a vacuum for the carpets, and a gorilla doll for Gay Htoo, which he carried in his arms for the rest of the afternoon, beating his chest and roaring as Alex had taught him.

"This is too much," I said with every bag they opened. "No, no, too much!" But I didn't mean it, and they knew. It was like Water Festival and Christmas combined, and before the afternoon was out, I had more possessions than ever before in my life.

"Welcome to America," Alex said, and he laughed. It was a laugh with many feelings, I think: The pleasure of helping another, because Alex had a heart to match his stomach. Amused surprise, that I might think this was a real sacrifice. (I didn't, really, though I will always be grateful for their help.) Embarrassment, that they had so much, and I so little. And, for the same reason, pride.

On Sunday they drove Gay Htoo and me to their church, a stone castle floating in a lake of grass. How silly I felt, in my hand-sewn longyi with no thanaka for my cheeks, beside these beautiful ladies with shoes that matched their dresses and handbags that matched their shoes. How small I felt beside these men in their broad suits and ties. How poor I felt before the church's thick carpets and arching chapel, its stained glass and bright banners and bulging organ. I thought of the church in Kah Law Ghaw, with its bamboo walls and a blue plastic tarp for a roof, the way we'd celebrated after our church had raised the money—about five American dollars—to buy that tarp. I thought of the day a British camp volunteer, a young woman who had scandalized our English class by teaching in sleeveless shirts, tried to explain the phrase "on holiday."

"A trip," she told the class. "You travel, to see something new, to have an adventure. If you could go on holiday, where would you go?"

"I want return my village," a man answered, and several people nodded.

"No, no," the volunteer said. "Somewhere new. Like Angkor Wat, or the Grand Canyon. Someplace you want to visit for fun."

I put up my hand.

"Like you visit refugee camp?" I asked.

"No," she said, reddening, "I'm here to help."

And at that moment I hated her, this lovely woman who'd left her job and her family to bring us textbooks and knowledge but then spent more in a week on alcohol than I would see in four years. That night I prayed to God to take my envy from me, and for penance I bought the woman a package of cookies I couldn't afford. Still the anger lingered, and that day with the Pritchards it followed me even into the house of my God.

*

We Karen have no family names, but when I applied for Gay Htoo's Social Security card, the rushed clerk listed him as "Htoo, Gay." (If only this man had warned me what this name would mean for my son's future: the taunts and shoves, the scrapes and bruises, the afternoons of him weeping in his room, until at last he declared his new first name to be Greg.) So when the first letter came from the school, it came addressed to "the parents of Htoo, Gay."

I sat for hours with the letter and my Karen-English dictionary, trying to work it out: immunizations, enrollment papers, school supplies. As Gay Htoo watched cartoons beside me, I parsed phrases like "three-ring binder" and "safety scissors" and "dry-erase markers," but though I could find each word, they added up to nothing. I counted the remainder of our resettlement money, but I had no idea what these items would cost.

On the television two American boys played joyously with a robot that fired plastic rockets from its hands. If only Gay Htoo could be one of these boys, I thought. I considered calling Alex and Belle, as they'd so often urged me to do, but they came less often now, and always in a rush, dropping gifts of groceries or toys on the counter and stopping only a moment for conversation. Belle would ask me about our food, and Alex would ask me about the plumbing, but even as I stammered my answers, blushing with shame at my English and with pleasure from their company, their eyes drifted back to the door, perhaps fixing on their next hurried good deed.

So in the end I was a coward: I left the letter on the table and didn't call. Two days passed, and then four. I caught myself waiting at the window and listening for footsteps in the hall, but all I heard was the thrum of the ceiling fan and the slide whistle of Gay Htoo's cartoons. When we'd first come to Milwaukee, he'd asked me every day to go play outside, missing the open spaces of the camp, but I was too afraid of murderers and police. Finally he'd stopped asking, and now we spent our days playing with his building blocks or practicing English but more often sitting side by side, watching cartoons, movies, and talk shows we barely understood and waiting for Belle and Alex to knock.

When I finally heard the bang at the door, I was frying pork for lunch. I ran from the kitchen without even turning off the stove.

"Please," I said, opening the door to Alex and Belle, "come in, come in."

But Belle smiled and shook her head. "We just wanted to drop off a few more things the congregation gave," she said, handing me a paper sack. (Board games and military dolls, I discovered later.) "We have to run."

The apartment filled with the smell of scorching chilies. I thought of the school's letter and tried to insist, but in the end it was Gay Htoo who saved us, bounding up behind me shouting, "Hello, hello, hello!" and giving his gorilla roar. Alex smiled, and Belle relented. They stepped into our kitchen, where I turned off the burner too late to save our lunch.

"Mmmm, smells good in here," Belle said.

Alex put a sack of children's clothes down on the table, and then, as I'd planned, he saw the letter.

"Uh-oh," he said to Gay Htoo. "Looks like somebody's starting school."

Belle looked over her husband's shoulder. "They ask for more every year, don't they?"

"Please," I asked, "what is 'three-ring binder'?"

Alex smiled, picked up the letter, and folded it. "Let us take care of it," he said, and I felt a rush of guilt for how easily my plan had worked.

"No," I said, "I will pay. But I do not understand all—"

"Nope," Alex said. "Taken care of," and he tucked the paper away into his pocket.

School was two weeks away, and Gay Htoo and I practiced the ten-block walk each morning, past the check-cashing shops and the gas station and the barred windows of our neighbors, down through the park with its basketball hoops and creaking swing sets, along the ragged sidewalks and up to the gate that would separate me from my son for the first time in his life. Derek had arranged it so that I would start work the same day as Gay Htoo's schooling— half shifts sorting laundry at a downtown hotel. Otherwise I think I would have stood on that sidewalk all day, watching for a glimpse of him in the windows.

"I don't want to go, Mommy," he said, but I saw the way he brightened at the sight of the playground's plastic castles, and I knew he was only telling me what I wanted to hear.

"You must be brave like your father," I told him mechanically, and then, as an afterthought, "Say it in English." And to my surprise, he did. He would be a great scholar, I told him, a headmaster or a professor, and on our way home I let him play on the swings.

Days passed with no word from the Pritchards, and each night I checked the calendar and fidgeted the sleeve of my blouse. Gay Htoo and I walked the five miles for Sunday worship, but I didn't see them in their usual pew; they had gone to the early service, one of their friends told me. Belle called the next day to say Alex would come that evening with the school supplies, but then she called two hours later to say they'd forgotten their daughter's tae kwon do lesson and asked if Alex could come Friday instead.

"Yes, very good," I said. "Thank you." When I marked the day on my calendar, I saw it was only three days before Gay Htoo's school began.

*

On Friday we didn't take our walk to the school because I didn't dare to leave the apartment for fear of missing Alex. I turned down the volume of Gay Htoo's cartoons, and we tried to play Chutes and Ladders on the living-room carpet. Though we couldn't understand all the rules, Gay Htoo enjoyed hopping the cardboard children from square to square, and we raced them from one end to the next. At the slightest sound from the hallway I rushed to the peephole. Six o'clock passed and then seven. We ate one of Belle's casseroles for dinner, as if this would summon her and Alex's presence, but the macaroni was bland and soggy, and still no one appeared. At 8:00 I put the card with their cellphone numbers by the phone, and at 8:30 I picked the phone up and put it to my ear, just to hear its buzz.

I put Gay Htoo to bed and stepped to the window, but the city was dark now, the streetlights of our block flickering or broken, and I saw no one. They have forgotten me, I thought. With all their riches and all their promises of help, they had forgotten me. I hefted the phone's receiver in my hand and listened to the dial tone until a woman's voice scolded me into hanging up. Then I thought of the fences of the refugee camps, the plans I had made there for my son. I have been a modest Karen long enough, I told myself, and I lifted the receiver again and pressed the numbers to make the first phone call of my life.

Alex's recorded voice fooled me for several moments. I hung up, and then immediately regretted it. Was this rude, I wondered, to call without leaving a message? I considered calling him again, but instead I called Belle. She didn't answer either. At last, with no other ideas, I called the church. The receptionist, Carol, was still there.

"Hello," I said. "Is Alex Pritchard there, please?"

"Oh, Naw Me Me," Carol said, her voice cracking. Behind her

I could hear the soft chirrup of voices and another ringing phone. "You'd better turn on the television."

"What number?" I asked, meaning, *What channel?*

"Sweetie," she said, "it's everywhere."

Alex was dead. I watched the news until 2 a.m., but still I didn't understand why. They showed a yearbook photo of a boy and a photo of a gun. They showed weeping neighbors and witnesses and photos of the dead (seven of them at first, though later the total was raised to eight). They showed a hundred police cars and a video-rental store festooned in yellow tape, but still I couldn't connect them into an explanation. It was only when I stopped listening for words and started watching the frightened eyes of the reporters that I understood: they couldn't explain, either, not in any way that mattered.

I thought of the day the Burmese soldiers shot my mother, the way her body fell like a sack of rice. I thought of the artillery shells that landed around us as we fled, smashing houses like eggs. I thought of the land mine that tore Saw Htoo Kyaw's leg off, and the bullet that opened Naw Wah Paw's forehead and the way her body ran for three more steps before spinning to the ground. I thought of crouching in the ferns, breast-feeding Gay Htoo to keep him silent as I watched the soldiers rape Naw Mary and cleave her head from her body. I was so frightened that the urine ran freely down my legs, but even then I made no noise, no noise at all.

I thought of Alex, and I hoped it had been quick.

Gay Htoo and I set out the next morning to see for ourselves the growing mound of flowers we'd seen on the television—I with a bag of apples and my city map, and Gay Htoo with his gorilla. I watched for the numbered signs, and we took one bus and then another, looking out the window as the apartments grew into houses and the sidewalks turned into lawns and the black faces changed to white. Not since the day we'd come to Milwaukee had we seen so much of the city at once, and Gay Htoo knelt on the seat with his hands to the window, naming the objects we passed in Karen and then, when he could, in English. In my pocket, just in case, I carried the caseworker Derek's phone number, but I was determined not to call.

I didn't need to. We could see it from the bus: the idle police cars, the television cameras, the somber men and women, the flowers spreading before the yellow police tape as in a mountain field. We stepped off the bus, and I led Gay Htoo along the display. We saw mums, roses, and gladioli, the air thick with their smell. We saw pictures of the dead, clipped from newspapers and websites. We saw signs from churches and elementary schools and a card from the staff of the Whitefish Bay Taco Bell. We saw a wreath from a university, a teddy bear clutching a heart the size of its chest, and a child's drawing of angels rising from the video shop's sliding doors. And though I carried a heavy sorrow in my heart, I felt envy there as well, that this city could afford such luxury for its victims, while the dead of my village were left unburned, a feast for worms and wild pigs.

"Why is Alex there?" Gay Htoo asked me, pointing to his picture.

In my daze I hadn't known how to explain. "Because he passed away," I tried. "He's with God now, so he can't come to visit us anymore."

Gay Htoo considered this for a long time, looking at the flowers and candles.

"Like my father?" he finally asked.

"Yes," I said. "Like your father."

*

I woke from a dream of my husband's touch to a soft knocking at my front door. As always my first thought was to run, but in a moment I realized where I was and who it must be. I still had my refugee habit of sleeping fully dressed, so I slid my arm from beneath Gay Htoo, slipped from the bed, and went to the door.

"I'm sorry to come by so late," Belle said, trying to smile. With her face stripped of makeup, she looked old enough to be my mother. I wanted to take her in my arms, but I didn't know what American grief would allow. "I couldn't sleep. I had this." She opened a plastic bag to show me pencils, markers, scissors, a three-ring binder.

"Please," I said, "come in." I led her to my kitchen and pulled out a chair, glancing at a clock: 3 a.m.

"The girls are asleep," she told me, and I was surprised to smell cigarettes on her. "My sisters are with them. But they just…" Her sentence dropped away, and she sat. So this is what it took for her to come to a refugee for friendship, a small, bitter part of me thought. But then I remembered the school supplies, and I pictured her tossing alone in bed without the warmth of Alex's bulk beside her, and I didn't care what had brought her. I sat beside her and enwrapped her hands in my own.

"I'd left the girls' DVDs in the car," she said. "I called him at work and asked him to drop them at the store." And then she fell back into silence, and we sat hand in hand, the clock ticking above us, until I spoke.

"I have lost many people," I told her. "In my family and in my village. It is never easy. But the husband, this is the most difficult." The English words rose one after another to my lips, unafraid, the way I spoke in my dreams. "Alex was a good man," I said. "He helped us, and he helped many others. When you are good, my mother said, your good lives on after you die."

Belle gripped my hands tighter, and though I could feel the bite of her fingernails, still I didn't let go.

"We survived," I told her. "You will also."

Belle turned her head, and I worried that I'd offended her, but still she clutched me, and at last I saw the tears dripping from her face.

"I should get back," she said. "The girls might wake up." But she didn't move her hands, and this is how we sat as she told me about Jamie's boy trouble and Zoë's gymnastics and the day that Alex drove three hundred miles to propose to her and three hundred miles back to school the same night, and I told her of my husband, Saw Isaac, and his family's fruit orchards and his birthmarked cheek and the hymns we sang beside each other in church, until Gay Htoo woke to the breaking dawn and the sound of our voices and emerged sleepily from the bedroom. Belle and I laughed with insomniac delirium and showered him in school supplies and then lifted him to the ceiling, my glorious son, one day from the start of his American schooling, and he looked down upon us as proudly and as somberly as a king.

THIRTY MORE
DISTINGUISHED STORIES

"Not Even Lions and Tigers" by Steve Amick. First appeared in *Cincinnati Review*.

"In Casimir's Shoes" by Steve Amick. First appeared in *Michigan Quarterly Review*.

"The Beauty Engine" by Nick Arvin. First appeared in *Midwestern Gothic*.

"The Sunflower State" by Matt Baker. First appeared in *Southern Humanities Review*.

"Art is Art" by Debra Brenegan. First appeared in *Natural Bridge*.

"Single Occupant House" by Richard Burgin. First appeared in *Pleiades*.

"Black Coat" by Susan Connors. First appeared in *Pearl Magazine*.

"This is Not a Fairy Tale" by Ashley Cowger. First appeared in *Peter Never Came* (Autumn House Press).

"The Pool" by Adam Dowd. First appeared in *River Styx*.

"The Good Father" by Jack Driscoll. First appeared in *AGNI Online*.

"Regarding Donor #5873 and Him or Her" by Matthew Hamity. First appeared in *Carolina Quarterly*.

"Offspring" by Ann Harleman. First appeared in *Southwest Review*.

"No Contest" by Heather Herrman. First appeared in *Alaska Quarterly Review*.

"Self-Destruct" by Dustin M. Hoffman. First appeared in *Southeast Review*.

"No Wants, No Returns" by Alexander Lumans. First appeared in *Yalobusha Review*.

"Overflow" by Tim Melley. First appeared in *The Sun*.

"The Gar of Much Bay" by Eric Neuenfeldt. First appeared in *Southern Indiana Review*.

"The Lent Boy" by Lori Ostlund. First appeared in *Iowa Review*.

"The Polish Bride" by Tracy Pearce. First appeared in *Colorado Review*.

"Too Much Anthropology" by Don Peteroy. First appeared in *Cream City Review*.

"Bellwether" by Mark Robert Rapacz. First appeared in *Water~Stone Review*.

"Everything in Its Right Place" by Adam Theron-Lee Rensch. First appeared in *Glimmer Train Stories*.

"Grown-Up Land" by Richard Smith. First appeared in *Narrative Magazine*.

"The Goddess Complex" by Christine Sneed. First appeared in *Notre Dame Review*.

"Stargazer" by Eliot Treichel. First appeared in *Narrative Magazine*.

"The Lesson" by Marc Watkins. First appeared in *Boulevard*.

"The Current State of the Universe" by Theodore Wheeler. First appeared in *Cincinnati Review*.

"Zoom" by Mark Wisniewski. First appeared in *Antioch Review*.

"The Getaway Driver" by Nick Yribar. First appeared in *Glimmer Train Stories*.

"Our Atrocious Miracle" by Mabel Yu. First appeared in *MAKE*.

CONTRIBUTOR
BIOGRAPHIES

ELIZABETH (BETSY) BEALS was born and raised in Windsor, Illinois. Her business, Beals Photography, is based out of Clinton, Illinois.

KATE BLAKINGER's fiction has appeared in *The Gettysburg Review*, *Harpur Palate*, *The Iowa Review*, and other magazines. She earned her MFA at the University of Michigan, where she was awarded the Meijer Postgraduate Fellowship. She has also received grants and fellowships from the Elizabeth George Foundation, Jentel, and the MacDowell Colony. She lives in Philadelphia.

STEVE DE JARNATT grew up in the small logging town of Longview, Washington. He attended Occidental College, graduated from The Evergreen State College, and recently completed the Creative Writing MFA program at Antioch University Los Angeles after a long career as a writer and director in film and television. The indie cult film, *Miracle Mile*, is among his many credits. His story "Rubiaux Rising" (Santa Monica Review, Spring 2008) was selected for *The Best American Short Stories 2009*, guest edited by Alice Sebold.

CHRIS DENNIS grew up in southern Illinois. He holds an MFA in Fiction from Washington University in St Louis, where he also received a postgraduate fellowship. His work has appeared in *Granta Magazine*, *Super Arrow*, and *West Branch*.

MARY STONE DOCKERY is the author of one collection of poetry, *Mythology of Touch* (Woodley Press, 2012). She is also the author of two chapbooks, *Aching Buttons* (Dancing Girl Press) and *Blink Finch* (Kattywompus Press). Her poetry and prose have appeared in many journals, including *Midwestern Gothic*, *Gargoyle*, *Thrush*, *> kill author*, *Mochila*, and others. She is the co-editing founder of *Stone Highway Review* and also reads poetry and prose for *Echo Ink Review* and *Gemini Magazine*. She lives in Lawrence, Kansas.

GINA FRANGELLO is the author of the forthcoming novel *A Life in Men* (Algonquin Books), as well as two other books of fiction, *Slut Lullabies* (Emergency Press, 2010) and *My Sister's Continent* (Chiasmus, 2006). She is the co-founder and Executive Editor of the independent press Other Voices Books, as well as the Fiction Editor of *The Nervous Breakdown* and the Sunday Editor of *The Rumpus*.

ROXANE GAY lives and writes in the Midwest.

ELIZABETH GONZALEZ was born in Indiana and lived for many years in Waterville, Ohio. Her stories have appeared in *Hunger Mountain*, *Post Road*, *Trigger*, *Best American Nonrequired Reading*, and other publications. She lives in Lancaster, Pennsylvania, with her husband and two daughters.

JUSTYN HARKIN lives in Chicago. He grew up within the shadow of the city, and frequently writes about characters from the Northwest Indiana "Region" and the Illinois Fox River Valley.

MARK MAYER is the R. P. Dana Emerging Writer Fellow at Cornell College in Mount Vernon, Iowa. "The Evasive Magnolio" is the first piece published from a collection of stories about the afterlives of circus figures.

MARY MORRIS is the author of fourteen books: six novels, including *Revenge*; three collections of short stories; and four travel memoirs, including most recently *The River Queen*. In 2015, her new novel, *The Jazz Palace*, set in Chicago in the 1920's, will be published by Nan A. Talese/Doubleday. Her numerous short stories and articles have appeared in such places as *The Atlantic*, *Ploughshares*, *The Paris Review*, and *Narrative*, where "Standards" first appeared. The recipient of the Rome Prize in Literature, Morris teaches writing at Sarah Lawrence College. She was born and raised in Chicago, and now lives in Brooklyn, New York. For more information, visit her website: www.marymorris.net.

BONNIE NADZAM's debut novel, *Lamb* (Other Press), won the Center for Fiction's 2011 Flaherty-Dunnan First Novel Prize. Her work has appeared in *Granta*, *Harper's*, *Epoch*, *Orion Magazine*, *The Iowa Review*, and others.

SUSAN POWER is an enrolled member of the Standing Rock Sioux tribe and a native Chicagoan. She is a graduate of Harvard Law School and the University of Iowa Writers' Workshop, and she is the author of three books: *The Grass Dancer* (a novel), *Roofwalker* (a story collection), and *Sacred Wilderness* (a novel). *The Grass Dancer* was awarded a PEN/Hemingway prize in 1995 and *Roofwalker* a Milkweed National Fiction Prize in 2002. Her short stories and essays have been widely published in journals, magazines, and anthologies, including *Best American Short Stories 1993*, *Atlantic Monthly*, *Paris Review*, *Southern Review*, and

Granta. Her fellowships include an Iowa Arts Fellowship, James Michener Fellowship, Radcliffe Bunting Institute Fellowship, Princeton Hodder Fellowship, and USA Artists Fellowship. She lives and teaches in Saint Paul, Minnesota.

SARAH ELIZABETH SCHANTZ lives on the outskirts of Boulder, Colorado, with her family. Her story "The Sound of Crying Sheep" won the 2011 Jaimy Gordon Prize in Fiction hosted by *Third Coast*; the story prompted her first novel, *Fig*, coming out April 2015 from Simon & Schuster. Among other awards, Schantz recently received the Fall 2012 Orlando Prize in Short Fiction hosted by A Room of Her Own. Her work can be found in *The Los Angeles Review*, *Alligator Juniper*, *Hunger Mountain*, *Midwestern Gothic*, and the new anthology of contemporary fairy tales, *Modern Grimmoire* (Indigo Ink Press, 2013). She has an MFA in Writing & Poetics from the Jack Kerouac School of Disembodied Poetics and is currently working on her second novel, *Roadside Altars*. She collects Edwardian-style nightgowns, Lotus slippers, Blue Willow, and antique marbles.

GREG SCHUTZ holds an MFA from the University of Michigan, has received fellowships from the Provincetown Fine Arts Work Center and the Kimmel Harding Nelson Center for the Arts, and was a 2013 tuition scholar at the Bread Loaf Writers' Conference. His stories have appeared in such journals as *Ploughshares*, *Sycamore Review*, *The Carolina Quarterly*, *Third Coast* and *Colorado Review*, and have been named among the distinguished stories of the year by both *Best American Short Stories* and *Best American Mystery Stories*.

SHARON SOLWITZ has published stories in such magazines as *Tri-Quarterly*, *Ploughshares*, and *Mademoiselle*; they have received awards that include the Pushcart Prize, the Nelson Algren, and the Katherine Ann Porter. She has published a novel, *Bloody Mary*, and a story collection, *Blood and Milk*, both with Sarabande Books. Her collection received the Carl Sandberg award and the Midland Authors prize and was a finalist for the National Jewish Book Award. She teaches creative writing at Purdue University and lives in Chicago with her husband, poet Barry Silesky. Her story "Alive," published in this volume, also appeared in *Best American Short Stories 2012*.

IAN STANSEL's collection of stories, *Everybody's Irish*, was published in 2013 by Five Chapters Books. His work has appeared in numerous journals, including *Ploughshares*, *Cincinnati Review*, *Ecotone*, and the *Antioch Review*. He holds an MFA from the Iowa Writers' Workshop and a Ph.D. from the University of Houston.

RACHEL SWEARINGEN's stories have appeared in *American Short Fiction*, *Kenyon Review*, *AGNI*, *Massachusetts Review*, and elsewhere. Recipient of a Rona Jaffe's Writer's Award and the Mississippi Review Prize in Fiction, she lives in Minneapolis.

DEBBIE URBANSKI grew up in Chicagoland and then lived in Minnesota for several years. Her fiction has appeared in the *Kenyon Review*, the *New England Review*, the *Southern Review*, the *Indiana Review*, *The Sun*, the UK science fiction magazines *Interzone* and *Arc*, and the *Alaska Quarterly Review*. She now lives with her husband and two children in Syracuse, New York, which is a nice place, but she still misses many things about the Midwest.

ALEXANDER WEINSTEIN is the founder and director of The Martha's Vineyard Institute of Creative Writing. He is a recipient of The Lamar York Prize and The Gail Crump Prize in Fiction. His short stories and translations have appeared in *Cream City Review*, *Chattahoochee Review*, *Notre Dame Review*, *Pleiades*, *Sou'Wester*, *World Literature Today*, and other journals. He is a professor of Creative Writing at Siena Heights University, and lives in Ann Arbor, Michigan with his son, Peter.

A former Peace Corps Volunteer, **DAVID YOST** has served on development projects in the United States, Mali, and Thailand. His fiction has appeared in more than thirty publications, including *Ploughshares*, *Southern Review*, *New England Review*, *Witness*, and *The Sun*. His anthology *Dispatches from the Classroom: Graduate Students on Creative Writing Pedagogy* was published by Continuum in 2011.

EDITOR
BIOGRAPHIES

ROSELLEN BROWN has published ten books: stories, poetry, and five novels. Her work has appeared in half a dozen *Best American Short Stories*, *O. Henry Prize Stories*, and Pushcart Prize anthologies. She teaches at the School of the Art Institute of Chicago.

JASON LEE BROWN is the author of the historical novel *Prowler: The Mad Gasser of Mattoon*, as well as the poetry chapbook *Blue Collar Fathers*.

SHANIE LATHAM is Assistant Professor of English at Jefferson College in Missouri and an editor at *River Styx Magazine*.